"Sylvia."

A chill crept along my spine. It was the wrong name in his mouth, but it perturbed me no less. When he met my gaze, the anger fled from my bones, replaced with pounding terror. His eyes were flinty, colder than rain on my skin. I forgot Rory, Adel, the dead soldier. I forgot Mahair in its entirety.

I was a ten-year-old Heir sitting at an ancient oak table as the sky erupted in fire, as black lightning bolts struck the earth. I was shivering, starving, covered in ash and blood in Essam Woods. Reaching for the woman who bent over me, the sun pouring through her like she was little more than a netted shroud on its glorious surface.

I had encountered death in every incarnation of my life, but I had never looked it in the eye until now.

THE JASAD HEIR

THE SCORCHED THRONE: BOOK ONE

SARA HASHEM

orbit

orbitbooks.net

Copyright © 2023 by Sara Hashem
Excerpt from *The Phoenix King* copyright © 2021 by Aparna Verma
Excerpt from *The Sun and the Void* copyright © 2023 by Gabriela Romero Lacruz

Cover design by Lisa Marie Pompilio
Cover illustration by Mike Heath | Magnus Creative
Cover copyright © 2023 by Hachette Book Group, Inc.
Map by Tim Paul
Author photograph by Sara Hashem

Orbit
Hachette Book Group
1290 Avenue of the Americas
New York, NY 10104
orbitbooks.net

First Edition: July 2023
Simultaneously published in Great Britain by Orbit

Orbit is an imprint of Hachette Book Group.
The Orbit name and logo are trademarks of Little, Brown Book Group Limited.

The Hachette Speakers Bureau provides a wide range of authors for speaking events. To find out more, go to hachettespeakersbureau.com or email HachetteSpeakers@hbgusa.com.

Orbit books may be purchased in bulk for business, educational, or promotional use. For information, please contact your local bookseller or the Hachette Book Group Special Markets Department at special.markets@hbgusa.com.

Library of Congress Cataloging-in-Publication Data
Names: Hashem, Sara, author.
Title: The Jasad heir / Sara Hashem.
Description: First edition. | New York, NY : Orbit, 2023. | Series: The scorched throne ; Book one
Identifiers: LCCN 2022057400 | ISBN 9780316477864 (trade paperback) | ISBN 9780316477963 (ebook)
Subjects: LCGFT: Fantasy fiction. | Novels.
Classification: LCC PS3608.A789747 J37 2023 | DDC 813/.6—dc23/eng/20230314
LC record available at https://lccn.loc.gov/2022057400

ISBNs: 9780316477864 (trade paperback), 9780316477963 (ebook)

Printed in the United States of America

LSC-C

Printing 2, 2023

To Hend, for being my first reader, friend, and little sister.

And to every eldest daughter who chooses to be brave.

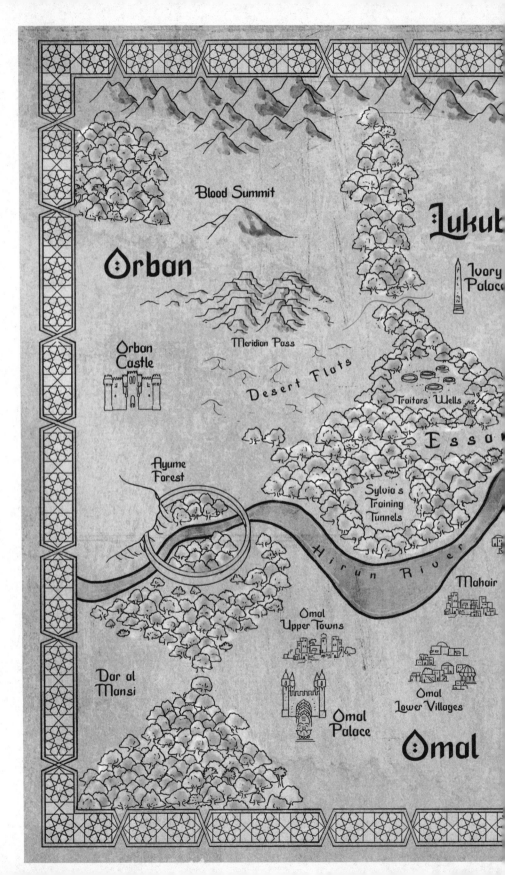

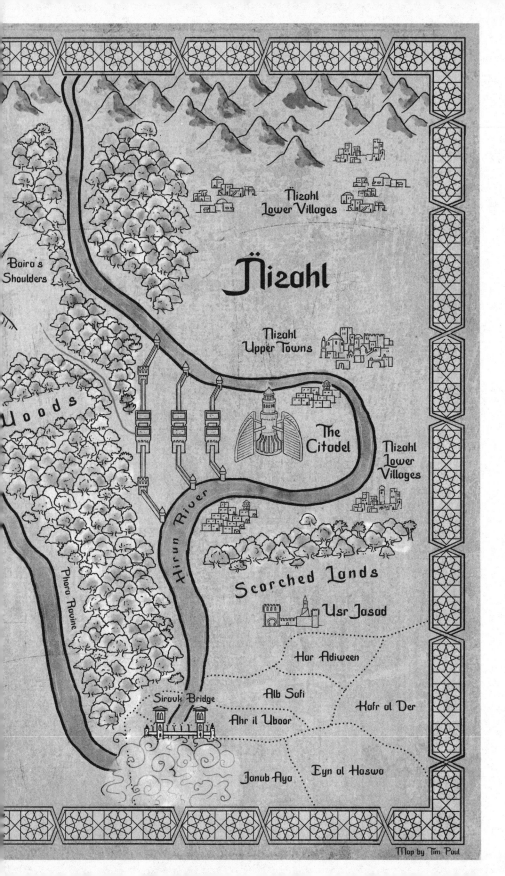

Map by Tim Paul

CHAPTER ONE

Two things stood between me and a good night's sleep, and I was allowed to kill only one of them.

I tromped through Hirun River's mossy banks, squinting for movement. The grime, the late hours—I had expected those. Every apprentice in the village dealt with them. I just hadn't expected the frogs.

"Say your farewells, you pointless pests," I called. The frogs had developed a defensive strategy they put into action any time I came close. First, the watch guard belched an alarm. The others would fling themselves into the river. Finally, the brave watch guard hopped for his life. An effort as admirable as it was futile.

Dirt was caked deep beneath my fingernails. Moonlight filtered through a canopy of skeletal trees, and for a moment, my hand looked like a different one. A hand much more manicured, a little weaker. Niphran's hands. Hands that could wield an axe alongside the burliest woodcutter, weave a storm of curls into delicate braids, drive spears into the maws of monsters. For the first few years of my life, before grief over my father's assassination spread through Niphran like rot, before her sanity collapsed on itself, there wasn't anything my mother's hands could not do.

Oh, if she could see me now. Covered in filth and outwitted by croaking river roaches.

Hirun exhaled its opaque mist, breathing life into the winter bones of Essam Woods. I cleaned my hands in the river and firmly cast aside thoughts of the dead.

A frenzied croak sounded behind a tree root. I darted forward, scooping up the kicking watch guard. Ah, but it was never the brave who escaped. I brought him close to my face. "Your friends are chasing crickets, and you're here. Were they worth it?"

I dropped the limp frog into the bucket and sighed. Ten more to go, which meant another round of running in circles and hoping mud wouldn't spill through the hole in my right boot. The fact that Rory was a renowned chemist didn't impress me, nor did this coveted apprenticeship. What kept me from tossing the bucket and going to Raya's keep, where a warm meal and a comfortable bed awaited me, was a debt of convenience.

Rory didn't ask questions. When I appeared on his doorstep five years ago, drenched in blood and shaking, Rory had tended to my wounds and taken me to Raya's. He rescued a fifteen-year-old orphan with no history or background from a life of vagrancy.

The sudden snap of a branch drew my muscles tight. I reached into my pocket and wrapped my fingers around the hilt of my dagger. Given the Nizahl soldiers' predilection for randomly searching us, I usually carried my blade strapped in my boot, but I'd used it to cut my foot out of a family of tangled ferns and left it in my pocket.

A quick scan of the shivering branches revealed nothing. I tried not to let my eyes linger in the empty pockets of black between the trees. I had seen too much horror manifest out of the dark to ever trust its stillness.

My gaze moved to the place it dreaded most—the row of trees behind me, each scored with identical, chillingly precise black marks. The symbol of a raven spreading its wings had been carved into the trees circling Mahair's border. In the muck of the woods, these ravens remained pristine. Crossing the raven-marked trees without permission was an offense punishable by imprisonment or worse. In the lower villages, where the kingdom's leaders were already primed to turn a blind eye to the liberties taken by Nizahl soldiers, worse was usually just the beginning.

I tucked my dagger into my pocket and walked right to the edge of the perimeter. I traced one raven's outstretched wing with my thumbnail. I would have traded all the frogs in my bucket to be brave enough to scrape my nails over the symbol, to gouge it off. Maybe that same burst of bravery would see my dagger cutting a line in the bark, disfiguring the symbols of Nizahl's power. It wasn't walls or swords keeping us penned in like animals, but a simple carving. Another kingdom's power billowing over us like poisoned air, controlling everything it touched.

I glanced at the watch guard in my bucket and lowered my hand. Bravery wasn't worth the cost. Or the splinters.

A thick layer of frost coated the road leading back to Mahair. I pulled my hood nearly to my nose as soon as I crossed the wall separating Mahair from Essam Woods. I veered into an alley, winding my way to Rory's shop instead of risking the exposed—and regularly patrolled—main road. Darkness cloaked me as soon as I stepped into the alley. I placed a stabilizing hand on the wall and let the pungent odor of manure guide my feet forward. A cat hissed from beneath a stack of crates, hunching protectively over the half-eaten carcass of a rat.

"I already had supper, but thank you for the offer," I whispered, leaping out of reach of her claws.

Twenty minutes later, I clunked the full bucket at Rory's feet. "I demand a renegotiation of my wages."

Rory didn't look up from his list. "Demand away. I'll be over there."

He disappeared into the back room. I scowled, contemplating following him past the curtain and maiming him with frog corpses. The smell of mud and mildew had permanently seeped into my skin. The least he could do was pay extra for the soap I needed to mask it.

I arranged the poultices, sealing each jar carefully before placing it inside the basket. One of the rare times I'd found myself on the wrong side of Rory's temper was after I had forgotten to seal the ointments before sending them off with Yuli's boy. I learned as much about the spread of disease that day as I did about Rory's staunch ethics.

Rory returned. "Off with you already. Get some sleep. I do not want the sight of your face to scare off my patrons tomorrow." He prodded in the bucket, turning over a few of the frogs. Age weathered Rory's narrow brown face. His long fingers were constantly stained in the color of his latest tonic, and a permanent groove sat between his bushy brows. I called it his "rage stage," because I could always gauge his level of fury by the number of furrows forming above his nose. Despite an old injury to his hip, his slenderness was not a sign of fragility. On the rare occasions when Rory smiled, it was clear he had been handsome in his youth. "If I find that you've layered the bottom with dirt again, I'm poisoning your tea."

He pushed a haphazardly wrapped bundle into my arms. "Here."

Bewildered, I turned the package over. "For me?"

He waved his cane around the empty shop. "Are you touched in the head, child?"

I carefully peeled the fabric back, half expecting it to explode in my face, and exposed a pair of beautiful golden gloves. Softer than a dove's wing, they probably cost more than anything I could buy for myself. I lifted one reverently. "Rory, this is too much."

I only barely stopped myself from putting them on. I laid them gingerly on the counter and hurried to scrub off my stained hands. There were no clean cloths left, so I wiped my hands on Rory's tunic and earned a swat to the ear.

The fit of the gloves was perfect. Soft and supple, yielding with the flex of my fingers.

I lifted my hands to the lantern for closer inspection. These would certainly fetch a pretty price at market. Not that I'd sell them right away, of course. Rory liked pretending he had the emotional depth of a spoon, but he would be hurt if I bartered his gift a mere day later. Markets weren't hard to find in Omal. The lower villages were always in need of food and supplies. Trading among themselves was easier than begging for scraps from the palace.

The old man smiled briefly. "Happy birthday, Sylvia."

Sylvia. My first and favorite lie. I pressed my hands together. "A consolation gift for the spinster?" Not once in five years had Rory failed to remember my fabricated birth date.

"I should hardly think spinsterhood's threshold as low as twenty years."

In truth, I was halfway to twenty-one. Another lie.

"You are as old as time itself. The ages below one hundred must all look the same to you."

He jabbed me with his cane. "It is past the hour for spinsters to be about."

I left the shop in higher spirits. I pulled my cloak tight around my shoulders, knotting the hood beneath my chin. I had one more task to complete before I could finally reunite with my bed, and it meant delving deeper into the silent village. These were the hours when the mind ran free, when hollow masonry became the whispers of hungry shaiateen and the scratch of scuttling vermin the sounds of the restless dead.

I knew how sinuously fear cobbled shadows into gruesome shapes. I hadn't slept a full night's length in long years, and there were days when I trusted nothing beyond the breath in my chest and the earth beneath my feet. The difference between the villagers and me was that I knew the names of my monsters. I knew what they would look like if they found me, and I didn't have to imagine what kind of fate I would meet.

Mahair was a tiny village, but its history was long. Its children would know the tales shared from their mothers and fathers and grandparents. Superstition kept Mahair alive, long after time had turned a new page on its inhabitants.

It also kept me in business.

Instead of turning right toward Raya's keep, I ducked into the vagrant road. Bits of honey-soaked dough and grease marked the spot where the halawany's daughters snacked between errands, sitting on the concrete stoop of their parents' dessert shop. Dodging the dogs nosing at the grease, I checked for anyone who might report my movements back to Rory.

We had made a tradition of forgiving each other, Rory and me. Should he find out I was treating Omalians under his name, peddling pointless concoctions to those superstitious enough to buy them—well, I doubted Rory could forgive such a transgression. The "cures" I mucked together for my patrons were harmless. Crushed herbs and altered liquors. Most of the time, the ailments they were intended to ward off were more ridiculous than anything I could fit in a bottle.

The home I sought was ten minutes' walk past Raya's keep. Too close for comfort. Water dripped from the edge of the sagging roof, where a bare clothesline stretched from hook to hook. A pair of undergarments had fluttered to the ground. I kicked them out of sight. Raya taught me years ago how to hide undergarments on the clothesline by clipping them behind a larger piece of clothing. I hadn't understood the need for so much stealth. I still didn't. But time was a limited resource tonight, and I wouldn't waste it soothing an Omalian's embarrassment that I now had definitive proof they wore undergarments.

The door flew open. "Sylvia, thank goodness," Zeinab said. "She's worse today."

I tapped my mud-encrusted boots against the lip of the door and stepped inside.

"Where is she?"

I followed Zeinab to the last room in the short hall. A wave of incense wafted over us when she opened the door. I fanned the white haze hanging in the air. A wizened old woman rocked back and forth on the floor, and bloody tracks lined her arms where nails had gouged deep. Zeinab closed the door, maintaining a safe distance. Tears swam in her large hazel eyes. "I tried to give her a bath, and she did *this*." Zeinab pushed up the sleeve of her abaya, exposing a myriad of red scratch marks.

"Right." I laid my bag down on the table. "I will call you when I've finished."

Subduing the old woman with a tonic took little effort. I moved behind her and hooked an arm around her neck. She tore at my sleeve, mouth falling open to gasp. I dumped the tonic down her throat and loosened my stranglehold enough for her to swallow. Once certain she wouldn't spit it out, I let her go and adjusted my sleeve. She spat at my heels and bared teeth bloody from where she'd torn her lip.

It took minutes. My talents, dubious as they were, lay in efficient and fleeting deception. At the door, I let Zeinab slip a few coins into my cloak's pocket and pretended to be surprised. I would never understand Omalians and their feigned modesty. "Remember—"

Zeinab bobbed her head impatiently. "Yes, yes, I won't speak a word of this. It has been years, Sylvia. If the chemist ever finds out, it will not be from me."

She was quite self-assured for a woman who never bothered to ask what was in the tonic I regularly poured down her mother's throat. I returned Zeinab's wave distractedly and moved my dagger into the same pocket as the coins. Puddles of foul-smelling rain rippled in the pocked dirt road. Most of the homes on the street could more accurately be described as hovels, their thatched roofs shivering above walls joined together with mud and uneven patches of brick.

I dodged a line of green mule manure, its waterlogged, grassy smell stinging my nose.

Did Omal's upper towns have excrement in their streets?

Zeinab's neighbor had scattered chicken feathers outside her door to showcase their good fortune to their neighbors. Their daughter had married a merchant from Dawar, and her dowry had earned them enough to eat chicken all month. From now on, the finest clothes would furnish her body. The choicest meats and hardest-grown vegetables for her plate. She'd never need to dodge mule droppings in Mahair again.

I turned the corner, absently counting the coins in my pocket, and rammed into a body.

I stumbled, catching myself against a pile of cracked clay bricks. The Nizahl soldier didn't budge beyond a tightening of his frown.

"Identify yourself."

Heavy wings of panic unfurled in my throat. Though our movements around town weren't constrained by an official curfew, not many risked a late-night stroll. The Nizahl soldiers usually patrolled in pairs, which meant this man's partner was probably harassing someone else on the other side of the village.

I smothered the panic, snapping its fluttering limbs. Panic was a plague. Its sole purpose was to spread until it tore through every thought, every instinct.

I immediately lowered my eyes. Holding a Nizahl soldier's gaze invited nothing but trouble. "My name is Sylvia. I live in Raya's keep and apprentice for the chemist Rory. I apologize for startling you. An elderly woman urgently needed care, and my employer is indisposed."

From the lines on his face, the soldier was somewhere in his late forties. If he had been an Omalian patrolman, his age would have signified little. But Nizahl soldiers tended to die young and bloody. For this man to survive long enough to see the lines of his forehead wrinkle, he was either a deadly adversary or a coward.

"What is your father's name?"

"I am a ward in Raya's keep," I repeated. He must be new to Mahair. Everyone knew Raya's house of orphans on the hill. "I have no mother or father."

He didn't belabor the issue. "Have you witnessed activity that might lead to the capture of a Jasadi?" Even though it was a standard question from the soldiers, intended to encourage vigilance toward any signs of magic, I inwardly flinched. The most recent arrest of a Jasadi had happened in our neighboring village a mere month ago. From the whispers, I'd surmised a girl reported seeing her friend fix a crack in her floorboard with a wave of her hand. I had overheard all manner of praise showered on the girl for her bravery in turning in the fifteen-year-old. Praise and jealousy—they couldn't wait for their own opportunities to be heroes.

"I have not." I hadn't seen another Jasadi in five years.

He pursed his lips. "The name of the elderly woman?"

"Aya, but her daughter Zeinab is her caretaker. I could direct you to them if you'd like." Zeinab was crafty. She would have a lie prepared for a moment like this.

"No need." He waved a hand over his shoulder. "On your way. Stay off the vagrant road."

One benefit of the older Nizahl soldiers—they had less inclination for the bluster and interrogation tactics of their younger counterparts. I tipped my head in gratitude and sped past him.

A few minutes later, I slid into Raya's keep. By the scent of cooling wax, it had not been long since the last girl went to bed. Relieved to find my birthday forgotten, I kicked my boots off at the door. Raya had met with the cloth merchants today. Bartering always left her in a foul mood. The only acknowledgment of my birthday would be a breakfast of flaky, buttery fiteer and molasses in the morning.

When I pushed open my door, a blast of warmth swept over me. Baira's blessed hair, not *again*. "Raya will have your hides. The waleema is in a week."

Marek appeared engrossed in the firepit, poking the coals with a thin rod. His golden hair shone under the glow. A mess of fabric and the beginnings of what might be a dress sat beneath Sefa's sewing tools. "Precisely," Sefa said, dipping a chunk of charred beef into her broth. "I am drowning my sorrows in stolen broth because of the damned waleema. Look at this dress! This is a dress all the other dresses laugh at."

"What is he doing with the fire?" I asked, electing to ignore her garment-related woes. Come morning, Sefa would hand Raya a perfect dress with a winning smile and bloodshot eyes. An apprenticeship under the best seamstress in Omal wasn't a role given to those who folded under pressure.

"He's trying to roast his damned seeds." Sefa sniffed. "We made your room smell like a tavern kitchen. Sorry. In our defense, we gathered to mourn a terrible passing."

"A passing?" I took a seat beside the stone pit, rubbing my hands over the crackling flames.

Marek handed me one of Raya's private chalices. The woman was going to skin us like deer. "Ignore her. We just wanted to abuse your hearth," he said. "I am convinced Yuli is teaching his herd how to kill me. They almost ran me right into a canal today."

"Did you do something to make Yuli or the oxen angry?"

"No," Marek said mournfully.

I rolled the chalice between my palms and narrowed my eyes. "Marek."

"I may have used the horse's stalls to...entertain..." He released a long-suffering sigh. "His daughter."

Sefa and I released twin groans. This was hardly the first time Marek had gotten himself in trouble chasing a coy smile or kind word. He was absurdly pretty, fair-haired and green-eyed, lean in a way that undersold his strength. To counter his looks, he'd chosen to apprentice with Yuli, Mahair's most demanding farmer. By spending his days loading wagons and herding oxen, Marek made himself indispensable to every tradesperson in the village. He worked to earn their respect, because there were few things Mahair valued more than calloused palms and sweat on a brow.

It was also why they tolerated the string of broken hearts he'd left in his wake.

Not one to be ignored for long, Sefa continued, "Your youth, Sylvia, we mourn your youth! At twenty, you're having fewer adventures than the village brats."

I drained the water, passing the chalice to Marek for more. "I have plenty of adventure."

"I'm not talking about how many times you can kill your fig plant before it stays dead," Sefa scoffed. "If you had simply accompanied me last week to release the roosters in Nadia's den—"

"Nadia has permanently barred you from her shop," Marek interjected. Brave one, cutting Sefa off in the middle of a tirade. He scooped up a blackened seed, throwing it from palm to palm to cool. "Leave Sylvia be. Adventure does not fit into a single mold."

Sefa's nostrils flared wide, but Marek didn't flinch. They communicated in that strange, silent way of people who were bound together by something thicker than blood and stronger than a shared upbringing. I knew because I had witnessed hundreds of their unspoken conversations over the last five years.

"I am not killing my fig plant." I pushed to my feet. "I'm cultivating its fighter's spirit."

"Stop glaring at me," Marek said to Sefa with a sigh. "I'm sorry for interrupting." He held out a cracked seed.

Sefa let his hand dangle in the air for forty seconds before taking the seed. "Help me hem this sleeve?"

With a sheepish grin, Marek offered his soot-covered palms. Sefa rolled her eyes.

I observed this latest exchange with bewilderment. It never failed to astound me how easily they existed around one another. Their unusual devotion had led to questions from the other wards at the keep. Marek laughed himself into stitches the first time a younger girl asked if he and Sefa planned to wed. "Sefa isn't going to marry anyone. We love each other in a different way."

The ward had batted her lashes, because Marek was the only boy in the keep, and he was in possession of a face consigning him to a life of wistful sighs following in his wake.

"What about you?" the ward had asked.

Sefa, who had been smiling as she knit in the corner, sobered. Only Raya and I saw the sorrowful look she shot Marek, the guilt in her brown eyes.

"I am tied to Sefa in spirit, if not in wedlock." Marek ruffled the ward's hair. The girl squealed, slapping at Marek. "I follow where she goes."

To underscore their insanity, the pair had taken an instant liking to me the moment Rory dropped me off at Raya's doorstep. I was almost feral, hardly fit for friendship, but it hadn't deterred them. I adjusted poorly to this Omalian village, perplexed by their simplest customs. Rub the spot between your shoulders and you'll die early. Eat with your left hand on the first day of the month; don't cross your legs in the presence of elders; be the last person to sit at the dinner table and the first one to leave it. It didn't help that my bronze skin was several shades darker than their typical olive. I blended in with Orbanians better, since the kingdom in the north spent most of its days under the sun. When Sefa noticed how I avoided wearing white, she'd held her darker hand next to mine and said, "They're jealous we soaked up all their color."

Matters weren't much easier at home. Everyone in the keep had an ugly history haunting their sleep. I didn't help myself any by almost slamming another ward's nose clean off her face when she tried to hug me. Despite the two-hour lecture I endured from Raya, the incident had firmly established my aversion to touch.

For some inconceivable reason, Sefa and Marek weren't scared off. Sefa was quite upset about her nose, though.

I hung my cloak neatly inside the wardrobe and thumbed the moth-eaten collar. It wouldn't survive another winter, but the thought of throwing it away brought a lump to my throat. Someone in my position could afford few emotional attachments. At any moment, a sword could be pointed at me, a cry of *"Jasadi"* ending this identity and the life I'd built around it. I recoiled from the cloak, curling my fingers into a fist. I promptly tore out the roots of sadness before it could spread. A regular orphan from Mahair could cling to this tired cloak, the first thing she'd ever purchased with her own hard-earned coin.

A fugitive of the scorched kingdom could not.

I turned my palms up, testing the silver cuffs around my wrists. Though the cuffs were invisible to any eye but mine, it had taken a long time for my paranoia to ease whenever someone's idle gaze lingered on my wrists. They flexed with my movement, a second skin over my own. Only my trapped magic could stir them, tightening the cuffs as it pleased.

Magic marked me as a Jasadi. As the reason Nizahl created perimeters in the woods and sent their soldiers prowling through the kingdoms. I had spent most of my life resenting my cuffs. How was it fair that Jasadis were condemned because of their magic but I couldn't even access the thing that doomed me? My magic had been trapped behind these cuffs since my childhood. I suppose my grandparents couldn't have anticipated dying and leaving the cuffs stuck on me forever.

I hid Rory's gift in the wardrobe, beneath the folds of my longest gown. The girls rarely risked Raya's wrath by stealing, but a desperate winter could make a thief of anyone. I stroked one of the gloves, fondness curling hot in my chest. How much had Rory spent, knowing I'd have limited opportunities to wear them?

"We wanted to show you something," Marek said. His voice hurtled me back to reality, and I slammed the wardrobe doors shut, scowling at myself. What did it matter how much Rory spent? Anything I didn't need to survive would be discarded or sold, and these gloves were no different.

Sefa stood, dusting loose fabric from her lap. She snorted at my expression. "Rovial's tainted tomb, look at her, Marek. You might think we were planning to bury her in the woods."

Marek frowned. "Aren't we?"

"Both of you are banned from my room. Forever."

I followed them outside, past the row of fluttering clotheslines and the pitiful herb garden. Built at the top of a grassy slope, Raya's keep overlooked the entire village, all the way to the main road. Most of the homes in Mahair sat stacked on top of each other, forming squat, three-story buildings with crumbling walls and cracks in the clay. The villagers raised poultry on the roofs, nurturing a steady supply of chickens and rabbits that would see them through the monthly food shortages. Livestock meandered in the fields shouldering Essam Woods, fenced in by the miles-long wall surrounding Mahair.

Past the wall, darkness marked the expanse of Essam Woods. Moonlight disappeared over the trees stretching into the black horizon.

Ahead of me, Marek and Sefa averted their gaze from the woods. They had arrived in Mahair when they were sixteen, two years before me. I couldn't tell if they'd simply adopted Mahair's peculiar customs or if those customs were more widespread than I thought.

The day after I emerged from Essam, I'd spent the night sitting on the hill and watching the spot where Mahair's lanterns disappeared into the empty void of the woods. Escaping Essam had nearly killed me. I'd wanted to confirm to myself that this village and the roof over my head weren't a cruel dream. That when I closed my eyes, I wouldn't open them to branches rustling below a starless sky.

Raya had stormed out of the keep in her nightgown and hauled me inside, where I'd listened to her harangue me about the risk of staring into Essam Woods and inviting mischievous spirits forward from the dark. As though my attention alone might summon them into being.

I spent five years in those woods. I wasn't afraid of their darkness. It was everything outside Essam I couldn't trust.

"Behold!" Sefa announced, flinging her arm toward a tangle of plants.

We stopped around the back of the keep, where I had illicitly shoveled the fig plant I bought off a Lukubi merchant at the last market. I wasn't sure why. Nurturing a plant that reminded me of Jasad, something rooted I couldn't take with me in an emergency— it was embarrassing. Another sign of the weakness I'd allowed to settle.

My fig plant's leaves drooped mournfully. I prodded the dirt. Were they mocking my planting technique?

"She doesn't like it. I told you we should have bought her a new cloak," Marek sighed.

"With whose wages? Are you a wealthy man now?" Sefa peered at me. "You don't like it?"

I squinted at the plant. Had they watered it while I was gone? What was I supposed to like? Sefa's face crumpled, so I hurriedly said, "I love it! It is, uh, wonderful, truly. Thank you."

"Oh. You can't see it, can you?" Marek started to laugh. "Sefa forgot she is the size of a thimble and hid it out of your sight."

"I am a perfectly standard height! I cannot be blamed for befriending a woman tall enough to tickle the moon," Sefa protested.

I crouched by the plant. Wedged behind its curtain of yellowing leaves, a woven straw basket held a dozen sesame-seed candies. I loved these brittle, tooth-chipping squares. I always made a point to search for them at market if I'd saved enough to spare the cost.

"They used the good honey, not the chalky one," Marek added.

"Happy birthday, Sylvia," Sefa said. "As a courtesy, I will refrain from hugging you."

First Rory, now this? I cleared my throat. In a village of empty stomachs and dying fields, every kindness came at a price. "You just wanted to see me smile with sesame in my teeth."

Marek smirked. "Ah, yes, our grand scheme is unveiled. We wanted to ruin your smile that emerges once every fifteen years."

I slapped the back of his head. It was the most physical contact I could bear, but it expressed my gratitude.

We walked back to the keep and resettled around the extinguished firepit. Marek dug through the ash for any surviving seeds. Sefa lay back on the ground, her feet propped on Marek's leg. "Arin or Felix?"

I slumped on my bed and set to the tedious task of coaxing my curls out of their knotted disaster of a braid. The sesame-seed candies were nestled safely in my wardrobe. The timing of these gifts could not have been better. As soon as Sefa and Marek fell asleep, I would collect what I needed for my trip back to the woods.

"Are names of the Nizahl and Omal Heirs."

"Sylvia," Sefa wheedled, tossing a seed at my forehead. "You have been selected to attend the Victor's Ball on the arm of an Heir. Arin or Felix?"

Marek groaned, throwing his elbow over his eyes. Soot smeared the corners of his mouth. Neither of us understood why Sefa loved dreaming up intrigues of far-flung courts. She claimed to enjoy the aesthetics of romance, even if she didn't believe in it herself. She had wedded herself to adventure at a young age, when she realized the follies of lust and love did not hold sway over her.

I sighed, giving in to Sefa's game. Felix of Omal would not recognize a hard day's work if it knelt at his polished feet. I had listened to his address after a particularly unforgiving harvest. He brought his handspun clothes and gilded carriages, leaving behind words as empty as the space between his ears. Worse, he gave the Nizahl soldiers free rein, reserving his resistance to intrusion for Omalian society's upper classes.

"Felix is incompetent, cowardly, and thinks the lower villages are full of brutes," Marek scoffed, echoing my unspoken opinion. "I would hesitate to leave him in charge of boiling water. At least the other Heirs are clever, if still as despicable."

At "despicable," my thoughts swung to Arin of Nizahl, the only son of Supreme Rawain.

Silver-haired, ruthless, Heir and Commander of the unmatched Nizahl forces. He had been training soldiers twice his age since he was thirteen. I had always thought Supreme Rawain's bloodthirst had no equal, since it wasn't his kind heart responsible for murdering my family, burning Jasad to the ground, and sending every surviving Jasadi into hiding. But if the rumors about the Heir were true, I could only be glad Arin had been an adolescent during the siege. With the Nizahl Heir leading the march, I doubted a single Jasadi would have made it out alive.

The constant presence of Nizahl soldiers was common to all four kingdoms. An incurable symptom of Nizahl's military supremacy. But the sight of their Heir outside his own lands spelled doom: it meant he had found a cluster of Jasadis or magic of great magnitude. I struggled to repress a shudder. If Arin of Nizahl ever came within a day's riding distance from Mahair, I would be gone faster than liquor at a funeral.

"Sylvia?" Marek asked. Marek and Sefa wore a familiar frown of concern. Black strands had drifted into my lap while I unbraided my hair. I rolled them up and tossed the clump into the fire, where I watched it curdle into ash.

"Sorry," I said. "I forgot the question."

As it always did, the thought of Nizahl curved claws of hatred in my belly. I wasn't capable of sending magic flying in fits of emotion anymore. All I had left was fantasy. I imagined meeting Supreme Rawain in the kingdom he'd laid waste to. I would drive his scepter through the softest part of his stomach, watch the cruelty drain from his blue eyes. Plant him on the steps of the fallen palace for the spirits of Jasad's dead to feast upon.

"Ah, yes, an Heir." I paused. "Sorn."

"The Orban Heir?" Sefa lifted her brows. "Your tastes run toward the brutish? A thirst for danger, perhaps?"

I winked. "What danger is there in a brute?"

CHAPTER TWO

Long after decent people were asleep, I crept out of the keep. I wrapped both arms around the basket's middle as I sped down the hill. My hood hung low over my forehead. Loose curls gathered at the base of my neck, warming me against the wind. I hated leaving the keep without my hair in a braid. The curtain of curls was the perfect weapon for an enemy wishing to swing me around like a cattle hoop. Marek and Sefa's impromptu visit had rushed my schedule.

Night had thickened over Mahair, and a dense fog hung over the shuttered shops. In three hours, Yuli would rouse the boys sleeping in the barn to muck the grounds and release the cows for their feeding. Children would line up outside the bakery, latticed wooden trays propped on their shoulders to carry breakfast back to their families. Mahair, like the rest of Omal, thrived best in the daylit hours.

I paused at the end of the hill and scanned the path. We lived right behind the vagrant road, but the vagrants knew better than to trouble me. The soldiers were the real problem. I couldn't risk running into the patrol again. They changed shifts only twice: once at dawn and again at dusk.

After assuring myself of the road's emptiness, I picked up the basket and resumed walking. A wagon's wheels had gouged enormous tracks. I walked inside its tread, hiding my footprints within the unsettled dirt. A silly precaution, given Mahair's rigid sleep schedule.

Very few homes or businesses bothered to invest in outdoor lanterns, and if they did, they used the kind shaped like a shell and filled with just enough oil to illuminate their immediate surroundings. The sole lantern on this entire road hung from a balcony six buildings down.

What I remembered of my childhood in Jasad wouldn't fill a poor man's pocket, but I knew we were a night people. Just as no two villages in Omal were alike, every wilayah in Jasad kept slightly different customs. In the evenings, daughters of wealthy families relinquished their finery for their street clothes and chased each other for miles. Men gathered for tea and table games, their laughter and good-natured shouts audible throughout the street. And in every wilayah, magic swept the air. It animated the sky, rumbled in the ground. I was born to a place where magic meant joy. Celebration and safety.

Lost in thought, I crossed the street. A prickly pear fell from beneath the blanket I'd tossed over the basket. "Dania's bloody axe," I swore, scooping up the vengeful fruit with the bottom of my tunic. The sesame-seed candies had added to the volume of this week's emergency supplies. Why did I even put them in the basket? As though I'd be in the mood for sweets if the need to flee Mahair arose. I pictured myself indulging in a little treat while I hid in a ravine full of the ashes of the dead.

A disintegrating wall of mud-and-straw brick barricaded Mahair from the woods. I gingerly felt along a cornerstone. Plumes of dust exploded from the pressure. Awaleen be damned, but I hated this village sometimes.

The wall was a relic of days past, when monsters crawled between the borders of the kingdoms, feeding on the traces of magic scattered between the trees. Terrible creatures with horns longer than my arm and tails like a polished sword. More thoughtful monsters, with lovely faces and a beckoning hand, drawing you sweetly to your bloody end. Magic had permeated Essam for most of its existence, and where magic settled, monsters spawned.

A wall would hardly have deterred the monsters if they wanted to enter the village, but I suppose its presence gave Mahair some measure of peace. I rubbed the dust covering the words etched into the limestone:

May we lead the lives our ancestors were denied.

My grandmother had told me the monsters were already dying out when Nizahl descended on the woods in powerful, crushing waves thirty-three years ago. The siege was long and deadly. Monsters had fled into villages on the outskirts of the woods, slaughtering entire populations.

I pressed close to the wall and kept moving. The purging of monsters was not the first piece of Nizahl's campaign against magic, but it was certainly the most effective. To the other kingdoms, they were burying their dead not as a consequence of the former Supreme's poorly planned siege but because of magic. Magic made monsters, and monsters killed without discrimination.

It was the first real stroke of doom over Jasad's image.

I peeled myself from the wall to squeeze past the stacks of straw blocking the path. Children tended to get sneaky maneuvering into Essam, so random blockades had been erected around the village to pen them in.

A donkey lazily twitched a fly from its ear, flaring giant nostrils at my appearance. Finally! I exhaled at the sight of a crack in the rows of brick. I preferred to use the wall behind the vagrant road, but the encounter with the Nizahl soldier had unnerved me. At this hour, the patrol was harder to shake than fleas on a dog. The hole barely fit my basket, but it would squeeze me into the woods without needing to risk the main trail.

The donkey brayed, irritated with my prolonged presence. My heart somersaulted into my throat, and I hurriedly shoved my basket

through the crack. Someone might stick their head outside to check
for intruders and see me skulking on their grounds.

This was the excuse I gave myself for nearly rending my arm from
my body to get through the hole. It had nothing to do with the old
Jasadi superstition that donkeys brayed at the sight of evil spirits.
Absolutely nothing.

I grabbed the basket and continued into the woods. I sidestepped
the twigs and mud puddles, barely avoiding walking headlong into
a tree. I despised making the monthly trip to the ravine, burdened
with the food I judged least likely to perish in the dank underbrush.
Especially during winter, when the wind carried out its personal
vendetta against my thin cloak.

I reached the row of trees marked with the Nizahl raven. It was
against the rules to cross the line without explicit permission.
Nobody sane would risk trespassing and giving the bored and
bloodthirsty soldiers an excuse to cut them down.

The raven stared at me. Discomfort trickled in my belly. I was
suddenly acutely aware of the silence of the woods. The impenetrable darkness.

If I hadn't spent five years of my life living in these woods, I might
have turned around and run straight back to Mahair.

"You think you are the most frightening creature in these woods,
but you're not," I said to the raven. "I am."

Tightening my grip on the basket, I crossed the line of Nizahl-
marked trees and continued walking. This trip—and my trespass—
was necessary. I lived against the will of those who would see me
dead for the magic in my veins. Never mind that my veins were the
only place my magic existed. The cuffs meant I could not so much
as squash a mosquito with my powers, let alone use it to defend myself.

I glanced at my wrists. The cuffs glimmered an overly smug silver.

When I took a step around a patch of wet moss, my foot failed to
land. A shriek rose and died at my lips as the ground gave way.

"Ugh." I lifted my dripping sandal out of the mud. The ravine was still another three miles ahead. Sighing, I moved the basket to my other arm. I would have to hurry if I wanted to get back before Raya did her morning bed checks.

As I walked deeper in the woods, my muscles began to relax. The lines in my brow and the tight curl of my lips eased. These woods... they knew me as I knew them. The branches overhead seemed to wave in greeting. A gang of white lizards scuttled over my foot and up the side of a tree. The slight smell of rot lingered in the mist, underscoring the warmer notes of wood and dew.

I hummed a jaunty Lukubi tune I'd overheard in the duqan and reviewed my tasks for the next day. Preparations for the wal-eema had spun Mahair into a frenzy. Celebrating the Alcalah was no small affair. I shuddered, thinking of the influx of strangers that flooded the village during the last waleema three years ago. Restraint alone had prevented me from running into the woods until it ended.

A splash caught my ankle as a sesame-seed candy tumbled out of the basket and into a puddle. Kapastra's twisted horns, these candies were a *curse*. I bent down, wrinkling my nose against the scent of excrement and rain. Maybe I could leave the flies to enjoy this one.

I straightened, reaching for the basket—and found myself face-to-face with the Nizahl soldier from Zeinab's street.

My heart slowed. Each beat thundered in my ears.

"Sylvia, apprentice to the chemist Rory, healer of poor elderly Aya. Did I get it right?"

For a split second, as the safety of the woods and the terror of discovery shattered together, I thought: *Who is Sylvia?*

A smirk played on his lips. He was waiting for me to lie. My physical appearance wasn't enough to condemn me as a Jasadi. He'd needed more, and I had crawled through a hole in the wall and given it to him. Now he wanted to be entertained by a fumbled excuse for why I had ventured past the raven-marked trees in the middle of the night, basket of food in tow.

The resolve, once it settled, was soothing. The fear retreated. It had been a long time since I'd killed anything bigger than a frog in these woods.

I straightened to my full height, standing eye to eye with the soldier. "Not a coward, then."

He blinked. "What did you say?"

I adopted a light, conversational approach. "I wasn't sure. The one decent thing I can say of your ilk is that you die early. Yet here you stand, your age written into the lines of your skin. You were either a coward or too clever for your own good." As I spoke, I untied the clasp of my cloak. I folded it carefully and set it atop the basket. "You watched me. Followed me far enough that nobody would hear me scream."

The Nizahl soldier remained unperturbed. "Even if they could hear you scream, they would not come to your aid. Nobody cares for the whimpers of Jasadi scum."

I closed my eyes briefly. With two words, the soldier had eliminated any chance of him leaving these woods alive. Feigning innocence did not matter now. As soon as the accusation of *Jasadi* was leveled, only a Nizahlan court could absolve it. This soldier would put me in the back of a wagon and drag me to Nizahl, where I needed zero hands to count the number of Jasadis who survived the trial. I'd learned over the years most did not even survive the journey. The detained died in convenient accidents or in retaliation against "unprovoked" attacks.

The soldier's hand hadn't budged from the hilt of his blade. "You will not even try to deny it?"

I shifted my feet. Slightly, only to confirm the cool hilt of my dagger pressing against my ankle. "Would it matter?"

He freed his sword from its clasp, pointing it at my chest. "Surrender peacefully and you will face a fair and just trial in the courts of His Wisdom, Supreme Rawain."

"Is that so?" I laughed. "Only two months ago, an Orbanian merchant illegally trading in Jasadi body parts was brought to your Supreme's fair and just courts. He confessed to crushing and selling Jasadi bones to those eager to ingest traces of magic. His patrons, blessed with the brains of a goat flea, believed Jasadi remains were flush with health benefits. Your precious tribunal released the merchant with a warning and a hearty chuckle. He helped people *eat Jasadis* and walked free."

The soldier's expression didn't waver. Of course not. All he heard were more whimpers of Jasadi scum.

I stretched my neck. "Identify yourself, soldier. I would like to know what name to mark on your grave."

"This is your last warning. Surrender. And if you try to use your magic on me, be informed it will result in a sanctioned execution."

"'Nizahlan idiot' it is, then."

The soldier lunged, swinging the broad end of his sword in a powerful arc. Impressive. If it landed, it would sever my head quite cleanly.

It had been a long time since I'd fought to kill, but my instincts remained. I rolled into the soldier, grabbing his sword arm and slamming it against my knee. His fingers spasmed. Before he could drop the sword, a blow caught my gut, knocking me to the side. I steadied myself on a tree and coughed. Damn it to the tombs, he wasn't going to make this easy.

There was no time to recover. The sword slashed inches from my ear, nearly slicing my shoulder. I twisted away at the last second, leaving his sword wedged in the bark. I freed my dagger from inside my boot while he pried his sword from the tree.

We lunged at the same time.

I moved with the vindictive speed of a wasp, avoiding his deadly swings. Each time I succeeded in moving close, he evaded me. It was the most frustrating dance. Too close to throw the dagger, too far to plunge it into him. His sword caught the edge of my tunic, the rip of my sleeve cutting through our labored breathing.

"Why do you not use your magic?" he growled. "Your kind has one advantage, yet you squander it. I will not think you virtuous for withholding."

"Rest assured, I would love to use my magic to peel your flesh and boil your eyes. Virtue. Ha! I have many weaknesses, but virtue is not among them."

He wrapped both hands around the hilt of the sword and swung. I threw my weight to the side, catching myself on a knee. Before I could stand, the sword was under my throat. He grabbed a fistful of my hair, yanking it hard enough to bring tears to my eyes. Hot breath wafted over my cheek. "How long did you live in that disgusting little village, fooling everyone into believing you were nothing but an apprentice? But I could see the foul stain of your magic. That your kind continues to exist is a testament to how insidiously you have snuck into our societies. Jasadis are the rot in our ranks."

My cuffs tightened. They reacted sometimes—to certain insults or emotions. They were too random and varied for me to figure out the pattern. All it did was remind me that my magic existed, skimming under the surface of my skin, but remained impossible to access.

If I had the choice to reach into my body and tear it out, I wouldn't be sitting here, swallowing past the blade at my throat.

"Then I suggest you do a better job," I said, and dug my teeth into the hand holding the sword.

"Agh!" He hurled me away and I sprung to my feet. Strands of my hair hung from his fist.

I threw a glance at the sky. In two hours, dawn would stripe across the horizon. Mahair would rouse for a new day, and a different pair of Nizahl soldiers would arrive to relieve the evening patrol. When this soldier didn't appear, it would be a matter of minutes before chaos fell upon the village.

I am not ready to leave. The traitorous thought filled my throat with ash. I had stockpiled food in a smelly ravine for the express purpose of preparing for a situation like this. Hesitation was a luxury I rarely indulged. Mahair wasn't meant to be permanent. I had escaped these woods five years earlier with blood on my hands and one clear goal: I would never be trapped again.

But it would not be this soldier who drove me from the village. He would not win that honor.

I kicked hard and fast, connecting with the crook of his arm. He howled as my boot slammed against bone. The sword dropped. He clipped the side of my head with a forceful blow, but I twisted my chin in preparation. I surged forward and plunged my dagger deep into his lower belly. The angle could not have been worse. I quickly yanked the blade through the resistance of skin and muscle, slicing him open from hip to hip. A lesser gut wound would leave him writhing in agony for hours, and I took no pleasure in torture.

He staggered, a scream foaming with the blood on his lips. His hands went to the stream of red coursing from his wound. The soldier collapsed to his knees.

"Be grateful that in death, nobody will try to sell your bones for a hearty broth." I grimaced at the bloody dagger. It hadn't seen this much excitement in a long time.

"Th…they will find my…body." He spat a mouthful of blood onto my boot. "You will not…escape judgment."

My dry eyes stung when I closed them. Even in the throes of death, this soldier thought he was my moral superior. Because he didn't have magic? Because he was born in a Nizahlan home and I was born in a Jasadi one?

If only he knew the truth. If only he was capable of believing it.

"How many others…have you k-killed? How many?" he rasped.

The secret slammed against the inside of my teeth, eager to attack.

I wiped my dagger with the piece of sleeve he'd torn and tucked them both into my boot.

"Not nearly as many as you hope. You think I fear the judgment of Nizahl?" I stepped toward the soldier, batting away his feeble attempts to hold me off. My hands settled against each side of his face, cradling it. "Your soldiers cannot take me to your kingdom and put me before a court, because I do not exist. According to your history texts, I died almost eleven years ago. I burned to death alongside my grandparents and a dozen others. I believe my crown was taken for display in a war monument. Tell me, how can the dead stand trial for the living?"

He stared at me, uncomprehending, for a second before any remaining blood leached out of his face. "Impossible. You lie."

"Frequently." I smiled without any humor.

"The Jasad Heir perished in the Blood Summit. Everyone saw the blaze take her and the Malik and Malika. You cannot be her. She burned."

"You are correct, soldier," I said. "The Jasad Heir did burn in the Blood Summit. She was a better person. Susceptible to such notions as honor and virtue. She would have tried to save her kind. Protect them from the likes of you, even if it spelled her own destruction.

"But your Supreme killed her." I stroked a finger down the soldier's cheek. "And Sylvia replaced her. I do not heal. I do not lead."

I tightened my hands and twisted sharply. The snap of the soldier's neck echoed in the silent wood. "And unlike her, I am excellent at staying alive."

He fell forward, his body hitting the earth with a dull thump.

I stood over him for the time it took to quiet my breathing. He was dead. He would not expose me. I killed him.

Rovial's tainted tomb, I *killed a Nizahl soldier.*

I looked at the sky and nearly screeched. I had an hour and a half at the maximum before I lost the cover of darkness.

Dry leaves blew onto the lifeless soldier's back. I lacked the proper tools and time to dig a grave, and I couldn't leave him here—Nizahl soldiers would come crawling through every lower village in Omal searching for the killer. Even the ravine, hidden away as it was, would be compromised. I could think of only one way to prevent them from descending on us like a swarm of death.

I grabbed the soldier's shoulder and hauled him onto his back. "You drank your weight in ale last night. You wandered too far into the woods and stumbled upon the river. Everyone knows the riverbanks require careful navigation, and you were anything but careful. It only takes one misstep. You were found floating in the water, probably near the southern embankments, body broken from the boulders under the tide."

Not the worst plan, but also not my best. I sat on my haunches and pressed my lips together. I needed time to disguise his wounds and drag him to the river. At least two miles stretched between us and the nearest riverbank. Even if I somehow managed to finish arranging him on the rocks before the soldiers' shift change, I wouldn't get back to Mahair in time. They'd catch me past the raven tree line and throw me in the back of the nearest cart headed to Nizahl.

My stomach turned. I couldn't finish this alone. I needed help.

Sliding my cloak over my shoulders and picking up the basket, I shot one more glance at the body. "I'll be back."

Then I ran. Faster than I had run in over five years. I had lived in these woods, yes, but I hadn't been alone. I was with the woman who rescued me after the Blood Summit and trained me to survive. A Qayida who once led Jasad's army into countless battles before being exiled. Hanim would add a dozen new scars to my back if she knew the risk I was taking.

I weaved between the trees, pushing labored air from my nose. I didn't bother avoiding the main trail this time, not when fortune had clearly chosen to spit on my efforts tonight. I sprinted up the hill to the keep and circled the garden. Please, *please* let Marek have left his window open. He had trouble sleeping without a breeze, but it was an unseasonably cold night.

An inch separated the window from its hook. Without stopping to process my relief, I pushed the window the rest of the way in and climbed through the narrow opening as soundlessly as possible. My boots left muddy tracks on his boar-hide rug.

I silently cheered at finding he'd dumped an inebriated Sefa on his bed and fallen asleep on a stack of coats. Trying to wake Sefa without rousing the other girls sharing her room would have grayed my hair. I set the basket aside with shaking hands.

My heart dropped to my feet as I contemplated the sleeping figures. My friendship with these two had happened against my will. I had worked hard to prevent myself from forming any attachment that couldn't be severed at a moment's notice. Tonight would change everything. Tonight, I was trusting them.

And if I was wrong, Mahair would be forever lost to me.

I yanked the pillow out from under Sefa's head. Terrified brown eyes flashed open, relaxing only after registering my hooded face. A kick to Marek's ankle, and I had a confused, drowsy audience of two.

"How fast can you run?"

CHAPTER THREE

Marek and Sefa stared at the soldier's body. Ants crawled over the crusted blood on his chin.

Sefa spoke first. "Your knife work is excellent."

"Sefa!" Marek snapped.

"It is! You work with animals; you know how hard it is to cut so deep and so long into the underbelly. She did it while under attack. It's impressive."

"Were you?" Marek said to me. His golden hair stuck out in every direction. "Under attack, I mean?"

They hadn't asked questions when I dragged them from their beds and forced them to run at full speed into the woods. Even when we passed the line of raven-marked trees, they had plunged after me without a second's hesitation. I owed them some part of the truth. The pieces I could spare, at least.

"Yes. He would have killed me if I hadn't killed him. I breached the raven-marked line to collect some ingredients I forgot for Rory, and he would not accept my explanation." I gestured at his fallen sword. "They'll put me on trial if I do not mask his death as an accidental fall into Hirun."

The violence of Nizahl soldiers required little elaboration. Everyone had felt the lash of their terrible power at some point. What my non-Jasadi friends did not need to know was how he accused me of more than merely trespassing. They might feel more sympathy for the soldier if they knew what kind of hand had felled him.

I described my plan, mindful of my race against the dawn. Every instinct rebelled against letting them help. If they made a mistake, it would be my neck. Teamwork, however, was a necessary evil to see this night through.

"Preparing him will not be a delicate affair. If you doubt your tolerance, you can wait behind those trees. I only need your help with carrying his body to the river."

"This is a bad omen. A bad, bad omen. The Alcalah is only seven weeks away. Isn't it meant to bring prosperity and good fortune?" Sefa appeared transfixed by the unnatural angle of the soldier's neck. "What if this means the Awaleen are closer to waking from their slumber?"

"Don't be a fool." Marek collected branches to spread over the blood-dampened earth. Impressive forethought. "The Awaleen's sleep is permanent. If a tournament as bloody and random as the Alcalah could influence the Awaleen, they would have cracked out of their tombs and killed us centuries ago." Marek scattered the branches with more force than necessary. The mention of the Alcalah must have prodded an old wound. I wondered if Marek had ever joined the legions of competitors vying for a position as their kingdom's Champion. "Think carefully, Sefa. If the Alcalah or its Champions had the power to bring good fortune, the Supreme would have called it magic and eliminated it after the war. What we are witnessing here is the result of a Nizahl soldier's hubris."

Sefa shivered. In our rush, she and Marek had left the keep without any shields against the wind. She looked small and profoundly pathetic. It wouldn't do—I needed her in action-ready condition.

I shoved my cloak toward her. "Avoid getting it bloody."

As I moved to the soldier, a hand thrust forward, halting my path.

"Sylvia, you cannot think you have the strength to break this man's back." Marek crossed his arms over his chest. "I have seen you struggle to lift a crate of apples."

I choked on a bark of laughter. Oh, but there was not any sport in winning a game the other side wasn't playing. "You saw what I wanted you to see. Sefa, please find as many small, jagged stones as you can fit in the cloak's pockets."

"Let me do this part," Marek argued.

I took a fortifying breath, releasing it through my nose. He was trying to help, I reminded myself. "I can handle it. Alone."

Flipping the body facedown on the ground, I grabbed the arms and hoisted the body back. Sefa turned green. I couldn't blame her. The body was on its knees, pulled back by its arms, its mutilated and mud-stained torso pointed in her direction. A macabre sight, to be sure.

"At least we do not plan on eating him," I grumbled to myself. Marek shot me a bewildered glance.

Keeping a firm grip on the body's elbows, I planted my boot at the base of his back. Sefa scurried into the trees, covering her ears. Marek watched with a skeptical frown.

A sinister voice bloomed in my mind. *In a matter of hours, you may have destroyed the identity you spent years building. You cannot even protect your own pathetic, pointless life,* Hanim whispered in my ear. My darkest thoughts always spoke in her voice. Years had passed since I last heard my former captor. That I heard her now could not signify anything good.

I heaved the body's arms toward myself. Breaking a grown man's back at this angle required a significant amount of force. Hanim had compared it to pretending I was trying to shove my foot *through* the person and toward the ground just ahead of them. The arms needed to be pulled back far and held fast. Otherwise, the shoulders would pop loose, and the back would remain undamaged.

I slammed my boot downward against his back. The thunderous crack sent Marek's brows disappearing into his hair. Satisfied, I dropped the body onto its broken bones and pointed at the gash on the soldier's belly. "This cut is too clean. I need you to make it seem as though he sustained the damage from the boulders in Hirun."

Marek accepted my dagger with a slow smile. "I can't break a grown man's back, but I can certainly whittle a messier wound."

I left him crouched beside the soldier and went to find Sefa. I stumbled on her apologizing to a colony of ants for stealing the rocks they were hiding behind. "I am almost finished," she said.

Suspicion thickened into a brick in my chest. Aside from her spat of superstitious paranoia, she seemed utterly nonchalant. So did Marek. I had dragged them out of the village in the middle of the night to help me mangle a soldier's corpse and carry it to the river. I'd seen them react with more horror to the discovery that I routinely forgot to water my fig plant.

I slid into a crouch, grimacing at the sight of my cloak dragging against the ground. It swallowed Sefa's small frame. "Speak plainly. Why are you doing this for me?"

Undeterred by my harsh tone, she blew gently on the rocks in her palm, flaking away the loose debris. "Despite your strong resistance to the concept, we *are* friends."

"Friendship has its limits."

"Perhaps."

"I wouldn't do this for you or Marek."

The corner of her mouth lifted like I had said something amusing. "I know."

"If I'm caught, I will be executed. You would be thrown to the mercy of a Nizahlan tribunal for helping me."

"If you are hoping to light a fire of fear in me, you are too late. It was lit long ago." Sefa tucked the rocks in her pockets. "Be at ease, Sylvia. Before it ever came to a tribunal, I would promptly follow you into death."

Sefa and I stood at the same time. Only a Jasadi would have need for such a disturbing vow, but Marek and Sefa did not have a trace of magic. Living as closely as we did, I would have seen it. What cause did they have to fear Nizahl?

I evaluated Sefa as though seeing her anew. "What aren't you telling me?"

"Now, Sylvia. You may have my loyalty without cost." The rest of the rocks tumbled into her pocket. "But you must earn my secrets." She smiled, whites of her teeth bright against her skin.

I caught my breath as an earth-shattering possibility shook through me. A possibility winding into everything I thought I knew about Sefa and Marek. Marek, who leaned on his *a*'s and *l*'s when he spoke in anger. Who complained about the weather in Mahair as though it were any different in the rest of Omal.

"Marek called the tomato by the wrong name," I said suddenly. Remembering. "A week after I came to the keep, I saw you two in the kitchen. He asked you to pass him an oota. Omalians call tomatoes 'tamatim.' I thought it was strange, and I kept a close eye on him for the next month. I heard him call a slew of vegetables by other names. Lukubi, Orbanian, Nizahlan names for vegetables. He said Yuli was making him practice for the visitors who come on market days. But he was just trying to cover, wasn't he? He was trying to cover the very first slip."

Sefa forcefully clapped the dust from her hands. Her face was unreadable. "The corpse will be more challenging to carry after it stiffens. We should go."

You have been so preoccupied with your own secrets, you did not bother to see theirs, Hanim murmured. *Pathetic.*

I wanted to drag Sefa back and shake her until the truth fell out. If what I suspected was true…but no, I couldn't. I wouldn't. The lives we led before reaching Raya's keep were not discussed. As long as their secrets couldn't harm me, I would not ask. Curiosity was always repaid in kind.

Marek had done a commendable job turning the lines of the

wound jagged and uneven. We scattered rocks into the open meat of the body. Hopefully by the time they found the soldier, the fish would have made quick work of the exposed skin flap.

The run to the river felt eternal. I carried the front while Marek and Sefa supported the rest of the body. The trees closed around us eagerly, the ground dipping lower with every dozen steps. I spotted Marek shuddering. The deeper we ventured into Essam, the more it felt like the teeth of a beast too vast to comprehend were closing around us.

We stopped only twice to catch our breaths, all too aware of the crisp morning breeze and pinkening sky.

Sefa began to sing, her warbling voice covering the squelch of our footsteps. "The Awaleen came sight unseen, to survey the empty land. Abound, abound!"

"Sefa, please," Marek groaned. I didn't recognize the melody, but he clearly did.

"Above the hills and valleys to the west, Kapastra laid her crown. Mother of Omal, Beast Tamer of blue, abound!"

"She won't stop," I warned Marek. My boot went through a rotted log. Crickets exploded from the hole, hopping over my leg. Their indignant chirps joined Sefa's incessant tune.

"Beam of beauty, sharper than ruby, Baira, Baira, Baira," Marek intoned flatly. "To Lukub she took her light, abound, abound!"

"Battle beat in Dania's bones, and in Orban she sang its bloody song. Abound, abound!"

A cricket jumped onto the corpse's cheek. I watched it crawl into his nose and grimaced. I could predict what came next in the song. Or rather, who didn't.

In the early days, the four original kingdoms—Lukub, Omal, Orban, and Jasad—had been flush with magic. Nizahl came after the Awaleen's entombment, created to arbitrate peace between the other four kingdoms. But the centuries passed, each taking a little more magic with it, until only Jasad's magic remained. Nizahl's armies grew, scaring Lukub and Omal, even battle-hungry Orban. But not Jasad. Not even Nizahlan armies stood a chance against Jasad's unassailable fortress.

At least, they shouldn't have.

To my surprise, Sefa's song continued, albeit softer and more reserved. "Rovial heard the hum of Jasad and gave his soul to keep her awake. Abound! Abou—"

"Quiet." I stopped walking and listened. There it was, the best song of them all—the gurgle of Hirun. We broke through the trees, skidding to a halt at the edge of the riverbank.

"Oh," Sefa breathed. "I have never seen Hirun with its banks so far apart."

Hirun wound through every kingdom like a mighty serpent, sustaining life across the land. In some areas of Essam, the river stretched no wider than a tree trunk. Here, the opposite bank of Hirun was at least half a mile away. The full moon's reflection rippled on its dark surface.

"I'll take him." Marek rolled the body down the riverbank, mindful of his weight on the damp earth. He grunted as he carried boulders to place around and beneath the body.

I could feel Sefa's gaze boring into the side of my head. "Can I ask you a question?"

My teeth hurt from grinding down the answer I wanted to give her. "I suppose."

"Why did you need to break his back? Isn't a broken neck enough to make it seem like he slipped?" Sefa asked. I could hear only curiosity in her voice, but I still paused before responding.

"If they decide to investigate his death as a killing, the broken back means they will be searching for a man."

Her lips parted. "Because of the force needed to cause such a break."

"Yes." It felt beyond strange to share this part of myself. The balance of our relationships had shifted, and I no longer knew where we stood.

If you were the girl I raised you to be, you would finish them here, Hanim said. I scraped a hand down my face. When would she go away?

Once Marek finished arranging the body, Sefa helped him out of the riverbank. I lingered out of reach. A touch right now would snap the last of my already fraying calm.

"We need to run. Fast as you can. We won't be in Mahair in time for the shift change, but we need to be within the boundary of the raven-marked trees." I picked at my wrist, gaze somewhere above their heads. "Thank you. This favor will not be forgotten."

We ran against the dawn. Sefa stumbled more than once, but Marek remained near with a steadying hand. I focused on avoiding the puddles. There was no guessing how deep they went, and they had already caused plenty of trouble. A broken ankle was exactly what this catastrophe of a night needed.

I tried to put my suspicions about Sefa and Marek's backgrounds out of my head. It was too big a thread to unspool in my current state of mind.

We crossed the raven-marked trees without incident. A collective exhalation passed between us. "We should walk the rest of the way," Marek said. "We're wearing the sweat of the guilty."

"Neither of you are guilty," I said sharply. "If it comes between protecting me or yourselves, make a smarter choice than the one you made tonight."

"Is she trying to protect or insult us?" Sefa asked Marek. "I can never tell."

"Both, I think."

"We have all heard the rumors about the random disappearances happening across the kingdoms in the last year," I said. "This was just another disappearance."

"Those rumors aren't true." Sefa glanced around, more alert than she'd been a moment ago.

"Maybe not, but their existence might buy us some time."

As we reached the end of the trail, a wagon rumbled past us, stacked with towers of crates bound together with water-stem rope. The smell of fresh aish baladi drifted from the main road as the kids threw loaves of the dense flatbread into baskets or onto the wooden lattices propped on their shoulders.

The warm scent of wheat tugged at my memory. How many mornings in Usr Jasad did I spend with crumbs on my clothes, burning my tongue on aish baladi hot from the palace ovens? The bread was more common in Jasad's rural communities, but my mother had asked the bakers to prepare us two loaves each morning. So many of Jasad's customs had been adopted by the other king-doms. Jasad's food, art, traditions—pretty spoils of war for the cir-cling scavengers.

I turned away from the bakery. Jasad was gone. Mourning a kingdom I barely knew was a disservice to the life I had built.

"It's my turn to pick up the fūl for breakfast," Sefa said. "If I go home without it, Raya will mop the keep with my neck."

"We don't have the pot," Marek said.

"Hamada is nice. He'll let me borrow his extra pot."

"*Nice*," Marek repeated with derision. "Only oil, salt, and black pepper this time, all right? Nobody likes lemon on their fūl except you and Fairel."

Sefa rolled her eyes. "I'll ask for it plain so you can season it your way. Your wrong way, I might add."

We stopped at the fūl cart. Hamada dismissed Marek and me with a glance, homing in on Sefa. While he poured the steaming beans out of a massive metal jug and into a lidded pot, I surveyed our surroundings. The shift change had happened twenty minutes ago. Even if they allowed the soldier a few minutes for tardiness,

they would not have waited twenty minutes before calling in reinforcements. Dread swelled in my chest. Why did I come back? I
should have left the soldier and kept running. I knew how to hide
in the wilds of Essam. I had had a basket of food and a head start. I
could have eventually found my way into the lower villages of Lukub
or Orban and started over. What kind of simpleton was I to stumble
back to the cage and hope they didn't close the lock?

They would barricade any entry or exit within Mahair. Every
home would be combed for Jasadis. Trade would halt. They might
even cancel the waleema, one of the greatest sources of income for
the village.

"Soldiers disappear frequently," Marek murmured. I flinched,
surprised to find him openly watching me. "They will not waste
resources on a middling Omalian village until they are certain he
was killed."

"They have plenty of resources."

"Not with the Alcalah only a few months away. They divert a
massive retinue of soldiers into the woods to protect the Nizahl
Heir while he searches for a Champion."

I stared at Marek. I had the scars on my back to testify to the
thoroughness of Hanim's education. She had ensured I studied the
dialects of each kingdom, the common language shared between
them, their habits and history. Yet I had less than a cup's worth
of knowledge about the Nizahl Heir. Hanim hadn't talked about
him beyond telling me he'd kill me without losing his breath unless
I made my magic work. Given her fervent hatred for my grandparents and Supreme Rawain, I imagined it stung to see the ways
the Supreme succeeded where she had failed. He raised a warrior,
and she...she raised the person who'd be spotted from a watch-
tower fleeing the battlefield with the other soldiers' food.

Some of my regret subsided. If I'd gone running into the woods
and encountered Arin of Nizahl, the question of my fate would have

been instantly decided. Jasadis did not leave an encounter with the Nizahl Heir alive.

How did Marek know how many soldiers Nizahl diverted while its Heir chose his Champion for the Alcalah? My earlier suspicions returned with a vengeance. "You certainly seem familiar with Nizahlan customs."

His raised eyebrow was pointed. "As do you."

"You're sure they will not raise the alarms unless they find a body?" I badly wanted to believe him.

"Sure enough."

"Will one of you take a handle?" Sefa wheezed. Hamada had filled the pot to the brim with fūl. Sefa staggered, and some of the beans dribbled over the side. Marek and I snatched the handles, and we returned to the keep unscathed.

Raya shouted at us for ten minutes about the filthy state of our clothes. As soon as she finished, the three of us split up. Me to bathe, Sefa to help with breakfast, and Marek to change for a day of hard labor.

As I dragged the towel over my body, I wished I could rub the tension from my limbs through sheer force. I was strung tight in a way I hadn't been since my first few months in Mahair. I wrapped my wet curls in linen pants, tying the ends at the nape of my neck. Not even dropping onto my bed helped me relax. Outside my door, a flurry of footsteps and conversation signaled the start of the new day.

The younger girls in the keep did not like me much. I lacked the gentle, nurturing touch that came so naturally to Sefa. Though I tried to be softer with them, I possessed the maternal instincts of a bloodthirsty cockroach. Yet for some unfathomable reason, I found their presence grounding whenever fear tightened its noose around me. Raya would rather die than let these children feel the pressure of the responsibilities she carried on their behalf. She made sure they were free to worry about urgent problems like who could claim the prettiest dress in the monthly donation carts or who could carry the biggest goat the farthest. These orphaned girls were as close to happy as their circumstances permitted.

"You shouldn't hide the realities of the life they face outside this keep," I'd said once, a few days after I turned sixteen. I'd been sharpening the kitchen knives by the fire while Raya counted her weekly earnings for the sixth time. "The more responsibilities you place on their shoulders, the better they will become at bearing them."

She'd looked at me so long that I'd started to tense, tightening my grip on one of the knives. Dark circles hollowed the space under Raya's eyes. "Children are not meant to bear the woes of this life, Sylvia. It breaks them. They will spend their adult lives doing everything in their power to never feel the weight of the world again."

Exhaustion tugged at me. I hadn't slept in two days, but each time I closed my eyes, I saw Nizahl soldiers riding into Mahair with swords and torches.

Any illusion of safety here had been shattered.

You are the Jasad Heir. Safety was not written for you, Hanim said.

I shoved my face into the hard pillow. I mentally recited the herbs I would pack for Rory and planned the best spot to set up our table for the waleema.

When nothing else worked, I resorted to a practice as old as the scars on my back. I pressed my cold palm against my heart and counted the beats.

One, two. I'm alive. *Three, four.* I'm safe. *Five, six.* I won't let them catch me.

I stand alone at the head of a vast ballroom. An audience of faceless Jasadis waits breathlessly for my address. My bodice is in the shape of a lotus flower, curling out and around my ribs. Jasad's iridescent symbol is etched on my skirt. The head of a falcon and gold wings sit on the body of the sleek black cat. A gold kitmer, a feline of pure magic and legend. The kitmer circles within my dress, agitated.

On my head rests a crown.

"Queen Essiya! The lost Heir has returned to reunite Jasad!" shouts a man of twisted shadow and smoke.

"Magic will prosper once more!"

I try to flee, but I am immobile beneath the weight of the crown. Golden thread stitches my lips shut. I silently bear their exultation, their relief, as it batters me from every side. Savior. Hero. Queen.

Red drips down my chin as I force my lips apart, pulling the stitches taut. An iron tang fills my mouth, trying to drown out my words at their inception. "Please, I am not who you seek! I can't help you!" I drop to my knees.

The stitches tear, beautiful golden threads fluttering to the ground in a bloody heap. My freed voice rings in the empty ballroom.

A strong grip lifts me to my feet. "Essiya, you're going to wrinkle your dress."

Shock ripples through me. I stand over my mother by nearly a full head. The shoulders I used to climb are half the width of mine. I have curves in the places where she's slim, and I am strong where she's soft. "I'm taller than you," is all I can think to say to my dead mother.

Niphran's laugh is music. "Only by a little. You take after your grandmother in shape."

The ballroom dissolves around us. We stand on the surface of a frozen lake stretching for miles on every side.

Orange flames dance at Niphran's legs. "A kingdom cannot fall when its Heir still stands. You cannot outrun your duty, ya umri. It is an inheritance by blood." I scour for the source of the fire that steadily eats at her body. There is none. "More than that," Niphran continues, as though she's not burning alive two feet away, "it is an inheritance by right. Who we are, who we might have been, our identity as a kingdom—do the people who have lost their home mean nothing to you?"

I pound my foot against the hard surface beneath us, but it does not break. We are surrounded by water, and yet my mother burns.

"Don't leave me," I gasp. They already took her once. I reach for Niphran, cringing back as the fire blazes higher.

"Then save me."

"It won't crack!" I drop, hitting the ice with my fists. My knuckles split in vain. The layers of ice are too thick, too deep.

The inferno roars, swallowing Niphran whole, but her words are clear. "Shatter it."

"I don't know how!" I raise my fists to beat against the ice again—and stop.

My wrists are bare. Where my cuffs should be is smooth skin.

The fire licks into the sky, consuming the night in its monstrous glow. It illuminates thousands of shadow people, standing still at the shore. Watching. Judging.

"Essiya!" Niphran shrieks.

I scramble back, throwing an arm over my face.

The flames burst. We are consumed.

CHAPTER FOUR

Four days went by without anyone calling for my execution. The pair of Nizahl soldiers patrolling Mahair continued their route, visitors for the waleema kept pouring in, and I continued terrorizing frogs for Rory. If I didn't have bruises and a missing clump of hair, I might wonder if I hallucinated the entire night.

Worry shadowed me relentlessly. I didn't trust the peace. Nizahl soldiers would not simply forget the disappearance of one of their own.

Two days before the waleema, Raya pounded on our doors, descending into a rare fervor of agitation. None of us could fathom why. Her fabrics sold with stunning success at regular market, never mind a waleema that only took place every three years. Noblewomen from the farthest towns in the four kingdoms sent their servants to bid for Raya's extravagant gowns. With everyone eager to dress their best for their kingdom's Alcalah festivities, the gowns would sell for more than enough money for Raya to bring in another orphan or two from the streets.

At the bottom of the hill, Marek loaded the wagon. The canvas usually covering the back had been peeled away, giving him room to stack the crates.

"You're late. Rory has probably reduced the patrons to tears already." Marek hopped into the driver's seat.

"As long as he hasn't thrown his cane at anyone, I would call that a good morning. Where's Fairel?"

Marek pointed at the figure of the tiny girl running full tilt down the hill, her back bent under the weight of a wooden chair. I hid a smile. Raya gave every girl in her keep a choice: work or learn. Most chose learning, but nine-year-old Fairel had stuck her little chin forward and said, "I would rather be the best at one thing than know a little about a lot of things." In the three years since, she had taken her role as watcher of Nadia's chairs with a seriousness reserved for those handling the instruments of battle.

Fairel hurled herself into the back of the cart, chair in tow. "Here! I'm here!"

Marek chuckled, clicking his tongue at the horses. Six girls climbed into the back, arranging themselves in the cart. I jiggled my leg as we lurched into motion, fingers dancing on my knee. Dread filled my chest the closer we rumbled toward the main square. Another reason to hate the busy Alcalah season was the threat of recognition.

I always kept my ears open for any rumors about the Heir of Jasad. Not a single whisper suggested the world thought Essiya was any less dead than the rest of her family. Most of those at the Blood Summit had perished during the attack—including Isra, Supreme Rawain's wife. Only the Queen of Omal, Supreme Rawain, and Sultana Bisai had lived. Sultana Bisai was dead now, the Lukub crown passed to her daughter, and the other two royals wouldn't cross paths with a lowly orphan. It didn't stop me from checking for the reassuring weight of the knife tucked in my boot whenever Mahair had visitors.

The blue cottage rose on our right. Its owners were old and childless. Not many were interested in buying property here, not with a keep full of orphans to the left and the vagrant road to the right. It would be an excellent home. There would be space for Sefa and Marek. Perhaps a small garden for my fig plant.

I directed my gaze forward. Sefa's fanciful musings had clearly seeped into my common sense. Longing for the impossible was a task best left for fools.

The cart jerked as the path grew rockier. The children chasing the cart fell back, scuttling in the opposite direction. Heeding their parents' warnings against venturing into the vagrant road.

"How do you feel?" Marek asked quietly.

I knew what he was really asking, but I did not have an answer suitable for his ears. "Hungry. Maya shouldn't be allowed to prepare breakfast for anyone but her enemies. I still have eggshell in my teeth."

Marek was silent for a long moment. I hoped we'd seen the end of the conversation.

"Five years. Five years of friendship, Sylvia. And we are friends, despite your many efforts to distance yourself from us. Yes, I noticed. I am a talent at understanding people, but you…you baffle me. Five years of friendship, and do you know the only word I would use to describe you?" He glanced at me. "Mild. Just…mild. Which might have been the end of the story until two nights ago, when I watched you singlehandedly sever a man's backbone without flinching."

Mild. I examined the word, testing the fit. It amused me. Perhaps Hanim's whip was reserved for mild-mannered girls, and the scars on my back a generous reward for my tepid temper. My first week in Hanim's tiny cabin, I threw my food at the wall and promptly burst into tears. I was still a rebellious thing, full of spite and the indignations of slighted royalty. Though I'd seen my grandparents burn with my own two eyes, had heard the messenger declare Niphran's death with my own ears, reality had yet to sink its claws into my chest. Jasad's disgraced war captain had stood silent as the grave as she waited for me to wipe the last of my tears.

"Go to the corner," she said, "and lift your arms."

Frightened of her blank eyes, I'd kept my arms raised until the scream in my shoulders dulled into a whimper. I counted the cracks in the wall, memorized the writing on my cuffs. The pain eventually settled, becoming as constant and forgettable as the pulse in my neck. I found a way to think through it.

Mild, indeed.

Undeterred by my silence, Marek continued, "Have you heard the news? They say the Nizahl Heir was spotted near the border to Gahre."

The spike of fear his words drove into my chest irritated me. Gahre was another Omalian lower village sitting a mere hour away. The news of his arrival would have ridden in long before the Commander's horses. I unclenched my fists. "Chatter of idle merchants, I'm sure."

"Yes," Marek agreed, glancing askance at my twitching fingers. "It's Omal's turn to represent Nizahl in the Alcalah this year. The Heir is probably gracing our humble villages to find his Champion." Marek's derisive tone communicated exactly what he thought of such an idea.

Hosted once every three years, the Alcalah invigorated every kingdom from the highest crown to the wildest vagrant. The tournament consisted of three grueling trials meant to celebrate the sacrifice of the progenitors of our kingdoms. The location of each trial rotated between the four kingdoms and culminated in a Victor's Ball. If Mahair's obsession with the Alcalah was any indication, the kingdoms built their lives around this event. I couldn't count the number of times I had listened to Rory's patrons walk around the shop and fantasize about dancing at the Victor's Ball or cheering in the audience of one of the Alcalah's trials.

Nizahl was the only kingdom not to choose a Champion from among its own people. Shortly after burning Jasad to the ground, Supreme Rawain had generously announced Nizahl's plan to foster peace by choosing a Champion from a different kingdom every

Alcalah. Besides, Nizahl possessed an unfair advantage. They conscripted their youth into the army from adolescence, and their most incompetent soldier could easily match another kingdom's best.

"He wouldn't choose a Champion from a lower village," I said. "I'm sure he has some arrangement with the Omal Heir. A preselected Champion the royal family favors, perhaps."

"Felix can't pick the snot from his nose. The Nizahl Heir certainly will not be asking him his thoughts on picking a Champion."

I made a disgusted sound at the image. "Every Champion he's chosen has won the Alcalah. I doubt he would agree to train an incompetent just to curry political favor. Even if the Nizahl Heir did decide to choose a lower villager, he would find it a challenge to convince them to accept such a fatal role." For all they loved to speculate about the Alcalah, lower villagers had too much sense to willingly compete in a tournament that left more than half its Champions dead. At least, I hoped they did.

Marek shrugged, navigating the wagon around a stretch of foul-smelling ponds dotting the road. "It might be worth the risk. If they become Victor, they win a retinue of guards, an upper-town home in every kingdom, riches to last their lifetime."

"It's not worth the risk unless you're an oat-brained noble whose sole purpose for competing is to prance around and claim you're celebrating the sacrifice of the Awaleen."

The myths behind the Alcalah were utter nonsense. The four original siblings were beings of pure magic—the first magic. The Awaleen had created the kingdoms and ruled over them for millennia before Rovial, Jasad's Awal, went insane and killed thousands. Magic-madness, the storytellers claimed. The inevitable consequence of powerful magic. To contain their brother and protect their kingdoms, the Awaleen consigned themselves to an eternal slumber beneath Sirauk Bridge. What exactly did the Alcalah seek to celebrate? The bloodshed or the burial?

Aware of my rising frustration, I fell quiet, smoothing my skirt down around my knees. The pale sunlight reflected brightly from my cuffs. It was a blessing to be the one person capable of seeing or feeling them. Their shine would have seared holes into Marek's periphery.

"The Commander's last two Champions were a Lukubi stone-mason and an Orbanian beggar. Both became Victor."

"Marek, enough." I didn't wish to talk about Nizahl or the Alcalah anymore. Anger was far slower to fade than it was to kindle, and I didn't have the energy to spare.

"They say meeting his eyes can freeze a Jasadi's magic in their veins," Marek continued. "Supposedly, he can sense it by touch alone."

The very thought threatened a reappearance of my eggshell breakfast. Most days, I excelled at willfully forgetting Jasadis were hunted like rabid animals. There was nothing I could do for them. There was barely anything I could do for me.

"What you describe is impossible. Do you mean to say the Commander has magic himself?" My tone went harsh, roughened by the tableau Marek's words painted.

"Of course not. I am just saying—"

"What you are saying is treason. We have committed more than our fair share of that lately, don't you agree?"

The crowd thickened as we neared the main square. People weaved around Marek's wagon as it moved through a crowd clad in blue and white. As soon as he stopped, I took a deep breath and jumped down. I kept my cloak wrapped tight and my head low. Every accidental shoulder-bump or arm-brush sent a thousand pinpricks of revulsion throbbing through me. I couldn't walk to Rory's shop fast enough.

The bell over the door jingled. I waited for Rory to poke his head from the back room. When a minute passed without the click of Rory's cane, I rounded the counter and pushed the curtain aside.

"Go away," he said without turning around. Rory sat perched on two upturned crates, three bowls on the table and the bucket of frogs at his feet. I wrinkled my nose at the odor. Dania's dusty bones, I was too late. He never worked with the frogs during the day, when the stench of blood and sour alcohol wafted through the rest of the shop. Not unless his distaste for humanity overwhelmed his common sense.

"Now, Rory," I began, infusing my voice with patience I didn't have. Of all the weeks for him to throw a fit, he had to choose the week of the waleema? "I think you should——" Before I could continue, a basket hit my chest. Rory didn't look up from the bowls.

"I need more ingredients," he barked. "Not your opinion."

I glared at the side of his head. "The last time I went into Essam in a skirt, the rash on my thigh took a week to fade." I would prefer cleaning my teeth with a lizard's tail over selling to dozens of strangers, but unlike Rory, I did not have the luxury of pitching expensive tantrums. "I'll mind the shop myself. You can stay back here."

Rory ignored me, flipping a limp frog onto its back. Unbelievable. I snatched the basket. There was no piercing his thick skull when he fell into these moods. Outside, the main road bustled as those who'd arrived ahead of the waleema explored Mahair's limited offerings. So many visitors with pockets begging to be emptied. Cursing Rory under my breath, I picked up my skirt and turned toward the woods.

"Stop! Jasadi!"

The scream knifed through the din of the main road.

I froze. My legs tensed, preparing for a hard and brutal run. I bent my elbows at the crook, bunching the muscles at my shoulders. A second more, and I would have been a blur of fabric disappearing into the woods. A second more, and I wouldn't have seen the baker's father thrown into the dirt.

The crowd surged behind me. Arms pressed against mine,

bumping and elbowing for a view of the Nizahl soldiers standing over the flour-dusted man in his seventies. It wasn't me they had caught. It was him.

A Nizahl soldier with a chest shaped like an ale barrel loomed over the scrawny old man. Adel, I thought. His name was Adel. He always put extra sesame on my bread rolls.

"You are accused of the possession and active use of magic. You will be taken to Nizahl, where your kingdom of origin will be confirmed. If the investigation brands you a Jasadi, you will stand trial in our Supreme's fair and just courts."

"Please, I—I have lived here for forty years. I've lived in Omal almost my entire life. I raised my family here. My magic is nothing, barely a drop!"

"You admit you have magic. You admit you are a Jasadi."

"I was only born in Jasad," he wept. "Decades before the war."

"I saw him use his magic!" the woman who'd screamed shouted. I didn't recognize her. She must be one of the visitors. "He touched a burned loaf of bread, and it repaired itself."

My cuffs tightened around my wrists. Fool—why would he use his magic within sight of others? Careless, so needlessly careless!

"He un-burned bread? That was his crime?" a furious, gruff voice said. Yuli. He must have known Adel for years. Maybe even hired his sons to work on his farms. "Adel is one of us."

He is not one of them. He is one of yours, Hanim hissed. *Do something, Essiya. Save him!*

I remained motionless. Interfering would only result in two deaths instead of one. I couldn't help him. I did not owe him my life simply because he was born a Jasadi and I was born the Jasad Heir. He should have been more careful.

"Come with us." The shorter Nizahl soldier hoisted Adel to his feet, ignoring his cries at the crushing grip on his arm. "You can state your claims to the tribunal."

"Stop! You're hurting him!" Yuli's shout mixed with others. A strange thought crossed my mind, threatening to tilt the ground beneath me.

What if they had all already known?

If Adel had lived here before the war, he might have told people he was a Jasadi. Easily, without fear, in the halcyon days before his identity and birthplace could summon the bells of death. In a village as small as this, someone must have noticed his magic. Adel's family owned the bakery. They operated it for decades. Could it be possible Mahair had collectively decided not to report Adel despite the severe penalties of knowingly harboring a Jasadi?

Panic filled Adel's blanching face. He shook, forcing the soldier's grip tighter. I saw it coming before it happened.

Be smart, I wanted to beg him. *Hold steady, Adel. Do not let the panic win.*

"No!" Adel screamed. The air tightened, flowing toward the quaking Jasadi. Like the band of a slingshot, Adel's magic pulled itself taut. Silver and gold swirled in his eyes. In the quivering moment where Adel's magic was pointed and poised, I glanced at the soldiers. They knew it was coming. They were *eager* for it.

Adel's magic exploded.

The crowd shrieked as the soldiers were flung to the ground. Adel heaved, staring at them with uncertain eyes.

Had I not been fixed to the spot, I might have yanked at my hair. Why wasn't he running?!

Adel sprinted toward the woods. If he made it past the wall and beyond the raven-marked trees before the soldiers could catch him, he might have the slightest chance of escaping.

He is a soft man. He will not survive in the woods. If the soldiers do not catch him, a different predator will, Hanim said. I could feel her disappointment as if she stood right beside me.

The question of Adel's survival skills would never be answered. The barrel-chested Nizahl soldier drew to his feet and pulled a short blade from his hip. Adel was running in a straight line. The soldier reared his arm back.

I closed my eyes.

Look! Hanim shouted. *At the very least, they are owed the right to be seen.*

I looked. I looked as the knife buried itself between Adel's shoulder blades. I looked as the old baker crashed forward, mere feet from the wall. And I looked while the shorter Nizahl soldier caught up to Adel and buried the Jasadi beneath a storm of vicious blows and kicks. The wet, fleshy thumps were harder for some onlookers to bear than the snapping bones. When again the soldier stood, an empty-eyed pulp lay where Adel once had.

A sob broke out. The visitor who had pointed the finger at Adel avoided the sight of his carcass, maintaining her defiance.

At the edge of the crowd, I saw Rory. He was staring at Adel. White-knuckled hands gripped his cane. Was Rory's shock because of disgust? Was it grief?

"We will load his body into the wagon," the barrel-chested soldier said. Blood soaked his upper right thigh. Adel had thrown him *hard*. "When we return, we expect full cooperation in locating his children. Any resistance will earn you a trip to Nizahl."

The shorter soldier glanced dubiously at the other man's leg. It could barely support its owner's weight. They murmured briefly to one another before turning back to us. "I will remain here to ensure none of you attempt to protect the Jasadi's children. We need a volunteer to help carry the body to the wagon."

No one spoke. Only someone of astoundingly poor intelligence would volunteer to walk into the woods with a Nizahl soldier and the brutalized body of his victim.

"I can carry him."

Heads swiveled toward me. My mouth closed with a snap. What had I just done?

The uninjured soldier took in my build and height. He pressed his lips together, and I almost laughed. He didn't want to choose me. I was taller than him and broad-shouldered. If a conflict ensued, I would make a fiercer opponent than an elderly baker.

As reliable as the rising and setting of the sun, the hubris of men was a winning bet. "Fine. Take his head."

For once, moving away from the crowd failed to bring relief. I wondered if Sefa and Marek were watching, silently screaming at me for my foolhardiness. They didn't understand. They thought I belonged in the crowd of onlookers.

Hanim wanted me to feel guilty for Adel's death, to shake with righteous rage and a thirst for revenge, but all I felt was despair. More than anything, I wanted to belong in the crowd of onlookers. I didn't want to be here, sliding my hands under Adel's shoulders and lifting him from the pool of his own blood. His head rolled onto my shoulder, leaving slick trails of red along my neck. The soldier faced the woods, holding Adel's legs under one curled arm. We walked. I barely noticed when we passed the raven-marked trees. I carried Adel's fragile body and tried to see nothing but the path ahead. The river babbled to our right, splashing gently against the boulders studding the small riverbank.

"Here," the soldier said. I startled; I'd been staring at the back of his head and vividly imagining caving his skull in. We lowered Adel to the ground. "I'll bring the horses. Stay by the body." He shot me a warning glance before vanishing into the trees.

I crouched by Adel's body and pressed two fingers against his eyelids, drawing them down. Sefa would cry. She was good with emotions. She welcomed them as they came, without allowing them to linger or deepen. Anger did not settle inside her like shards of glass, cutting her open on the way down. I wished I had her tears. Adel deserved them.

But Rovial's tainted tomb, how had he been so stupid? He'd confessed his magic in seconds, used his precious little stores of it to seal his fate. At least if he'd let them capture him, he could have tried to escape during the trip to Nizahl.

I should just leave. I hadn't known this man. His blood was not on my hands.

Of course you want to hide. That's what you do best, Hanim sneered.

My teeth ground together. I needed her out of my head. What would satisfy her? What could I do for this Jasadi that would rid me of Hanim's voice?

An idea struck. An idea twice as idiotic as volunteering to carry Adel's body into the woods. But if it meant purging myself of Hanim…

I hurried to the riverbank. Kicking my sandals off, I picked my footing between the boulders. Hirun was a moody river. I had to trust it not to undercut my balance and pull me into its currents.

I debated how to carry water back. Any I scooped into my hands would slosh out while I climbed from the riverbank. Time was not on my side. The soldier could return at any minute.

Finally, I dipped the bottom of my skirt in the water, drenching an inch of the fabric thoroughly. I hurried to Adel's side, lifting my skirt to keep the bottom from absorbing dirt.

My lessons with Hanim had covered Jasad's funereal rituals. She had been so convinced she could mold me to rule a kingdom Nizahl had already wiped from existence. What a waste of her time and mine.

I wrung a length of the skirt. The water trickled over Adel's hand. I moved to his other hand, then his feet. They had beaten him raw. Every drop slid away red.

I reached his face. I did not recoil from touching him. My aversion to physical contact was reserved exclusively for the living.

They'd ruptured his eyes; blood still trickled from under his eyelashes. His magic had barely supported pushing the soldier a single time. I had once sat in Essam, much like I did now, listening to

Hanim rant about how Jasad's magic was already weakening when Nizahl attacked. How in a few generations, our lands would be as barren as the other kingdoms, and Jasadi children would be born without any magic in their veins.

I dabbed water onto his cheeks and forehead. I had stomped out Hanim's lies as soon as I was free of her, casting them to a dark corner of my mind. But looking at Adel's thin face, the bones of his forehead crushed into his hair, it was hard not to believe her words held some measure of truth.

I squeezed the last drops from my skirt and used them to wipe the blood from Adel's chin. "Min dam Rovial, min ra'ad al Awaleen," I began in Resar. If we were in Jasad, someone would have placed a date pit on his tongue. A farewell to his finished body, and a sign of gratitude for all it had given. I dusted a pebble against my vest and pressed it into his mouth. "Irja'a ila makan al mawt wal haya, ila awal al Awaleen." *Return to the place of death and life. To the first of the Firsts.*

I hoped Adel wouldn't mind my performing a Jasadi ritual. He had spent his life largely in Omal. Jasad might not have meant anything to him. Hanim had not taught me the Omalian death rites, but I hoped they were somewhat similar.

"Ila al mawt niwada'ak, wa na'eesh haya bakya fi fikrak. Yikun ma'ak—" I paused. *To death we leave you, and we shall live our remaining life in remembrance. Be with you*...what? I closed my eyes, reciting the sentence again in search of the missing pieces.

"A'malak we ahbabak," came the smooth, measured voice above me. "I believe those are the words you seek."

I went still. I had forgotten to listen for approaching footsteps.

I opened my eyes to boots standing a few inches from Adel's head. My gaze crawled higher. Over the violet ravens embroidered on the bottom of a long black coat. Over a lean, broad-shouldered body shrouded in a Nizahlan uniform finer than any I'd seen before. The infamous black gloves encased his hands. A thin scar reached from the bottom of his throat to his jaw. If all this still did not sway my recognition, his eyes would have rung the final bell: pale blue and wintry. I had seen their likeness only once before.

Arin of Nizahl stood above me, watching me administer Jasadi death rites to a slain man.

I am found.

The world flipped, leaving me spinning through emptiness. Nausea surged in my gut. I leapt to my feet, forgetting the heaviness of my skirt. How was he here? When did he arrive?

I opened my mouth. To explain, to lie, to scream. A puff of air passed my lips, and nothing else.

Steady, Essiya. Remember the first rule, Hanim murmured.

It was too late. The panic had already spread. I was numb with it.

When I died, would anyone perform the Jasadi rites over my body?

A soft neigh accompanied the appearance of two horses led by the other soldier. His eyes flew comically wide at the sight of his Commander. He hadn't known he was coming. If the Nizahl patrol hadn't anticipated the Heir's arrival, then why was he here?

A pulse of pure terror shot through my bones. The dead soldier. What if they'd found his body?

The soldier dropped to a knee instantly, visibly nervous. "My liege."

"I assume he is yours." The Nizahl Heir gestured to Adel's body.

The soldier swallowed. "He used magic to attack us. We had no choice."

"Did you tie him down? Blindfold him?"

"N-no."

"Did he use magic a second time?"

The soldier shook his head. A tremor ran through him.

"I see." The Nizahl Heir's stare was cold. "Bury the body and meet me at your post."

While they spoke, my instincts had sluggishly recovered. The Nizahl Heir wouldn't be in Mahair over the death of a single soldier. He couldn't know my true identity, either, unless the dead had learned to speak in the last few days. Marek said the Heir was spotted in Gahre, so Mahair wasn't the first Omalian village on his route. He had seen me speaking Resar and performing the Jasadi death rites, but not using magic.

I could salvage this.

The soldier collected Adel's body and staggered past the trees, leaving me alone with the Nizahl Heir.

When he turned to me again, I bowed my head. "I ask Your Highness's leave to explain what you witnessed."

The Heir tipped his head, causing a lock of silver hair to come loose from the tie at the nape of his neck. "You have it."

"I am not a Jasadi." I took a slow breath. Truth was perception. I couldn't change my actions, but I could alter how he interpreted them. "I have no magic and no ties to the scorched kingdom. Though I have known Adel for years, the truth of his nature remained hidden to Mahair. To me. The savagery of his death…upset me. I only wanted to pay him a kindness by performing the death rites of his people."

"Is it common to learn Jasadi death rites in your village?" He sounded curious. Conversational.

"No." I pretended to hesitate. "I learned them in Ganub il Kul, before the war. My tutors placed a high premium on speaking the old languages and understanding the practices of every kingdom."

A year or two before the siege, Nizahl had tried to foster a comradery between the kingdoms by creating a camp in the middle of Essam called Ganub il Kul. The camp would heal divisions between the kingdoms by unifying hundreds of their children in a shared education. No one in the royal families sent their children, of course. My grandparents had scoffed at the idea and discarded Supreme Rawain's flowery invitation.

My favorite attendant, Soraya, had not been so dismissive. "Be wary of evil men's kindnesses, Essiya. They always grow from poisonous roots."

The second week of the war, every child still in Ganub il Kul was slaughtered. The murders were brutal, inhuman. And Supreme Rawain blamed it on Jasad. Any kingdom hesitant to point its sword at Jasad changed its tune quickly after Ganub il Kul.

"Your accent is perfect. Your tutors must have been proud."

I studied the Heir. I could not puzzle out whether he believed me or was merely playing along. His features remained smooth and perfectly polite. I could have been describing the best scrubbing technique to remove a stain from cotton, for all he had reacted.

"Truthfully, I caused them great distress. As you can see, I rarely put my skills to good use."

"Ah," the Heir said, with a slight quirk of his lips. "Your first piece of honesty."

I struggled to control my breathing. He didn't believe me. Four Nizahl soldiers broke through the bracket of trees. Two were astride mounts, and the others pulled theirs along. They glanced at me, promptly disregarding my presence.

"Sire," panted the first to arrive, bowing. "We've been searching for Your Highness."

"You've found me," he said. "Do you bring news?"

"No, my liege. It was as the blacksmith said. The boy has been released."

Sire. Your Highness. My liege. How many more? Jasad had one or two honorifics for its royalty at most.

The Commander's expression didn't change. "Excellent. Hand me my reins, Jeru. We will accompany the lady to Mahair."

I had succeeded in retreating several steps. The Commander's announcement halted me in my tracks. "I can assure you that's not necessary."

The soldiers were irritated with my response. "Accept His High-ness's kindness, girl," the brawny one snapped.

The curly-haired one—Jeru—handed the Heir the reins to a black horse. The Heir studied me with his unsettling eyes. I wanted to stab them out of his head.

Bowing stiffly, I pasted on a gracious smile. There was only one right answer. I wouldn't be like Adel, reacting first and thinking second.

"Of course. Thank you, my liege. I humbly accept your offer."

"Wonderful. Do you ride?"

I dug my empty fingers in my cloak. What was his angle?

"I've had little occasion, but I can make do. Sire."

He took a second set of reins from Jeru. I assumed he would mount, but he lifted his right hand and began to pluck the fingers of his glove loose. The soldiers stilled.

The Commander extended his bare hand in my direction. "Allow me." There was no mistaking his intention.

Marek's voice. *He can sense it by touch alone.*

It wasn't possible. Nobody but Jasadis possessed magic anymore. But why else would he remove his glove?

I counted my breath in time with my steps and gritted my teeth. The choice was a simple one. I pull my magic from the surface and pray the cuffs do as they were designed, or I reveal myself as a Jasadi and live long enough to scream.

I thought about Supreme Rawain's wink at the Blood Summit, moments before the screams began. Gedo Niyar shoving me from the table. Molten gold sliding over Teta Palia's eyes as her magic wrapped around the table. The roar when the table exploded, killing Teta and Gedo and engulfing anyone nearby in flames.

It was only later that I understood why the Malik and Malika chose such a gruesome fate for themselves. Accounting for the bod-ies of the dead when they lay in charred, unrecognizable pieces is a tricky task indeed. The record was taken, and ten-year-old Essiya's name was listed among the deceased.

His father had spilled enough of my family's blood. I would not grant the son the same privilege. Drift by drift, my magic ebbed back, the heat fading from my cuffs. My chest burned, as if I'd swallowed the sun.

I took the final step forward and folded my hand over the Commander's.

He was unexpectedly warm to the touch. If I hadn't been watching as keenly as I was, I might have missed the flicker of bemusement rippling across his stoic features. It was there and gone, but the meaning was unmistakable.

The Nizahl Heir was not a man who often found himself in error.

I raised my brows in a mockery of concern. "Is anything the matter, my liege? You've grown pale."

I meant to land a barb, though it seemed only the growling soldiers felt the weight of my insolence. It would be in my best interest to keep far from the brawny one if I didn't wish to suffer a fatal fall from my horse.

The Commander remained infuriatingly unruffled. "My natural complexion, I assure you."

To my horror, he held his horse's reins to the east. "You can't mean to come to Mahair yourself," I blurted.

"Sire!" the guard exploded. "If you would allow me to answer this insult—"

"Vaun." The Commander aimed a quelling glance at his guard. "I've long meant to pay Mahair a visit. I have heard it is an honest and hardworking village. Have I been misled in this belief?"

I stared at him. Marek was wrong. They were all wrong. Arin of Nizahl's greatest power did not lie in any supernatural ability. If I offered any resistance, I would raise their suspicions. If I agreed, he would say his visit to Mahair was on my invitation. He was three steps ahead in every direction I turned.

I pictured his mind as a thousand tiny serpents, moving in a rhythmic, seething coil. A snare within a snare, and I was caught fast within it.

"Not at all, my liege," I said. "Mahair welcomes you."

We rode into the village, outlined against the setting sun. The crowd from earlier had thinned. A hush fell over the remaining stragglers. If the silver hair and crest on his horse did not declare the Nizahl Heir, the unequivocal air of authority did. His soldiers flanked him in the colors of their kingdom, cutting space through the street.

I was the outlier. An Omalian commoner riding in the Heir's cavalry. I shrank into myself as we moved, wishing my hair was not braided back from my face. Between this and my offer to carry Adel into the woods, my anonymity had been compromised more effectively than if I'd danced naked through the main road.

I brought my horse to a stop when we reached Rory's shop front.

"I am expected here," I said. "Thank you for the honor of your escort." I hitched my leg to the side of the mount and dropped to the ground. "I do hope you enjoy your time in Mahair."

When the Commander dismounted and handed the reins to one of his men, my budding optimism that this nightmare was over died.

"Allow me to explain your extended absence to your employer."

Did he expect I'd lead him into a room riddled with evidence of magic? I strangled the basket's arm and tipped my chin. "Your thoroughness is a merit to Nizahl."

I hoped Rory had left his eviscerated frog experiments scattered over the counter. I wanted *something* to assault the Heir, even if just his sense of smell. I passed ahead of him, giving Vaun a wide berth.

The bell above the door jangled with each entering guard. A cavalcade of uniformed doom. Rory sat on a bedraggled cushion, sorting salves and scribbling in his tattered record book. At my entrance, relief slackened his thin frame. "There you are, Sylv—my liege!"

"Your name is Sylv?"

"Only twice a month," I said. Rovial's tainted tomb, what harebrained specter had possessed me?

"Sylvia!" Rory balked. "Forgive her, Your Highness, she is young and foolish. Hand me my cane, Sylvia, I can't—" He leaned over, toppling the book from his lap.

With an unpleasant jolt, I saw why Rory was adamant to reach his cane. He'd cast it aside after lowering himself onto the cushion, and he could not kneel to the Heir without its support.

The Nizahl Heir seemed to draw the same conclusion. "Be at ease," he told Rory. I was briefly surprised he'd dismiss Rory from his duty to kneel. But then, what was one more supplicant when you had thousands? "Your apprentice has not failed in her duties. We delayed her."

"Certainly, it is forgotten," Rory said, clutching his cane against his chest. The chemist quaked like a newborn foal. "Please, it would be my honor to prepare a tea for Your Highness and your men."

"His Highness wished to see me returned safely," I said hurriedly. "We mustn't impose on any more of his time."

The Commander's mouth twitched. My efforts to see the back of him seemed to be as entertaining as they were transparent. I was relieved when Vaun turned his head to speak quietly in the Commander's ear. When he stepped back, the Commander tipped his chin and said, "Another time. Enjoy your evening.

"Sylvia." A chill crept along my spine. It was the wrong name in his mouth, but it perturbed me no less. When he met my gaze, the anger fled from my bones, replaced with pounding terror. His eyes were flinty, colder than rain on my skin. I forgot Rory, Adel, the dead soldier. I forgot Mahair in its entirety.

I was a ten-year-old Heir sitting at an ancient oak table as the sky erupted in fire, as black lightning bolts struck the earth. I was shivering, starving, covered in ash and blood in Essam Woods. Reaching for the woman who bent over me, the sun pouring through her like she was little more than a netted shroud on its glorious surface.

I had encountered death in every incarnation of my life, but I had never looked it in the eye until now.

"Your Highness." I averted my eyes.

The Commander and his guards withdrew. I waited until the thunder of beating hooves disappeared to turn to Rory. He'd climbed to his feet, but I doubted it was the exertion leaving him ashen.

A heavy silence remained in the Heir's wake. When Rory finally spoke, it was low and racked with horror. "You led them into Mahair."

I blinked. "I did not *lead* them here. I was helping with Adel, and they happened upon me. He insisted on escorting me to the shop. What would you have had me do, Rory? Shove the Commander into Hirun and steal his horse?"

A storm waged inside the old man. My worry deepened. The sight of the Nizahl Heir would surely send Mahair into unmitigated hysteria, but I had not expected Rory to fall among them.

Despite his tantrums, Rory held ground as a man of medicine and fact, subservient to the callings of higher reason. Though the Supreme was no friend of science, I doubted he would send his son to mete out justice against a small village chemist.

"Rory," I said slowly. "What are you hiding?"

Resignation weighed down the proud line of his shoulders. "I am not the one hiding, Essiya."

CHAPTER FIVE

The ground rocked beneath my feet. Instinct struck, and my dagger was in my grip before sense could follow. Tears welled in my eyes. I didn't want to hurt Rory.

The last person to call me Essiya was Hanim. Jasad's exiled Qayida found me bruised and matted in ash after the Blood Summit. How I had quaked in relief to hear my name in her mouth, anticipating a quick exit from the unforgiving woods back to Usr Jasad. Instead, she kept me in the woods for five years as Jasad burned.

The name Essiya brought darkness wherever it went.

"Put that down!" Rory snapped, swatting his cane against my leg.

My words emerged soaked in grief. "How did you find out?"

I was so careful. But it wasn't enough. Hanim was right. It would never be enough. No matter where I went or how hard I tried, Essiya would follow.

"I knew you the moment I saw you, starved and bloody and shivering at this door. Niphran's daughter, Heir of Jasad. Essiya."

"Don't call me that!" I shouted. My blood pounded in my ears. "How?"

Concern colored Rory's voice. For himself or for me? "I have a history with Jasad, one that existed long before you. Be at peace. Only I could have known you by sight. Fate's hand drew you to my door that night."

I had not realized how heavily I leaned against the wall until my legs ceased their support and sent me sliding to the floor. Dizzy, I said, "You told me fate is comfort for the content and a misfortune for fools."

My knuckles were white around the dagger. It belonged lodged in Rory's throat, stemming the poisonous truth. I needed a minute. Just a minute, to collect my thoughts.

"The Commander will sense your magic. He'll execute you." I finally deciphered the strange note in Rory's voice. He was frightened for me. I was contemplating slicing his throat, and he was stewing in worry. "If he discovers who you really are—"

"My magic is hidden from him. He won't know I am—I'm a Jasadi." I swallowed hard. "The Heir of Jasad died with the rest of the royal family. There is nothing to discover."

Rory's lips pursed. "You can't be certain. He has an unnatural aptitude for—"

"He touched my hand and found nothing, Rory." I pinched the skin between my brows. A torrential migraine brewed between my temples. "I am not a novice."

Rory's confusion soothed some of my frayed corners. He did not know about the cuffs. I still had some secrets. "I don't understand."

A more important question rose to the surface. One I should have asked five years ago, but Rory hadn't pressed, and I hadn't offered. "Why did you never ask me whose blood I wore the night I arrived in Mahair?"

"I knew it wasn't yours," he said evenly. "I cared little past that."

Rory, who threw apocalyptic fits every time one of his experiments went slightly awry, who nitpicked over proper storage temperatures, who regularly turned his hands different colors digging around baskets of plants I'd scrounged from the dankest corners of Hirun—that Rory didn't care?

I pushed aside a basket of wrapped vials and clambered to my feet. "I don't understand. Why didn't you care where I had vanished for five years if you recognized me? Or how I survived the Blood Summit?"

Rory's grip tightened on his cane, but his features remained languid. "There is much we do not know about each other yet, Essiya."

My jaw clenched. "I told you—"

"My apologies. Sylvia." Disdain dripped from his voice.

The visceral reaction I experienced whenever I heard my birth name was absurd. She was not an entity separate from myself, a fiction in the tales of bards. But neither was she truly real. Not anymore.

"Answer my question," I growled.

"Watch yourself. I owe you no answers."

"Give them to me anyway."

We scowled at each other. Finally, through gritted teeth, Rory said, "I didn't want to know."

"Didn't want to know what?"

"How you survived," he burst. "Your grandparents killed so many at the Blood Summit. I did not want to know what lengths they took to ensure you walked away."

I stopped short, shock rippling through me. "You think—" I clamped my mouth shut. Of course he thought Malik Niyar and Malika Palia had arranged the events of the Blood Summit. Everyone else believed it.

"What exactly do you know of what happened at the Blood Summit?"

For a moment, Rory looked unsure. "The messenger entered the hall with news of Niphran's murder in Bakir Tower. Stabbed to death. The Jasad crown used the chaos to attack the other royals, but their grief over their Heir caused their magic to go awry. They couldn't control what they created. It cost many lives and led to the war."

I pulled at the fringed ends of my braid, avoiding the insistent tug of my memories. After the Blood Summit, the scholars asked all the wrong questions. They wanted to know whether the messenger referred to my mother as "dead" or "slain." Whether he'd arrived on horseback or by carriage. Not why the Malik and Malika of the most successful kingdom in the lands would bother trying to assassinate the other royals, especially in such a reckless outburst. Why they would risk bringing their granddaughter and second Heir to a summit they intended to destroy.

Hurt sharpened my tone. For all his genius, Rory was as susceptible to Supreme Rawain's lies as everyone else.

"I see. Because my grandparents were apparently smart enough to orchestrate the most violent massacre on royals seen in a hundred years, but not smart enough to survive it. Go on, Rory. Finish the tale."

"I do not think—"

"Continue your tale, Rory." My cuffs pulsed in warning. "You will not like my version of it."

Rory sighed, making nervous circles around the cane's handle. "Supreme Rawain rallied the other four kingdoms against Jasad. They found a way through the fortress. Left without a Qayida or any Heirs, Jasad fell to the invading forces."

"I can finish for you." I pushed off the counter, and the chemist's expression tightened with unease. Good. "Nizahl's armies reduced Jasad to rubble. They threw bodies into holes and burned the homes they left behind. Every Jasadi who survived is in hiding, their magic made a capital offense." I trembled. My cuffs tightened around my wrists, warm with my vibrating magic. "No one asked, Rory! No one wondered. How does an unassailable fortress fall?"

Once given voice, the question bloomed in my mind like blood in a clear pond. Hanim hadn't cared about the deaths at the Blood Summit; she hadn't really cared when the siege began, either. But when the tide of war turned in Nizahl's favor, what reduced her to a frothing rage was Supreme Rawain's victory. With my grandparents gone, she had truly believed Jasad would bring forth a new dawn of political freedom. She had imagined herself leaving Essam

Woods when Jasad was at its weakest, welcomed with open arms to the kingdom that had exiled her with a convenient Heir to put on the empty throne and manipulate.

But my magic didn't work. And when the fortress fell, Supreme Rawain's forces were joined by Omal's, Lukub's, Orban's. Envy over Jasad's prosperity, its magic, had hardened into a hate no one could have anticipated. No one except Supreme Rawain.

And so Jasad's Heir suffered in the woods while the throne of magic sat empty in the newly scorched kingdom. In her captured corner, the soft girl who had known a bird by its song and calmed at the touch of another was burned away.

I am what remains.

"The Jasadis' story deserves to be told in whole," I said. "They are not something distasteful to be split up into pieces you can swallow."

"I never said—" Rory stopped short, brows drawing together. "What do you mean, *they?*"

A light knock sounded at the door. We both went silent, our argument falling to the wayside in favor of trepidation. Had the Nizahl Heir returned?

Rory's elbow caught my stomach, pushing me behind him. What did he think he would do against the Commander?

He could turn you in, Hanim whispered. *The chemist works with dangerous substances every day. Think of how easy it would be for him to accidentally ingest a lethal dose. No one would suspect you.*

Killing Rory would only cause more problems. Mahair might not second-guess the accidental death of a soldier, but two accidental deaths in the span of a week?

Rory went five years without speaking my true name. He would not betray me to the Heir now.

"Rory? Are you there? Oh, please be here, Mistress Nadia will have my hide if I return empty-handed."

I tucked my dagger back into my boot while Rory opened the door. Fairel drooped in relief, lifting her skirt to step into the shop. Loose curls bounced around her round face. "You gave me a fright. I have a list from Mistress Nadia."

I tried to smile at Fairel. Rory grunted, "Talk to Sylvia. Damn this day," and disappeared behind the curtains.

Nobody roused at my footsteps through the darkened keep. I kept my tread light. Tomorrow was the day before the waleema. This was probably the most sleep the girls would get for the next two days. The groans of the old, waterlogged walls would hopefully disguise any sound I made outside.

I carefully shut the rusted back door behind me and walked to the side of the keep. Kneeling on the damp ground, I dug my fingers into the soil and tore out the roots of the fig plant until my wrists ached and dirt crusted my fingertips. I shouldn't have planted it to begin with. Even at full growth, these trees would never be like the fig trees in Jasad. The fig trees used to soar to more than thirty meters in Usr Jasad's gardens. When the trees were saplings, the architects infused the branches with magic. Weaving them into complicated, mesmerizing patterns as they flourished.

What kind of idiot was I to think I could stay here forever? Long enough for a fig plant to sprout, for the blue house to become mine, for Rory to give me his shop. Mahair didn't belong to me. Any roots I planted could only ever rot.

I stamped on what was left of the plant and scattered its mangled remains down the slope. Fig trees had no place here, and it had been cruel to let it hope.

This is what he wants, Hanim whispered. *No matter how docile you pretend to be, a feral animal shows its true colors in captivity.*

I pressed my palm over my heart and tried to focus on counting. I was not a captive.

One, two. I'm alive. *Three, four.* I'm—

"Oh," came a small voice. Fairel stuck her head out from behind the bushes, holding a watering pot. "I thought you might be Raya. Was that your plant you dug out?"

I squinted at the child, utterly thrown by her presence. My current mood should not be borne by anyone, let alone Fairel. I wrapped my arms around my middle. "Go inside, Fay. It's past bedtime."

She lowered the watering pot to the ground. Her chin jutted out, and I braced myself for the argument. "You're upset. I can tell. Why don't you talk to me like you talk to Sefa and Marek? Is it because you think I'm little? I will be twelve in two months and six days."

I couldn't help myself. "You think I talk to Sefa and Marek?"

"More than me. Twelve is big, you know."

"I know." When I turned twelve, Hanim enchanted lions to chase me through Essam so I could practice my climbing skills. I had her to thank for my ability to scale a tree in under a minute. I sighed. "Would you like to take a walk with me?"

Fairel glanced at the hushed streets beyond the hill. "Now? The patrol will yell at us."

Then I would flay their skin from their bodies and feed it to them. On how many occasions had I allowed myself to be belittled and demeaned for the sake of safety? All for nothing. I could not budge an inch beyond the village. Not when the Nizahl Heir had placed me firmly in his crosshairs.

"I'll protect you."

Like you protected Adel? Hanim laughed. I gritted my teeth. She was so hungry for my guilt. When would she realize I had none? She had wrung every drop out of me long ago.

"Okay." The trust on Fairel's face disturbed me. More than age or maturity, the ability to trust remained the greatest relic of youth. I hoped to be long gone before I witnessed the world take it from her.

Of all the young wards in the keep, Fairel was my undisputed favorite. So much so that when she reached for my hand, I let her hold it all the way to the bottom of the hill before gently pulling away.

"Why do you always pull away?" Fairel clasped her arms around her middle. Mimicking me from earlier. Kapastra's scaly throne, I couldn't imagine a more disastrous scenario than Fairel modeling her behavior after me.

We ducked into a narrow alley, allowing the darkness to swallow us. Neither of us needed help navigating the uneven path. A shower of pebbles rained into our hair. I shepherded her away from the deteriorating wall, wishing I could as easily guide her from this question.

I could have lied. I would have, had it been anyone other than Fairel and her hurt tone. "I do not have fond memories of being touched. My body recognizes it as a threat." It hadn't always, but Fairel didn't need to know how I'd loved being swung up in Dawoud's arms as a child. I would spend hours hanging on to Usr Jasad's chief advisor while he conducted his business in the palace. Dawoud would walk into meetings with me dangling from his neck and carry on his conversation without batting an eye, as though the other person would be in the wrong for noticing the hyperactive seven-year-old clinging to him.

Hanim had bled those memories from me. She left them gray, so everything to follow could be a dark, dripping red. Whips tearing against my back and shoulders. Nights of hanging by my feet from a sturdy tree branch, not unlike a slab of meat from the butcher's hooks, with a dagger placed in my hand to fight any curious animals. On those nights, I could have easily bent in half and sawed at the ropes lashed around my feet. Another layer of Hanim's punishment—knowing I had the ability to free myself, but not the bravery.

"I would never threaten you," Fairel said, horrified.

Oh, but only this child could make me laugh in the temper I was in. "I know you wouldn't. But my body interprets the sensation the same, no matter who it is coming from."

A clatter echoed from the other end of the alley. I put a hand in front of Fairel and listened. A rat scurried next to my foot, overturning a pile of pebbles in its path.

Just a rat. I ushered Fairel forward, my arm hovering protectively a few inches behind her back.

The alley opened to the flickering illumination of lamplight. Fairel's head swiveled, taking in the uncharacteristic stillness of the main road. A muddy dog loped to the front of the butcher's shop, sniffing at the discarded bones.

Preparations for the waleema were almost complete. Lanterns connected by silver twine hung from the balconies lining the plaza road, creating a roof of light over the village. Shop owners had laid out lovingly braided reed rugs, dyed in muted shades of Omal's blue and white. Incense burned in almost every balcony, warding away the evil eye of the new visitors. I breathed in the smoky scents of lemongrass and rose and exhaled on a smile.

In the unlikely event the Nizahl Heir did not kill me, I wanted to preserve my happy moments here. I had precious few of them left. As soon as the Supreme's son gazed upon my face, this village was lost to me. After his horses cleared Omal's lower villages, I would disappear into Essam.

"Look." Fairel tore ahead, pointing at a splash of vibrant red. "They have almost finished repainting the wall."

A painting stretched over the tallest and sturdiest wall in the main road. On it, the Awaleen towered over us. We craned our necks at the four figures representing the first and truest source of magic in the realm.

"The Awaleen's story is different in Omal," Fairel said.

"Which part?"

Fairel fidgeted with her sleeve. "Mama told me a different story about how they were entombed."

I paused. Fairel never spoke of her parents.

Raya had brought her home from a market trip almost three years ago and dumped the nine-year-old into my lap. As the oldest in the keep, Marek, Sefa, and I helped with the new girls, especially in the first few months when all they did was weep. But Fairel hadn't cried. She had attached herself to me instantly, ignoring my numerous attempts to trade her off to Sefa. Whether it was her steely determination or the fact that she was nearly the same age I was when I watched my grandparents burn, I'd softened far too quickly.

"What did she tell you?"

Fairel brushed the bottom of Kapastra's image. Omal's Awala was drawn in boisterous colors and painstaking detail. Serpentine creatures with forked tails and reptilian eyes curled at her feet. Roche-lyas. The revolting snakelike lizards were Omal's symbol, centered on the kingdom's flags. The Beast Tamer of Omal glared down at me, as though sensing my disgust for her favored pets.

"Omalians believe the Awaleen created the entire world. The kingdoms, Essam Woods, Hirun River. Kapastra's magic brought Omal its bountiful soil and docile animals. Her sister Dania's axe delivered fearsome beasts and the thrill of hunting to Orban. Baira's beauty resulted in Lukub's wealth and good fortune; Rovial's heart poured prosperity into Jasad. So the Omalians say," Fairel said. She flattened her palm against Baira's ankle. "But Mama told me that the world and its beauty existed before the Awaleen, and the four siblings were simply first to enter it with magic. She agreed that they brought life to the land and ruled united for many years. Siblings fight too much, though, so they parted ways to find their own kingdoms. They lived happily for many years."

A loose curl bounced around Fairel's freckled nose. She moved her hand to Dania, Orban's Awala, who had her axe thrust into the sky. Baira had a hand pressed to her midnight-dark skin while she lounged back on her throne, watching her siblings with a mischievous expression. And finally, Rovial. Jasad's Awal.

"Mama told me nothing in this world is meant to be limitless. Nature will find a way to exact a cost. I suppose it is true. She had seven children. More than anyone else in our village." A choked laugh. "And I was the cost."

Oh. My surprise arrived and evaporated in the same breath. Fairel was Orbanian. I'd assumed Raya brought her from another lower village in Omal, but the truth made more sense. Austerity and humility were not pillars of Omalian society, but Orban prided itself on living by the scarcest of means, even if it entailed losing hundreds to starvation every year. I could not imagine the kind of straits a mother with seven mouths to feed must have endured to expel her youngest.

Fairel's hand curled into a fist. "The Awaleen's magic was boundless. None of them had noticed the effects of the magic on their minds over the years. They were becoming colder. Cal—callu—"

"Callous?"

Fairel nodded, brows rumpling with concentration. She seemed determined to recite the story precisely as her mother had. My hand twitched at my side, driven to reach for the girl. *Your mother loved you,* I almost said. *She filled you with stories.*

"The Awaleen could have remained in rule for many more years if it had not been for Rovial. The Awal of Jasad lost his humanity to the magic-madness. He had killed thousands by the time the other Awaleen realized. His evil runs in the magic of all Jasadis."

I struggled not to flinch. Fairel had said she would never threaten me, but Orbanians inherited their Awala's skill and thirst for battle. Today, I was Sylvia. Tomorrow, I might simply be a Jasadi.

Oddly enough, I felt fierce pride at the image of Fairel as a grown woman with the power to challenge me.

Blissfully unaware of my thoughts, Fairel continued, "The Awaleen could not kill their brother. His magic was too strong to destroy without also destroying the kingdoms and everyone in them. It was Dania's idea to contain his magic instead. She convinced Kapastra and Baira that they should entomb themselves with Rovial to ensure the continued survival of their descendants. Dania feared Rovial's magic-madness would eventually catch up to the rest of them."

I craned my neck to peer at my Awal. He was always drawn in profile, with his face turned away in shame. Even Jasad in its glory days hesitated to celebrate him. The blood he shed during the years before the entombing, the lives he stole, were a blight on Jasad's records. They ignored that Rovial's madness was only sped along because of how much magic he had poured into Jasad, into its soil and trees and people. The other kingdoms lost more of their magic with each generation after the entombment, but not Jasad. Rovial had given more of himself, of his magic, than any other of the Awaleen.

In the end, he gave more than he could afford to lose.

The rest of the story remained the same throughout the kingdoms. Masons and architects worked side by side to build a tomb to contain the Awaleen. Chemists from Lukub perfected a draught to put the Awaleen to sleep, so the centuries might pass them in ease. The four kingdoms, determined to learn from the mistakes of their predecessors, appointed a man to create an independent army to balance the power of the kingdoms. This new kingdom would be known as Nizahl, and they would serve as arbiters for the conflicts between the four other kingdoms.

"The Awaleen were buried beneath Sirauk. Mama called it the Boundless Bridge, but my father said it was the Death Crossing, a bridge shrouded in so much mist and shadow that none who began the crossing ever finished."

"My mother—" I stopped. Fairel waited, features open and

innocently curious. I hadn't spoken about my mother with anyone but Soraya. Whereas my grandparents had flinched at the mention of Niphran, my attendant had taken me to see my mother in Bakir Tower once a week. I believed she feared I would one day start to think of my mother the way the rest of our kingdom did. The Mad Heir of Jasad. The Wailing Widow. A tragedy to be tossed in a tower and forgotten. "My mother told me hundreds of people came to cross the bridge shortly after the entombment, thinking they could whisper their wants and secrets to the sleeping Awaleen. The bridge is so long, it took weeks before anyone realized none of them finished the crossing." Their bodies simply vanished, devoured by the mist shrouding Sirauk.

Fairel shuddered. "How terrible. Then why do we celebrate the Awaleen with the Alcalah?"

Because it is the nature of humanity to celebrate the things that want to kill them.

We resumed our walk. I guided us off the main road, onto the street hosting Daron's tavern and the visitors' tents. I would never bring Fairel down this road under normal circumstances, but the Nizahl patrol would be eager to prove themselves to their Commander, and there was no glory in harassing drunkards leaving the tavern.

"The tournament is a remembrance. We thank the Awaleen for their sacrifice and honor them by sending our most worthy Champions to compete in the Alcalah."

Fairel slapped a mosquito from her ear. She peered up at me. "Do you think I might become Champion someday?"

I skidded to a halt, gaping at her. "Most of the Champions die, Fairel."

"They die brave. It is a worthy sacrifice," she said. "Just like the Awaleen."

I thought of the watch guard frog in my bucket and knelt to Fairel's eye level. "There is no such thing as a worthy sacrifice. There are only those who die, and those willing to let them."

The next morning, I went straight to Nadia's duqan for extra chairs. I had forgotten to reserve two chairs for tomorrow, meaning Rory might find himself standing behind his booth for the entirety of the waleema.

Three women strode past me, massive clay pots balanced on their heads as they walked from door to door, freeing their hands to carry bundles of sweet-smelling mint. Shop owners swept the dust off their front steps and knocked spiders from their water-logged awnings. The butcher's sons knelt on the ground with a soapy bucket, scrubbing the bloodstains and shooing away the dogs. A group of children half the size of the knives they were wielding sliced the peels off chopped-up sugar cane stalks. No one's gaze lingered on the bakery's stone oven, cold from days of disuse.

Adel's half-Jasadi children, who had never even visited Jasad, had evaded capture. In a day or two, the stone oven would probably light beneath the hands of a new owner. Adel and his family would become another shocking Jasadi story, more evidence of the lower villages' lack of vigilance.

I spat the shell of a melon seed like it had done me a great personal offense and rolled my sleeves over my cuffs.

The bell over Nadia's shop jangled. "Sylvia!" Fairel greeted. She scurried to fetch her mistress.

"We take care of our own before any of those donkeys from Gahre," Nadia said as Fairel carried out two chairs. She refused to let me pay her, a frustrating sort of reverse-haggling the elders of Omal too often engaged in. Accepting her generosity without argument would also be grounds for offense, so I did not leave until I had persuaded her to come into Rory's shop for three free bottles of ointment for her knees.

Fairel helped me carry the chairs. "Is it true, Sylvia? Have you met the Nizahl Heir? The Commander?"

I groaned. It had been less than five hours since I saw Fairel. Had news traveled so quickly? "Fay."

She bit her lip. "Forgive me, I should hold my tongue, but it's all so exciting, isn't it? An Heir in our village, searching for his Champion! The girls say he's odd-looking. Handsome, though. Very handsome. Have you ever seen hair colored so strangely? Like moonlight. What do you think?"

"I think you're never too old for a spanking." We rounded the corner, coming into view of the shop.

Fairel's chair fell from her suddenly limp grip, hitting my foot. I cried out, hopping to the side. "Fairel! What has gotten into you?"

I followed the source of the girl's stupefaction. Standing at the door of his shop, Rory held himself stiffly near the Nizahl Heir and his guard. The three men in the rear appeared to be suppressing smirks, which explained why Fairel was blanching. Her words had carried.

She dropped to her knees, shaking like an autumn leaf. The sight brought a sour taste to my mouth. "My lord, I didn't intend any disrespect. Silly gossip—you're very pleasing to behold, truly—they just meant your hair was odd. And your face is just *lovely*, honest, the best I've ever seen. Silver is an unusual color for Omal, you see—"

A lightness of spirit had not visited Vaun since we last met. He scowled at the girl. I scooted in front of her, matching his glare with my own.

"Your Highness. I see you have chosen to continue honoring our humble village with your company."

"It is I who have the honor," Arin said. To Fairel, he nodded. "You may rise."

Fairel nearly toppled on the length of her skirt. I steadied her elbow, squeezing tight lest she find inspiration to dive for further prostrations. At the Commander's steady gaze, she folded close to my side. My muscles clenched, resisting the urge to fling her off.

"Silver is an unusual color for any kingdom," he said. "Thank you."

When I could bear it no longer, I peeled Fairel off my person. "Go. Nadia is waiting for you."

Fairel set off at a run. The Heir and I regarded each other. His hair was tied back at the nape, not a single lock astray. His soldiers had made no effort to blend into the populace, laced in the dark hues and overcoats of Nizahl. The street was unusually still. Despite their curiosity, the residents of Mahair possessed a healthy sense of caution. They pressed inside their shops and windows, climbing atop one another for a glimpse of the Heir and his guard.

"Mahair will certainly lack in excitement when you depart, my liege," I said, gesturing at the windows. "Whenever that sad occasion may be."

The Commander glanced at the shops, causing a scramble as people ducked away from the windows. "Then it is fortunate I intend to remain in Mahair until the end of the waleema."

I forced myself not to react. Only a guilty person would take this news poorly. The treaty Nizahl signed with the other kingdoms didn't allow them to hurt just anyone—only Jasadis.

"I am surprised you seek to explore the lower villages," I said, proud when my voice didn't crack with anger. "There is not much to find in our corner of Omal. Certainly not a Champion."

"I disagree," he said. "There is plenty to be found, if one knows where to look."

The Commander (*Arin*, his name was Arin, his mother hadn't named him Commander or Nizahl Heir) stepped toward me. I prepared myself. I was coming to realize that every exchange with this man was consciously directed, designed to entrap.

He addressed his next words to Rory. "Her services as an apprentice must be unparalleled if she is twice employed."

Twice? I glanced at Rory. He looked similarly mystified. I took additional work only over the summer, when Yuli paid handsomely for seasonal farmhands.

Wait. My entire body stiffened. He couldn't mean my route, could he? He had been in the village for less than a day. I hadn't seen anyone since Zeinab and her mother. What if they told him my cures were like magic? Kapastra's fanged rochelyas, perhaps I was too good a crook.

"My services are unexceptional, my lord. I have simply been blessed."

"Sylvia, where is the herb basket I asked for?" Rory spoke up. Sweat had collected in the lines of his forehead. Despite my rising nausea, I suppressed a small smirk. Who knew how poorly Rory reacted under pressure?

"I forgot to fetch it. My mistake. Your Highness, if you'll excuse me, there are items—"

Arin didn't bat an eye. "I am happy to escort you. My guards can set up your chairs in the meantime."

The guards shifted, displeased about parting with their Commander. Arin's pointed glance brooked no arguments. It would be a lie to say I wasn't a little smug. Rory made such a performance of my failure to dissuade Arin from escorting me from the woods. Now he could see for himself there was no victory in a battle of wills with the Heir. It rankled, how effortlessly we had been spun into the precise situation we sought to avoid.

"You have made almost no impression on the other villagers," he said once we passed Nadia's storefront. I had no idea where I was taking him. "I find it peculiar. An orphan girl without ties to this village until the age of fifteen. No origins, no story."

I stayed quiet. He was probing. If he knew anything, I would be tied to the back of a wagon.

"I must have a forgettable disposition."

Three steps. In the distance, the clanking bell of a fruit cart.

"Or you have magic."

He halted when I did. His brow arched at my expression. "You're shocked. Did you think I was taken in by your show in the woods?"

"If I've mistakenly led Your Highness to believe—"

Arin waved aside my objection. "Don't embarrass yourself."

My nails dug into my palms. "You don't have proof." As though he needed it. As though anyone would dare question him. A single word on his tongue held more power than a thousand objections on my own.

"True," he conceded. "Either you are a study in restraint or these villagers are as unaware as they are dull."

My cuffs burned. I mocked the villagers daily, had probably expressed the sentiment myself, but I *could*. I was one of them.

"If *unaware* means we do not brutalize defenseless old men in the middle of the street, then yes. I suppose we are." It took all my effort not to snarl.

The Commander tilted his head. "Not restraint, then." He moved toward me. I arrested my breath, belatedly remembering the magic building against my cuffs. Would he sense it frothing under my skin? I would not be able to dampen it fast enough.

I calculated my odds of survival. Cornered as I was, he could snap my neck or slit my throat before I could conjure any kind of functional attack. I would be able to scratch him, maybe, before my body crumpled at his feet.

"Now, it would be a simple matter if I had sensed your magic by the river. Magic is often eager to make itself known. The stronger the power, the faster the response. It takes only a single touch."

A gloved finger hovered under my chin. Though he didn't move to close the distance, my trepidation spiked. A world of danger lived in that inch of space.

"The trouble is, your magic doesn't seem to behave as it should."

A day ago, Marek had shaken his head and said *mild*. Ten years of whittling away common vulnerabilities and leashing my violence. Ten years I felt willing to waste for the chance to stab Arin of Nizahl in the eye.

I gritted my teeth hard enough to crack. "Investigate as you wish, sire. I am afraid it will be time poorly spent."

The Nizahl Heir withdrew his hand. "Perhaps. But a temper that ignites as quickly as yours leaves ashes in its wake. I need only follow the trail."

CHAPTER SIX

The morning of the waleema dawned in complete, unbridled chaos. Daleel, one of the few good cooks in the keep, had baked loaves of fino for breakfast. I hurried to slice the steaming bread along the side and spoon scrambled eggs into its lumpy center. I escaped with my sandwich just as the horde of girls descended on the kitchen.

At the bottom of the hill, Sefa spotted me just as the first wagon destined for the main road departed with her aboard. She pointed a warning finger at me as it rumbled away. "Behave!" she shouted. I hadn't spoken to her and Marek for more than a few minutes since the night in the woods. I usually struggled to secure alone time at the keep, but I had recently found myself with an excess of it. They'd been missing from dinner yesterday, and I'd caught Marek in the hall whispering urgently to Sefa the night the Heir arrived. At my approach, they had both hurriedly straightened and bid me good night.

Their strange behavior worried me. What if the Heir's arrival had sent them into a panic? They might be tempted to turn me in and protect themselves. After all, helping me hide a murdered soldier was not much better than committing the killing itself.

I waved down the next wagon. I'd keep an eye on both of them, lest the bonds of friendship find themselves mysteriously frayed.

The wagon rattled over the bumpy ground, crates sliding with each dip and lean. I hopped out as soon as we reached the outer throng of the square. Booths lined each side of the main road, backed by merchants dressed in the colors of their kingdoms. They shouted as I passed, pointing at their fruits and jewelry and scarves. The crisp air carried music and the notes of burned sugar and grease. The visitors from the Omalian lower villages swarmed the main road in shades of white and blue. A mass of children sat in a circle, playing with dolls in the images of the Awaleen. A woman with a red triangle scarf tied over her curls slapped a few thieving hands from her ghorayeba platter and hollered for Yuli. Yellow coins sewn into the scarf jangled with her motion.

"I wonder if I sing the beautiful woman a song, will she dance?" A man roughly my age plucked his lute as he approached. The sweet strum of the instrument transported me to quieter nights, standing barefoot in Hirun as the river flowed around me. Several paces behind him, his partner giggled as she drummed her tubluh. "Will you give my music the honor of moving your spirit and body?"

"Certainly," I said. "I am going to move my body far away."

Skirting the crestfallen lute player, I almost knocked over a young man holding a tray full of steaming cups of reddish chai above the crowd. The sounds of the lute and tubluh followed, the melody weaving through the air, twining with the cries of the hawking merchants.

"An ula for your kitchen, ya anisa? Engraved by the finest artist in Lukub!"

"Abayas, abayas, come try on your new abaya! Embroidered by Orban's Hany Barrow himself!"

My brows shot up. What merchants with the full privilege of their sanity would come to Mahair all the way from Orban or Lukub? The closest border for Orban required six weeks' travel west, not including the voyage through the desert flats. Three weeks if they cut through Essam, but such shortcuts were rarely taken. Over thirty years later, and the siege of monsters remained too fresh.

Stuck between Nizahl and Orban, a border-locked Lukub had recently expanded its territory south, into the woods. The trip to Mahair from Lukub would take a mere week traveling south—but only by braving the woods. Otherwise, any Lukubi merchant with eyes on Omal's lower villages would need to circle through Orban or Nizahl to reach us.

Perhaps they intended to remain in Omal until the waleema in the upper towns. I heard the Omal palace preferred to host their own waleema a day or two before the Alcalah's second trial.

Rory had given me permission to explore the booths before joining him. I didn't have much interest in purchasing trinkets I couldn't take with me when I fled, but circling the road would give me an opportunity to scan for Arin and his guard. I compared daggers from Gahre masons, sampled powdered jellies, and chewed on nuts hardened in sugar syrup. I was maintaining my frugal self-control until I reached a merchant with barrels full of sesame-seed candies. I had devoured the pile Sefa and Marek gave me in a fit of stress.

Oh, what did it matter? I filled my basket and poured ten coins into the merchant's palm. Either the Commander would transport me to Nizahl to die at trial or I would flee this village as soon as he left. His arrival had plunged my already uncertain future into bleak nothingness. I had earned the right to fill my belly with as many of these candies as I could.

Marek hustled behind the tavern's collar-shaped booth, pouring ales faster than should be possible. Yuli must have loaned Marek out for the day. He waved, gesturing invitingly at an overflowing cup of ale. I shook my head at the offering with a shudder. Intoxication had always lacked any appeal. My uglier insticts were difficult to control on the best of days; I dreaded to think what could happen with my inhibitions lowered and my tongue loosened.

Since I had already planned to spy on Marek and he appeared on the verge of collapse, I heaved a sloshing barrel into my arms and set

up a serving space next to him. I lost myself in the routine of scooping and pouring. The attention of so many strangers scraped against
my nerves, but they were better than Mahair's residents, who had
taken it upon themselves to try to gossip with me about the Nizahl
Heir. Increasing the general inebriation level of the crowd would
serve me well.

When the surge lapsed, Marek flung himself to the ground, pressing his cheek to the well-beaten rug. "Sylvia, I love you," he said. "I
will bring you flowers and sesame-seed candies until the day I die."

I nudged his head with my boot. "I would rather have the candies
and a portion of your earnings."

Marek laughed, rolling onto his back to look at me with dancing
eyes. "How un-Omalian of you to ask me for money."

"How un-Omalian of you not to accept."

His smile slowly disappeared. A solemnity passed between us,
heavy with words unsaid. Neither of us belonged to Omal, yet neither of us laid claim to our true kingdoms. I doubted Marek or Sefa
had considered the possibility I was a Jasadi. I had not performed a
single act of magic in the entire time they had known me. But they
must have suspected I was more than I claimed.

Marek's replacement arrived to relieve us. We lounged in Nadia's
borrowed chairs and watched two men grappling on the platform.
The fights were my favorite part of the waleema. Mahair's craftsmen
constructed a raised platform for the matches taking place between
the first and last hour of the waleema, with the last hour reserved
for serious contenders. Buckskins and boiled leather cushioned the
platform, preventing a hard fall from cracking open any skulls. Men
and women hoisted themselves into the ring for a chance at victory.
There could be no celebration of the Alcalah without a competition,
and Mahair preferred the physical kind.

"Are you competing?" I asked Marek.

He lifted a shoulder. "Could be."

I stifled a snicker. He'd be in the ring within an hour. I'd always wanted to compete. Indulge the tempting opportunity to win the prize and buy myself a new cloak with nothing more than an hour's effort. But I could not risk exposing my skill.

You mean exposing your savagery, Hanim said. *Would they treat you the same if they knew you could snap a man's neck without a thought?*

I shoved a candy into my mouth, crunching until I drowned out Hanim's voice. I wound my way back to Rory's booth. A cheer rose as performers leapt from roof to roof, swiping long torches to light the lanterns hanging over the road. A rosy haze illuminated the mosaic of fire above us. Children chased each other, dodging legs and swinging baskets, their laughter ringing louder than the lute players' cheery melody. Mahair in its full glory.

For the next hour, my voice grew hoarse explaining the purpose of each oil and ointment to the visiting Omalians while Rory snored lightly on my right.

By the time Fairel crashed into the booth, I was ready to hurl a jar at the next person who asked why we used frog fat in the plaster. Someone had tried to braid Fairel's short hair into twin tails. The resulting braids curved over her ears like a ram's horns. A smear of what I fervently hoped was chocolate covered her nose, and she wore a clean, lovingly tailored frock woven in Omal's white and blue. I had seen her running between the booths all afternoon, dragging around the chairs Nadia loaned to the Gahre merchants. Her Orbanian work ethic at full play.

"Are you busy?" She vibrated with anticipation. "Raya said I can watch the matches if I have company."

A lemon would shudder at the sour pucker on Rory's face. "Why would you go with Sylvia? There are plenty of small urchins gathering at the matches."

Fairel lowered her eyes. "Sylvia is my only friend, and I want to watch them with her."

Rory and I glanced at each other, sharing in the unease of *me* being anyone's only friend. He waved a hand. "Off with you, go."

I gritted my teeth before taking Fairel's small hand and weaving through the crowd. I had on loose white pants that rose high on my abdomen and cinched at my ankles. Two slits cut into the sides of my tunic allowed me to knot it just above the band of my pants. Though gowns were the standard fare for a festival, I had dressed in case of a sudden need to flee.

Each person on the platform dedicated their fight to Kapastra. No Omalian Champion had triumphed in the Alcalah for over ten years, but reality did not prevent excitement from buzzing around the villagers. Even if their Champion lost, the Nizahl Heir was choosing his Champion from Omal. An Omalian had twice the chance of winning the Alcalah, even if they did so in Nizahl's name.

The crowd undulated, crowing as a short woman with shaved hair knocked Yuli's son to the leathers. Odette, the butcher's daughter and the waleema's reigning fighter.

"Why don't you fight?" Fairel asked. "You're strong. I helped you clean Yuli's stables one summer, remember? You carried the heaviest crates and controlled the biggest horses."

I glanced at Fairel, surprised. I took care not to reveal my strength; she must have snuck up on me.

I was at a loss. Why *didn't* I fight? The Nizahl Heir was already in Mahair. He knew me as a swindler, an orphan, a liar. Discovery arrived in my village despite my best behavior—recent murder of a Nizahl soldier aside. Why not join the challengers? My magic certainly wouldn't react one way or the other.

I shook away the petulant musings. I planned to save self-pity for my deathbed, and not a minute before.

"It wouldn't be kind to the others," I said.

Fairel speared me with a glance entirely too mature for her age. "Since when are you kind?"

My mouth opened. Fairel said it matter-of-factly, without skipping a beat. "I like it about you. Sometimes, I do not want to be kind, but Raya says we must treat others better than they treat us." She scrunched her face to mimic Raya's characteristic scowl. "*We must value our differences and lead with a welcoming hand.* If someone slaps my welcoming hand, why shouldn't I slap them back?"

I laughed so hard I snorted, startling the couple ahead of us. I caught my breath, nearly descending into a new fit of giggles at Fairel's braided horns.

"Oh, I need to check on the chairs!" Fairel yelped, dashing away before I could stop her. Wiping tears of laughter from my eyes, I debated whether to follow Fairel or hunt down the girl selling basboosa studded with roasted almonds and drenched with so much sharbat I'd smelled it from three stalls away.

My neck tingled. I brushed my fingers over my braid.

Someone was watching me.

I scanned the crush of revelers moving through the main road. I would bet my right elbow the Nizahl Heir had joined the waleema. He was here somewhere.

If my suspicions about Marek and Sefa were true, Sefa might have information about the Nizahl Heir. I needed to understand how exactly he possessed an ability to sense magic. Did it require his hands, or was it any skin-to-skin contact? Was he immune to magic?

I tracked down Marek, cheerfully bruised after his beating from Odette. "Where is Sefa?"

He sobered instantly. "Why? What's the matter?"

I suppressed a groan. Were it not so infernally annoying, I might find his constant protectiveness over Sefa sweet. "I ask your leave to speak to her, oh wise Marek."

Marek rolled his eyes. "I saw her with Raya. A patron is trying to halve the price of a gown with 'wobbly stitching.' She would probably appreciate a rescue."

I swiped my basket from under the booth and edged around the crowd, straining to find Sefa's head. But Sefa was not the person I saw approaching me, a gray hood pulled over his telltale silver hair.

As it had by the river, the rest of the world bled its colors, turning gray to outline the Nizahl Heir in sharp relief. He glided through the throng. The cacophony of the waleema faded as my senses narrowed on the threat.

His guards wore similarly bland clothes. The disguises would crumble under any scrutiny, but people were moving around the Nizahl brigade without a second glance.

"Your Highness." I bowed my head. "An honor to see you taking part in our humble waleema."

"The honor is mine alone, Sylvia."

He said my name with subtle contempt. A five-letter accusation. An acknowledgment of my most successful lie.

Arin's attention slid to my basket. "Quite the bundle of sesame-seed candies you've acquired."

I eyed him. A predilection for tooth-rotting sweets was hardly unique to Jasadis.

"I seem to have come upon my own sample of the candy." He reached into his pocket and I tensed. Surely he would not try to injure me at a crowded waleema?

The Nizahl Heir pulled out a sesame-seed candy. Its distorted pink wrapping plucked at my memory. Unless requested, these candies weren't typically sold with individual paper wrapping. The wrapping protected the hardened sugar from melting, but the onerous task of folding the paper dissuaded most merchants.

"I believe it belongs to you."

At my bewilderment, Arin flipped the candy onto his gloved palm. "I found it floating in a puddle two miles past the raven-marked trees. Strange, is it not? How might such a candy have fallen so far into Essam?"

Oh no. Oh no, no, *no*. Sour fear surged into my throat. I had dropped a sesame-seed candy the night I crossed the raven-marked trees. I'd hesitated to fish it from the pungent puddle. Seconds later, the Nizahl soldier had confronted me. I never retrieved it.

His expression was a study in civility. He might have been inviting me to tea instead of accusing me of trespassing. Where the Supreme manipulated with charm and grand speeches, his son could be chiseled from pure ice.

Everything inside me screamed at me to act. Shove my blade into his chest, hurl coins into his eyes and run, *something*. We'd taken the soldier's body not too many miles from where the candy fell. All I could do was hope Hirun had done its job and carried the corpse to a different part of the river. Without a body, this piece of candy alone couldn't link me to the soldier's disappearance.

Adopting a guileless, unaffected tone, I said, "Am I the only person in Mahair who enjoys sweets? Perhaps one of your soldiers had a craving."

The scar cutting across his jaw caught the lantern light when he tilted his head. A wound made doubly disturbing by the fact that it was meant to kill. And by appearance alone, it should have succeeded.

"Try again," he said.

"What?"

"Think of a better lie. You're capable of it."

I gritted my teeth. If he aimed to prick my temper into revealing the truth, he needed a stronger arrow. "I apologize if my honesty is without adornment."

He tucked the candy back into his pocket. I wanted to snatch it away and dash it under my boot. Thanks to my cuffs, exposing me as a Jasadi would be a lofty task. But I had concealed the soldier's death hastily, without a quarter of the care I'd spent on concealing my identity. Either offense ended with my death.

An invisible noose tightened around my neck. If he intended to slowly chip at my sanity, his progress could not be faulted. I had always imagined my discovery as a brief, brutal affair. Like Adel's. I had prepared myself for the lion, not for the circling vulture.

His implacable demeanor infuriated me. Enough for my tongue to loosen and say, "When will I have proven my innocence to you?"

"Your innocence?" Though his smile didn't falter, the veneer of detachment dropped. He looked at me like sheer willpower alone prevented him from tearing me limb from limb.

This man is going to kill you, Hanim whispered. *If not today, then someday soon.*

Arin raised a gloved hand. I didn't flinch as he drew a leaf from my braid. When he spoke, it was almost soothing. Rueful. "You cannot prove what doesn't exist."

A faraway shout. "The horses!"

The Commander turned his head. He paused, features going blank as he listened for something beyond my ears. I remained fixed to the spot, struggling to convince my pounding heart we were not seconds from death.

"Sire?" Jeru shuffled closer.

The musical troupes abandoned their instruments, plunging the festival into a confused silence. The blare of trumpets shook the air.

Movement rippled around me as one by one, the people of Mahair, drunks and children alike, dropped to their knees. Arin swept his hood back.

"Visitors," Arin said.

CHAPTER SEVEN

The villagers scattered as a carriage bearing the Omalian crest rode through the center of the road, led by horses saddled in white chains. Giant wheels, lacquered in sparkling blue and white gems, fought their own weight as they spun over the uneven dirt. The carriage stopped in front of the platform, and two guardsmen flanked the door as the steps unfurled.

I angled my body behind the wall, just out of sight. Only Arin and his men remained standing. I spotted a puzzled and stained Fairel, clutching a yam sticky with molasses in her fist. "Fairel!" I hissed. I wanted her far away from whoever was about to step out of that carriage. Oblivious, Fairel slipped behind one of the chairs, nibbling at her yam.

A tangle of emotions somersaulted in my chest when the Omal Heir descended. He was smaller than I had imagined him. I searched for any family resemblance in his feathered dark hair or the proud nose sitting below darting hazel eyes.

At a glance, no one would ever assume I shared blood with the Omal Heir.

My father was born Emre, Heir of Omal. Three months after I entered the world, an arrow cleaved his throat open during a hunting trip for my mother's birthday. Although Emre had left behind a rightful Heir—me—my grandparents had balked at the possibility that I might inherit Omal's throne before I inherited Jasad's. With my mother grieving in Bakir Tower, no one stopped the Malik and Malika from renouncing my claim to the Omal throne. For its part, Omal was all too eager to strip me from their line of inheritance; I imagined the rumors of my grandparents' role in Emre's death played a part.

Felix was my father's nephew. The laws of Omal's lineage should have prevented the throne from ever passing to him, but the murder of most of the royal family at the Blood Summit complicated matters. Though Queen Hanan would hold the throne until her death, I'd heard my paternal grandmother had all but sequestered herself in her palace. Leaving Omal in Felix's highly incapable hands.

No one in the village liked Felix, and for good reason. From the stories I'd heard, he had less political acumen than a rabid goat. They clearly weren't wrong; there must have been miles of empty space in that giant head of his if he thought riding into Mahair in a carriage worth more than the entire village was the right move.

But an idiot Heir was still an Heir, and I mapped my escape. If I cut through the vagrant road, I could circle the crowd and sprint to the keep in under twenty minutes.

Arin met Felix by his carriage. Felix bounced on his shiny shoes. "So it is true. I heard you were patronizing our lower villages. It would have been remiss of me not to welcome you myself."

"A generosity not soon forgotten," came Arin's mellifluous response. "Mahair is wonderful. A true tribute to its kingdom."

"It has been too long since last we met." Felix extended his hand to Arin. I cringed.

How could the Heir of the largest kingdom in the land be so unstudied in Nizahl's customs? Inviting a touch from the Nizahl Heir carried dangerous implications. A child with the faintest trace of royal blood would know better. Two things were widely known about Arin: he was never seen without his gloves, and he did not touch unless he meant to kill. Fantastical gossip, I'd thought. Just more village nonsense. Now I wondered if Felix was aware of his fellow Heir's ability to sense magic.

My brow furrowed. How had *Marek* been aware of it?

Arin's gloved hand closed around Felix's briefly. "Indeed. Shall we move to more private quarters to continue our reacquaintance?"

Felix glanced around. "Has the waleema concluded?"

"Nearly." The first signs of impatience leaked into the Nizahl Heir's tone. He glanced at the kneeling crowd. "You must be weary from your journey."

"Nothing a hearty brew cannot fix," said the royal dunce. He instructed the rider to house the horses with Arin's and not "leave them alone with a half-wit stable hand."

Maneuvering a carriage in such a tight space irritated the horses. They harrumphed, hooves clomping in a wide loop. One of Nadia's chairs stood directly in the path of the carriage's wheels. My heart dropped. I knew what would happen as soon as the rider reined the horses back, but I was too late.

"Stop! Stop!" Fairel shouted, launching herself toward the chair. I vaulted to my feet, braced to watch her get split in two. Yuli grabbed Fairel's frock before she could intercept the carriage's path. The chair splintered beneath the wheels, and Fairel shrieked. Spooked, the horses reared, sending an Omalian guardsman crashing into Felix. They went down in a heap.

Dusty and red with embarrassment, Felix slapped aside the guard's hand and clamored to his feet. He glowered at Fairel. "Come here."

Pulse pounding, I took a step from the shadows. The crowd sobered, watching Yuli unwillingly release Fairel. Bowed in front of the Omal Heir, her braids coming loose from their upturned horns, she was as much a threat as a river gnat.

"I apologize sincerely, my lord," Fairel hurried to say. "The chairs—they're my responsibility, you see, my mistress tasked me with their safe return—"

Felix shoved Fairel in front of the horses.

Later, I would wonder whether I might have acted differently had it been anyone other than Fairel, who was mine since the day Raya brought her to the keep. If under alternate conditions, I might have stayed hidden and merely added this kernel of rage to the collection.

The villagers screamed as the clustered horses kicked at Fairel, and the sound of breaking bones fired across the main road. My magic seethed forward, and I gripped my dagger, Felix's viscera bright in my mind's eye. I was moving for Felix before the horses had finished their assault on Fairel's still body.

Arin moved faster. I hadn't taken more than a step, and he was already there, blocking my path. He knocked the dagger from my hand. My magic did not approve, howling as the horses trotted past Fairel, their hooves red with her blood.

The pressure on my cuffs tightened, familiar pain roaring beneath my skin, and then—the impossible.

The dagger shuddered into the air and flew. My magic hummed, keeping the dagger's course true. I gasped, the incomprehensible sight made more confounding by the cuffs' unchanged presence around my wrists.

Arin didn't turn around to see the dagger embed itself into Felix's thigh, not even when the other Heir screamed. He didn't turn at the shouts from the guardsmen or the sobs as the village physician crouched by Fairel's prone form.

Inches separated me from the Nizahl Heir. I stood close enough to see the dark victory eclipsing the frost in Arin's eyes. I had done it—given him the evidence he needed.

Horror thrilled down my spine. I tried to jerk back.

When he spoke, the words brushed my temple. "If you wish to keep your head today, stay still."

His hand closed around my wrist. My livid magic danced beneath the surface of my skin but did not break through a second time.

The Heir turned to ten of Felix's guardsmen brandishing their swords in my direction. The villagers who weren't occupied with moving Fairel's splayed limbs onto a stretched calfskin watched with apprehension. Apprehension *for* me. They thought I had thrown the dagger. They hadn't seen Arin knock it from my hand before it flew. A trickle of relief tempered some of the nausea churning in my gut.

Congratulations, it was only the Nizahl Heir who saw you use magic! Hanim yelled. *No one important.*

"Arrest her!" Felix screeched. "For her attack on the Heir of Omal! Where is the physician? Leave the girl! Can't you see I've been stabbed?"

Fairel's sudden, strangled cry pierced through me. I tried to go to her, but Arin's grip on my wrist didn't falter.

The Omalian guardsmen moved, but Arin's men closed in front of us. Murmurs rose from the crowd. Heirs raising arms against one another was tantamount to a declaration of war.

"What is this?" Felix asked, and though his retinue blocked him from sight, his voice pinched with bewilderment. "Instruct your guards to stand down! I am after the girl, not you."

I tried to yank my hand away. If I fled into the woods fast enough, I could climb a tree near the bend of Hirun and wait out any pursuers. I still had food waiting for me in the ravine. I would keep company with its ghosts while I devised my next steps.

"My men are not protecting the girl," Arin said. "They are protecting your kingdom from incurring the full wrath of the Citadel."

"Move!"

Felix's protectors melted to the side, exposing the Omal Heir leaning against the carriage steps. The dagger jutted out of his thigh. The Nizahl guardsmen veered to the side, swords pointed at the Omalian guardsmen. Felix ignored me, which was just as well, as my perplexed expression would likely ruin whatever story Arin was spinning.

"Why?" Felix demanded. "Who is she to you?"

I spied Rory in the crowd, tending to Fairel. A bone jutted out of her right leg. Sefa knelt at his side, rubbing a clear liquid beneath Fairel's nose. The girl's pain-stricken eyes drooped shut, leaving her body still. Rory wrapped a cloth around the exposed break with a confidence his petrified features did not share.

They both stopped when they saw who stood behind the guards' barricade. Rory went the color of the bone protruding from Fairel's thigh, and Sefa clapped a hand over her mouth.

Arin didn't react. In fact, it appeared as if the lot of us had vanished from his sight. Clear blue eyes flicked from side to side. I braced myself, for I had reason to worry. Wasn't this how the most lethal corners of his mind worked? Chasing a million futures, probably calculating the far-reaching impact of each moment?

"Sylvia of Mahair is protected from harm under amnesty laws," he said.

Felix blinked. Ah, there was our familial resemblance—confused grimaces. "How?"

"She is Nizahl's chosen Champion for the Alcalah."

The Commander's control over his soldiers was commendable, for none of them flinched at this staggering announcement. Only Vaun's hold on his sword budged, as if keeping it aimed forward required every ounce of his discipline.

The ground shook as Mahair surged to its feet as one, the air exploding with their exaltations. They struggled to identify me the ensuing chatter, everyone rushing to claim familiarity. "Raya's ward! Rory's apprentice!"

Then, "Nizahl's Champion!"

Felix's lips parted. "You cannot be serious. A lower village brat? One who just assaulted me? There are a thousand better choices."

"I choose her," Arin said. Final.

Felix opened and shut his mouth. Just as I thought he would be stupid enough to argue, he snarled. "Withdraw!" he snapped to his guards. "We cannot harm a Champion."

Arin dropped my arm instantly. Vaun and the bald guard outpaced the Heir as he strode away, cutting a path through the onlookers. The Omalian guards hoisted Felix onto a taut buckskin, carrying him a few paces behind Arin.

I was not the Commander. My mind was not suited for elaborate deceptions and chilling foresight. A few moments ago, I had been primed to abandon Omal forever or die. I could not find footing in the steep spiral of this new development.

Jeru and the other guard remained. "The Commander would like you to wait for his return at a private location."

I balked. "What?" Were they responding to some invisible signal he issued? Had he planned this?

"I have to see Fairel," I said, the words coming from a faraway place. "Rory cannot treat her alone."

"This is not a request," Jeru said. "The people do not need another spectacle."

"You're right." I giggled. Hysteria closed tighter and tighter in my chest, crystallizing into shards under my breastbone. "They have seen more than enough."

The room they thrust me into straddled Mahair's border, pungent from the odor of nearby livestock. The door slammed shut, leaving me alone with my whipping panic.

"No, no, no," I repeated, pacing the length of the room. The Nizahl Heir could not name me Champion, not after he saw my magic. He *knew*. He had the evidence he sought against me. The Commander would never knowingly assign the honor of Champion to a Jasadi. It must have been a tactic to delay Felix. Hunting me had taken more than two whole days' worth of effort—it seemed fair he would want to kill me himself.

I needed to get out of here. Where in the tomb-damned earth had they taken me? Dozens of maps covered the walls of the room, names and dates scrawled on their surfaces by the same hand. A single straight-backed chair was tucked near a table barely wide enough to support a cup of tea. A glass cabinet stretched along the left wall.

I yanked at the cabinet's handles. The locks held fast. Behind the glass sat replicas of the Awaleen's most famed possessions, some of which I recognized, some I was glad not to. The tree branch Dania swung into the heart of a new mother. An axe forged to resemble Dania's, rusted with blood. The sight of a ragged doll hewn from animal hide repulsed me a step backward. The doll leaned at a forward angle, childlike eyes drawn onto its rigid flesh. I didn't remember the doll in any of the Awaleen's stories.

I studied the cracked lines of its skin and pursed my lips, distracted by a vague recollection from Hanim's lessons. The doll wore Orban's flag from the ancient Battle of Zinish. Lukub had won by using magic, which Nizahl had expressly forbidden in times of war. The magic Lukub's captain drew upon to defeat the Orbanians during the Battle of Zinish was too awful to recall, an evil that consumed the land like a mighty pestilence. Some of the Orbanian soldiers had been torn apart, their bodies warped and condensed into—

—into small, humanlike dolls.

I tore my gaze away, pressing two fingers to my lips to fight a surge of bile. No wonder the battle ended the way it did. Nizahl, who rarely muddied their boots in territorial feuding, had marched through Lukub. Only the clever and quick politics of the then-Sultana kept Nizahl from tearing Lukub apart. The Battle of Zinish had led to a peace accord between Nizahl and Lukub. One each subsequent Supreme and Sultana upheld.

Of course, the Battle of Zinish took place when magic was

forbidden only as a weapon of war. Peace was an option for them. Peace, which my magic had permanently forsaken by hurling a dagger at the Omal Heir.

If I could repeat this evening, I would never leave Rory's side. We would bundle up whatever we had not sold at the booth and go back to the shop. Maybe we could have heated enough water for two mint teas in the back room and laughed at the children tripping over one another in the street.

I would not be in this room of war relics, standing in the ashes of my second life.

Escape was the only option. Even if Arin condescended to listen to an explanation, his mercy would not extend beyond staying my execution until after a trial.

I paced the room. If Arin maintained his pattern of dismissing his guards, he would be the only obstacle between me and freedom. His guards would patrol the perimeter, and even if they spotted me running, they would not give chase. They had pledged to protect their Commander, and they would go straight to him. Once they realized I'd slain him, well, I would need to run very far and very fast indeed.

I glanced down at my torn and bloodstained clothing. Sefa still had my cloak. The dagger I kept in my boot had found a new home in Felix's leg. I would vanish without taking so much as a sesameseed candy with me.

Tears pricked my eyes. I felt utterly, achingly alone.

I pulled at the handles of the cabinets again. I hurled my body against the glass, but the thick surface didn't bend. If the cabinet could withstand the passing centuries, my paltry efforts would not break it.

The doll's eyes seemed to follow me. Mocking my failure.

I knew what I needed to do, but it would hurt. Was it too much to hope for a bloodless solution, just once? By Sirauk's cursed depths,

I had not come this far to be foiled by a pane of glass. My magic lay dormant, unaffected by my efforts. I could not fathom how it had escaped my cuffs, and I did not have time to waste hoping for two impossibilities in the same night.

I grabbed the slit on the bottom right of my tunic and yanked down. I tore the amount needed to completely wrap my elbow and lower arm.

Sweat beaded at my forehead. I closed my free hand around my other wrist and raised my cushioned elbow to shoulder level. "No broken bones," I ordered. Life with Hanim had made for some strange habits, including speaking to my body as though it could hear me.

I swung my elbow into the glass as hard as I could. Pain exploded into my arm, reverberating through me until I tasted it behind my teeth. Using my grip on my wrapped arm to angle my right side forward, I hurled my body weight behind my elbow at every hit. If I stopped now, I wouldn't start again. The agony radiating in my arm wrestled with the reality of confronting the Nizahl Heir without a weapon, and I swung until blood soaked the tunic strips.

A crack formed in the glass. Small, barely consequential compared to the sheer size of the weapons cabinet. I drew my arm back, choking down a whimper, and slammed my elbow into the fissure. The bottom half of the glass shattered. I turned my head as shards rained onto the ground, covering my face with my bloodied arm. Bloodied, but not broken.

I shoved my arm through the pane, reaching for the rusted axe behind the Lukubi doll. My nails scraped the handle, my fingers struggling to close on it. Had I mangled my elbow to miss the Awaleen-forsaken axe by mere inches?

Footfalls sounded outside. A low murmuring rumbled at the door. I craned for the axe, but I would need to break more of the glass to reach it.

I swore and grabbed the first weapon I could fit through the jagged edges. A short blade, half the length of my battered forearm, sharp despite its years. Not as good as an axe by half.

Twin footsteps grew loud, then faded in the distance. The two guardsmen assigned to my door departing on their Commander's orders. I tucked the blade into the waist of my pants. The handle burrowed into the small of my back.

He was here.

I peeled the wet strips of fabric from my arm and flicked them aside. I had played his game from the moment he stood over me at the river. The boring, unassuming village ward. A girl either naïve enough to perform burial rites on a fallen Jasadi or clever enough to hide her magic for five years. Until my magic reacted, I was simply Sylvia.

My magic tore the illusion of Sylvia to pieces and rebuilt her to represent one word only: *Jasadi.*

I straightened my shoulders. The chase had ended, and the Nizahl Heir was merely another monster at my heels.

The door opened.

CHAPTER EIGHT

The shadows in the room silhouetted the Nizahl Heir. The lanterns flickered with the rush of wind accompanying his entrance. He shut the door behind him, removed his coat and lifted it to the hook. Ease in his movements, as though we were two companions meeting for a meal.

I was sweating to rival one of Felix's overworked horses. I feared the slickness of my palm against the blade's smooth handle.

This was not like the soldier in the woods. I could not assess him for weaknesses to exploit or avenues of attack. I was a bird flying into the heart of a windstorm, and the millisecond of surprise between my attack and his defense would decide the outcome of my flight.

When he finally glanced up, it was to look beyond me, closing in on the cracked opening in the war cabinet.

My blood beat in my ears.

The Nizahl Heir's gaze met mine. Whatever he saw brought a cold smile to his lips. Relics of every kingdom's gruesome history surrounded me, and only this man drove ice through my heart.

"There you are," he said. "We meet at last."

I closed the distance between us in a single bound. Terror churned in my veins, carrying the momentum of my swinging knife. Had my opponent been any other, my aim would have been true. I had acted fast, and I would have struck him at an angle from which there was no recovery. My greatest trouble should have been pulling the dagger from the stubborn clutch of his corpse.

But my opponent was not any other.

Arin caught my knuckles in a flash. Without a flicker of hesitation, he snapped my wrist to the side.

I choked on a scream at the crunch of bone. My limbs went lax in the bright bloom of pain. The dagger clattered, falling from my grip.

He pulled me closer, sliding his hand to my elbow. His breath touched my temple. From the outside, my body curving into his, it could have resembled a lover's embrace.

"Is this all you have to offer me?" he whispered.

He hurled me back. I slammed into the cabinet, glass raining down around me. When I hit the ground, a few of the cabinet's effects fell with me.

Among them, the axe.

Glass crunched under his boots. "Sylvia of Omal, I find you guilty of wielding magic against another."

We were skipping the pretense of explanations, then. I turned onto my elbow with a groan and grabbed the axe. My shoulder, already aching, popped under the weapon's weight. With a grunt, I swung at Arin's legs.

He sidestepped, but not quite fast enough. Satisfaction surged through me at the slash of blood beading on his left thigh.

It lasted until he slammed his boot down on my hand. Agony blackened my senses, and the axe dropped from my limp grip.

But of course, he wasn't done. Arin crouched by my head, and in my failing lucidity, he was death himself, arriving to reap my soul. To finish what the Supreme began and destroy the last of Jasad's royal line. I clawed at him, a dying rabbit clasped in the vulture's claws, heedless of the crushed glass embedding itself deeper into my skin.

The Commander threw a knee over my bucking body, pinning my mangled hands above my head.

I was held fast, helpless to resist as he raised a gloved hand to his mouth and caught the leather in his teeth. He tugged at each finger meticulously, and the glove slid loose. It dropped onto my chest, and my magic seethed forward, fracturing against my cuffs.

"There is nowhere left to hide," he said softly, and curved his bare hand against the side of my face.

The bones of my splintered wrist imploded beneath the unbearable strain of my cuffs. I was eaten alive from the inside out as my magic beat against me, seeking an outlet that did not exist. Tears ran down my temples, pooling between the Arin's fingers. What was he doing to my magic?

A ring of blue survived in eyes gone pitch-black. His lips parted, features awash in wonder. "How are you hiding this?" he said, voice low and accusatory. "I can feel—how can you—"

The door opened, almost hesitantly, and I glimpsed Jeru blanching before Arin snarled an order, and another surge of agony scattered my thoughts. He was flaying me alive with nothing more than a searing touch. What brand of cruelty was this? What manner of murder?

A soft touch against my forehead forced my eyes open again. Niphran smiled down at me.

"Can I come home?" I wept. "Please?"

Her skin was fragments of the sun, her shifting eyes stolen from the surface of the sea. "Fight."

I twisted weakly. Arin's hand dug deeper, curling into my hair. His eyes were blank, swallowed whole by darkness.

"I cannot!"

Did the Nizahl Heir have magic? How else could he be doing this?

"He is reacting to your magic, and it is stealing him from his right mind," Niphran said. The sun inside her shone brighter, blinding me. "He will kill you if you do not resist."

I sank into the raging froth of my magic. It battered against me, growing more enraged with each ineffectual attempt at gaining freedom. His touch drew at my magic without an avenue of release, leaving it shrieking just beneath my skin.

"Do not resist who you are," Niphran murmured. The sun engulfed her, a white inferno bursting forth and flooding the room in an unbearable brilliance. "Essiya."

They have taken enough. Nizahl will not destroy what is left of my family.

The ground shook beneath me. The cabinet rained debris as the maps on the wall fluttered wildly. I screamed with a thousand voices as something crumbled inside me. A whisper of relief eased the pressure on my cuffs, and Arin flew into the wall on the opposite side of the room. He caught himself before hitting the ground.

The earth rocked, tilting the cabinet forward.

It was not Niyar's or Palia's face I conjured as the cabinet groaned, but Rory's scowl. Sefa's musical laughter. Marek rubbing soot from his roasted peanuts and offering a handful to Fairel.

Alarm flashed across Arin's expression, now devoid of its delirium. The cabinet yawned forward. I had enough time to close my eyes before something collided with the side of my body, hurling me into nothingness.

I swam circles in the velvet darkness of the lake. The creatures dancing down here were much more intriguing than anything waiting for me on the surface.

Wake up, said a disgruntled fish with six lavender tails. It used Rory's voice.

I frowned and swam toward a large bolti with Dawoud's stern nose. *You cannot sleep any longer, Essiya.*

Who was Essiya?

I started to tell the Dawoud bolti it was mistaken—my name was Sylvia, probably—but the water rushed into my mouth, choking me. I kicked up, reaching for the waning, shimmering surface of the water. Almost there. If I could just reach the sunlight...

With a gasp, I bolted upright. A shout rose and died in my throat. Pressing a hand to my racing heart, I struggled to calm myself as my eyes adjusted to the dimness of my new setting.

The room of relics had vanished. This room was smaller, containing only a mirror, a rocking chair, and the cot beneath me. No war cabinets or weapons. Thick, mossy vines weaved over the dirt floor, explaining the scent of damp decay. The walls had been erected directly around the floor of the woods. I sniffed, searching for a note of manure or rotten eggs to determine my distance from Hirun, and instantly regretted it. An overwhelmingly foul odor gagged me. If this was death, my soul hadn't wound up anywhere good.

On the off chance I was still among the living, I pressed my hand over my nose, sipping the air in tiny, careful pulls. From the size of the vines winding over the ground, this room had been built a long time ago. Perhaps he enjoyed killing me so much that he moved me somewhere new to do it again.

I reached to scratch my shoulder and flinched. My wrists. The Commander had snapped the right one and crushed the other, and I distinctly recalled my cuffs grinding the bones of both to dust. Bewildered, I rotated them. Nothing—no pain. Baira's blessed hair, had I finally gone mad?

My torn clothes had been replaced by a simple linen gown. The thought of one of the Nizahl guardsmen stripping my clothes while I slept made me grit my teeth. I cast an assessing glance over the room once more, searching for anything I could use as a weapon.

Because your last endeavor to kill the Heir was so exceedingly successful, Hanim bit out.

Who said anything about trying to kill him again? My intentions began and ended with getting out of this room. I turned on the cot, setting my feet on the ground. They settled over a bulbous, springy surface. I frowned. Odd, why would the vines be—

I looked down and screamed. My legs violently recoiled, knocking my knees against my chin.

Stretched on the ground beside my bed was the soldier I killed.

A bone of his snapped neck protruded from the waxen glaze of his skin. Insects skittered in the open gash under his belly. My stomach turned as his lips pulsed, parting briefly as a roach escaped onto his cheek.

I had seen many corpses, but never quite this far into death. Yuck. He must have been a nightmare for the guards to carry. I stretched my leg to hop over him when something much more unsettling caught my eye.

On the soldier's chest lay a wrapped sesame-seed candy.

The door opened. Jeru and Vaun entered, moving to opposite sides of the frame. They stood at attention.

Arin strode past them. With his hair swept tidily from his face and his vest meticulously laced beneath his coat, it was hard to imagine someone with such self-possession had nearly strangled me to death.

His attention found my face and settled, eradicating the small hope I had indulged that perhaps the soldier's body had been in this room before I arrived. Arin wanted a reaction.

I had a split second to decide which one I should give. I could give him innocence, feign shock and horror at the mutilated corpse and maybe break into tears. I could offer the Heir subdued distress and ask him what happened. Every option I considered fell flat, because they all inevitably led to the same consequence: my death. He had declared as much in the war room.

I bent down and plucked the candy from the soldier's chest. I studied it between two fingers, bringing it to my nose for a sniff. Filth and sugar.

"I think you misplaced this," I said, casual.

No response. I may as well have spoken to a stone. He wanted a reaction? Well, that made two of us. I flicked the candy. It fell against his boot. "I do not care much for sweets, myself."

Vaun stepped forward, a hand on the hilt of his sword. Jeru grasped his elbow.

"Out." Arin did not raise his voice or move his eyes from mine. A sour-faced Vaun wrenched his elbow away and stormed out. Jeru followed, closing the door behind him.

We were alone.

I bit my lip. The urge to break the silence battered me, an unfortunate relic from my time with Hanim. Silence was danger. The more still he was, the more unsettled I became. I forced myself to hold his gaze. The blackness was gone, replaced with his placid blue. Not a suggestion of the savagery I had witnessed remained in his frosty disposition. One question pushed and pushed, forcing itself into creation.

"Is Fairel—" I cleared my throat. "Is Fairel alive?"

Arin arranged himself on a long-backed wooden chair, crossing his ankle over his knee. His gloved hand dangled loosely over his bent knee.

"Yes," he said. Relief crashed through me, and I exhaled. I wanted to press further, inquire after her condition and recovery. But my affection for Fairel had plunged me into this disaster, and I could not move forward while she weighed on me.

She was alive. Raya and the other girls would not leave any of her needs unmet. The villagers would come to the keep with food and supplies. Despite their apathy concerning Adel, Mahair's villagers knew how to support their own. If she had died at her own Heir's hands, the village would never have recovered. The lower villages tolerated much from the Omal crown. Killing their children would be the torch to light resentment's kindling.

Fairel would be taken care of. I could do nothing more for her.

"How am I alive?"

He tilted his head. The perfect polish of his expression had worn away, leaving faint distaste in its place. If his actions in the war room were any indication, few emotions were strong enough to overwhelm

Arin of Nizahl's command of his body. Which meant the look of
faint distaste masked a much deeper hatred.

"Your magic saved you. Knitted you back together. You have slept
for eleven hours."

What a preposterous concept. My magic could not be convinced
to dislodge a stone stuck in my boot, let alone repair broken bones
and knit new skin.

I spoke without thinking. "My magic tried to kill me."

A charged silence preempted his careful words. "You speak as
though your magic has a will of its own."

A fly buzzed over the corpse's exposed insides. I was out of plans.
If our roles were reversed, his silver tongue might bend this situation
to his favor, weave glittering nets to evade his certain doom. But my
own tongue was brutish, lacking fluency in the speech of serpents.
I was versed in subterfuge and escape, and he had quite definitively
proven I did not have a prayer of besting him at either.

I needed to change the direction of his questions. Exposing my
cuffs and their hold over my magic might give the Heir momen-
tary pause, but the law was clear: I possessed magic, and its presence
would corrupt me regardless of its actual exercise.

*You cannot mention your cuffs. Any information you give this man, no matter
how inconsequential, will return to haunt you,* Hanim warned.

For once, I agreed with her. No one had reason to believe Essiya
of Jasad was alive. If Arin even *suspected* my true identity, he would
slit my throat in the same time it took to blink.

"Why am I alive?"

"Good," he said. "You have arrived at the right question."

"You knew I was a Jasadi the moment you met me."

"I do not make accusations indiscriminately."

I picked at the quilt's threading, keeping his glove hidden from my
sight. I couldn't forget the weight of it falling on my chest, the red
pain of his bare hand. "Why not allow the Omal Heir's guardsmen

to kill me at the festival? It would have been justly earned, and your task completed in efficiency."

A more perfect solution could not have presented itself. Yet he had blocked me before I had taken a step toward Felix. The price for magic was my head. What difference did it make which sword lopped it off?

"Your fate lies in my hands. Not in that wastrel's fumbling guard," he said. His level gaze found mine. "Not in yours."

I burned blisteringly hot, then cold. He thought I brought the cabinet down on purpose? "Satisfy your hubris, then. You are my arbiter to the afterlife. End this cleanly."

"Your infantile mastery of your emotions has done you no credit. I could have seen you dead a thousand times since I arrived, but there you sit, insolent as ever."

I scooted to the opposite side of the cot. The thick scratch of vines beneath my feet was a welcome replacement for the soldier's body, and I stood.

Arin did not react as I approached. Why should he? My hair fell down my back in unkempt knots, and I was lost in this sack of a gown. I was truly Niphran's daughter. The madwoman in the tower births the madwoman of the woods. It would take less than nothing for him to block an attack. To plant his boot on my throat and press.

"You could have seen me dead a thousand times, but you haven't."

If I were the Nizahl Commander, what would keep me in an obscure Omalian village to hunt down one impotent Jasadi for this long? What benefit could I gain from preserving her life?

His was a deliberate game, removed of the incendiary trappings of emotion.

Before arriving in Mahair, the rumors placed Arin in Gahre. If he'd found the soldier's body, then he must have been traveling south along Hirun. Along the outer edges of the lower villages.

I thought of the inexplicably stationed cabinet of war relics, leagues away from the Citadel. Our very first meeting—hadn't the guards mentioned releasing someone? The layers knit together, and it hit me with such clarity that I placed a bracing hand on the wall.

"This isn't about me at all, is it?"

I laughed, the sound grating and overly loud. I had played his game as Essiya, a girl who merited such attentions from the Nizahl Heir. But Sylvia was nothing. No logical reason existed for why the Commander of the Nizahl army himself should devote his energy toward my capture.

The truth is always in the beginnings, Hanim murmured. *What is his basic truth?*

Arin of Nizahl had trained thousands of soldiers on identifying and combatting Jasadis. The raven-marked trees, patrols, and trials were his prerogative. Where the Supreme just conquered and killed, his Heir turned Nizahl's power into a political stranglehold on the other kingdoms.

Two obligations could compel the reclusive Nizahl Heir from his kingdom: choosing a Champion for the Alcalah and hunting a Jasadi threat of extraordinary danger. I'd assumed the wrong obligation brought him here.

"There is another Jasadi. Maybe a group," I said. Slowly, the pieces slotted into place. I couldn't believe how stupid I had been. "You've used the guise of choosing a Champion to hunt them down undetected." The copious maps mounted in the war room, covered in lines and scribbles. "You're after *them*. I am only convenient."

I drew closer. A herd of deer stampeded on my chest, warning me back, *Haven't you learned anything?* But if my suspicions were right, I had nothing to fear. Not yet. I leaned into the Commander's space, gripping the arms of his chair. I gazed down at him, stirring the hair at his temple with my words. "I am alive because you need me, don't you?" I lingered close enough to count his silver lashes. "And you're *furious.*"

Arin smiled, pulling his scar tight. "Finally."

CHAPTER NINE

Arin stood. I retreated, tripping over the edge of the threadbare carpet, but he moved around me.

He knelt by the soldier. A black gloved finger tapped the corpse's throat. "It puzzled me at first. A broken neck, a broken back, and a disguised six-inch knife wound dealt to an area of the torso thick with muscle. Such excess. To what end?"

I crossed my arms over my chest. Did he mean to unnerve or flatter me?

"What I did not question was the use of magic in his murder. Only a Jasadi could have the capacity to eviscerate and break the back of a seasoned soldier." Arin's hand shifted to the soldier's vest. He reached into its pocket. "And then I found this."

Arin unfurled his palm, revealing tangled strands of curly black hair.

Not just any hair. Dania's dusty bones, that boar of a Nizahlan died with a handful of my hair.

My scalp stung with a phantom ache. After I bit him, hadn't he used his grip on my hair to hurl me away? I had seen the strands caught in his fist, but I assumed he dropped them. When had he gotten the chance to tuck them into his vest? Why would he?

"When defeat becomes a possibility, Nizahl soldiers are trained to collect evidence of their killer." Arin turned his palm over. The strands floated onto the soldier's chest. "I was seeking a Jasadi with long, curly black hair and a fondness for sesame-seed candies. And who did I see at the river, speaking Resar over a dead Jasadi?"

The *one* time I tried to be kind—

You weren't being kind. You thought it would get me out of your head, Hanim snorted. "Well? Don't leave me in suspense." Knowing he had no immediate plans to kill me had done a great deal to loosen my tongue.

The side of Arin's mouth twisted up. How pathetic I must have seemed to him. Like a bug running so quickly from an approaching shoe that it stumbles onto its back, arms and legs writhing in midair.

"You're abnormally strong. You lie well enough to fool an entire village. Despite your attempts to prove otherwise, I believe you possess an agile mind." He unfurled to his full height, and the shift was unmistakable. This was the moment he had foreseen as Felix's guards leveled their swords at us. The crossroads he had already traveled and planned out.

"You will train and serve as my Champion for the Alcalah. When you have finished the trials, freedom is yours."

My breath hitched. I must have heard him wrong. "Freedom?" I could barely shape my mouth around the word.

"I will not hunt you. Every village in every kingdom will hail you as the Alcalah's Victor and offer you home and hearth. You will be assigned a retinue of guards for the rest of your days, offered more wealth than you can spend in ten lifetimes." The lilt in his Nizahlan accent lengthened as he spoke. "I offer you a new life."

I scarcely dared to believe it. I would never need to vacate this identity. Sylvia's fame as the Alcalah's Victor guaranteed Essiya's ultimate erasure. After all, it would be unthinkable that the Champion riding beneath Nizahl's banner was also the dead Heir to the kingdom Nizahl brutally razed from the earth. That wealth and liberty could outweigh such a loyalty.

Whose blood could run so cold?

"You must be truly desperate to catch them," I said, "if you are willing to offer me this."

The endless possibilities streamed before me. I could return to Mahair with enough money to buy the shop from Rory and a home of my own. Feed Raya's wards and take care of Fairel. I could purchase a horse—a stable of them—and take Marek to the places he dreamed of visiting. Chase adventures with Sefa.

I could visit Jasad.

There is no Jasad, Hanim said harshly. *Why would you go visit the Scorched Lands?*

It was a slap of cold reality. Hanim had taken great pleasure in telling me of the war between Jasad and Nizahl. When the tide of war turned in Nizahl's favor, Hanim would draw frantic runes at our feet. Dirt would twirl in the air and coalesce into moving images of the war. A hundred miles away, we watched flames char the palace's grand pillars. Children torn screaming from their beds as hoofbeats thundered into wilayah after wilayah.

"How can I trust your word?" I asked. "You have but to gesture in my direction after the trials are complete, and a dozen of your company will be upon me."

"Are you suggesting I would order our Champion executed after she has earned Nizahl victory?" he asked. "That I would dishonor my kingdom by revealing our Champion as a Jasadi and admitting I allowed an abomination to stand in Nizahl's name?"

He raised a shoulder. "Anything is possible, I suppose."

Arin lifted a golden ribbon from the pillow. It must have fallen from my hair while I slept. He slid the strip of gold between his fingers. "Allow me to spare you further strain and answer your next question. What keeps you from escaping? No supervision is flawless. You might very well decide to forgo the nuisance of the ordeal and simply vanish."

This time, it was he who closed the distance between us. He lifted his arms and paused. He was giving me an opportunity to steel myself against the instinct to flinch away.

Irritation at his contradictory behavior simmered. Arin would hand-feed me to wolves without a second of regret, yet he would not breach the boundaries of my body.

Gathering the long ropes of my hair in his gloves, he said, "The decision is yours, suraira. I will not be your warden. However, Sayali and Caleb may have a more vested interest in your participation." He deftly twined my curls together. The silk ribbon trailed across the back of my newly freed neck.

Suraira?

I couldn't focus with him so close. My muscles were tense, braced for attack. "I have never met a Sayali or Caleb," I managed.

He chuckled softly. "My apologies. You know them by other names." He finished tying my hair. A velvety press of leather on my chin guided my gaze up to his. More frustrating than even the twisted maneuverings of Arin's mind was his Awaleen-forsaken beauty. Trying to ignore it from this close was like glaring at the sun and pretending not to smell your eyes burning. I cataloged each facet of him as one studies the sharpness and shape of their executioner's scythe. The strong contours of his jaw, the elegant line of his throat. I wanted to rip the pretty illusion apart and reveal the beast I'd seen in the war room.

"The Citadel's High Counselor has searched long for his stepdaughter and her blond lover after they left him for dead and emptied his coffers. Should their location be made known to him, I imagine they would be hung for their crimes. Maiming and robbing a High Counselor is punishable by nothing less. They wouldn't even need to factor in her lover's defection from the army."

My eyes narrowed. I genuinely did not have an inkling what he was talking about. I wouldn't associate with any Nizahlans, let alone fugitives. I opened my mouth—and went utterly still.

If you are hoping to light a fire of fear in me, you are too late... Before it ever came to a tribunal, I would promptly follow you into death.

My nails dug into my palms. "Sefa."

Her blond "lover" could be none other than Marek. Hadn't I questioned their history? Wondered after Marek's specific knowledge of Nizahl's customs? To be fair, not even the farthest limits of my imagination could have conjured the possibility of Sefa as the stepdaughter of the Supreme's High Counselor.

"You would hinge their lives on my compliance?"

Like a stone against the surface of still water, the brutal efficiency of his plan rippled through me. If I left, he would haul Sefa and Marek to Nizahl to account for their crimes. Crimes I doubted had any basis in truth. Sefa wept at the sight of limping stray dogs and taught the girls in our keep how to braid their hair. She wouldn't brutalize and rob her family. Marek... Marek might, but not without a reason.

If the High Counselor was anything like the Supreme, he would chain their carcasses on the Citadel's gates. Their flesh would be a feast for the carrion-eaters.

A mirage standing by the river, a bare hand extended for mine. An impossible decision. And just as I was trapped then, I was wholly cornered now.

"Hundreds of lives hinge on your compliance," Arin replied. "They are two of many. Yours is counted in the number. If you do not triumph in the Alcalah, the protection you are granted as a Champion will disappear. Felix is a prideful man. There will be no safety for you anywhere in Omal. If any patrol captures you in another kingdom, Felix will have the right as your true Heir to drag you to stand trial in his courts." He didn't need to finish. We both knew Felix would never suffer me to live long enough to stand trial after I lodged a knife in his leg and humiliated him.

There was more. There had to be. One doubt circled stubbornly to the forefront. "Why me?"

He withdrew, releasing me from his strange thrall. A beat of silence passed, and I gritted my teeth. Another instance of information he deemed privileged to himself only. He preferred to spin me where he aimed, ground me in half-truths and suspicion.

"You were fate's choice, not mine. While I hunt the Jasadis who have slaughtered a legion of innocents from Orban to Lukub, they hunt you."

After Arin left, the guards blindfolded and led me from the room. I strained my ears for the babble of the river or the rumble of carriages, any marker of our location. The crunch of leaves underfoot did not leave plenty for me to work with. Fresh air replaced the foul odor of decay, and I wondered who would be left with the miserable task of burying the deteriorated soldier.

"Will we be much longer?" I complained. Walking blind at the mercy of Nizahl guards wrought havoc on my nerves.

One of them exhaled. "Not much."

"Do not indulge her," came the other's retort. The bald one? "Log." They nudged me to the left.

"You saw him, Wes," Jeru said, defensive. "I have never seen our liege in such a state."

I tried to diminish my presence. They were speaking as though they had forgotten I stood between them. I was curious to hear what they had to say in the absence of their master.

A pregnant pause, then, "I have. Seen him in a similar state, I mean. I was appointed to his guard when he was sixteen."

Apparently, this meant something to Jeru, because he bumped into me. "I thought only Vaun was present for that."

"Vaun has been by his side since they were both old enough to carry a sword. They were friends long before Vaun became his guardsman. I was there when it happened, too.

"You should believe better of our Heir," Wes continued, stern. "To think him capable of such a thing…"

Baffled as I was trying to parse out what could have happened to Arin at sixteen, it took me a second to catch up. "Oh dear, did you think *lust* overcame your Heir?" The very notion of the icy Nizahl Heir allowing a physical urge to overcome his ruthless control made me cackle.

"He was on top of you. The mistake could've been made by anyone," Jeru snapped. "Wes is right. I should have known better."

I couldn't help myself. Angering Nizahlan men was just too diverting. "Are you calling your Commander frigid?" I winced at the resulting clench on my arm.

"You trespass your bounds," Wes spat.

The events of the last two days had driven me into delirium. "Then redraw your maps, soldier. Haven't you heard? I'm your Champion. The rules changed. No, they disappeared." They lifted me again. The heels of my borrowed calfskin shoes brushed the prickly tops of a bush.

The rustling signs of nature faded into eerie silence. Our footfalls changed, taking on an echo. "If it brings you relief, Jeru, Wes is right," I said. Distracted, I dragged my heels, bewildered when the calfskin slid without catching on any loose dirt or puddles. The terrain had gone flat and smooth. Similar to the roads leading to Omal's upper towns. Where were we?

"Your Commander was hardly moved by passion, although I suppose sensing my magic changed that." His feverish reaction still lingered in the vault of unanswered questions. How could the strictest discipline fray into such a mania? Niphran's specter had said he was reacting to my magic. Was it an anomaly of birth? The way some children sense death or a coming storm—was that how he sensed magic?

But then, why had my magic reacted to his touch?

Jeru and Wes stiffened. I continued, unperturbed. If they did not already know I was a Jasadi, they would learn the truth soon. "I think he was annoyed I tried to stab him."

Wes choked. "You *what?*"

"Oh, don't fuss. He disarmed me immediately. The most I managed to do was graze him with the axe."

"Graze him," Jeru repeated, several decibels above his normal register. "It is a miracle you have survived as long as this."

"You have no idea," I said. "Where are we?"

The blindfold fell away. Swiping my hair from my face, I surveyed our surroundings. We stood in the dead center of a clearing between four towering trees. I made a slow turn, unease trickling down my spine at the unnatural symmetry. The rain had followed us as soon as we started walking, yet we stood completely dry in this pocket of space. The rain hit an unseen barrier at the apex of the trees and sluiced over the sides of the invisible walls.

I spun in the void, reaching for the rain that didn't fall. Extraordinary. For a sphere of protection to be woven into the fabric of the woods so seamlessly, a dozen Jasadis must have pooled their magic.

I didn't recognize our surroundings. If I had truly slept for eleven hours, they would have had time to take me entirely out of Omalian territory. The majority of Essam was unclaimed by any kingdom.

"If you're quite finished," Wes said. "Slacken your muscles and brace your knees."

I'd heard those instructions before, typically right before Hanim shoved me off a bluff. I glanced at Jeru questioningly. He pointed at my knees.

The ground crumbled beneath us, and I dropped straight down.

Landing on my heels, I coughed at the explosion of dust. The guards hit the ground smoothly.

He wanted to train me underground? Baira's blessed breath, I would need a miracle tonight. Each passing minute made my prospects of escape more and more unlikely.

Not that it mattered. Unlikely or not, I did not plan to spend a single night in this...living grave. I had a complicated relationship with luck, but after the last few days, it owed me.

They led me through a complicated series of tunnels. The halls narrowed the longer we walked, until I had to duck my head to avoid brushing the ceiling with my hair. Stale air tickled my nose. Alabaster tiles covered the walls, their edges emanating an iridescent light. I grazed my fingers over the glowing tiles with no small amount of awe. The evidence of magic was everywhere. Who had these tunnels belonged to? Even Jasad's wealthiest wilayahs wouldn't have expended the amount of labor and expense needed to build all of this beneath Essam. An underground network of this scale was beyond their eccentricities.

Just as I started to think the goal was to suffocate me, the hall ended at the threshold of a towering silver door. Etched along the door's round frame were intricate gold letters, winding through and into one another. Was the writing...Resar? I squinted at the letters, trying to make out any words. I couldn't stand this Resar writing style, where the words were written to appear elegant and, as such, made almost unintelligible.

Before I could decipher more than the word *nahnu*, Jeru and Wes extended their fists in unison and knocked twice. A piercing shriek sounded as the door heaved to the side.

When I hesitated at the threshold, Wes prodded my arm. "Go on."

With leaden dread, I stepped through the door. The sight that greeted me nearly took me to my knees.

High above us, a glass ceiling swirled with pillowy clouds. They moved around an invisible wind, floating halfway down each side of the enormous room, at which point a lively, verdant courtyard overtook the walls. The courtyard of Usr Jasad.

Every detail of the palace had been captured. Seven gold pillars soared toward the clouds, supporting the awning curving around the front of the magnificent palace. Beneath them, the staircase stretched almost a quarter of a mile wide, one banister at the first pillar and the second at the last. Silver flames danced beneath the translucent steps, chasing the footsteps of the climbers. I'd spent countless hours darting around those steps, trying to outrun the flames. Guards wearing Jasad's uniform patrolled at the foot of the stairs. In the courtyard in front of the Usr, children chased a rabbit hopping in midair, just out of their limited reach.

Beneath the shade of a fig tree, Niyar flipped the pages of his book. Palia stood on the palace steps, watching him with her hands on her hips.

The scenes were alive. As though I could reach out to pet the rabbit or pluck a ripe fig from the dangling branches.

The mirage wavered almost imperceptibly. Niyar's thumb halted on the page; the children's arms blinked from existence. A flicker of time, and the scene began again. A perfect moment looped for infinity.

"These tunnels were discovered a year before the siege. We believe they were commissioned as a school for talented Jasadis during Niyar and Palia's reign," Jeru said. "For those whose magic made them promising candidates for the Jasad army."

Palia's chin lifted at something—a breeze, a bird's song, the children's laughter—and the permanent furrows in her brow smoothed for a brief instant. My heart squeezed. I never thought I would see my grandmother again.

A soft mat replaced loose soil, absorbing our tread. I allowed myself another lingering glance at the specter of my grandfather. His royal ring caught the sunlight, the golden kitmer glinting on his finger. I struggled not to turn around when we exited to the hall.

"This room is yours," Wes said, gesturing at a door indistinguishable from the dozen others lining the hall. "The kitchen is around the corner, three doors past the lavatory. You will report to the training center after first light. There is only one exit, and it is monitored. Questions?"

Several, but I started with, "How do you suppose I shall see first light from a windowless underground room?"

Wes glanced at Jeru. His mouth pinched. "Your...kind. Have an attunement to nature."

I nodded, somber. "Of course. Most mornings, the sun—I call her Beatrice, actually—taps my shoulder and invites me to tea with her and the mountains. She's quite the gossip. Tragically, however, I don't know how well my 'attunement' will hold against several layers of dirt and stone."

The cough Jeru stifled in his fist skirted suspiciously close to a laugh. If Wes soured any more, they could squeeze him over a broth.

"Someone will come to fetch you," he said.

"Excellent." I shouldered the heavy door open, coughing at the resulting billow of dust. The room was bland, perfunctory: crumbling walls and bare floors carrying a constant chill, and a circular table near the wardrobe with two sturdy wooden chairs. My back ached simply looking at the narrow bed in the center of the room.

Jeru and Wes lingered outside the threshold.

"We were instructed not to enter your quarters under any circumstance," Jeru explained. "For your comfort."

My comfort, which roughly translated to "no guards in the room so Vaun can't smother you in your sleep."

"What if I'm dying?"

"Why would you be dying?"

"Perhaps an insect crawled into my throat. I'm choking, frothing at the mouth. Will you watch from the threshold?"

"Yes," Wes said. "Try not to swallow any insects."

I sniffed the sheets, relieved when I couldn't detect the cloying scent of mold. How would I wash these? How would I bathe? Unless the soldiers intended to transport basins for my daily use. I imagined Vaun sloshing my bath water over his uniform and felt momentarily cheered.

The guards left, closing the door behind them. I collapsed onto the lumpy bed, jaw aching from hiding my tension from these Nizahlan snakes. I'd memorized our movements as we walked through the complex, but I had no idea how I would climb out once I reached the exit. The drop had been close to eight feet. Even if I managed to pull myself out, where would I go? I lacked the faintest clue as to where in Essam they had taken me. Nizahl maintained its surveillance of the kingdoms by keeping hundreds of secret locations sprinkled throughout Essam. Most were unoccupied, but without knowing for certain where the locations were and which were active, the kingdoms were compelled to behave. I could run directly into a busy Nizahlan stronghold as soon as I fled.

A part of me wondered if it wouldn't be more prudent to remain in the complex until a more reasonable means of escape presented itself. Immediately, I brushed the prospect aside. The Nizahl Heir claimed he needed me to compete in the Alcalah to capture these mysterious Jasadi groups, but I very much doubted he would tolerate me to live the six weeks between now and the Champions' opening banquet. As soon as Arin found a solution that did not require my continued existence, he would dispose of me with the same efficient brusqueness of a captain decapitating a lamed warhorse. And if he discovered I was once Essiya of Jasad…I shuddered.

I would not pin my life on a promise from the Nizahl Heir. Sefa and Marek would be fine. By now, I was sure they had packed their life in Mahair and fled. Arin's threats against them would go unfulfilled.

I kicked off my shoes, grimacing at their state of disrepair. Hardly fit for fleeing through the woods. And if Arin was to be believed, it wasn't just him I would be running from. These mysterious Jasadi groups "hunting me" would also be giving chase. Here was the trouble: I didn't believe him. Why would a Jasadi group be interested in me? Recent exceptions aside, I didn't have magic, and only Rory knew my true name. Arin wanted to use me as bait when my proximity to these Jasadis was entirely coincidental. Assuming they'd discovered I was a Jasadi, I doubted their interest was more than fleeting. He'd probably exaggerated the threat simply to incentivize against an escape.

Resolved, I changed into the clothes they had set out. The seams strained; they were obviously made to accommodate a woman of more diminutive dimensions. The pants had been designed to hang loosely on the wearer, so they fit me closely but not uncomfortably. I tore the pinching sleeves from my arms and used them to tie my hair into a high bun. I would not have time to slow for branches catching in my braid.

The colors brought the taste of ash to my tongue. Black and violet. They had dressed me in the colors of Nizahl.

Why wouldn't they? You are the Commander's puppet now. He can do with you what he wills, Hanim said.

"His will is strong. It always is, in the self-righteous," I said to the empty room. The gray walls echoed my hollow words.

"But the will of the damned is even stronger."

CHAPTER TEN

Six hours. Six agonizing hours I waited, ear to the door. Listening for patterns in their patrols. I had left to relieve myself midway through and emerged into an empty hall. I'd almost left right then, but I encountered the fourth guard at the bend. "The washroom is in the opposite direction," he'd said.

I hadn't heard footsteps in forty minutes. By my best estimation, it was the middle of the night. Perhaps the guard responsible for strolling by my room had fallen asleep.

With a litany of excuses ready on my lips, I cracked the door open. Silence. A peek in the hall confirmed my hope: the guards were gone.

I untied one of my torn sleeves from my bun and wrapped it around my knuckles. I hated not having my dagger. Still, anything could be a weapon in the right hands, and this length of sleeve would strangle a guard at least half as effectively as a rope.

I kept close to the walls. The stillness in the complex unnerved me. Decades of dust swirled in the stagnant air and tickled my nose. The back of my throat itched with a sneeze.

I raised two fingers and pressed them against the inner corners of my eyes. The urge to sneeze eased. Soraya had taught me the trick a few days after she became my attendant. She had caught me slipping out of the Usr, sugar-coated kahk shoved in my pockets and shoes abandoned to go play in Hirun. Instead of chastising me, Soraya had tucked my mane of curls behind my ears and said, with a conspiratorial smile, "Next time you try to sneak out of the Usr, take me with you."

When the fortress fell, Soraya had burned in Usr Jasad. So had Dawoud.

And instead of rising from the ashes to save the rest of your people, you hid, Hanim goaded.

I pushed into the training center with more force than necessary. I studiously avoided the moving images of my grandparents and their palace on the walls. Why did I owe more to Jasad than Adel or anyone else? I couldn't access the magic that marked us from the rest of the kingdoms. I had lived outside of Jasad longer than I had lived within it. They weren't entitled to my protection or my life just because I'd been born to the wrong bloodline.

Halfway through crossing the mats, a glint in my peripheral vision stopped me in my tracks. An engraved wooden chest nearly the size of my bed occupied the left wall.

I glanced around the empty training center. Just a quick peek.

I braced my shoulder against the lid and heaved. With a soft click that sounded like a roar to my nervous ears, the chest opened. A veritable arsenal took up the space inside. Throwing spears, hunting spears, javelins, crossbows, three kinds of axes, and every type of sword and dagger known to man.

One similarity became clear the longer I perused. These weapons belonged to Jasad. All their handles bore some aspect of the kitmer, from its falcon head on the feline body to the golden wings. The Nizahl Heir meant to train me as Nizahl's Champion using Jasadi weapons.

My cuffs tightened, and my nails curled into the wood at the sick comedy of it all. A normal Jasadi would balk at lifting a Jasadi-forged weapon in their enemy's name, but the *Heir* of Jasad? Essiya would rather have died than demean her entire family so spectacularly.

I glanced at my cuffs and shook the specter of the Jasad Heir from my head. She *had* died, in every way that mattered.

Tucking two daggers into my boot, I left the weapons chest open and hurried to the silver door. Jeru and Wes had knocked on it at the same time. I rapped both knuckles against it and paused. The door did not react.

I threw my weight against it. The bottom scraped against stone, shrieking with each inch I shoved it open. Subtle.

I didn't waste my advantage waiting to see if anyone heard. I slipped into the narrow hall and sprinted. Kapastra's scaly throne, how had anyone willingly lived in this tomb?

You have grown soft in Mahair, Hanim scolded. *Listen to you, panting from a little run!*

I finally stumbled into the spot where we'd dropped into the complex. Light leaked from the edges of a circle in the dirt ceiling. Too high for jumping. I looked for a rope, a foothold, anything I could use to climb. Nothing but crumbling dirt.

Frustration howled the longer I searched. This is how they would catch me. Not dodging them with skill and cleverness in Essam, but in a dead end, like a rat with its head stuck in a hole. I pulled one of the daggers from my boot and hacked at the wall. He had trapped me in Essam just as Hanim had. Planned to use me, just as Hanim had. I wanted to laugh—who could have known the Nizahl Commander and the Qayida of Jasad had so much in common?

I hacked the wall with my dagger again. The blade wedged against stone, resisting my pull. Really? I almost used the second dagger to stab the first until inspiration hit me with the force of a rabid bull.

My fit of rage had lost me a dagger, but it also created a foothold.

I checked the firmness of the dagger in the wall and pulled my other blade from my boot. I backed up, evaluating the distance between the ground and the dagger. Then I ran forward and leapt.

My right boot caught the blade's handle. I twisted my middle and swung with my other dagger, using my seconds of leverage to stab the center of the circle. The dirt crumbled. Moonlight flooded through the opening.

I hit the ground with a grin. Almost there.

I tucked my free dagger into my boot and took another running leap. This time, I didn't turn. I reached back until my hands found the edge of the circle. I dangled in midair, grateful I had had the foresight to free my arms from the constraint of sleeves. Grunting, I clenched the muscles in my stomach and pulled my head and shoulders through the circle. I clawed at the ground, drawing the rest of my body out and onto solid earth.

With a triumphant huff, I kicked dirt into the opening. Escaping this accursed complex was as close to a birthing experience as I ever intended to get. The moon shone brightly, streaming past the naked branches rustling overhead. The only witness to my rather impressive feat.

The strange bubble of protection between the four symmetrical trees did not resist when I walked through it. As soon as I did, the unbearably cold wind battered me. Darkness unraveled in each direction I turned.

Every hair on Raya's head would turn white if she saw me. Simply staring in the direction of the woods at night had spooked her, and here I was. Devoured by the dark.

I started jogging east. With each step, worry edged out my elation. If Arin hadn't transported me across Hirun, then I would find myself running in the direction of the mountains. Otherwise, east was my best chance at locating the river.

I flexed my wrists and leapt over a pond the size of a cow. Why had my cuffs tightened in the training center? What had upset my magic? Nearly thirteen years with these cuffs, and I had yet to discern a recognizable pattern to my magic's reactions. Before the incident with Fairel, I would have ignored it. My magic had a long history of disappointing me.

It was impossible not to think of Hanim as I ran through Essam, navigating the dark by instinct alone. She would rouse me in the middle of the night for runs exactly like this one. Blindfolded and cold, I'd hike a mile from the warded hovel we called home. At the bottom of the river's runoff, Hanim would point at an expanse of frozen dirt and order me to dig a hole wide and long enough to lie in using only my magic. Reasoning with her was futile. Any reminder of my trapped powers enraged her. So I would get on my knees and dig, muscles cramping against the cold, until my fingers were useless and bloody or the sun rose. Whichever came first.

A distant howl raised the hair on my arms. Essam Woods did not treat its guests tenderly after dusk.

Another howl, closer this time. The sky opened in sheets of rain. Unease slithered down my spine. I listened hard through the patter. The air grew heavier, and my hurried step could not shake my mounting dread.

I was being watched.

I tripped over an exposed root and caught myself on a tree. My fingers danced across the rough surface, scrabbling for a hold. Patterns were cut into the bark. Odd, it almost felt like—

Gasping, I reeled back. It wasn't—it couldn't be. This tree shouldn't be here. It belonged on the other side of Essam.

Rain sluiced over my trembling body. I groped frantically along the thick grooves, wiping my face against my shoulder. The longer I searched, the easier it was to breathe again. What was I thinking? This tree looked a little similar, but—

Beneath my left palm, the striations in the bark shifted. I traced the unnatural grooves and crouched, heart seizing, to confirm what I already knew.

Whittled into the raised surface of the bark was a crooked number. *1,822*

I whimpered, stumbling back into a bed of brambles. The tree stretched, mutating, the numbers growing taller and wider. I crawled back on my elbows. The tree towered over me. A canvas on the sky, swallowing me whole. The branches weaved together, twisting like serpents in a nest.

From the base of the tree, a viscous black puddle streamed out, foaming toward my prone form. I slapped at my body, clamping my ears shut and pressing my lips together to bar its entry. The shadows beneath the tree merged. A woman with flesh dangling in moldering ropes off her body and a gaping throat filled with maggots loomed over me.

Hanim.

I considered it a mark of personal victory that only when the maggots fell onto my face did I start to scream.

Essiya, she hissed from the gashed slice of her mouth. *How deep can you dig?*

I bucked against the invisible restraints shackling me to the ground. How could this be real? She shouldn't be here.

How far did you dig?

Gnarled fingers rotted at the roots danced across my neck. The putrid smell of decay filled my nose. I twisted, gagging, which delighted her.

How long did it take you?

I snarled, and her demeanor changed in an instant. She bent to my face and roared, drenching me in ichor and rage. I cried out, at the cusp of relinquishing the answers she sought.

It took 1,822 days to dig a hole. Nine feet deep. Eight feet wide.

I'd carved the numbers into the tree with my dagger. 1,822 days spent with Hanim. 1,822 days of wishing I had died with the rest of my family.

You were right. I was glad to have practiced digging that hole.

1,822 days of planning my escape.

It made an excellent grave.

CHAPTER ELEVEN

I was screaming, eyes shut tight, when the odor of rotten meat abruptly vanished.

I stayed frozen on the ground. Was she gone? I finally gathered the courage to crack my eyes open. The insects had vanished, and so had Hanim's specter.

Heart in my throat, I forced myself into a seated position. The slash in Hanim's throat had peeled back at the edges, curling like a second set of lips below her chin. It couldn't have been her actual corpse—death magic had been eradicated centuries ago, in a rare moment of agreement between the kingdoms. Hanim's appearance had been replicated down to the details. Her long black hair, always pulled into a severe braid, and the way one eyebrow was slightly fuller and longer than the other. I had almost forgotten that Hanim was once beautiful.

Someone had conjured a likeness of her. Someone who knew how she died...and who killed her.

The dangerous Jasadi groups. What if he had been telling the truth?

Another worry lodged like an arrow in my gut. The "legions" Arin claimed the groups had slaughtered. What if the rumors about disappearances happening across the kingdoms weren't rumors at all?

You thought the Jasadis wouldn't hurt you? Hanim said, and my entire body flinched until I realized her voice was inside my head. *You say you owe them nothing. If you are not their ally, you are their foe. You do not get the luxury of indifference in war.*

War. I shook off the mud on my palms as forcefully as I wished to shake Hanim's ravings from my head. Nizahl had defeated Jasad in its own lands. Jasadis were scattered, hunted, afraid. Any tales of them scheming for a new war came from the mouths of lunatics. They were outnumbered and outmatched. The only war left was to survive.

A branch snapped. I spun around. The puppeteer for the magic-ridden corpse must still be nearby. Why had they stopped before finishing me?

In the distance, a new sound raised the hair on my arms.

Hoofbeats.

Understanding hardened in my chest. There was only one person whose presence would scare a powerful Jasadi into ceasing their attack.

"May this night be damned right to the tombs," I seethed, heaving to my feet. The world spun.

I couldn't outrun him. I knew Essam better than almost anyone, but so did he. My best chance was to find Hirun and hope a ravine or gully appeared. Though with luck's best efforts working against me, I would probably run right into the Jasadi trying to kill me.

I hurtled through the woods, heedless of the crunching leaves and my wheezing breath. He would know where I was headed no matter how well I masked my tracks. Spindly branches slapped against my face and naked arms, leaving thin white lines on my skin. Pockets of mud studded the ground, growing larger the farther east I traveled. The moon flickered between the branches, illuminating slivers of Essam between the stretches of shadow.

The scent of spoiled eggs and resin soured in my nose. Yes, yes! Hirun was near.

But so were the hoofbeats.

The wind carried his smooth voice through the dark. "You must have an appetite for failure."

Too close. He was too close. I pumped my arms. My bun unraveled, curtaining my vision in curls. I just needed to reach the river. It couldn't be far.

A streak of mud caught my boot, shooting me forward. I careened right to the edge of a steep, pitch-black riverbank. I gasped, throwing my weight away from the crumbling cliff and crashing to the ground. Idiot! I had forgotten the small cliffs curving around the western bank of Hirun, eating into Essam with uneven, jagged lines.

My fingers skimmed against the bristly surface of a tree trunk. I scrambled upright, maintaining my hold on the tree. The dull roar of Hirun greeted my ears like the fondest song.

He couldn't bring his horse. It was too slick to risk riding. He would almost certainly approach on foot. Unfortunately for him, I did not intend to wait around.

I put my dagger between my teeth and pulled off my boots. They tumbled over the edge, crashing on the boulders below. I watched them disappear with a heavy heart. The last thing I brought with me from Mahair—gone.

You will have plenty of opportunity to be sentimental from the grave. Climb! Hanim snapped.

A thin calfskin slipper covered the bottom of my foot and curled over my toes. I was grateful for its protection as I found a foothold. With an eye to the stones at the bottom of the riverbank, I started to climb.

The sole skill I had developed as the Jasad Heir came from my affinity for climbing. Afternoons sneaking from Usr Jasad to the courtyard outside and scaling our towering date and fig trees. I would climb to the very top and wave at Bakir Tower, imagining Niphran could see me from her tiny window. That Niphran would *want* to see me.

With a groan, I heaved myself onto the first branch thick enough to support my weight. I threw my leg over it and buried my face in the tree, heedless of the striations and hardened sap digging into my cheek. Let the dark swallow me from his sight. Let him forget to look up. Better yet, let him slide in the mud and right over the riverbank.

Below, unhurried footsteps crossed the spot where the mud stole my footing. I caged my breath.

"This is your last opportunity to minimize the damage you have done tonight," Arin said. His voice came closer, and I struggled not to move my head. Had he spotted me up here?

"Show yourself, suraira."

Suraira again. I made a note to investigate the meaning of the Nizahlan word if I lived to see a new day. I was fluent in every kingdom's original language, but certain dialectal words evaded me.

A long pause. A spider skittered over my elbow and onto my wrist. I didn't dare breathe.

The soft neigh of his horse perplexed me. Had he brought it out here? The terrain could barely support a human's weight.

"I was mistaken in my original assessment of you. A Jasadi capable of hiding her magic from an entire village is restrained. Clever. But you insist on running in the dark, chasing monsters you are not prepared to face." His tone hardened, shedding its false amiability. Each word fell like the swing of an axe. "You want to be hunted?" A branch snapped somewhere below me. "Then I will gladly grant your wish."

A strangled cry tore through my teeth as searing pain cleaved my calf. "Son of a——" My hand flew to my leg, and there, inches above my ankle, was a knife. He *stabbed* me?

The knife throbbed with the blood flowing from my wound. Tossing aside my failed attempt to stay hidden, I pulled one arm from around the tree and turned to scour the ground for the Heir.

How had he thrown a dagger with such force and accuracy that it found my leg?

My stomach turned to stone. With the reins in one hand and a hold on the lowest branch of the tree behind him, Arin stood on his horse's saddle. The cliff curved mere feet from its hooves. If it spooked, it could hurl its rider straight over the edge.

The moonlight weaved through his silver hair, loosened from its meticulous tie. Without his coat, freed from his perpetual mask of politeness, Arin of Nizahl was every inch a monster.

And he was staring directly at me.

Death had always scared me more than its fair share. I had watched it steal everyone I loved. I had guided its hand in taking the lives of others. But one thing scared me more than death ever could: capture. Losing myself in the will of another, feeling my purpose crushed and re-molded to fit someone else's plans. Hanim had torn the Heir of Jasad to parts. She needed a weapon, so she assembled me into one. The night before I escaped, I had pressed a dagger against the throbbing vein at my neck. Death was a door, I told myself. An escape. One slice, and I would be free.

I killed Hanim that same night.

Arin was too strong for me to kill. What good was his offer of my freedom if it was a lie, a honey-soaked trap for the witless bear?

I wouldn't be trapped again. I had cut and bled and fought for my freedom. I would rip his head from his shoulders with my teeth before I took his shackles.

Gripping the hilt of the dagger, I yanked it out of my leg, burying my cry in my shoulder. A fool's move, to be sure. Depending on how deep the knife had wedged itself, removing it without a readily available tourniquet would endanger the entire limb.

Another knife slammed inches from my hand. Arin had ridden closer, looping the end of a rope around the base of my tree. "It is not mere caution stilling your magic, is it?"

I stifled my groan. Baira's blessed beauty, was his goal to evoke my magic by riddling me with knives? I didn't understand how it healed me last time, and I doubted it would bother to save me twice.

My leg cramped in protest as I hauled myself to the next branch. Blood dripped down the bark like grotesque sap. The wound bled freely, slicking the back of my heel. All I wanted to do was press my forehead to the tree and catch my breath again, but I didn't have time. I anchored one arm around a thick fork of branches. With the other, I threw the bloody knife straight at the Heir.

My aim met true...in a sense. The knife sailed past Arin and sliced into his horse's flank. It shrieked, rearing onto its haunches. Had Arin been seated, he would been thrown directly over the river-bank, his body smashed into the stones at the bottom.

I made an unintelligible noise of frustration as the rope in his hand went taut. He swung off the horse with disconcerting grace and landed at the base of my tree. His horse galloped off into the woods.

"You can't use your magic. Someone or something has blocked it off." Arin's laugh, devoid of any warmth or humor, sent shivers along my spine. He retreated from my tree, and to my horror, began to climb the one right next to it. "How utterly miserable you must be."

Why was he climbing the tree *next* to mine? I froze, unsure whether to climb higher or drop to the ground and outrun him on foot. He balanced himself on a branch parallel to mine, and I realized his intentions a split second too late.

A new dagger slammed into my arm, pinning me to the tree. I screamed, the sudden agony whiting out my vision.

You will not do this, Essiya, Hanim commanded. *You will not allow the Supreme's Heir to finish what his father started.*

My cuffs tightened. I swallowed a sob. Everything hurt. I forced myself to look at the dagger. One good turn: it hadn't hit bone.

But the next one might. He would cut and cut and cut at me until

I crawled down in defeat. My blocked magic was an experiment to him, another string to tug and twist. He thought it would heal me. I did not know how to explain that my magic cared less about my suffering than he did.

"I will not be trapped again," I whispered.

A path to the finish appeared before me. A way to end this, one way or the other.

I stuffed the torn sleeve in my mouth and grasped the hilt of the dagger. One breath. Two. I yanked the dagger from my arm, my muffled shriek reverberating in my ribs. My hand convulsed. Oh, it hurt, it *hurt*. Through blurry eyes, I watched the dagger tumble to the ground.

"You can climb down and end this whenever you want," Arin said.

I spat the sleeve from my mouth. Fury cleared the haze of agony from my mind. He was so assured, so confident he would win. Why wouldn't he be? Shedding Jasadi blood was his birthright.

For once, spite motivated me faster than fear. I peeled myself from the tree trunk. With my uninjured arm, I pushed myself away from the branch's root. I scooted back—to the edge of the branch, directly above the riverbank. One stiff wind, and I would tumble over the side and splatter my insides on the stones below.

"What are you doing?" Astonishment underscored his harsh tone. He slid to the bottom of the tree and took a step toward me.

"Stop!" I shouted. "One more step and I'll push myself off. You may think my magic might heal a few stab wounds, but can it knit together a broken body?"

In a blink, his expression went calm and steady. I wanted to slap it off. Did he discard his frustration like a stray eyelash or merely push it down?

"You have lost a great volume of blood. I expect you have minutes until you faint. I will not be fast enough to catch you," he said.

"Good."

He took a step forward. Did he think I was making empty threats? I sealed my free hand around the branch and dropped to the side. I went airborne.

The branch crackled ominously, bending under the weight of my body. The veins in my hand bulged with the strain of holding on. I dangled from the branch and felt the inexplicable urge to cackle. If this was how magic-madness felt, I understood why Rovial had wanted to burn the world down.

Arin had darted closer, but not close enough. If he took another step and I let go, I would hit the rocks before he reached me. A fuzziness had already begun to encroach on the margins of my sight.

His manner remained unmoved. He proceeded as though we were sitting down to share a pleasant meal together. "What do you want?"

What I meant to say was "Your severed head rotating on a spit."

What came out was significantly worse.

"Freedom. Real freedom." The branch whined. I slid farther down, tightening my sweat-slickened fingers at the last minute.

"I offered you freedom, and you ran away."

I scoffed. The beat of my heart slowed, becoming as heavy as the rest of me. "I have no need for your empty promises, Commander. Throw your clouds to the sky. I will keep my feet planted in the earth."

"How can I convince you my word is true?"

I stared at him with open bewilderment. I had prepared to die in the river with the knowledge that the Heir's offer of freedom meant nothing. Was this another game?

He started talking before I could form a coherent response. "Hundreds of people have disappeared in the last seven years, taken by two groups. Forty-seven of them have been found dead. Likely killed by the same people who took them—Jasadi rebels calling themselves Mufsids."

At some point, he had maneuvered closer. The woods had narrowed onto Arin, wreathing him in shadows, and I could not distinguish how much of it was due to my failing lucidity. Mufsids. I'd never heard the name before.

"You said...two." My mouth resisted the onerous task of forming a sentence. I blinked, and when I opened my eyes, I had slid to the very last inch left of the branch.

"The others are the Urabi. A second Jasadi group, less violent than the Mufsids. The Mufsids and Urabi chase Jasadis throughout the four kingdoms, competing to recruit them for their cause. Whoever the Mufsids can't successfully recruit, they murder. The Urabi steal their target without any trace, whether they come willingly or not. Both groups have only competed for the same person if they held some important post in Jasad. Nobles, army officials, council members."

Important post?

A distant alarm sounded behind the wall of my fatigue.

"And you think...they want...me?" It took everything not to close my eyes. If I did, they would not reopen, and I was starting to worry I had made a grave error in judgment. What if everything the Heir said in the cabin was the truth?

"I am certain they do. Once I see my plan to the end, freedom is yours. If you do not believe in my honesty, believe in my loss. If it is revealed I allowed a Jasadi to stand as Nizahl Champion in the Alcalah, it will cast my reputation and my throne into ruin."

Skepticism etched itself into every line of my face. The best way to ensure no one ever found out his treason was to simply dispose of me after he captured the Mufsids and Urabi.

He plucked the next thorn of uncertainty before I could speak. "You will be constantly surrounded by guards if you win the Alcalah—independent guards from every kingdom who do not obey any command but yours. Not even mine."

It didn't matter. We both knew that if he wanted to kill me, he would.

Yet I found myself struggling to believe he would risk plunging his own kingdom into turmoil by murdering his Champion. If he accused another kingdom of killing me, it would be grounds for war. Even Felix, whose intelligence I admired less than a rutting pig's, had not dared to lay a hand on me after Arin's declaration.

The world swayed. My fingers strained around the branch. I could no longer keep the darkness at bay.

"I believe you," I slurred.

My last recollection before my hand slackened and my body dropped was of the Nizahl Heir running, sliding in the mud trail, and the collision of our bodies over the edge of the cliff.

ARIN

He was alive. Bleeding quite profusely, but alive.

Good. His calculations hadn't failed him.

Arin exhaled, rolling his shoulders with a wince. The river lapped at his legs. The Jasadi lay unmoving against him. He had caught her at a precise angle, using the curve of the riverbank to slide to the rocks instead of tumbling straight down.

The moon spared little light to see her with. Arin turned to the side, laying her inside a shallow puddle. Still no movement. Water lapped against the boulders, lifting her hair into a cloud of black curls circling her face. Combined with the deathly pallor of her skin, the effect pricked a rare bead of disquiet in the Nizahl Heir.

Blood spread in the river from the wounds in her arm and leg. She wasn't healing.

Nothing could be easy with her. The possibility of her magic not healing her on its own had occurred to him, but he had hoped he was wrong. Arin pulled off his gloves and hesitated. The last time he brushed against her magic, it had consumed him. The utter loss of control was not a memory he would soon forget.

Her chest was barely rising. If she died, he would lose his best chance to lure the Mufsids and Urabi to the Alcalah.

Sharp rocks dug into Arin's knees as he loomed over the girl. With no small amount of distaste, he grasped the Jasadi's hands. If she were awake, he had no doubt she'd claw his palms raw. She had the temperament of a deranged goose. Every interaction he'd shared with her had thoroughly convinced him he was not dealing with a stable woman.

The hunger seized him as soon as their hands touched. Howling through Arin, digging into him with a thousand whittling blades. His teeth cut his bottom lip open.

Her magic—it was strong. Too strong. He should have guessed as soon as he touched her in the Relic Room that something about her magic was amiss. Nobody could have hidden power of this caliber from a nosy village of Omalians. Not unless a separate force prevented her magic's expression. It mystified him, and he loathed being mystified.

The torn edges of her skin reached for each other. Watching her wounds knit shut amazed him no less the second time. Her magic roiled beneath his touch. As soon as the color returned to her skin, Arin dropped her hands, exhaling harshly. Leashed violence shuddered through him, filling his mouth with rust. Her magic's influence. Arin took no satisfaction in brutality for its own sake, nor did primal impulses typically succeed in overwhelming him. This bloodthirst was a product of her magic. He did not know how, but he intended to find out.

"Sire? Are you here?" Jeru's call barely rose above the river's babbling.

The river pulled at the Jasadi, eager to whisk her away. Arin caught her arm and immediately recoiled. She'd torn the sleeves off her tunic? Fleeing into Essam Woods under the siege of winter, arms bared to the elements, was a superbly efficient way to end her time among the living. Arin grabbed a fistful of the fabric at her collar and dragged her to the rocks beside him.

"Are you a donkey's bastard? If the Jasadis are near and hear you calling for your Commander, they will make finding him first their priority." Vaun's incensed voice was much more distinguishable.

"You don't think the riderless horse may have already alerted them?"

"Look. There is blood on this tree." Ren.

It did not take them long to spot Arin and the Jasadi at the bottom of the riverbank. To his guards' credit, they hid their reaction to the bizarre sight of Arin pinning the unconscious Jasadi with a grip on her collar. Jeru skidded down the slope, a rope fastened around his middle. Shock finally flickered over his face at the full tableau waiting by the river. "My liege, you're injured."

"Nothing is broken or severed. Take the girl and send her back to the tunnels with Ren immediately."

Jeru obeyed, bending to scoop the Jasadi into his arms. As soon as he lifted her, she began to writhe.

"No, no!" she shrieked. Her eyes moved rapidly behind her closed lids, chasing invisible threats. "Do not touch me. Don't!"

Jeru struggled to hold her. She spilled out of his arms. Jeru only barely prevented her from dashing her head against the rocks. "Should we tie a rope around her?" Jeru asked desperately. She'd splashed him to the knees.

Arin scowled. How could she be this aggravating even in her sleep?

She was still twisting, eyes closed. "Please, please," she whimpered, with such terror that it gave Arin and his guard pause.

Secrets. So many secrets. She was wreathed in them.

"Prop her shoulders," Arin ground out. His collection of injuries was beginning to demand attention.

Jeru did as he asked, despite the Jasadi's renewed thrashing. They wouldn't be able to get her out of the riverbank if she did not lie still.

Her slurred voice echoed in his head. *I believe you.* As though Arin cared to win her confidence. She was caustic and contradictory. Every time she opened her mouth, she pulled Arin to the very limits of his patience. This Jasadi was the human equivalent of spilled ink over the meticulously drawn lines of his map. Whether he could refrain from breaking her neck until the end of the Alcalah was one question for which Arin had no answer.

"Tell Wes to leave a cold cloth over her forehead to reduce any swelling," Arin said. His arm twinged when he bent it.

"What swelling?" Jeru clenched her wriggling shoulders.

Arin struck the Jasadi. Her head snapped to the side.

Finally, she was still.

CHAPTER TWELVE

I glared at the guards through the eye their Commander hadn't blackened. The bruising looked far worse than it felt, but I took satisfaction in Jeru's guilty frown each time he glanced at me.

The rest of the guards ignored me. Wes, who I had woken this morning to find hovering over me with a cold cloth (to which I had garbled, "Did I swallow any insects?" and promptly earned his departing back), spooned a mealy, pale gruel into his mouth. Vaun and Ren were talking in low tones on the other side of the kitchen.

I poked at the gruel. It sprang back into place. Dania's war-hungry axe, I had eaten some truly gruesome fare while living with Hanim, but this? If this was what Nizahlans regularly ate, it was no wonder they were such an angry people. They were hungry.

"You should eat," Jeru said, breaking the seal of silence.

"Then give me food." I pushed the bowl away. The spoon dropped with a clatter, spattering gruel over the table. "This is cow vomit."

Tension wired the thick cords of Vaun's neck. He did not look in my direction, and I wondered if it was to keep himself from dismembering me.

"It helps if you add salt." Jeru nudged a small platter toward me.

"I would truly rather eat the salt."

Vaun turned around. Ren put a hand on his chest.

"Is there a problem?" Arin materialized from the shadows, leaning against the kitchen's arched entrance. The guards snapped to their feet.

He wore the black coat from the first day I met him. The violet ravens stitched along his sleeves made me faintly ill. Not a single lace in his vest missed its loop. The only imperfection to the Nizahl Heir's refined appearance was the purple bruise on his cheekbone.

I might have supposed the marks of our voyage into Essam ended there, on an insignificant bruise, were it not for him leaning against the wall. For anyone else, leaning would be casual, not worth a second glance. But I could not fathom the tightly wound Nizahl Heir slouching, never mind *leaning*. He had borne my deadweight as we slid down the riverbank. The rocks might have flayed his back raw.

I palpated the corner of my black eye and tried not to feel smug.

The specter of last night rose in the kitchen, thickening the air. My escape attempt hadn't helped my relationship with the guards.

"I cannot be expected to live like this," I said, a hair too loudly. "This food is barely suitable for vermin."

Ignoring Vaun's murderous glare, I listed my grievances. They had stewed over the hours. "The lavatory was clearly intended to function with magic. Have you seen it? Abominable. My current stench alone could be used as a weapon. I have no garments, and the sole company I am permitted to keep is a handful of soldiers whose conversational skills peaked in the womb."

Arin unbuttoned his coat. "Good morning to you, too."

I scowled, gesturing to the windowless walls. "I have seen no evidence of either."

Jeru released a sound between a laugh and a strangled hiccup. He covered his mouth.

Arin tipped his head to Jeru and Wes. "There are parcels near the stairs. Take them to her room."

Parcels?

"Are they for me?"

"They're for the vermin." He glanced at my bowl. "Are you finished?"

I pushed away from the table. "Evidently."

We walked to the training center. I fidgeted with the sleeves of my borrowed tunic, still too tight around my biceps. I avoided the walls alive with birds and my dead family.

"How long has your magic been blocked?"

My head whipped toward him. Arin uttered it as he had "You have magic" or "I choose her." Absolute. With the conviction of one who never speaks in vain.

"Do you find these bold, sweeping inquiries satisfying? Catching the recipient off guard and startling the truth from them? Is that your strategy?"

He didn't blink. "Generally, yes."

"Might I ask how you've reached this conclusion?"

"The power I felt when I touched you in the Relic Room should have torn me to pieces," he said calmly. I stilled. We had yet to openly discuss the details of what had occurred in the war room. "Instead, it barely stopped me from killing you."

Niphran was right, I marveled.

"Are you typically so overcome when you sense magic?"

"Nothing was typical of my behavior." Disturbingly pale blue eyes studied me. "Yours is not a simple magic."

Another diversion. I imagined the Nizahl Heir's tutors must have been driven mad at his expert evasions of any clear reply.

He went on. "Jasadi magic cannot be hidden from me. I should have detected it at the river, when you placed your hand in mine. At the very least, it should have reacted last night. Pain and peril are two of the surest ways to ignite magic. Yours reacts to mine in unusual ways. I can sense it, I can draw it close, but it will not leave the limits of your body."

He frowned at a cobweb on top of the weapons chest before redirecting his attention to me. "That is how I've reached my conclusion."

"Your touch boiled my magic. It nearly killed me," I said flatly.

"It saved you. Twice."

Aha. "And how can a nonmagical touch do such a thing, Your Highness?"

A glimmer of approval passed over his features. I had neatly walked him into my own trap.

"Under normal circumstances, it can't. I sense magic because I am immune to it, and I can drain the magic from a Jasadi with the same touch that seems to ignite yours."

I did not try to hide the horror written on my face. He could drain magic with a touch?

My cuffs tightened around the sudden force of my magic. How many Jasadis had he robbed of the very advantage for which they were hunted? How many had felt their magic stripped from them in the moment they needed it most?

"I don't understand."

He watched me coolly. "You don't need to."

"Explain what you mean by 'draining magic,' and I will answer your query."

Surprise darted in the Heir's eyes, gone before I could chase it. He had expected me to ask how his touch came to be its own weapon. And indeed, I should have asked that. The mechanics of how he drained magic did not affect me; my cuffs prevented him from doing more than pulling my magic to the surface. Damn it to the tombs. The stupid moving wall had thrown me off-balance. Affected my judgment.

"Jasadi magic is not a bottomless well. Every Jasadi has a finite supply from which to draw. Imagine one uses their magic sparingly, easing the drudgeries of daily chores. Another spends their allotment on some spectacular display. For the first Jasadi, replenishing their magic is not an issue, because they never reached the bottom of the well. The one who drained their magic by commanding a horse to fly or rain to fall must wait, helpless, until time renews their supply." He raised his gloved hand to his temple, brushing it with a featherlight touch. "I possess the ability to drain the well temporarily. Time will still replenish their magic, but by then——"

"You will have already caught or killed them." My cuffs throttled my wrists, so urgently did my magic beat against my veins. Was it reacting to Arin or to Arin's words?

"Yes." He remained composed in the face of my loathing. Had I not heard the hatred in his voice last night, I might have believed his indifference. But at least now I had an answer for why my magic reacted so strongly to his touch. He couldn't drain my magic, but he could bring it surging to my cuffs.

He removed a handkerchief from his coat and brushed it over the spiderweb. "Your turn."

I wanted him to choke on his intestines as I fed them to him in pieces. He did not deserve my secrets.

Then do not give them to him, Hanim urged. She seemed buoyed I had chosen to ask a question on the Jasadis' behalf instead of my own. *Escape again and join the Jasadis he is hunting.*

Cold water splashed over my rage at the very notion. No, I had made my decision. My best route to freedom was through the Nizahl Heir. I hadn't forgotten what Arin said yesterday. The Mufsids and Urabi chased the same Jasadi only if they had held an important post in Jasad. They either suspected who I was...or they somehow already knew.

"I do not remember a time when my magic flowed free."

He clasped his hands behind his back. "Can it be fixed?"

I shook my head. If he pressed, I did not know if I could devise a lie capable of withstanding his scrutiny.

"It is an unusual cruelty. Your magic feels strong."

I almost laughed. If only he knew. My grandparents would not have cuffed an average magic, nor would Hanim have been so desperate to unleash it. Abnormal magic defined my life. "You would know. Unusual cruelty is your specialty."

Arin moved on without comment, though I was sure the matter of what suppressed my magic would be revisited. He seemed to tuck new information into the frightful web of his mind until he had collected all its threads. "The Champions' Banquet will be held in Lukub in six weeks' time. From there, we will depart for the first trial in Orban. We have until then to make you fit for this role."

He walked to the corner of the room, crouching in front of the weapons chest I'd pilfered yesterday.

Clouds moved leisurely in the facsimile sky above us. "I still don't understand why I must compete as Champion to lure the groups you seek. If they are the same ones who attacked me in the woods, they already know where I am."

I crossed my arms over my chest, resisting the urge to shudder. The rotted corpse howling with Hanim's voice would haunt me forever.

Arin froze. He straightened, turning toward me, and only bewilderment prevented me from stumbling back. "What attack?"

The severity of his tone surprised me. I recounted the confrontation with the mirage of Hanim's corpse. Arin paced, and I could almost see him weaving this latest revelation into his web. "You did not recognize the corpse or see its summoner?"

"Correct." A half lie. "It disappeared at the sound of your horse. Do you think the attacker belonged to the Mufsids?"

Arin shook his head. "They would not kill you unless you had already refused their offer to join. Have you spoken to anyone unfamiliar?"

"Only the Nizahl Heir and four of his unfriendliest guardsmen."

Arin tipped his head back, gazing at the ceiling. Reminding himself of all the reasons he needed to keep me alive?

He pivoted on his heel, striding to the weapons chest again. I followed, pretending to view the weapons for the first time. I lifted a shield clearly crafted for someone born from giants and staggered under its weight. Painted on the front, the kitmer's wings stretched high as it soared into a mighty blaze. Its beak opened in a bellow. The pride of Jasad. Rovial's first companion.

Arin chose a curved dagger from the chest, weighing it in his palm. I lowered the shield to rest against my leg. Arin and knives were not—

With an almost unnatural swiftness, Arin lifted his arm and threw. I had enough time to glimpse the blurred form of the dagger cutting through the air, straight for my chest.

I didn't think. In a burst of motion, I clapped my palms together, catching the hilt before the dagger could bury itself in my heart.

I raised the knife to my eyes, checking to make sure I hadn't hallucinated the Nizahl Heir *once again* using me for target practice. I snarled, "Was yesterday's stabbing session insufficient for you?"

"Fascinating," he said. "That was a learned instinct. Who would teach an orphan girl to catch knives?"

"You aimed at my heart! What if it had met its mark?" I demanded. "Were you prepared to kill me on a guess?"

"Can you feel your magic?"

Unbelievable!

I flipped the dagger and hurled it. He caught it single-handed.

I beamed. "Now you've learned an orphan can throw knives, too. Isn't it *fascinating?*"

Arin tossed the twice-foiled dagger into the weapons chest. To his credit, he didn't seem bothered I'd thrown a knife at him. Arin lifted his chin, studying me with singular concentration. "What is your real name?"

I caged my breath, pinned in place by a thousand pinpricks of foreboding. I crushed the instinct screaming for me to swing the shield at his head and run. Half a decade of hiding ruined by the scheming of strangers. Not only had these groups implicated me as a Jasadi, they had also assured the Heir there was more to me than met the eye.

"I am not rich in names, Your Highness. I have only the one."

Arin lifted a brow. I fell quiet, donning an expression appropriate for the occasion: a little flummoxed, a little anxious. Deception was an art form I thought I'd perfected. It was easy to mold myself into what others wanted to see, but Arin had exposed the flaws in this particular skill set. Apparently my rage, when roused well enough, was the last truly honest thing I had left.

The Nizahl Heir tipped his lips up. I had seen more expressiveness from him in the last ten minutes than in the last three days combined. "Have your pleasure, suraira. Every truth has its time."

Foreboding trailed its finger along my neck. If he meant to rattle me, he'd succeeded.

Arin tapped the opened chest, moving on. "These tools will become your dearest companions in the months to come."

"Do you truly believe six weeks and a few weapons will help me become Victor? The other Champions have been training since the last Alcalah. They have a three-year head start."

"You have one advantage the other Champions lack."

"You must mean my irresistible charm, since we have established my magic does not function."

"Yet it was your magic that stabbed Felix and twice saved your life."

He picked up a rusted cutlass, extending the hilt in my direction. I took the curved sword, slashing it through the air experimentally. I had dozens upon dozens of questions, all momentarily replaced by the childish glee of swinging a sword. I passed my finger along the kitmer carved into the side, its falcon head held high.

"You would allow me to wield Jasadi weapons, even in private?" Was it his way of rubbing my cowardice in my face? If so, it was a wasted effort. Looking at the kitmer, imagining the Jasadis who'd held these weapons before me, I felt…nothing. I knew what I *should* feel. Hanim hadn't been shy about reminding me of how I failed Jasad, how Jasadis suffered at my incompetence. Shame is a dangerous feeling to manipulate. Pull at the string too many times, and it will eventually snap into apathy.

Arin slid his handkerchief over the dusty handle of another cutlass. "I would prefer my time wasn't drained in the sieve of your animosity for Nizahl," he said. "We will both be better served without the intrusion of divided loyalty."

The sword leaned heavily against my legs.

"Nizahl will never have any share of my loyalty."

Again, Arin did not rise to the insult. I wondered at it, sometimes, this imitation of patience. The coiled quiet of him.

"I did not mean Nizahl," he said. "Pick up the cutlass."

CHAPTER THIRTEEN

The first week tested my limits. How fast could I run on land? How nimbly could I maneuver in rushing water? How far could I throw? Every evening I fell into bed convinced I had reached the peak of exhaustion, only to be disproven the following night. If it hadn't been for the drawings Jeru delivered to my room, I would have written off the exercises as another peculiar viciousness of the Commander.

"What are these?" I asked as I spread the pages on my bed. Jeru dutifully remained behind the threshold. White chalk dusted the top of his curls.

"A collection of Lukubi artists created drawings of the tournament dating back centuries. A gift for Sultana Vaida. His Highness thought you should study them."

"In my plethora of free time?" I was intrigued despite myself. I unwrapped the strip of rabbit hide bundling the parchments. Some of the pages were yellow with age. "How did they come into the Heir's possession?"

"He borrowed them from her."

Of course. Because the ruler of Lukub, rumored to be the most vicious Sultana since the Howling Crown, was friendly with Arin. He borrowed precious parchments from her and probably advised her on the best torture techniques over a hearty meal.

Jeru veered down the hall before I could press for more.

The sketches were divided by trial, then by year. I flipped through the images of the first trial, my curiosity morphing into apprehension with each new set of Champions. The number of Champions dropped from five to four suddenly, and I knew the bottom sketches had been done after the Blood Summit.

I traced the shaded drawings of the forested Orban canyon. The artist had used a knife to press ridges into the trees, the grim-faced Champions posed beneath its sinister branches. Ayume was an Orbanian forest where the first trial would be held, brimming with the horrors wrought by Dania's ancient war magic. Dania was a master hunter, as austere in life as she was brutal in battle. Orbanians commemorated her with a trial testing physical endurance in the heart of the forest where she'd waged her most infamous battle.

A corner of the parchment chipped when I turned the page. Black chalk sliced across the cover, and the words *Dar al Mansi* titled the top. The second trial had changed in recent years. In the new one, Champions entered an abandoned village in Omal and fought off the magical creatures released within its borders. Not only did the Champions need to cross the village in one piece, they needed to acquire three trophies from their kills to proceed. The second trial served as a grisly celebration of Awala Kapastra and her vulgar pets, held in her home kingdom.

I followed the line of Al Anqa'a's fiery glass wings with my thumbnail. The sketches depicted Champions in the second trial carried away by the massive bird as claws sharper than any sword closed around the helpless Champions. Those who evaded Al Anqa'a were torn apart and eaten by the nisnas, a ghoulish humanlike creature with lumbering limbs on one side and spikes of dangling flesh on the other. The artist outlined the other monsters lurking in the periphery, jealously watching the nisnas reach a Champion first.

What was he hoping I'd learn from this? I flipped away from the second trial, sickened, to the third. The third trial would be held between the final two Champions remaining. In honor of Awala

Baira's talent for illusions, the Champions would be given elixirs to bring visions springing up around them. In a pit of sinking sand, the Champion with the strongest will would parse through the real and the hallucinations before the sand swallowed them whole or the other Champion cut them down.

Ten minutes later, I stormed into the training center and threw the paintings on top of the weapons chest. Jeru and Wes paused their swordplay, wearing the fatigue of new parents taking their squalling child to the shop. "Where is he?" I demanded.

Wes pursed his lips. "Not here. Why?"

I gestured at the sketches. "If Lukub is hosting the Banquet, then the third trial will be in Nizahl."

The guards exchanged a glance. "Yes," Wes said slowly. "Baira's trial will be held in Nizahl."

Jeru's thick brows drew together. "You are the Nizahl Champion; did you think you could avoid visiting the kingdom you're competing for?"

The question circled in my head. In the whirl of change, I had not stopped to consider I would be meeting Supreme Rawain again. The man who slaughtered my family, who eviscerated Jasad, would be delivered glory by the very same Heir he had failed to kill.

I walked out without another word. My surroundings dipped in and out of focus. If I failed in the Alcalah, Felix's ego would not rest until my head was mounted on Mahair's flag post. If I did win, I would be granted a Victor's immunity, but I would be spitting on the grave of every Jasadi cut down by a Nizahl sword. Which I could have borne, were it not for the fact that apparently, two groups of Jasadis probably suspected I was the Heir. Perhaps they were even stupid enough to want me at the helm of their pointless cause. What other reason could they have for chasing me? Certainly not the draw of my magic.

At some point, I had slid down the wall in the hallway. I wrapped my arms around my knees, and a part of me noted this fit could have been delayed for the ten steps it took to reach my room. I started to laugh.

If Arin knew the real reason the Mufsids and Urabi were competing, if he thought for even just one second that the Jasad Heir was alive and living two halls away from him—I laughed harder. They'd have to scrape what was left of me off the walls. He was not a man who played the odds, and the risk that the Mufsids or Urabi could capture me and lend legitimacy to their cause was too great.

Maybe they didn't hope to recruit me. It was entirely possible they simply wanted to kill me themselves. Take their well-deserved revenge on the Heir who had forsaken them.

"Careful, sire," came Vaun's voice, but it seemed to emerge from a narrow tunnel. "Her kind lash out during outbursts."

I trained you to lead Jasad, and he is training you to betray it. What freedom can you gain after this? Where can you go where Essiya won't follow? Hanim's words bled into my thoughts, until I could not distinguish what was mine and what was Hanim's. I became vaguely aware of a shape settling in front of me in the hall. I cringed, drawing my knees closer. *I hope you perish in the very first trial. Sylvia is worthless, and if you succeed as Nizahl's Champion, Essiya will be, too.*

How did they know where to find me? Why would they conjure Hanim's rotting specter if they meant to recruit me? I could not guess where to begin to make sense of any of it. There was only one truth amidst the chaos.

I should never have stayed in Mahair so long. I would not have loved Fairel nor cared for Rory's good opinion. Sefa and Marek would have remained untouched by the horrors of their past.

Everything you touch, you ruin, Hanim said.

When Hanim's voice had grown hoarse, and the disjointed laughter trickled to a stop, I slowly settled into myself. My shattered thoughts knit together, their seams red with Hanim's venom but mine once more. I unfurled from my pose, rubbing sensation into my tingling muscles. I was afraid of how much time might have passed.

The shadows shifted, and I nearly shrieked at the dark figure seated on a chair near the opposite wall. My vision adjusted to the dim light. I found myself staring into Arin's impassive face.

"Have you returned?" he asked.

I leaned my head against the wall. Vaun was nowhere to be seen, and I wondered how long Arin had sat there. "I never left."

He stood, the bottom of his coat rippling around his boots. "Yes, you did."

That night, I paced. Barefoot on the cold stone, hair freed from my braid, in the same dirty clothes I'd trained in. I traveled up and down the halls, losing myself in the complicated maze of tunnels winding through the complex. The blue light inside the walls followed me, so reminiscent of the gold streaks in Jasad's fortress that I bit my lip. Every now and then, I would spot one of the guards from the corner of my eye. They were keeping watch from a distance. I was grateful for the space.

My first year in Mahair, I'd skulked around the village every night until sunrise. Memorizing escape routes, finding the corners to duck into when Nizahl soldiers passed. The perimeters of the village had seemed enormous. I had spent ten years comfortable in the opulence and majesty of Usr Jasad, followed by half a decade living in a hollowed-out tree infused with Hanim's magic to fit exactly two cots and stacks of scrolls.

"Go back to your room. Now." Vaun's voice gave him away before he turned the corner.

I was too exhausted to handle Vaun. The other guards left me alone. Why couldn't he? "You first."

His lips curled back, and he stepped toe-to-toe with me. I ignored the urge to antagonize him further and ground out, "I can't sleep. Walking calms me down."

"I did not ask for your worthless opinion. Return to your room. If you leave again, I will drag you before His Highness myself."

Loathing trickled over my lethargy. I hated every Nizahl soldier, but Vaun—Vaun represented a type I despised above all else. The kind of soldier who thrilled in the ounces of power the colors on his uniform lent him. The kind for whom inflicting misery was not a byproduct of necessity, but the purpose. Vaun was a soldier who would learn about merchants selling Jasadi bones and give the offenders a wink.

I glanced at my cuffs. The silver shifted, tightening around my wrists. My magic was upset. Why? Why now and not during break-fast, when Vaun called me a dog's whore?

"I was not given orders from your Commander to remain in my room at all times," I said. I didn't flinch from his pungent breath or cower to his sad attempts to raise himself taller than me. "And I certainly do not take orders from you."

Wes appeared behind Vaun. The older guard rubbed his eyes and yawned. "Vaun, enough. Jeru and Ren are maintaining watch. We were not ordered to confine her."

Vaun didn't budge. Ah—now I understood. I turned my chin and met Wes's exasperated gaze. "He is baiting me. He wants me to attack him so he has an excuse to drag me before the Heir."

The furrow on Wes's brow deepened. He reached for Vaun's arm. Before he could make contact, Vaun settled a hand on my waist.

I tensed harder than if he had spit in my face. I pushed his hand off.

"Don't touch me," I hissed.

Keep your calm, Essiya, Hanim cautioned. *He is goading you.*

The next hand was on my arm. I tried to shove past him, but he clasped my elbow. His other hand went to my stomach, right above my navel. Any measure of composure sizzled to nothing.

Hanim tossed a rag. "Press it over the wound and stop crying. You shouldn't have let it catch you."

I turned my face into my hair. She hated the sight of my tears. I almost never cried anymore, but the pain—this pain eclipsed any I had known before it. My blood poured over my hands, soaking the rag in seconds.

Hanim crouched next to me and pried my hands away from my stomach. A sharp inhale whistled through her teeth. "Dania's rusted axe, Essiya, what did you do?"

"I w-wanted to let it get c-close enough," I moaned. Hot tears slid over my temples and into my hair. "I cut its head off. Like you said."

I faded in and out of consciousness as Hanim loomed over me, working to wrap my torso in strips of linen and rabbit hide. A bubble of happiness rose above my agony. She cared. She didn't want me to hurt.

A sting on my cheek pulled my eyes open. Hanim slapped me again. "You do not get to die," she snapped. Her eyes were pitiless. "Death is not for those with debts to repay."

"Sylvia! Sylvia, stop!"

I became aware of arms winding around my chest, holding me back. Vaun was on the ground, clutching his bleeding nose. I shoved Wes away. My back hit the wall.

"I told him not to touch me." I sounded delirious even to my own ears. "I told him."

Vaun surged to his feet and knotted a fist in my hair. He yanked hard, knocking me to the ground. "She will be taken to His Highness."

Wes watched Vaun maneuver my kicking form down the corridor with no small amount of disbelief. He didn't follow.

Vaun dragged me down the hall with both hands in my hair. The stone scraped and tore at me, and he moved too fast for me to try standing. I kept my hands in my hair, trying to minimize the pressure against my scalp. Each time I resisted, he yanked harder, and my eyes watered.

He released one hand to shove open a door. I was tossed onto a thick blue rug.

"My liege, I apologize for interrupting you so late in the evening. I discovered the Jasadi exploring the tunnels and behaving evasively. When I questioned her, she turned violent. She clearly has intentions to cause you harm."

I used the wall to hoist myself to my feet. Seated in an armchair by the window, very much looking like he'd planned to retire for the night, was the Nizahl Heir. Without looking up, he closed the text on his lap and set it to the side.

"He is lying," I said, but it emerged tired and without any fire. What did it matter? He would not take the word of a Jasadi over his own guardsman.

Arin ignored me. "Did she express these intentions to you?"

Vaun shifted. "No, of course not, but—"

"Was she wielding a weapon when you apprehended her?"

Vaun and I were equally baffled. "She means you ill, sire!"

"I am certain she does." He tapped the arm of the couch. The sight of Arin's bare hand was startling. "Many do. Arresting them all would be a lofty task indeed."

"She—"

"She is not easily provoked," Arin said. "Aside from her fits and failures of humor, the Jasadi is not prone to rabid reactionism."

I frowned. Failures of humor?

"He put his hand on my waist." I stared straight at Vaun, not bothering to hide my vindictive satisfaction. He had dragged me to the Heir only to have his own legitimacy questioned. "When I told him not to touch me, he put a hand on my stomach." I spoke the last part through clenched teeth, resisting the instinct to wrap my arms around my middle. "I am a weapon for the Heir, and you will treat me with the dignity you afford a sword, if not a person. *You* are not meant to wield me."

Arin's gaze slid to Vaun and hardened. Though his voice didn't change, a frigid chill swept through the room. "You put your hands on her."

Vaun dropped his chin, which I imagined to be the Nizahl version of wringing one's hands. "I had no other option, my liege. She would not return to her room."

I wanted to lunge at him, tear his sinew with my teeth and stomp his chest into a feast for the dogs. "I am here because I *chose it*, not because you have trapped me, you pus-ridden swine b——"

I fell silent as Arin approached. He was wearing a thin black shirt and pants, light fare compared to his usual layers of black and violet. Silver hair fell around his jaw, highlighting the fading bruise on his cheekbone. His ability to intimidate wasn't softened by his relaxed attire. Vaun fell to a kneeling position, lowering his head. "Forgive me, my liege. I acted without consulting you."

"Yes, that much seems apparent," Arin said. "Leave. We will discuss this at a more appropriate juncture."

Vaun glanced up. "What should I do with the girl?"

"You should do what I ask and only that." Again, Arin remained perfectly pleasant, but Vaun paled like the Heir had personally called for his beheading. "Go."

I massaged the roots of my hair with a wince. First the Nizahl soldier in the woods, now Vaun. My scalp had taken a beating in the last two weeks.

I remained close to the door, carefully avoiding glancing at Arin. I didn't want to risk exiting into the hall with Vaun still nearby, so I took my time studying the Heir's room. There wasn't much to see. A tall wardrobe, a bed only slightly bigger than my own, a tiny square table no wider than a book, and a much larger table covered in inkwells and partially unrolled maps. I wondered what he thought of the tiny table. They were once a staple in every Jasadi household, folded and tucked behind the furniture until a guest arrived. The host would place a saucer and an aromatic, palm-size cup of ahwa on that table, maybe slide a plate of biscuits or kunafa beside it. I'd loved the smell of ahwa, though the one time I'd tasted it I'd spat it right out. But Soraya would still sneak me empty cups from the kitchen so I could sniff the leftover dark sludge like a candle.

I couldn't seem to get Jasad out of my head lately. Surrounded by Nizahlans wasn't the optimal setting to be dwelling on my former home.

A small box at the corner of the small table held the Nizahl royal seal and a bottle of wax. I picked it up. The seal was untainted iron, heavy in my palm. Molded into the bottom were two swords clashing. A raven emerged where the swords met, its wings unfurling on each side. I traced its contours, mesmerized.

"Careful," Arin said. "Wax burns."

The seal fumbled in my grip. I dropped it, trying to claw at the fog over my senses. Navigating a conversation with the Heir drained me on a good day, and today was far from good.

"What do you use this for?" I held up the seal, expecting him to wrench it from my grip and toss me from the room.

"My maps." He satisfied a part of my prediction and held his hand out for the seal. I dropped it into his palm, careful to maintain distance from his bare skin.

"Can I see them?"

Arin regarded me for a long minute. I squared my chin, anticipating some remark on my literacy or intelligence.

He pivoted to the map table. I blinked at his back.

"Well?" he said. "Come and see."

I tripped over my feet in my rush. Dozens and dozens of maps sprawled over the table's broad surface. A pitcher full of a lavender liquid sat in the corner with the inkwells.

I couldn't believe he was allowing me to see this. The Commander's maps were almost as infamous as his gloves. Some of the sketches were undoubtedly collected by the Nizahl spies scattered across the kingdoms, but I doubted he placed a high value on them. His nature did not seem to allow for anything less than absolute perfection. And of course, absolute perfection could be rendered only by him.

"What do you want to see?"

"Anything. Everything."

"Decide."

The name flew from my mouth on reckless wings. "Jasad."

The Heir paused. I thought he would refuse until he pulled out a scroll tucked at the bottom of the organized stack and spread it over the table. The map covered the smaller maps beneath it. Fitting, since Jasad had possessed all the territory east of Hirun and north of Sirauk. Where the kingdom had once stood was the new Nizahl-approved name for Jasad.

Scorched Lands.

My cuffs strangled my wrists. This, at least, I could understand: my magic reacted to grief. Grief about a kingdom I had barely known before I lost it. Before it was used to define and damn me.

"I can feel my magic," I said with the detachment I'd use to remark on the weather. Reporting the fluctuations in my magic had been one of his first requirements after my escape attempt.

Arin dragged his thumb over the area where Hirun bisected Jasad's southern wilayahs. I might have thought he was uninterested if it weren't for the slight lift of his left eyebrow. "First Fairel, then your friends, now a map of the Scorched Lands. You haven't noticed a connection?"

Grief. Rage. Fear. But I usually felt all three without my magic reacting.

"No."

Arin hummed. He didn't believe me. It would have bothered me had I not been so confident my conjectures didn't matter. They were like the sketches drawn by the spies: glanced over and discarded in favor of Arin's own skill.

"Why did you defend me?" At Arin's glance, I clarified. "With Vaun."

He faced me, balancing a hip against the table. I trained my attention on the map of Jasad. I didn't want to ask, but I knew the question would eat at me. There were enough mysteries haunting my sleep.

"I did not defend *you*. I defended my laws." He tapped a scroll written in swirling script, pinned to the front of the table. *First Decrees of Arin of Nizahl, Commander in Power and Heir.*

It was a list of immediate revisions to the governing code of Nizahl soldiers. I scanned the list quickly, eyebrows rising higher with each line. The provisions in this scroll prevented Nizahl soldiers from acting as the final authority in judging a Jasadi. If a confrontation with one was inevitable, the soldier was to do everything in their power to prevent harm or death. Only if the soldier's life would be forfeit were they permitted to use fatal force.

I remembered the soldier responsible for killing Adel blanching at the sight of his Commander. Now it made sense. An entire village had watched him and his partner violate the Heir's decree and pummel Adel to death for merely tossing the soldier a few feet.

The next line made me laugh.

"Any physical or emotional mistreatment of Jasadi captives, including but not limited to beating, tying, cutting, spitting, baiting animals to attack them, sexual threats, sexual violence—" I snorted. "Vaun would sooner sexually touch a dead fish."

"He laid hands on a captive. His intentions are irrelevant."

My teeth dug deep enough into my lower lip to draw blood. "Stop calling me a captive. I am here by choice."

"I thought it would make it easier for you. Thinking of yourself as a captive might remove some of the guilt of betraying your own kind. Or is guilt beyond you?"

He thought he could prod at my loyalties, but I had none. Not anymore. Where loyalty might have existed lived only an echoing regret. Niyar's ashen face as he bid me to flee, Palia's scream behind me. My mother, assassinated alone in her tower. The bodies I had never buried.

Loyalty meant nothing when it was for the dead.

Arin continued, "Then again, perhaps it is a sign of your shrewd-ness that you care so little. Jasad was always damned. A kingdom so mired in treachery is the architect of its own ruin." He bowed over the map, bracing his weight on his knuckles.

Mired in treachery? Now I was sure he wanted a reaction. Jasad was the only kingdom without twisted court politics and double-dealing deceptions.

I turned to face him. This was the closest we had been without someone actively bleeding. I would be happy to rectify that.

"No one follows your edicts. Why would they? Your father con-trols the courts, and the soldiers know any Jasadi they capture will be put to death immediately. Jasadis are guilty by existence."

The scar curving beneath his jaw caught the lamplight. "Do you deny your nature?"

Disgust suffused my words. "What nature? If you mean my ten-dency to violence, it is no greater than yours."

To my shock, a small smile curved the corner of his lips. "Per-haps. But there will never come a day where my nature will overcome my mind. There is no magic in my veins that will turn poisonous and drive me to madness."

I shook my head. What was I doing, wasting my breath reasoning with Supreme Rawain's son? Rawain was hardly the first Supreme to work against Jasad—he was just the most successful. Jasadi magic had been hated and feared for centuries, and it was only a matter of time until they devised a reason to invade strong enough to over-power their guilt. The Blood Summit killed a dozen royals, including Supreme Rawain's wife—Arin's mother.

He would never suspect what I knew to be true. Arin would never believe his father was behind the deaths at the Blood Summit.

"For someone so convinced of his own brilliance, you do seem to neglect quite a glaring flaw."

He stayed quiet. Refusing to engage me. I didn't care.

"You think your mind is a blank slate, where you can build your own networks of information from scratch, through pure logic and reason. You ignore that each child enters a completely unique world, founded on different truths. We build our reality on the foundation our world sets for us. You entered a world where magic is corrosive and Jasadis are inherently evil. I entered one where turning a shoe into a dove made my mother laugh. Have you considered, in that infinite mind of yours, that the truly brilliant people are the ones who understand the realities we build were already built for us?"

My muscles locked in anticipation. Had I spoken with such impertinence to any other Heirs or royals, I would be on my knees with a sword at my jugular. Even my grandfather would have belted my hands, or at the very least banished me to my quarters.

Arin, expression thoughtful, poured the lavender liquid from the pitcher into a chalice and passed it. "Here."

With a sizable helping of bewilderment, I accepted the chalice. Better than a sword. I sniffed the drink. The smell burned my nose, far stronger than any ale in Mahair's taverns. Under Arin's watchful gaze, I tipped the chalice into my mouth, swallowing with a grimace. Ugh. Eating dirt after a fresh rain would probably taste better.

"You are not what I was expecting," Arin said. He drained his chalice and set it aside carelessly. It dawned on me, embarrassingly slow: this was not his first drink of the night. Each of these drinks was likely as strong as three ales. Even in a diminished state of reason, the man possessed more restraint than the entirety of the kingdom combined.

I hated him for more reasons than I could ever name. But his restraint—it infuriated me beyond sense. How do you predict the patterns of a river that never floods, never ebbs or flows?

Hanim's years of discipline had failed to corral my reactive nature. What training must he have endured to become this way?

Arin reached around me. I recoiled, acutely aware of his bare hands. But he only unfurled a new map, smoothing it over the first. I pulled in a breath. Was it—

JASAD, the new map proclaimed, the letters bold and golden. A line weaved around the border where our impenetrable fortress had once loomed, barricading Jasad from Essam and any outside threats. The fortress was keyed to every Jasadi citizen's magic to allow us to pass freely through the fortress, like it was nothing more than shining air. Anyone else was met with hard resistance.

I traced the lines of Usr Jasad, following it to the tiny letters pinning Bakir Tower. My home, then my mother's. Down I went, through the borders of Jasad's twelve wilayahs. An indescribable emotion rose in my chest. Jasad had existed. It had been real, once. More than *Scorched Lands*. It had been known for more than its fate.

"Read the names of the wilayahs," Arin said.

I flinched, shrinking from the map. The Nizahl Heir would not show me this out of kindness. He had an ulterior motive. But what?

I thought fast. The wilayahs were named in Resar. Jasad's dead language. He already knew I was literate in Resar thanks to the death rites I performed over Adel. What benefit could he derive from hearing me read the names of twelve vastly disparate wilayahs in Jasad?

Your accent is perfect.

Baira's bountiful beauty, how could I have missed it? My accent— or lack thereof. The wilayahs had slight dialectal differences in their speech and small variations in their naming systems. If he knew which wilayah I belonged to, he'd begin to cull the list of possible important figures I could be.

An idea unfurled its petals.

"Har Adiween," I began. I moved my finger along the wilayahs as I spoke. "Janub Aya, Eyn el Haswa, Kafr al Der, Ahr il Uboor." I continued until the very last wilayah, tucked right next to Sirauk Bridge.

"How odd," Arin said once I had finished. His hair fell like spools of silk between his fingers when he raked it from his face. "You seem to have developed an accent since you last spoke Resar."

I widened my eyes and flared my nostrils. Nuanced, minuscule indicators of fear. I had spun lies around Mahair as skillfully as a halawany spun sugar, but they were not Arin of Nizahl. They did not have senses honed against falsehood. "I—I do not have an accent. I misspoke. You make me nervous."

Arin tilted his head. "A sliver of truth in a stream of lies. But which is which?"

"I am not lying. I was nobody in Jasad."

The steadiness of his conviction worked opposite my own, unraveling me at the seams. I wanted to lash out, force the specter of discovery and certain death into his bones until the shadows on the wall were indistinguishable from the ones in his nightmares. But Arin was not Hanim, or any other adversary I had gritted my teeth against and overcome.

He was my discovery. He was certain death.

My cuffs tightened almost beyond the point of tolerability. Arin stepped closer. If he touched me in that moment, my magic would overwhelm him, just as it had in the Relic Room. The incensed throb of it skimmed along my skin.

"I do wonder just what you're capable of," he murmured.

"Be patient, my liege," I said. "You might yet find out."

This time, when the Commander moved toward me, it was a strike of lightning. He spun me around, pinning my arms behind my back.

"Is that a promise?" His voice was the whisper of a practiced sword leaving its sheath, soft and deadly. "Tell me, Sylvia of Mahair, how does a 'nobody in Jasad' learn to read Nizahl's old tongue?"

What?

He jerked my arms, pointing me toward the scroll pinned to the table. *First Decrees of Arin of Nizahl, Commander in Power and Heir.* Horror washed over me in thick waves.

The entire decree was written in a language Nizahl had not spoken in two hundred years.

I had been so distracted by the maps, I had forgotten to pretend I couldn't understand it.

"The Citadel records all new decrees in Nizahl's original tongue. I suppose they taught you a dead language in Ganub il Kul," he murmured in my ear. His sardonic chuckle sent chills running along my spine.

Arin released my arms. "If you have any ambitions in the art of deceit, I suggest you plan more carefully. There are few things more disappointing than a careless crook."

The dismissal was unmistakable. I had used a lifetime's allotment of carelessness already, and I would not spend any more by ignoring him. I fled from the room, pausing at the door. I glanced once more at the Commander. I emblazoned him as he was in that moment, standing over the map of the world. Its towering conqueror.

If Jasadi bones could speak, they'd warn Arin of Nizahl that nothing stays untouchable forever.

CHAPTER FOURTEEN

It took hurling a heavy bowl at Vaun's oversize head during supper for Arin to allow the guards to take me to the surface.

"Clear your head," he ordered from the top of his horse. He was going on yet another trip. Vaun and Ren mounted their horses. "We do not have the luxury of soothing your every tantrum."

I managed not to throw rocks at his disappearing back, comforting myself with the warmth of the sun against my skin. I hadn't been to the surface in ten days. Wes and Jeru accompanied me on the walk, kicking a pebble back and forth. It reminded me of Soraya and Dawoud during our afternoon strolls through the palace garden. I grimaced, batting aside the memory like a troublesome fly. In Mahair, I'd rarely dwelled on my life in Usr Jasad. I certainly hadn't allowed the memories to encroach on my consciousness. That moving wall and the Jasadi weapons must be unsettling me more than I thought.

My continued silence disturbed the guards. "It gets easier once you improve," Jeru said. "The beginning is always the worst."

Even Wes was inclined to offer reassurance. "The midnight hunting drills our first year—" Wes started, prompting a groan from Jeru. "I cannot count the number of times I lost myself in these woods, half-naked and confused."

"Holding a spear," Jeru added. "I woke up late once and grabbed a mop instead. Our unit leader found me waving it at a sparrow."

"Wait. Did you hear that?" Jeru stopped.

Wes's forehead puckered in concentration. "It's the river."

Jeru swiveled. "No, I thought I heard…I will catch up." He jogged into the trees before we could answer.

Wes and I resumed walking in a much less comfortable silence. We tended not to spend time together without Jeru's stabilizing presence.

"Is Jeru's family very wealthy?" I asked, apropos of nothing. The sudden interrogation technique seemed to work for the Heir.

Wes eyed me. "No."

"He is a kind man," I observed. "A liability in the Citadel."

For a long moment, I thought Wes wouldn't respond. I counted the prints our boots made in the mud. He answered at number forty-six. "His family comes from an impoverished village in Nizahl's southern provinces. He qualified for exemption from conscription and—"

Much as I hated to interrupt and risk Wes clamping shut again, I couldn't contain my shock. "There's exemption from conscription in Nizahl?"

"His Highness the Heir made it law five years ago. Unless there is an active war, Nizahlans may submit for exemption should their circumstances fit the criteria His Highness set forth. The southern provinces are in famine. Jeru was needed to keep his family from starvation."

"The Supreme allowed this law?" Skepticism colored the question. Supreme Rawain loved nothing more than soaking the earth in Jasadi blood and throwing adolescents into the army's gaping maw. A law providing relief to commoners—the easiest population to recruit—deviated from his agenda.

"His Majesty hadn't a choice," Wes replied, and I would have wagered all of Nadia's chairs that he sounded smug. "Nizahl's laws limit the Supreme's powers over the army. Once the Supreme appoints a Commander, those responsibilities transfer." He shook his shoe loose from the clutches of a shrub. "The Commander happened upon Jeru hours before his execution."

Execution? What in Dania's sacred skirt could Jeru have done to merit losing his frizzy head? "Did he murder someone? Burn a village to the ground?"

"He stole a bag of oats."

I opened my mouth, then clamped it shut.

"They leveled the charge against Jeru, though the real culprit was the stonemason's twelve-year-old son. The child's father had lost his arm in an accident, and his younger sister hadn't eaten in three days. The child stole the oats. Jeru told the patrol he did. Fortunately, His Highness had an appointment with a dignitary from the village. The child recognized the royal crest on his horse and pleaded for Jeru. His liege pardoned Jeru and offered him a position in the academy."

"What about his family?"

"His Highness set up a nimwa system for their village. It allotted every family a weekly amount of grains and milk. Jeru's family live off his wages."

Nimwa. The Nizahl dialect sounded gruffer leaving Wes's tongue. It reminded me of another word. "Wes, what does *suraira* mean?"

His thick brows met in a U-shaped wrinkle. It seemed to surprise him any time I displayed evidence of intelligent thought. Whether this was a byproduct of my constant complaining or his own preconceived bias was unclear.

"Suraira is said to be a demon of mishap protecting Sirauk," he said. "Some Nizahlans believe Suraira dwells beneath the bridge and emerges during a crossing to compel humans to their death."

I rubbed my arms, stepping over the carcass of a partially eaten rabbit. "Compel?"

Wes sighed, likely wishing he'd chosen sleep over this conversation. "No one is certain what occurs in the crossing. Suraira crafts her victims an image of beauty, decadence, freedom from their woes and burdens. She lures them into willingly leaping off the bridge and into the abyss. Every kingdom has outlandish stories about crossing Sirauk; Suraira is merely one of Nizahl's. How did you hear the name?"

Apparently, by being likened to a devious demon of mishap by his Heir.

Mist sprayed my face as we crossed the last line of trees. The gush of Hirun had never sung so sweetly. I jogged ahead, abandoning my slippers behind me. The first splash of cool water against my ankles was heaven.

I waded deeper. This river wound through every kingdom, and no one had ever traveled from one end to the other. Of all that had come and gone, Hirun remained unchanged. The only true axis in a land of shifting sands.

"Sylvia!" Jeru shouted. His voice was far away. Water surged around my waist. My feet had carried me farther than I intended.

A ball of tightly packed dirt hit the water and exploded in my face. A lump flew into my mouth. I hacked, pounding my chest, and lost my balance.

Wes and Jeru's shouts faded as the river catapulted my weightless body along. I flailed, struggling to keep my head above the murky water. A log bobbed ahead, directly in my path. Cheerfully waiting to behead me.

I ducked. Frigid water swept over me. My skirt dragged, pulling me deeper. I kicked it off and pumped my legs. When the river curved, I used the momentum to launch myself toward shore.

Hands reached forward, hauling me onto solid ground. I slapped them aside as soon as my knees were on dry earth and gagged.

"How did you run so quickly?" I rasped. I shoved my dripping hair off my shoulders, shuddering in disgust at the green webs tangled in the strands. "I left you on the opposite bank."

The pair crouching in front of me were not Wes and Jeru.

"Rovial's horned heifer," I groaned. "Are you two determined to die?"

Marek grinned. "We missed you, too."

I shook my head, shoving aside my glee at the sight of my two favorite fools. "A whiff of sense, a *drop*. That's all I ask. If the guards find you—"

"They won't," Sefa reassured. "Unless you plan on lounging for much longer."

Belatedly, I remembered my legs were covered only by the thin white shift I'd worn beneath my skirt. My hair fell from its braid, hanging in wet waves around me.

"Did you plan this?" Neither Marek nor Sefa attempted to touch me again, a gesture I appreciated now more than ever.

"We've been searching for you since the waleema," Marek said.

Dread pooled in the pit of my stomach at the mention of that accursed celebration. A name knocked against my skull, politely asking to be let out.

"Fairel. Is—did she—how is she?" I didn't notice my hand had found my heart. I counted the beats in my head, my body strung tight like it was anticipating a blow.

"She is still recovering," Sefa said, and I almost keeled over in relief before she finished her sentence. *She is.* Fairel still existed, still lived, and the rest were details.

"She and Rory are going to have matching canes," Marek said. "She misses you, but she is excited to know a Champion."

I shook my head, a fond smile on my lips. Maybe she would finally stop revering the Champions when she remembered she'd seen one of them shove burned bread into her dress to hide it from Raya.

Murky liquid dribbled down the nape of my neck. I squeezed mud from my hair and paused. "Wait, did you throw those damned dirt balls?"

"The dirt was necessary to get your attention, since those two guards never left your side. I didn't expect my aim to be so excellent." Sefa prodded me with the end of her walking stick. "Walk and complain, come on."

I slapped the stick aside. "I can't leave."

"They won't find you, Sylvia," Marek said, and the ferocity of his conviction startled me. "We're going to protect you."

I studied Marek's combative stance, Sefa's wary surveillance of the other bank. Oh dear. A fundamental misunderstanding had occurred somewhere between the waleema and now. Had they really spent the last few weeks searching for me?

"The Commander did not abduct me." At their disbelieving glances, I continued, "I am training to be his Champion."

Sefa's mouth hung open. "Tell me you don't *actually* mean to compete in the Alcalah. We thought—we thought you were stalling for time. Waiting for an opportunity to escape."

I stomped north, toward the spot in the river where I'd fallen. I kept a scattering of trees as a cover between us and Hirun in case the guards happened by. It wouldn't help anyone if these buffoons were accused of attacking the Nizahl Champion.

"Is he threatening you?" Marek asked. "He can't hurt you if you refuse the role. Turning down an honor isn't a punishable offense."

I tipped my head back and laughed. "There is no shortage of crimes to choose from, should the Heir wish to harm me." I was positive he maintained a running tally. Whatever expression I wore must have alarmed Sefa, because she thrust a bundle into my arms before I could speak.

"I washed it." It was my cloak, cleaned and repaired. My throat tightened. Sefa babbled, "It took three scrubbings to get the bucket clean after the grime and mud drained from your infernal cloak. There hasn't been much sun, so the wretch took a few days to dry. Does it smell all right?"

I did not trust myself to speak for a long moment. The image of Sefa on her knees in front of the water basin, scrubbing her hands raw against my cloak… "It's perfect."

"You can skulk wickedly around corners again," Marek said, with a grin of such fraternal fondness that I could hardly bear it.

A dangerous torrent gathered strength inside me. My cuffs were burning vises around my wrists. I made an idle note of it. "Your kindness would be better spent on someone else."

"Impossible," Marek said. "I've never met someone who needs it more."

This was far worse than I could have imagined. I had not earned this. Loyalty could be broken. These destructive fools loved me.

Love. Hanim mocked me. *A new name for an old insanity.*

When Arin threatened to expose Sefa and Marek, the tactic was only a piece of a much larger ploy. Without the offer of my freedom, without the threat of Felix's armies, I would have walked away. I might have searched for methods to secure Sefa and Marek's release, bartered and threatened to spare them from Nizahl's tribunal.

But I wouldn't have exchanged myself.

I stepped from the cover of trees, approaching Hirun with a stifled groan. Night had fallen, and the river's silhouette frothed in the darkness.

"We can hide you," Sefa blurted, darting away from Marek. She spoke fast, as though anticipating an objection. "Marek and I, we know how to move undetected. We have mastered the art of disappearance."

"Sefa!" Marek demanded. "Don't!"

Sefa splashed into the river, out of Marek's reach. "We're Nizahlan, Sylvia. I am sure you've gathered as much. What you don't know is after we fled Nizahl, we spent two years flitting between Orbanian and Lukubi villages, surviving on what we could get by cheating or stealing."

On my right, Marek sank to the ground, covering his head with his arms. A frog hopped onto his shoulder, its chest ballooning with a croak. A disbelieving chuckle slipped from my lips. "Do you mean to say you and Marek were vagrants?"

Sefa nodded vigorously. "Worse. Your route is nothing compared to our deceptions. We stole everything—jewels, clothes, farm tools. Then we sold them in the next village. We cheated our way into homes, charmed merchants and healers. Over and over, for years."

I shifted the cloak to my other arm and scooped the frog from Marek's arm. "What changed?"

Marek finally animated, lurching to his feet. He pointed at Sefa. "Go on, tell her. Tell her what changed."

The frog wiggled in my grip, unsettled by the tension whipping between the two. I released him on a boulder and enviously watched him scurry away. Sloshing onto the river's bank, Sefa worried her bottom lip. "There was an...incident...in one of the Orbanian villages."

Marek swung in my direction. "By 'incident,' she means we were caught in a scheme. While I was visiting a market, Sefa was beaten nearly to death. I stole a cart and barely outran the patrol. She was on her last breath when we stumbled into Mahair."

"We have led decent lives since then," Sefa interjected, largely ignoring Marek's ire. I couldn't blame him for his frustration; Sefa invited danger with startling frequency. "We can hide you from Nizahl soldiers."

I still didn't understand. "Why would you leave Nizahl in the first place? Sefa, your stepfather is the High Counselor."

The effect on Sefa was instant. Her eyes went dim and vacant. The luster drained from her face. So thoroughly blank did she look that I wanted to snatch my words back.

Marek moved, blocking my view of Sefa. Hostility rolled off him. "How do you know about the High Counselor?"

Having this conversation at the edge of the river, where anyone could sneak up behind us, wreaked havoc on my nerves. "The Nizahl Heir said you were wanted for assaulting and robbing the High Counselor." I withheld the reason he had shared the information with me. They would believe I had succumbed to the Heir's offer simply to save them.

Marek used both hands to scrub his face. "He said nothing else?" I couldn't mistake the undercurrent of suspicion in his question.

"What else should he have said?"

The golden-haired fugitive lowered his hands. His mouth twisted bitterly, and I braced myself. Marek could be incredibly vicious when it suited him. "Less than two weeks, and you already talk like him."

My shoulders went stiff. "What do you mean to imply, Marek?"

"Sylvia." Sefa interrupted the sharp insult I'd planned to hurl at Marek. Other than the tightness in her expression, she appeared mostly restored from the mention of the High Counselor. "I can explain later. But please, come with us. Let us help you."

I massaged my temples. "Do you believe me resigned to my own fate? If Felix didn't find me, the Nizahl Heir would." I thought of the Mufsids and Urabi. His determination to catch them outweighed his commitment to his own father's law. "He is a devoted hunter."

And you are determined to exist only as prey, Hanim murmured. *Complacency is spelled with the letters of your name... Sylvia.*

Sefa refused to accept defeat. "There are places we heard about during our travels. Lands lost to the mountains and Essam, beyond the reach of any hunter. They are only rumors, but—"

"Sefa," I sighed.

"Listen to me!"

My neck prickled. I spun around, but it was too late. Vaun tackled Marek to the ground. Ren caught Sefa, pulling her back against him with a dagger at her throat.

Arin materialized from the dark arch of trees, hands tucked behind him. "If she won't listen, I certainly will."

Marek hurled a filthy epithet at the Heir, words choking off when Vaun slammed his face into the ground.

"Get off them!" I cried out. I rushed forward, but Sefa's yelp as Ren's dagger dug into the line under her jaw halted me in my tracks. I whirled on Arin. "They have nothing to do with this!"

"Considering they've been bumbling around the woods in search of you since the waleema, I would have to disagree."

"You can't harm them. We have an agreement!"

In my periphery, I saw Marek stop struggling to stare at me.

"We do." Arin's attention moved beyond me, assessing our surroundings. "They will be kept in a secure facility in Nizahl until the Alcalah is over. They can irritate my soldiers to their hearts' content from there."

"No," Sefa whispered. Ren's arm went around her midsection as her knees gave out. Pure terror splashed across her face. "Please, please, no. He'll find me. He can go wherever he likes, access any building. He'll kill Marek!"

"You bastard," Marek spat. Vaun purpled, and the crack of his fist against Marek's jaw echoed in the dark wood. He raised his fist again, and Sefa screamed as Marek's head hit the earth.

Tendrils of agony snaked from my cuffs. "Stop!" I shouted.

They would die. They would be put into a wagon for Nizahl and never reach their destination. And I would have no way of knowing.

My fingers curled against the pressure swelling in my veins.

Marek spit blood directly onto Vaun's face. The hotheaded fool was going to get himself killed, and the only person who could stop Vaun seemed disinclined to intervene.

"Sylvia!" Sefa shrieked.

The ground shook. Overhead, a flock of birds left their roost in a burst. The pressure lessened on my cuffs. This time, the surge of magic was cleaner. Less agonizing as it slammed around, seeking an exit.

This time, some of it succeeded.

Ren shouted as he was catapulted backward, falling into Hirun with a splash. The current eagerly swept him away. Vaun's muscles locked, though his eyes still darted around in confusion. Marek shoved him aside, and the guard keeled over easily. My empty stomach contracted.

The eye that hadn't swollen shut in Marek's face widened. Sefa's breaths came too fast, juddering out of her shaking body. "Am I dead?" She patted at her throat.

"You're a Jasadi," Marek breathed.

Arin seemed to have forgotten about the two wards. He kicked Vaun's shin, but the guard could only quiver. A calculating gleam sparked in the Heir's gaze. Marek stumbled upright, helped along by Sefa. Before they could go any farther, Arin casually raised his blade. "I wouldn't recommend running," he said.

Marek sneered, shoving Sefa behind him. "Go! It's only one dagger."

I groped around in my cloak, a litany of curses on my lips. A single dagger was all he needed. Sefa would sever her own limbs before leaving Marek to die, and Arin probably knew it.

Sefa had turned out the pockets when she washed my cloak. Had she returned everything to its original place?

My fingers closed around a solid, cool shape.

It was exceptionally satisfying that my magic over Vaun broke at the same instant Arin found the tip of my blade pressed against his side.

"Vaun, if you take a single step, your Heir will be dead before the blade leaves his body," I said.

"I will feed your bones to the dogs," Vaun snarled. "Jasadi filth."

I pushed the dagger against the hard plane of Arin's stomach, tearing through his black vest. Arin glanced at the blade, then at me. He pursed his lips, looking vaguely annoyed.

There are two dozen ways he could disarm you, Hanim said. *Half of them involve your own blade buried in your body.*

I spoke fast. "My magic responds in their presence when it responds to little else. They know about my abilities now. They might reveal my magic if you send them to Nizahl. Any confidence is easy to betray under the right pressure."

"A sound argument for killing them," Arin said. Sefa had her arms around Marek's waist, holding him up. They watched us with the wariness of chickens on the butcher's block.

"Or keeping them in the tunnels."

Arin blinked, and I pressed my advantage. "It's the most practical option. They are the sole clue we have to my magic, and they can hardly spread my secret from the tunnels."

The fastest route to persuade Arin lay in logic, and from the furrow forming in his brow, I had him.

"Why lose a bargaining chip needlessly?" I pushed.

"And if they escape?"

"They won't."

Arin assessed the trembling Nizahlans. I held my breath, my palm slick around the dagger's hilt. Essam was unnaturally quiet, waiting with me.

Though his voice was soft, the wind carried his words like ice falling from a seething sky. "Do not waste this mercy," Arin said. "It will not be granted twice."

He dropped his arm. Relief coursed through me. The argument for sparing their lives had triumphed. A tenuous victory. If Sefa and Marek proved too troublesome, Arin's scale would shift in death's favor.

"Vaun, escort them to the tunnels," he said. "Remembering, of course, that they are our invited guests. No harm can come to them."

Arin's training was apparently worth its weight in gold, because Vaun managed to bow despite the protest lodged in his scowl. I nodded at Marek and Sefa. His flaws were many, but Vaun would not disobey a direct order from his Heir.

"Your Highness," Vaun said. He motioned at the dagger I still held to Arin's abdomen.

"Oh," Arin said, having deemed my threat inconsequential enough to forget. I scowled and slid the dagger back into the cloak's pocket. Marek and Sefa walked ahead of Vaun, leaning on each other.

Arin turned. From the way his brows crawled up his forehead, he hadn't taken a proper look at me until now.

"I lost my skirt in the river," I said primly.

"You're holding a cloak."

I crossed my arms. "I'm certain it has never been a consideration of yours, but wool is a difficult material to launder. Sefa spent hours—" I cut myself off with a huff. It was unexplainable, how effectively he roused my ire. "I'm keeping it dry."

He shrugged off his coat and held it toward me. I stared, uncomprehending.

"It's cold, and you are shivering." A touch of defensiveness crept into his tone. "Illness eats more time than I have to spare."

I rolled my eyes. His precious time. I accepted the coat, pushing my arms through the long sleeves. Since Arin stood a head taller than me, the coat fell to my feet instead of my calves. Arin's gaze lingered on my neck for longer than normal. When he reached forward, I cringed, tightening my grip on the dagger. I half expected him to close his hands around my throat. Instead, what he did was far more baffling.

He folded back my collar.

Fastidious to a fault, it seems, Hanim observed. *We might use it to our advantage.*

By the cursed tombs, I would never understand him. The man hardly stirred at a raised blade, but he couldn't tolerate a single crooked collar.

"We will work on improving your assault strategy," Arin said. He thumbed the ragged cut I had made in his vest with a frown. "You will need it when Ren fishes himself from Hirun."

Everyone in the keep knew Marek and Sefa bickered. They bickered about the best way to light a fire, how many thumps you need to properly beat a rug, what kinds of fruit seed tasted better roasted. Any notions the other wards entertained about the nature of Marek and Sefa's relationship were put to rest early on. Bickering was either an outlet for pent-up amorous frustrations or a consequence of prolonged exposure. The former resolved itself eventually, and the latter did not. Their bickering rarely escalated into full arguments. And before today, I had never seen Marek and Sefa shout at each other.

"We were willing to flee Mahair with her in tow and incur the Commander's wrath, but staying in a shelter with food, water, and beds is too much for you?" Sefa yelled.

I sat on Sefa's new bed, watching with a peculiar mixture of curiosity and regret. If Niyar and Palia hadn't killed Emre, I imagined watching my parents argue might have provoked a similar feeling.

"He thinks we're linked to her magic. He can use us against her!" Marek raked through his hair. "We can't stay here!"

"How would trying to escape help?" Sefa pounded the dust off the quilt at the foot of the bed. She aggressively folded it into a rectangle. "He would be committed to finding us, and we would be granted far less leeway than we have now!"

Marek covered his face, sliding down the door. Sefa watched him mutinously for a long moment. I tried to make myself smaller, less like a voyeur spying on their private moments. With a drawn sigh, Sefa left the quilt and knelt by Marek, gently prying his wrists apart.

"It's just until after the trials. What's one more adventure?"

I felt compelled to speak. "He wouldn't harm you as punishment for my disobedience." At Marek's fiery glare, I added, "Not out of compassion. Logically, hurting you two would ruin my goodwill and keep me from training efficiently. It might even motivate us to flee together. I am not denying that inflicting pain is another tool at his disposal. Just not one he'll turn to with other available options. But if you run, if you tell anyone about the tunnels…once the Commander reaches a decision, he cannot be dissuaded."

"You mean he'll kill us." Sefa giggled, snuffing the sound in her elbow. "What danger is there in a brute?" Sefa said, echoing the answer I gave her the night I killed the soldier. "I kept wondering what you could have possibly meant. You meant this, didn't you? The Nizahl Heir is polite, brilliant, handsome. He is the opposite of a brute, and a thousand times more dangerous for it, because you cannot know from which direction he will strike."

"You find that funny?" Marek peered at Sefa with concern. He pressed the back of his hand to her forehead.

Sefa toppled from her crouch, joining Marek against the door. She dropped her head on his shoulder. "No."

We sat there until Sefa's eyelids drooped and light snores vibrated in her chest.

Marek's lips tightened. "He knows who we are."

I smiled wanly. "Caleb is a nice name."

Marek's flinch nearly knocked Sefa awake. His expression shuttered, and a faraway sorrow lined his features. "It was."

His gaze hardened and snapped to mine. "We won't enter Nizahl. If you don't find a way to persuade him to release us before the third trial, we will take our chances in the woods."

"Understood."

"So. You're a Jasadi."

His discomfort was evident. Too many tales existed about Jasadis, expertly planted by Nizahl over the years to destroy any lingering sympathy for the scorched kingdom. Most people remembered Jasad before the siege, had traded outside the fortress and sent invitations to their waleemas. But even those old enough to remember Jasad at the peak of its power had succumbed to the distrust and fear sown in the last ten years.

"Do I frighten you now?" I was only partly joking.

Marek chuckled, sweeping Sefa into his arms as he stood. "No more than usual. I never much believed in the idea of magic-madness." He laid her down on the bed, brushing her curls from her forehead. "Sefa is quite angry, though. She wanted to know why you made her wash clothes by hand all these years."

Something tight and uncomfortable loosened in my chest. I had not realized how worried I was about their potential reactions. This was the first time being Jasadi hadn't cost me.

"Marek. What happened with Sefa's stepfather?"

The muscles in his back tightened. "It is not my story to share."

"I don't want to ask her." Not after that horrible emptiness had invaded Sefa at the mere mention of the man. "Please. Why are you both so afraid of returning to Nizahl?"

Marek stayed silent for long minutes. I was on the brink of accepting defeat when he said, in a voice filled with old fury, "Sefa's father died when she was eleven. Her father was Lukubi, but her mother was Nizahlan. Her mother moved them from Lukub to Nizahl and married the High Counselor a year after Sefa's father died. The High Counselor was powerful and well respected in the Citadel. He was not a good stepfather. He took…liberties with Sefa. Liberties a man does not take with a child."

Nausea rolled in my belly. I stared at Sefa's sleeping face and vividly imagined flaying the skin from a man I had never met. No wonder Sefa always startled so violently if one of the girls in the keep woke her up. Even many years and miles later, her instincts remembered.

"We escaped and swindled our way through the kingdoms. But we weren't careful enough. After the attack in the market, I carried Sefa to Raya's and held her hand while the healer's apprentice put her back together. When she woke, I told her we either settled in Mahair or she continued without me. No scheme was worth risking Sefa's life."

I was barely listening, stuck on rotating through everything Sefa had ever told me. Searching for clues. Signs of the horror she'd experienced. She was the liveliest girl in the keep. If anyone needed an opinion, Sefa would arrive with a thousand. The farmers disliked her for releasing their chickens if she disapproved of the state of their coops. She had befriended *me* against my efforts, and that was not an easily accomplished feat.

Marek, guessing my thoughts, patted the spot near my hand to catch my attention. "She will talk about it with you in her own time. Leave her be."

"I will." Hypocrisy did not rank highly on my trailing list of flaws. I would not ask for secrets from Sefa when I had no interest in repaying the confidence.

"Go bathe," Marek said. "You smell like the river."

"You knocked me into it!"

"That's no excuse." Marek shooed me from the room. He smirked at my glower before slamming the door shut.

I caught a whiff of myself and cringed. Marek hadn't been lying. When the hall fell dark and silent, I heated a few barrels of water and poured them into a wide wooden bath. Steam curled in white wisps from the stone floor. I lingered in the washroom late into the evening, trying not to dwell on Sefa's face by the river and the High Counselor's lies.

Checking the empty hall, I darted out, wincing at the slap of cold air. The Jasadis who stayed here before us had enchanted the walls to glow in the evening as a clever alternative to lanterns. The magic left over was faint, however, and did little to illuminate my path.

I rounded the corner and crashed into a firm body. A hand clamped over my mouth, shoving me into the wall. I clutched my towel. The waning light outlined Vaun's sneer.

"If you reveal your magic to anybody again, I will decorate these halls with your blood and tears," he growled. "The Heir will *not* be incriminated by you."

I licked a long stripe over his palm. He yanked his hand away with a sound of disgust.

"Should the need arise, the Heir can say he didn't know I was a Jasadi," I snapped. I had plastered myself to the wall already, but Vaun stepped closer.

"His Highness will not be made to look like a fool, either. A reputation like his will not be tarnished by atrocities like you." He leaned in, close enough for me to distinguish each bristly hair at the crown of his forehead. "And if you *ever* raise a knife to the Commander again—"

"You'll…what?" I met his glare with a maniacal one of my own. "Scold me in secret again?"

Vaun spat at my feet. With another hateful glare, he turned the same corner I had come from. I glanced at my cuffs. Not a trace of heat or pressure.

"Helpful as always."

If the Alcalah's outcome depended on my magic, we were all doomed.

CHAPTER FIFTEEN

History has a twisted sense of humor.

The day Jasad's fortress rose was remembered for all the wrong reasons. The newly appointed Qayida Hend had stood shoulder to shoulder with Malika Safa and Malik Mustafa. Behind them, a sea of Jasadis gathered on the hill that would become the courtyard of Usr Jasad. As one, they lifted their hands and poured their magic forth. Back then, magic was still as powerful in their veins as it was rich in the land. A conductor stood centered in the masses, guiding the flow of magic to the Qayida. They say on the day of the fortress's rise, the Qayida's entire body had burned silver and gold as she read the enchantment the Malik and Malika had toiled for years to produce.

The fortress had been a dream for Jasad since shortly after the age of the Awaleen. Protection. Peace. The monsters in Essam stalked their borders. Visitors came to stand at the edge of Sirauk, gazing upon the misty bridge and leaving bizarre offerings littered in Janub Aya. Trade had become unreliable, and the skirmishes with Omal were escalating. A fortress tuned to the unique magical marker of each of Jasad's citizens would allow us to move freely, but keep our kingdom secure from anyone—or anything—else.

The ground had quaked, knocking everyone but the Qayida to the ground. She had the magic of thousands flowing through her, and if she stopped, if she let it settle, it would incinerate her. With a roar heard all the way in the farthest corners of Lukub and Orban, the ground split. A wall the color of thick resin had surged from the earth, traveling past the hill, curving around Jasad's borders. The Qayida's scream was said to have filled the Malik and Malika's ears with blood. Gold and silver orbs burst from her chest, streaking inside the wall. The colors moving within the fortress would be known as Zeenat Hend, named after the Qayida who burned from the inside out to erect Jasad's impenetrable fortress.

I hadn't thought of Qayida Hend in years. Her bravery had guaranteed that each subsequent Qayida would be trusted with annually renewing the enchantment keeping the fortress intact.

I washed my face in the basin by the door. The water rippled with my reflection. I tried not to linger, but the sight of my face still stung. The hollows beneath my eyes were darker than date pits. My hair hung in a lusterless braid down my back. The face of someone who had failed to fulfill a legacy of sacrifice.

I shoved the basin away. Qayida Hend burned for her bravery. One of Jasad's foremost heroes. But if you asked me, Qayida Hend's death was an amusement of fate. She burned to raise magic, and centuries later, Jasad would burn so they could tear it down.

We mourn what history mocks.

In the training center, the Nizahl Heir did not bother with a greeting. He pointed at my legs and turned around, devoting his focus to the weapons chest. I should have been thankful for his silence. A serpent's tongue slithered only when it had poison to spread.

"Aren't Heirs supposed to travel with their personal chefs?" I asked, jogging past the wall with my grandparents. As usual, I averted my gaze. Guilt tightened my throat every time I looked at them, so I did my best not to.

Arin diligently arranged the day's tools on top of the chest. All I'd heard about the mysterious Heir prior to that fateful day in Essam had to do with his looks and his prowess in combat. It is significantly more enjoyable, I supposed, to wax poetic about the Heir's heart-wrenching beauty or his lethal grace than it is to dwell on this intense perfectionism.

A javelin wobbled on the chest. Arin scowled, moving it to the second row. After a moment of reflection, he nudged everything else an inch to the right.

Perfectionism might be too generous a term.

"Yes, typically. Why?"

I finished my circuits, bracing myself on my knees. "The guards can't cook," I panted. "I want a royal's chef."

"You're getting one." He held out the rounded end of the spear. "I eat what you eat."

"I am fully aware," I groaned. Had Arin not been so gallingly Nizahlan, I might have believed he was Orbanian, so uninterested was he in luxury and comfort.

The back of my neck prickled as he moved closer. "Spread your feet." He kicked my ankles apart in a succinct motion, momentarily catching me off guard.

I bounded forward, springing off my back leg to push my body's momentum into the spear. It sailed true, cracking the wooden board in the center.

"Did you see that?" I exclaimed. If anything would impress the unimpressible Heir, it would be throwing a spear with enough force to cleave a man's chest in two. "Half the Orbanian army cannot land a throw like that!"

He made me repeat it twenty-seven times before he was pleased. Our next task of the day required a trip to the surface. Arin refused to divulge details on what this particular training entailed or why we needed to complete it outside the tunnels.

Wes passed Arin a strip of fabric. "What do you know of the first trial?" Arin asked.

I shifted to the other foot, casting a nervous glance at the three waiting guards. "The first trial is held within a cursed forest in Orban. No one is permitted to enter the forest outside the Alcalah."

"Why can they not enter?" Jeru prompted. A blush rose high on his tanned cheeks when Arin glanced over.

"The forest is the site of a massacre from the age of the Awaleen. During the battle of Ayume, Awala Dania brought life to the forest. The trees, the lake, even the leaves—Dania enchanted everything in the forest to kill Kapastra's marching soldiers. Though the centuries have weakened Ayume Forest's curse, the poison of Dania's magic lingers."

Jeru looked suitably impressed.

"Correct," Arin said, plucking the fuzzy fibers from the cloth. I watched the deft movements of his fingers, oddly engrossed, until Arin continued, "The trial will be held at midday. History has shown that the Champions who do not reach the other side of the forest by dusk do not reach it at all. Our goal today is to have you navigate with magic as your only sense. You will follow me through the woods, and the guards will serve as decoys."

Kapastra's forked brow, it was a near replica of Hanim's old training. Except he wasn't resurrecting three-headed creatures to give chase. "My magic will not aid me. I'll be following on instinct alone."

"We will see." Arin raised the strip of cloth, preparing me for the coming contact. I was once again bemused at the strangeness of his personal code of ethics. "Close your eyes."

Smooth leather pressed against the wings of my cheeks. He pulled the fabric tightly over my eyes. Brush rustled around us as the guards presumably scattered, setting up posts to disorient me.

"How close will Sefa and Marek be?" Addressing Arin in the dark sent a shiver of unease down my neck.

"They will shift around the woods throughout the session. We need to determine whether their physical distance matters for triggering your magic."

Arin stepped away. "Try to follow me."

The woods went quiet as Arin vanished. The darkness didn't throw me as much as I had anticipated, and I walked with relative comfort. I trailed my hands from tree to tree, straining to hear footsteps. My magic remained removed from this venture, leaving my cuffs docile and dull on my wrists.

The crunch of leaves alerted me seconds before a shoulder slammed into mine. I careened, barely catching myself from a disgraceful tumble.

Branches snapped to my left, and I ducked. Needles rained down on my head. How did Arin expect me to find him while buffeted in every direction by his guards? My magic didn't care that Marek and Sefa were nearby.

The sound of my body became deafening the longer I stumbled along. My breaths were harsh to my own ears, my footfalls clumsy and loud. The stammer of my heart matched the pounding in my head. They weren't hunting me; they were toying with their conquered prize.

I shoved past the thought. I was not an eleven-year-old girl anymore, wandering Essam Woods in the night while monsters born of Hanim's spells gave chase. Terror had not induced my magic then, and it would not help me now.

Something wet and tacky hit my forehead. I gasped, wiping frantically at my face.

"Filth for filth," Vaun whispered, directly into my ear.

I lunged for him and met empty air. I failed to catch myself this time, landing hard on my knees.

A clicking hum preceded the scuttle of pointy legs over my hand. A munban. I thrashed, pushing to my feet too quickly and clipping my shoulder against a tree. I was surrounded by threats I couldn't see, and they were winning.

The next feint came from the right. I dove to the left instead, colliding with a distinctly human body. These were *my* woods. I fed this soil my blood and broken tears, sharpened its teeth on the fine flesh of monsters. In Essam, I reigned supreme.

Breathy noises leaked from my open mouth as I tightened my fist and smashed it into the side of what was hopefully a head. Did Vaun think I wouldn't kill him? I wasn't held to the same code of ethics as his precious Heir. I would rip his head from his shoulders and spit on his skull. I would crush what was left of him into the dirt, because his remains weren't fit to feed animals.

"Sylvia!"

The bloodsong wailing through me paused. For a terrible moment, I could not locate my mouth in the swirling savagery. "Marek?" I patted at the chest beneath me, checking for a guardsman's vest. It wasn't there. "Marek, I'm so sorry!"

I rolled away from him, but the urge to tear a living thing asunder and plant my fury into its quivering heart remained.

Approaching footsteps pushed me to my haunches. I crouched, ready to spring.

"Remove the blindfold," Arin said.

Awareness came too late, after I had already launched myself. A bone-crushing grip caught my arms before I could slam into the Heir.

"You," Arin said. "Take off her blindfold."

The cloth fell to the ground, and I blinked rapidly against the piercing light. Arin released me. His searching look resembled the one he'd worn when I dangled myself over Hirun. As though I'd failed some elusive test, but not in a way he had anticipated.

"Why did you wait?" he asked. "Why didn't you remove the blindfold yourself?"

My vision settled. The drum beating its feral tune faded, taking Hanim and her fiends with it. The hazy words leaving my mouth belonged to a different girl, addressed to a dead woman. "You didn't say I could. I have to follow the instructions."

Good girl, Hanim whispered.

In almost humorous unison, Marek and Arin's brows furrowed. Arin's smoothed again, but I knew his dangerous curiosity had been piqued.

"In the future, avoid touching the trees while you run," Arin said lightly. "Even the sap in Ayume can kill you."

The next morning, I walked into the kitchen to find the scent of Mahair surrounding me. Fruit displayed in colorful arrays, fresh cutlets of lamb, ground spices heaped in wooden bowls. I sorted through the food, some of which had passed from season months ago, with wonder.

"This was your doing, wasn't it?" Wes asked. I dropped into my seat, pulling a bowl of oats soaked in lavender and honey toward me.

"His Highness ordered a patrol to follow one of Raya's wards around the market and bring back items typically found at an Omalian table," Jeru added. "He's never shown any extracurricular interest in food."

"Maybe I should start complaining at the top of my lungs when I'm unhappy, too," Jeru mused. I crossed my legs, balancing a plate on my risen knee. Sefa inhaled a bowl of bileela, the milky wheat topped with raisins and sugar.

"You're not as attractive," Marek said. He pounded Sefa's back when she choked on her third bowl. I busied myself with food to hide my bewilderment. Why would Arin go through the trouble of bringing Omalian food to the tunnels when he couldn't care less what he ate?

I didn't voice my doubts aloud. Jeru and Wes had grown marginally more comfortable around me as the weeks passed. Marek and Sefa's arrival had helped, too. Ren continued to pretend I didn't exist, though, and Vaun...I wished Vaun would pretend I didn't exist.

"Marek's right," Wes agreed.

Jeru clutched his chest, toppling to the floor. "Wes, catch me! I'm wounded!"

I finished chewing a bite of gibna areesh enough to garble, "Try throwing knives at him, Jeru. He seems to like that."

All three guards turned to look at me. Wes put his head down on the table.

I cracked a boiled egg against Marek's forehead. Wes and Jeru balked. It was a time-honored tradition at the keep, cracking eggs on the nearest victim's forehead. I picked at the bits of shell and asked, "Did the patrol happen to find sesame candies?"

In unison, both guards scowled. Ah, I'd forgotten their last encounter with sesame candies took place when they removed one from the body of the Nizahl soldier I'd killed.

Marek inspected the colored berries with a frown. He plucked one from the stem, rolling it between his fingers. "This berry does not grow in Mahair," he said. "I cannot even name it."

"Let me see." Marek dropped the berry into Sefa's open palm. She studied the white fruit and shook her head. "I can't, either. Sylvia, do you know?"

I accepted the berry when she held it out. I split it in half and popped a piece into my mouth.

The dry, sour flavor bursting on my tongue brought with it an old interaction, too hazy to be properly called a memory. Hadn't Niyar tried to feed me a bowl of these white berries? It must have been before Soraya became my attendant and took over arranging my meals. I remembered Niyar going on and on about how special they were, how they only grew in the east of Jasad, and the nobles had taken to treating them like a delicacy. I called them "moon-vomit berries" and clenched my teeth when Niyar pushed one against my lips. When he would not desist, I shrieked, and my unrestrained magic threw the table and chairs into the wall. Someone had stayed with me after my grandfather stormed out—Dawoud, wasn't it? He'd dried my tears and lifted me into his arms. "Even queens must bite sour fruit sometimes, Essiya. Now help the servants fix this mess."

I hurled the fruit to the table, my pulse cacophonous in my ears. How could it be here? Nizahl had not left any portion of Jasad unscathed, and these berries' existence was confined to the wilayahs in the east.

"I do not recognize it," I whispered.

"Curious."

I jolted in my seat. Arin and Vaun stood framed in the kitchen's entrance. The Nizahl Heir glanced at the hastily discarded berry, and icy realization washed over me.

I was still being hunted. Arin would not stop until he uncovered my identity, culling the list of potential nobles in his systematic, efficient fashion.

My heartbeat slowed with new resolve. It wasn't enough to simply hope I'd hidden my tracks. He would keep walking this path, and my only option was to direct where it led him. If he wanted clues, then I'd leave ones that took him far away from Essiya, Heir of Jasad.

I already had a good start. He had seemed puzzled at my violent outburst when the guards chased me through the woods. Nobles did not descend into a feral state under such conditions: they rolled into a ball and wept.

Vaun grimaced at the berries as though they had personally insulted his mother. Arin moved on smoothly, the moment locked in his web. "Wear tighter-fitting clothes," he instructed. "You'll be going into Hirun."

CHAPTER SIXTEEN

Arin and Ren stayed away from the tunnels for the next few days.
I'd overheard the guards discussing the Commander's renewed
rotations in Essam to search for evidence that could help him learn
more about the Jasadi groups' movements. I was glad for a reprieve.
Others seemed to view the Heir's absence with less relief. I returned
from the washroom to find a smashed mess of fruit on my door.
Juice trickled onto the ground, threatening to draw several armies of
ants. I scraped a chunk from the top and held it to the lantern.

Jasad's white berry.

Vaun was not as inclined to bide his time as Arin. It was becoming a dangerous pattern with the guardsman. There were worrisome
ways he could harm me without directly violating Arin's orders. The
duty binding Vaun to Arin went deeper than that of the rest of the
guards. Jeru, Wes, or Ren would gladly throw their lives at their
Heir's feet, but they were not subject to the tumult of protectiveness
and rage plaguing Vaun.

On our walk to the tunnels, Wes had mentioned that Vaun had
been by Arin's side since childhood. Instead of flourishing into his
own person, the guardsman seemed to have grown around Arin,
branched into an extension of the Heir. Vaun believed in the Nizahl
throne, in his kingdom's ultimate supremacy, with the same fanatis-
cim driving his vitriolic hatred of Jasadis.

The answer hit me with the force of a gale.

Arin was to Vaun what Sefa was to Marek.

Which meant Vaun would stop at nothing to ensure the Heir's security, even if it meant going against Arin's will.

The thought bothered me through the next day. Arin had yet to return. After I finished my set of trainings, Jeru accompanied me to Hirun carrying two baskets of dirty clothes. I breathed in the river's scent and felt a knot in my chest loosen. It smelled terrible, as always, but a familiar terrible.

Jeru cursed as he sloshed around the river's shallow shore, trying to spread the clothes out on the rocks without losing them to the current. I considered offering to help, but I was enjoying a rare moment of sunshine and did not feel inclined to move. I leaned back against a tree and crossed my legs at the ankles, wishing I'd brought a treat from the kitchen.

Jeru finally managed to secure the clothes over the boulders and rocks. He scooped water into the empty baskets and poured it over the clothes. I didn't see Arin's coats anywhere. Shame. I would have loved to kick them to the fish.

I had just closed my eyes to bask in the sunlight when a shout struck me upright.

Jeru splashed in the middle of Hirun, struggling to keep afloat. The water flowed *around* him, leaving him fixed in the same spot.

Magic.

I bolted to my feet. An immaculately dressed woman stood on the banks of Hirun. Seven slits at the bottom of her abaya made the fabric seem to float around her legs, which were protected by gold-colored pants.

"We've been searching for you." She turned around. Silver and gold swirled in her eyes. "Mawlati."

Terror seized me in its grip and squeezed. The world spun, and I grabbed the tree for balance. She knew. She *knew*. Hadn't I suspected as much? I'd been so desperate to be wrong that I barely let myself consider what I'd do when I came face-to-face with the Jasadis hunting me.

Mawlati. I hadn't heard anyone but my grandmother called Mawlati. I never thought the title could belong to anyone other than her.

I forced myself straight. Weakness would win me no favor.

"Why do you call me Mawlati? The Jasad royal family is dead."

She chuckled. "So we all thought. We cannot fathom how you remained hidden for so long, but you need not fear anymore. We have come to help you reclaim the throne that was taken from you."

Denial was a doomed route. She would have already knocked me out without the grace of a conversation if she didn't know who I was. "Do you belong to the Mufsids or Urabi?"

She stepped delicately around a pile of munban nests. The colors of magic continued to seethe in her eyes, holding Jeru in the river. The strength of her magic, her clothing, her demeanor. I had grown up around power like hers. She had to be from the first or second wilayah.

Her nose wrinkled. "I have no association with the brigade of cowards who call themselves Urabi."

I wanted to pound my head against the tree. She belonged to the Mufsids. The Jasadi group Arin claimed left more dead Jasadi bodies in their wake than his soldiers.

"How did you find me?"

She stepped closer. I reached into my pocket, only to feel the lines of it sew themselves shut. The Mufsid wagged her finger. "I come in peace, Mawlati. I suggest you receive me in peace, as well."

"You are drowning the guard."

"No, not at all. Drowning would be too quick. I prefer to watch them choke over some time." She dabbed at her glistening forehead. The magic was taking its toll.

Jasadi magic is not a bottomless well. Every Jasadi has a finite supply from which to draw.

I had to keep her occupied until she ran through her magic. By the time it replenished, I would be long gone.

"I have no desire to join the Mufsids. You kill Jasadis."

The Mufsid gave me a look like I had just declared I dined on rat nails. "Yet you would align yourself with the Nizahl Heir?" She shook her head, raising an apologetic hand. "Forgive me, Mawlati. We know you are under duress and do not plan to complete the Alcalah as his Champion. I have come to take you. Our leaders are most eager to make your acquaintance."

I circled through a dozen approaches and came away empty. I couldn't exactly explain I intended to betray them to the Nizahl Heir. "If you wish to recruit me, why did you attack me with the specter of a dead woman?" The rotting corpse of Hanim looming over me still haunted my dreams.

Her thick brows pulled together. "We did no such thing. We would never. The Mufsids do not hide like the Urabi. Once we choose a path, we do not shy from it."

I swallowed. Jeru's thrashing had taken a turn for the worse, dwindling to lethargic writhing. He might not outlast this Mufsid's magic.

I studied her. In a way, I felt an echo of kinship with this Jasadi. We shared a mutual loss. A scar on our souls in the shape of our scorched home. "Why are you killing Jasadis?"

The sunlight caught the lighter strands in her brown hair. The gold and silver had slowed to a churn as her magic depleted from the effort of holding Jeru. "We are trying to *save* Jasadis. But some of our people believe it is better to hide, to live a life under another's control, than to stand up and reclaim what they took from us. We cannot allow those Jasadis to be weaponized against our movement."

"Why do you get to make that choice for them?" I shook my head. "And how do I factor into any of these plans?"

Brown had almost entirely replaced the other colors in her eyes. Soon, Jeru would be freed from the clasp of her power. He might hear this conversation. Hear her call me Mawlati.

Or she would kill him. Probably kill him.

"Are you not Essiya, once Heir of Jasad? Daughter of Niphran, granddaughter of Malik Niyar and Malika Palia? You were born to lead us. To fight at our helm."

Rust filled my mouth. I wanted to join Jeru in the river.

Tell her the truth. Tell her you are spineless and pathetic, that you believe you do not owe your kingdom your life, Hanim said.

"How did you know I was alive?"

Her annoyance grew with each question. It wouldn't be long before her patience reached its limit. "A new recruit decided to try a locating spell and discovered Qayida Hanim's body. We hadn't been able to track her since her exile. Whatever warding she used to prevent us from finding her collapsed when she died. They were insistent on investigating. Despite our misgivings, we agreed and spent the next year trying to track your magic, but it was like trying to catch a grain of sand in a storm. We finally found that horrible little Omalian village a month ago, but unfortunately, the information had leaked to the Urabi that we believed the Jasad Heir to be alive.

"Not everyone was pleased about the idea of recruiting you to our cause," she continued. "There was strong dissent in our ranks. Some who rightfully believe reinstating anyone raised within the corrupt walls of Usr Jasad flies in the face of our mission. They wanted to find you and kill you. But we believe your name—and most importantly, your magic—will serve a greater purpose than anyone realizes."

Corrupt walls of Usr Jasad? What was she talking about?

I did not have the luxury of time to process the information thrown at me. I had a plan that would hopefully see the three of us leaving this encounter alive.

Lies mixed with truth on my tongue, sealing together seamlessly. "The Nizahl Heir believes my power will help win the Alcalah for his kingdom. The Heir is like his father—power-hungry, obsessed with glory. He does not know who I am or that you hunt me. If I disappear now, all four kingdoms will devote their armies and efforts to finding you. The Alcalah is well protected, but I can create opportunities for you to find me. If I go missing during one of the trials, they will simply assume I died. Find a vulnerability in their security and take me then."

She frowned, but I could see the idea turning in her head. "I was told to bring you back now."

I pushed steel into my voice. "If you want me to lead, you need to listen."

The silver and gold in her eyes evaporated. The current finally pulled Jeru, carrying him downstream. I wasn't worried. He would catch himself on a turn and climb out.

The Jasadi inclined her head. "As you command, Mawlati. I do hope you remember this when the time comes to choose between us and our cowardly counterparts."

Cowardly, because the Urabi thought men like Adel didn't deserve to die for preferring to spend their life working in an Omalian bakery over joining a doomed rebellion? Then again, the Urabi wouldn't have left Adel alone, either. Jasadis spent their lives watching for Nizahl. How devastating it must be for the attack to come from within, from over your shoulder instead of across enemy lines.

She stopped near my shoulder as she passed. "Until next time."

I gritted my teeth at the underlying threat. She spoke to me as though I owed her a long-standing duty. Essiya would always be an anchor around my neck, chaining me to a fate I never wanted or asked for.

I met her gaze with a stony one of my own. "Only if you catch me before they do."

A knock came at my door in the middle of the night.

I sat straight up, the blanket spilling to my waist, and squinted around my dark room. What now? Nothing good could come from a visit at this hour.

Arin stood on the other side of the door. Mud stained his boots, and his windswept hair fell in a silver shock over his forehead. He must have returned to the tunnels and come straight here. It was satisfying to see the fastidious Heir so disheveled. Despite his best efforts, Arin was still human.

"Is everything all right?"

"There is a matter of some urgency I would like to discuss with you," he said. "May I enter?"

I waved him inside, settling into a cross-legged position on the bed. I hadn't been able to sleep, anyway. The words *corrupt walls of Jasad* pounded like drums each time I closed my eyes. It made no sense. If the rest of the Mufsids were like the woman I'd met, then most of them once belonged to the wealthiest, most powerful wilayahs in Jasad. What quarrel could they have had with the crown keeping them in their riches?

After deliberating briefly, Arin claimed the chair in the corner.

"Jeru spoke to you," I said.

"He did." The Heir tapped his knee. "What did she say to you?"

I didn't hesitate. I had played this coming conversation in my head from the moment the Mufsid left the river. "How can you sense magic?"

Arin paused. Amusement crept into his face. It baffled me, how much he seemed to enjoy being cornered or outpaced. Every exchange with the Nizahl Heir was a game. A battle of wills on a blood-soaked field with him as the last man standing.

"You want to trade?"

"Yes." I pointed an innocent smile at him. "You told me every truth has its time. Let this be yours."

"I could force it from you. Painfully."

Front strike. Obvious and easy to block. Too easy.

"We only have three weeks left until we leave for Lukub. My magic still isn't working. You cannot afford to waste training time while I recover from your torture."

"But I can afford your friends' time." He tipped his head. "Who shall I start with, Sefa or the boy?"

"You will not have my full cooperation if you torture them. You might even run the risk of motivating them to escape, which would be a waste of your resources and loss of a training tool."

I was enjoying myself. I had had little opportunity to be truly cunning in Mahair. It felt like flexing a muscle I had forgotten existed.

I had never met anyone quite as *still* as Arin of Nizahl. The man could be carved from stone. "I have a theory."

I raised a brow. "Congratulations."

He ignored me. "I propose a different trade. Tell me about the Jasadi by the river, and I will share my theory behind your attack in Essam."

Oh, a fatal blow. I pulled at the frayed ends of my gown while I considered my options. Learning why he possessed a strange sensitivity to magic was important, but not urgent. It would not serve me unless he also mentioned how one could develop an immunity to his touch. But the person who attacked me in Essam knew me, knew my history with Hanim, and wanted to kill me for it.

A sigh escaped my lips. "I accept your trade." And so he once again remained alone on the battlefield, my shadow of resistance chased to oblivion.

He knit his hands over his stomach. Leaned back. "Next time, you might have more to bargain with."

"I don't need your consolation."

"Would you prefer my mockery?"

"Just your theory. Or your well-crafted lie. They are probably one and the same."

Thunder cracked over his expression, bright and startlingly violent. Oh, I had pierced his granite layers, had I?

"I do not *lie*. Who do you think you are, that I would tarnish my integrity to fool you?"

"I am your Champion. Your student. You work hard to provoke my magic into existence." This time, it was me who remained calm. "I have unfortunate news about your integrity, Commander."

The ripple of anger dissolved as quickly as it appeared. His expression smoothed into the mask I had learned to approach with extreme caution, and Teta Palia's old caution rang in my ear. *A tree without roots is like a river without a current, Essiya. A sign of disrupted nature. Of chaos. If something is not made to bend, what can it do but break?*

I did not think Arin of Nizahl could be broken. But I did think he could be pushed far enough to break everyone else.

When he spoke again, it was toneless. A recital of facts. "My theory concerns the number of Jasadis after you. The Urabi and the Mufsids maintain a general pattern. The Urabi recruit or abduct useful Jasadis. The Mufsids take the willing Jasadis away and slaughter the rest. On the few occasions in which they are after the same Jasadi, the identity of their target remains a mystery. You are the exception, because I reached you before they did."

"Is your theory about why they are after me?"

Arin's lips twisted wryly. "A theory is a possible answer to a posed question. I have an answer to why they are after you."

"That I was a noble, or some important Jasadi figure? Do you truly suppose a noble could survive as a village peasant for years?" I shook my head, quickly changing the subject. "What is your theory?"

"Someone from the Mufsids or the Urabi has gone rogue," Arin said.

I tugged the loose strands at the bottom of my braid free, curling them around my finger. "Rogue how?"

"The specter in the woods would have killed you if I had not been near. If the Mufsids and Urabi are attempting to recruit you, and you have not rejected them, why kill you? There must be a defector, most likely someone from the Mufsids. They must have a strong reason to want you dead if they are willing to go against their own group."

The implication was clear. I looked the Nizahl Heir directly in the eye. "I do not belong to the nobles."

He hummed. "So you say."

I threw the scrutiny back at him. "Why not dangle me in Mahair and lie in wait until they attack? The Alcalah will be swarming with people."

"The Alcalah will be heavily guarded, and there are weak points between trials where both groups will try to attack. Mahair leaves open too much room for mistakes. The Urabi send their most powerful Jasadis to recruit, and it only takes moments for them to subdue their target and whisk everyone away. If you become Victor, you will be constantly surrounded by guards, protected in upper-town homes. The Alcalah is their best chance to capture you."

"What about the Champions' Banquet? Would it be better for them to attack me at the Ivory Palace than during the Alcalah?"

"Enough questions. Tell me about the Jasadi."

I folded my knees to my chest and wondered, not for the first time, if our souls had a shape. If they were like the sheep hanging from the butcher's hook, and each decision I made hacked mine down to its dangling, bloody bones. But I refused to believe it was a failure to prioritize my own freedom, even if Hanim's voice insisted to the contrary.

I opened my mouth and told Arin everything. How the Jasadi mentioned there had been dissent in their ranks regarding my recruitment. The lie I told her about leaving an opening for the Mufsids. I molded the story in the shape closest to the truth, slicing the pieces of *Essiya* and *Mawlati* like mold from a loaf of bread.

Arin had sat forward while I spoke, his elbows bracing on his knees. The eerie mask had dropped in favor of something I never thought I'd see: bewilderment.

"You chose to stay. Here, in this stone prison, training for a tournament that has a roughly two in three chances of killing you," he said slowly, disbelieving. "The Mufsids have evaded me for years. They are your best chance of hiding from Felix and me. Why would you stay?"

I set my jaw. "I told you. I am here by choice. I chose my freedom, and you are my best chance at achieving it."

"At the cost of your own people?"

"They are not my—" I caught my breath, horrified. Rovial's tainted tomb, I had almost said it. Almost spoken a secret worse than Essiya, worse than Hanim. I ground my teeth, sudden tears of frustration pricking the back of my eyes. "Why should I owe them my life? Why is it acceptable for others to choose themselves, but it is selfish when I do it? I didn't ask for this. I do not want it."

Abruptly, I stood, aghast at revealing a sliver of my deepest doubts to the person most likely to use them against me. "You should go."

"Sylvia." The use of my name—his first time since Mahair—brought my reluctant gaze back to his. Arin regarded me with earnestness. A shadow of understanding. "Tell me who you are."

Shock rendered me mute. I had an opening. I'd displayed honesty by recounting the Mufsid's conversation and an accidental show of vulnerability—apparently the right balance of ingredients to appease Arin's guarded mistrust by an inch. If I stumbled, if he caught a whiff of dishonesty, he would never lower it again.

"You will not believe me."

He waited.

"My father was Waleed Rayan." I packaged the name with a hint of longing, a dose of sadness, and a heap of reproach. The emotions of a betrayed but once-beloved daughter. At least, I hoped. I was never anyone's daughter. My father vanished from the world with an arrow in his throat, and my grandparents hurled Niphran into Bakir Tower when she sought to follow him.

"Waleed Rayan. The Justice of Ahr il Uboor." Arin tapped a finger against his knee. "You mean to tell me you are Mervat Rayan, daughter of the third most powerful family in Jasad?"

I had chosen Mervat Rayan for three reasons. First, we were the same age. Her parents visited Usr Jasad often, leaving me with the onerous task of entertaining the girl. Waleed Rayan was important enough to be widely hated, so Arin would understand the significance of recruiting Waleed's daughter. Second, I had disliked her. She wouldn't climb the date trees with me or chase my pet caracal through the gardens.

Third, I knew for a fact Mervat Rayan and her family were dead. They had come to pay my grandparents a visit before we left for the Blood Summit, and Gedo Niyar invited them to remain in Usr Jasad until we returned. The moment the fortress broke, the Supreme's soldiers had slaughtered every single person in Usr Jasad.

"I prefer Sylvia," I said.

And perhaps I was on the wrong side of exhaustion. Perhaps my encounter with the Mufsid left a deeper mark than I thought. "I know what you think of me."

The scar cut in sharp relief against his skin. Arin's eyes narrowed as I lifted my hand near his jaw. It was stupid, so tremendously stupid I knew I'd spend the rest of the night berating myself. I traced the air above his scar, my fingers a hairsbreadth from his face. He could not hide his scars behind a tunic or a gown.

The ones on my back were a mark of shame. Not Arin's. Whatever the cause, he wore this scar as he wore his gloves. Another barrier between him and the rest of the world.

"You would rather die protecting your own than live a half-life of hiding. I am fundamentally revolting to you, not only because

I am a Jasadi, but because you believe me a coward." I took one of his gloved hands in mine, turning his palm up. A thrill of terror raced up my spine when he did not withdraw. It felt like a forbidden triumph, doing this. Reaching forward and touching an Heir whose reputation for unapproachability had grown to mythical proportions. The urge to agitate him—to draw a reaction from the most reserved man in all the Awaleen-damned kingdoms—was too powerful to resist.

"Consider this, my liege: there are fates worse than death." I drew an arrow from the edge of his glove to the tip of his longest finger. "When the treaty became the most important result of the Battle of Zinish, nobody wondered what remained of the Orbanian soldiers who had suffered the consequences of the Sultana's magic. The ones who packed up their weapons, folded their uniforms, and went home to their families. Do you?"

"They dismembered themselves."

I smiled. "Nothing motivates humans faster than fear. It is a lesson your father adopted to its fullest extent. I have lived in fear. It has not motivated me to join the Mufsids or Urabi and march into a battle they may very well win, but at the cost of my dismemberment."

I folded his hand over his heart and stepped away. "I am not a coward any more than you are a savior."

Arin didn't move his hand for a long minute. "How very eloquent. I almost believe you."

He stood, and I caged my breath. If someone's sword ever brought this man to his knees, they would never bring him low. His power did not come from magic or status, but from an unassailable sense of self.

It might be the only thing I hated more than his bloodline.

Arin tipped my chin up, waiting until I stopped glaring at his forehead to speak. "You said you revolt me. You do, but not for the reasons you think."

A strand of his hair slid against his cheek, the silk of it sending a shiver of unease along my spine.

"I do not think it is fear motivating you at all. I could understand you, then. A cornered beast will lash out to protect itself. But you…"

His hand moved to my jaw in an unstoppable motion, turning my head to his. I could see every shade of blue in his pale eyes, count the silver lashes curling around them. I was caught fast in his hold.

"You are a creature of pure spite. You would not react out of fear, but out of fury. I think daily of chaining you to a wall and seeing which you would attack first—me, or the wall." His voice was low, threaded with…curiosity? No, it couldn't be that. Endeavors to unravel my identity nonewithstanding, Arin seemed to find me as noteworthy as a blunt axe.

I grabbed his arm, digging my fingers into his coat. If he made one more move, I would strike him in his unprotected throat.

"You. Definitely you."

"I almost believed you, Suraira. Almost. But you forgot one thing."

He moved a curl from my cheek. There it was again—the flash of curiosity.

"You gave me your name without asking anything in return."

CHAPTER SEVENTEEN

Two weeks before the Champions' Banquet, my magic continued to pose an intractable obstacle.

Arin wanted it to work. He had assured me on numerous occasions how efficiently death would find me if I competed against the
other Champions without my magic's help. To this end, our trainings escalated. In intensity and quantity.

On the sixth day until we were to leave for Lukub, I entered the
training center, winding my braid into a knot atop my head. I sensed
the wrongness in the air immediately. My apprehension rose at the
sight of the day's tools scattered carelessly in front of the trunk.

Arin threw a familiar dagger—Dania's dagger, from the war
room—upward and caught it. He did it again, catching the hilt at
each descent.

"What's wrong?"

He kept tossing up the dagger. I picked up the tools, trying to
remember how he liked to sort them. Did the three-pronged lance
go after the spear or hammer?

When Arin's silence lengthened, I rubbed the furrow above my
nose and said, "Why do you insist on torturing yourself?"

That caught his attention. He closed his hand around the dagger's handle. "Torturing myself." The tone itself, thin as a thread
and dripping in condescension, should have warned me away.

"I know what you do when you disappear to the surface. The
Mufsids and Urabi have claimed lives all over the kingdoms. Evaded

your most capable soldiers. That's why I'm here, isn't it? I'm your bait. Let them be lured instead of constantly giving chase."

Arin's humorless laugh echoed. "My bait whose magic could not induce a bird to flight."

I clenched my teeth. "I'm trying."

His dark mood was a tangible thing, whipping through the training center and leaving tattered trails in its wake. "No one can say you haven't given it all you have. It is only a shame all you have amounts to nothing."

Engaging him in this state wouldn't help anything. Arin could so easily chisel his ice into unbearable cruelty, cutting those in his way open from stem to stern. I couldn't predict it. Hanim's cruelty was artless, blunt, fashioned for hard and fast impact. I liked to think I was made of a hardier fiber, but it wasn't a theory I wanted to test.

Before I could leave, the door on the other side of the training center opened. Sefa and Marek spilled inside, in the middle of a heated argument.

Sefa picked up on the tension and fell quiet. Her gaze darted between Arin and me. "Apologies. We didn't mean to interrupt."

Marek, however, had the instincts of a goat flea. He raised a blond brow in our direction and drawled, "Lovers' spat?"

Later, I would recall how Arin blanched. How those two words seemed to deal him a debilitating blow. I would consider whether Marek's foolishness wasn't its own kind of intuition. In the moment, all I saw was Arin flipping his wrist and throwing the dagger.

It would have cut straight through Sefa's heart. Clean and efficient. She'd be dead before her body hit the mat.

Before the blade could find its mark, a powerful wave of nausea knocked me to my knees, and the world froze.

I pressed the back of my shaking hand to my mouth, struggling to keep my breakfast. All of them were unnaturally still. The dagger's tip had frozen two inches from Sefa's chest.

Supporting myself against the wall, I staggered to my feet. There was no predicting how long my magic would hold. Marek's features had frozen with the dawning of horror, Sefa's with irritation. Still stuck on Marek's asinine comment, completely unaware that two inches of empty air was all that stood between her and death's door.

I wrapped my hand around the dagger and tugged. To my relief, it came away in my grip. With the immediate threat eliminated, my rage seethed forth.

I swung around. Arin was pinned in place, arm still poised in midair.

"I should kill you where you stand," I snarled. I balanced the tip of the dagger at the underside of his chin. "Bleed you dry right here."

Arin and I had reached an impasse. I didn't dream of running him through with my sword nearly as often. On occasion, when he was contemplative or pretended to ignore me, I even tolerated his company. Killing my friend on a whim? What was the sense in it?

The tip of the dagger pushed deeper into his skin. "You aimed at Sefa," I murmured. "Not Marek."

Four weeks ago, my will might not have overpowered the urge to drive this dagger through the back of his head. Today, it was a narrow victory.

"Another test." The raw quality of my laugh scraped my ears. "Safer to wager my magic would intervene for Sefa than Marek."

Arin's gaze slid to mine. Had my magic even affected him? His dangerous mood hadn't changed, and I steeled my nerves against the urge to retreat.

"What if you were wrong? What if you had miscalculated?"

"Pointless questions are best left to the poets," Arin said. He forced me a step backward. I locked my jaw, glaring up at him.

Motion in my periphery signaled a newly animated Marek and

Sefa. Arin struck in a burst of movement, slamming the heel of his hand against the inside of my wrist and sending the dagger flying.

The Nizahl Heir's eyes were shards of lethal promise. "Point a dagger at me again, and it will be your last."

The fragile peace Arin and I had fostered disappeared.

To my consternation, his gamble paid off. Now that he knew my magic reacted to threats against Sefa or Marek, he found creative ways to ensure I felt genuine fear for them every session. He had Vaun take them for a walk to Essam, and my magic hurled a spade into the board. Another session, he described exactly how a tribunal would condemn Sefa for assaulting the High Counselor, and the methods they might choose to put her to death. I managed to levitate one of the war chests. Only for a second, while magic burned my cuffs and fear for Sefa tightened my gut.

Today, the war chest flew across the room, cracking against the image of Niyar. It flickered, revealing the white wall behind the animated painting, before re-forming.

Instead of rejoicing in this development, Arin seemed to grow grimmer. "Are you eating?"

I was thrown. "Yes?" Though the quality of food had improved from the milky wheat nonsense of the first week, the guards' talent for cooking had not improved with it. I had used Wes's bread as a weapon the other day.

"Jasadi magic is a well that replenishes at unpredictable speeds. If you reach the bottom of your well too quickly, you might be left powerless until it refills. You are scraping stone."

"I'm moving the chests." The rest was irrelevant. I had been weak and weary before. I could work through it.

I thought of Marek's body strung across the Citadel's gates. The pulse at my wrists didn't sting this time. The weapons Arin arranged on top of the chest hovered in the air for a millisecond, then flew into the wall on the far side of the center with deadly accuracy.

The perimeters of my vision blurred. When I opened my eyes, the fake sky greeted me.

Arin's head moved over the sun. He glowered at me.

"I'll need a moment," I said casually.

"You need more than a moment." He reached down, and the room spun again as I was hauled upright. My traitorous legs buckled. Arin caught me with an arm around my waist, his frown deepening.

Plastered to his side and weightless, I opened my mouth to shriek obscenities directly into his ear, then reconsidered. Why bother? I didn't have the energy for a respectable tantrum.

His body was a solid line against my own. This was the closest I'd been to a man I wasn't trying to stab. The closest I had been to anyone not actively trying to kill me, actually. How depressing.

I waited for the swell of panic to hit at his touch. I had chalked up its absence the last time he touched me as a fluke. I was too distracted wondering if he would snap my neck to consider panicking. But he was touching me now and—nothing. No panic.

Still plenty of discomfort, though. The moment we were near enough, I wriggled away, stumbling toward my bed.

Arin did not prevaricate. "Wes and Jeru will accompany you to Mahair. They will be nearby throughout the day, but I will instruct them to give you your privacy."

"Mahair? I've been asking you to let me visit for weeks, and you choose now? We cannot afford the time."

"It is less than half a day's ride away. I had them prepare the horses."

My jaw dropped. I had been less than half a day's ride away from Mahair this entire time?

I stared at Arin until it hit me. "You feel guilty." I burst into laughter, which promptly devolved into hacking coughs. "The famed Commander feels guilty for nearly killing a village girl. Don't worry, I don't think Sefa is upset with you."

"Are you quite finished?"

"Are you?" I countered. "My magic is weak and uncertain. We finally have an advantage, and the Champions' Banquet is in two weeks. We should be capitalizing on this." I formed a circle around my wrists, kneading my cuffs.

A vein in Arin's forehead jumped. "Don't misunderstand me. I wasn't offering. You *will* be going to Mahair tomorrow. If I discover you attempted to practice on your own—"

"If this is about Sefa—"

"I don't give a damn about the girl!" Arin shouted, shocking me into silence. The outburst clearly took him by surprise as well. He locked his jaw. I had never seen the Nizahl Heir struggle to express himself—I'd venture few had.

The tips of his gloved fingers formed a steeple on the table's surface.

"Martyrs don't survive the Alcalah."

"Can't you tell the difference between a martyr and a mercenary?"

"I thought I had employed the latter. You have proven me wrong."

I rubbed my temples, blocking out the incoming migraine and the tantalizing pillows in my periphery. "How? By doing everything possible to uphold my end of the bargain?"

When he didn't respond, I continued, compelled to defend myself. "There is much you don't know about me, but understand this: I will fight for my freedom until my last breath. You took it away, and you cannot fault how ardently I choose to take it back. Until you have felt hunted, less than human, rejected from the moment you were born for something you did not ask for and cannot control— until then, do not speak to me of martyrs and mercenaries."

I braced myself for the spiel I'd heard on countless occasions.

Everyone was so fond of remembering how magic forced the Awaleen into their tombs after Rovial devastated the kingdoms. They didn't mention how it breathed life into the barren lands to begin with. They spoke of Jasad in hushed whispers, of the hoarded magic that corrupted the very leaves on the fig trees. Of magic-madness building in Jasadi veins like a disease, threatening our grasp on sanity. Forgetting that before Jasad, Nizahl's powers were curbed, its function as an arbiter of peace strictly upheld. They had not enjoyed the unchecked powers Jasad's destruction had allowed them.

The Nizahl Heir repeated none of it. He looked at me steadily and said, "Understood."

Rory reacted to my visit with his flavor of effervescent glee. "You're late."

He chucked me under the chin, a wide smile winding over his face. "There are lavender bowls in need of sifting."

I grinned at him like a fool. "When aren't there?" I fetched an empty bowl and dropped onto the bench he'd had Marek carve into the wall for the elderly and expectant mothers, both of whom tended to frequent his shop. "How are you?"

The spectacles few knew he secretly wore slipped down the bridge of his nose. He flipped the page he was pretending to read. "Busy. I seem to have misplaced an apprentice."

"Dozens would gladly take my place if invited, old man. I'm not sure if you have heard, but people are under the impression you're an accomplished chemist."

"I have an apprentice," Rory said, finally meeting my eyes. "A loud, unpleasant, utterly deranged apprentice who I expected to run this shop after my death."

After his death? I raked over him critically, searching for any signs of failing health. He was fine, aside from a weakness for dramatics. "When I finish the Alcalah, I'll be able to buy the shop from you. You can sit on a chair outside and shout at people to your shriveled heart's content."

Rory put his book aside. "Do you truly believe you will live past the Alcalah? Past encountering the Supreme?" He glanced at the door. Wes and Jeru were patrolling outside the village, allowing me the privacy Arin promised.

I plucked out a sheaf of sage and shook it into the open bowl. "The Supreme will not recognize me."

"The Supreme is a more dangerous man than you can conceive. Nothing is certain."

The entire reason I'd originally wanted to visit Mahair was to escape these incessant doubts, not have them reinforced. "Even if he discovers my identity, he would not apprehend his own Champion. I will leave quickly and quietly, and the rest is on the Heir's head."

"The Commander would just let the Jasad Heir vanish into the wild? Think, Sylvia! If your existence is discovered, every Jasadi in hiding will rally behind your crown. You will give them a reason to rise and reunite. You are the greatest threat to his power. The Supreme wouldn't hesitate to slay you before the convened courts, Champion or not."

My hands shook. Rally behind me?

"What crown, Rory? Virtue of blood does not make me suitable to lead anyone."

"Blood cannot lead a kingdom," Rory said. His voice gentled. "Sacrifice can. A true ruler is one who puts their people before themselves. No matter the cost."

"That isn't me. It is not in my nature—"

"Of course it isn't. Altruism is no one's nature. It wouldn't be half as remarkable otherwise."

He took the sifted lavender. The sound of the pestle clacking against stone grounded me. I sorted the stalks into bundles, losing myself in the repetition.

"You look horrible," Rory said.

The next person to comment on my appearance would earn a swift punch to the throat. "That seems to be the general sentiment, yes."

"He cannot expect you to train as a Nizahl soldier would," Rory started, working himself up for a grand fit. "A village apprentice does not have the skills—"

"I am not only a village apprentice," I interjected. "The training isn't a problem."

"I cannot imagine the methods the Commander employs to train a Champion." He scraped the pestle with force.

"His methods don't leave me delirious or at death's door. That is more than I can say for others."

Rory halted. In all our revelations, I had never discussed the missing years between the Blood Summit and appearing at his doorstep. Perhaps living underground in the company of people who would dance on my grave had softened me to a kind face. I wanted him to know.

I picked up the next bundle of sage, keeping my gaze trained on it. "A former Jasadi, thrown from the kingdom in disgrace, found me in the woods after the Blood Summit. She knew who I was. Breaking open my magic became her singular obsession."

"Breaking open your magic?"

Oh. I had forgotten Rory didn't know about my cuffs. "My magic is...complicated. The waleema was the first time it expressed itself in over a decade."

For once, Rory did not interrupt my tale. He folded his hands over the curved top of his cane. After weeks of guarding my every word, it felt freeing to talk without reservation.

"We lived in the woods, somewhere warded to keep away other

Jasadis. She would acquire horrible spells to teach me how to fight. Enchant the water to boil and test how long I could touch the surface. Compel monsters to chase me through the woods. My magic didn't budge, not once, in all the years I spent with her. She would be livid to have failed where the Nizahl Heir succeeded."

Rory pushed himself to his feet. The sheer sorrow in his tone pierced through me. "She gave you those scars, didn't she? On your back?"

I briefly wondered when Rory would have seen my back until I remembered the night he found me at his shop. I'd been drenched in Hanim's blood, and he had given me a tunic to change into. He must have caught sight of my scars before he turned around.

I chuckled softly. "Hanim wanted her lessons to last."

Rory's head snapped to attention. "What did you say?"

"Am I speaking too quickly for you?" My smirk fled at Rory's mounting horror. "What?"

"Tell me you don't mean Hanim, Qayida of the Jasadi forces."

"One and the same. Rory, what's wrong?"

I eased a wobbling Rory into his chair. He didn't answer, clutching his cane in a white-knuckled grip. My concern grew. I fetched him a glass of water. Hanim's reputation clearly preceded her.

After he drained the glass, he cleared his throat. "That woman loathed your family."

I snorted. "Really? I hadn't noticed."

"No, no, she—" He coughed hard, shoulders curving inward. I thumped his back until the rattling stopped. Rory's poor heart must've been twice as strong before he met me.

He swatted my arm off. "Did she tell you why Niyar and Palia exiled her from Jasad?"

"She violated the tenets of war." My voice rose at the end, pitching the statement into a question.

"Yes, most certainly, and she committed treason."

I lifted my shoulder. Rory seemed to think this information should shatter my mind. I committed treason every day, merely by existing. The word had lost its sting. "How? The war crimes?"

"She was found guilty of conspiracy against the crown with an enemy party."

I took the empty glass, setting it on the counter. My voice was flat. "Enemy party."

"Supreme Rawain," Rory confirmed. "When he was only an Heir, they found records indicating he and Hanim had plotted to overthrow your grandparents and seize Jasad."

He must have been speaking in jest. If there was anyone Hanim hated more than my grandparents, it was Supreme Rawain. Why would she ever stoop to working with him against Jasad?

"I thought she hated Nizahl."

"Not at first." Rory grimaced. "Once she was discovered, Rawain and his father, Supreme Munqual, denounced her deceit. Your grandparents weren't interested in war, so they accepted Rawain's attempts at reconciliation. I imagine Qayida Hanim did not take kindly to losing her position and her home for naught."

"How long did she conspire with him?"

"They had been in communication for years. Her betrayal was not a revelation for your grandparents. They had long known of Qayida Hanim's disdain for the crown."

I scrubbed at my hair, pulling curls from my braid. None of it made sense. I hadn't thought twice about Arin calling Jasad the architect of its own ruin—he genuinely believed magic destroyed everything it touched. But the Mufsid woman describing the walls of Usr Jasad as corrupt?

Keeping on an untrustworthy Qayida was placing the entire kingdom at the knife's point and hoping it did not tip over. For all their faults, I had always believed in my grandparents' love for Jasad above all else. It had soothed the anguish of losing my magic as a child, knowing Niyar and Palia had cuffed my powers to protect our kingdom.

Rory read the confusion on my face. "I believe they were under the impression her role was superfluous. They were overly reliant on their magic and the fortress."

"It's the Qayida's duty to reinforce the fortress!"

Nausea rolled in my stomach as my cuffs tightened. *Grief. Rage. Fear.*

"The fortress. Do you think she—could she have?"

The jars behind Rory rattled, and the bell over the door swung wildly. If Hanim had collaborated with the Supreme to bring down Niyar and Palia, it was entirely possible she had schemed with others inside the kingdom. They had all lied to me. My grandparents, Hanim, my mother. What else had they hidden about Jasad?

"Hanim is not why the fortress fell," Rory said, prodding a jar of floating herbs with his cane. "Hanim was expelled from Jasad two years before the Blood Summit. The fortress was renewed annually. Renewing the fortress was always meant to be Niphran's duty. Your grandparents decided as soon as their daughter was born to appoint their Heir as Qayida in the Nizahlan tradition. Hoping it would show the might of the royal blood. Many wilayahs disapproved of breaking from custom, believing it dishonored the memory of Qayida Hend. The problem resolved itself after—" Rory cleared his throat.

After an arrow tore open Emre's throat and rendered Niphran incapable of leaving her bed, let alone serving as Jasad's Qayida.

"The wilayahs disapproved." I paced his shop, the pressure in my cuffs throbbing. "What else did they disapprove of?"

"I was not especially involved in Jasadi politics at the time, but your grandparents had a long history of causing uproars."

What if the Mufsids had existed before the siege on Jasad? The Urabi? What if one or both had conspired against the Jasad crown long before the Blood Summit?

But why would they want the fortress to fall? They could not control a kingdom that did not exist, and there was no chance of victory against Nizahl's armies without a fortress, a Qayida, or a single royal.

"Sylvia...why are you laughing?"

The irony, oh, delicious irony! All along, Hanim's hatred for Nizahl was personal. She wanted a pawn in her fight to reclaim a land she considered rightfully hers. How it must have burned to watch Rawain rise over Jasad while she rotted in the woods! What had he promised her for her betrayal? What had he offered?

Rory prodded his cane into my side, looking as though he wasn't sure whether to scold or soothe me.

"This is hardly a laughing matter. Hanim is not a forgiving woman. She'll be searching for you," he said. Adorable.

"She won't be searching for me." I wiped away the last of my tears. I needed a good laugh.

"You cannot know—"

"Hanim's dead," I said. "Although if anyone can exact earthly vengeance from beyond, it's her."

I returned Rory's wide-eyed gaze evenly. Whatever he saw in my eyes drained the color from his face.

"Essiya," he breathed, "what did you do?"

It flashed through my mind in an instant. A dagger slicing across a throat that never spoke a kind word. The slowing of a heart as broken and ugly as mine. A body shoved into a hole—a grave—painstakingly dug into the frozen ground.

How deep can you dig, Essiya?

Brushing crushed lavender from my cuffs, I smiled.

"I found you, Rory."

CHAPTER EIGHTEEN

I could not bring myself to visit the keep. Raya would try to feed me ten meals' worth of food and cluck over the state of my under-eye circles, the girls would beg for stories of the Heir and the training, and Fairel...Fairel would try to hide her pain so she didn't inconvenience me. She might babble too much, as always, but maybe not. Maybe she would stare at the ceiling and pretend she was alone like she had seen me do when I fell into my darker moods. It was selfish and weak, but I just couldn't bear to see how Felix had permanently altered Fairel. Not yet, at least.

My breath billowed in white clouds. I drew my cloak closer. Where were Wes and Jeru?

The horses' clomping came from the opposite end of the road. I turned, shivering, an acerbic remark ready on my tongue.

Jeru and Wes weren't the ones approaching with two horses in tow. Arin held out a set of reins, surveying the street behind me warily.

I suppressed a smile. Always searching for a threat. "Why are you here? Don't say more business in Gahre."

We mounted our horses. Arin scanned the trees, and I was sure his keen hearing strained for any odd noises. "Caution is an area where I am prone to excess," Arin admitted. "My faith in my guards has taken a beating."

"You? Paranoid? Steady me, sire, I may keel from my mount."

The corner of his mouth twitched. A small victory. I wondered if

I might someday see the Nizahl Heir smile without acting as though he'd be fined for it. "You should have sent Wes and Jeru. Seeing you scares the villagers."

"I have done nothing to frighten them."

I shot him a dry look. "You exist."

"Despite your most accomplished efforts."

I glanced over, surprised. The Nizahl Heir joked like a wary bird stretching its wings for first flight. Miracle of miracles.

The horse's hoofbeats quieted as we passed the wall separating Mahair from Essam. I relaxed on my mare, holding the reins loosely on my thigh. Lanterns in white and blue dangled from the row of trees closest to the wall. Clay miniatures of Kapastra's beloved rochelyas circled the bottoms of the trees. The blue-scaled protectors of Omal.

"Hazardous." Arin eyed the curtain of dyed sheepskin draped over the lowest branches. MEHTI, spelled the letters sewed onto the sheepskin. The Omal Champion.

"Celebratory."

"You are arguing with me again. You must be better." Our horses had drifted closer at some point.

"I feel better." Aside from the moment in Rory's shop, the dizziness and nausea hadn't made an appearance. Yesterday, I doubted I could have remained upright on this horse. "I won't say you were right, only that you weren't as wrong as usual."

A gleam of laughter brightened Arin's eyes. Being away from me for a few hours had apparently done wonders for his mood. "I'll take your renewed enthusiasm for disrespect as a good sign." My knee bumped into his before I straightened the reins, putting more space between our horses.

We wound past the spot where Hanim's desiccated specter had sheared several years from my lifespan. The more distance we put between ourselves and Mahair, the more it felt like I would never return. The chances that I would perish in Orban's Ayume Forest, during the very first trial, were incredibly high. My breath came fast, spilling in plumes of white. I would die in the Alcalah as the Nizahl Champion. Meet my fallen family wearing the enemy's colors.

"I enjoyed architecture," Arin said, rather abruptly. "In my youth. I memorized sketches of the Citadel and the other palaces."

I flushed with embarrassment. The Heir kept his gaze forward. "Architecture?" A detail-oriented pursuit worthy of a man who once spent forty minutes whittling all the arrows in the chest to match one another.

"Usr Jasad was my favorite." Arin steered his horse around a dead bird. "It was a marvel. Without magic, the southern wing would have collapsed." He shook his head. "A shame, its loss."

I could not believe my ears. "Breaking your cart's wheel is a shame. Coming home to find the good fruit's been eaten is a shame. What happened in Jasad was an atrocity."

"What happened in Jasad was well deserved." Spoken in a tight clip.

I drew on my horse's reins, coming to a stop. "Deserved? Your father reveled in Jasad's ruins. Razed what was left of the palace to the ground. You should have mentioned you were fond of it. Maybe he would have saved you a piece of the southern wing." I drew the horse to a halt. Fury tightened my cuffs, digging barbed tips into my skull. *Grief. Rage. Fear.*

A dozen feet away, Arin pivoted his horse, his lips pursing with resignation. We dismounted at the same time.

A lone bird squawked above us, coasting on the winding breeze.

"You don't have a clue what happened in Jasad."

I clenched my fists. "Is that right? Enlighten me. Was there a second kingdom your father gutted?"

The darkest winter night could not match the frost in Arin's voice. "I have allowed you to persist in your delusions of persecution long enough. We are not amoral executioners, and Jasadis are far from innocent."

I had pushed too hard this time. The mild irritation he exhibited whenever I insulted his father or Nizahl finally spilled beyond its brim. "Did you know Malik Niyar led a raid through Essam into southern Lukub during a territory dispute and used magic to strangle young Lukubi soldiers sleeping in their tents? How much have you heard about the enchantment Malika Palia cast over Omalian fields to rot their crops and sicken their livestock? Entire villages starved to death."

"Stop it," I said. "Lying is beneath you."

That only infuriated him more, and I had to quell the instinct to flinch away. "For hundreds of years, Jasad has bled its glory from the lives it ruined. One need only look as far as the last Malik and Malika, who killed their own daughter's lover—the father of her child—because an alliance with Omal meant an end to their blood-soaked prosperity. They threw the Jasad Heir in a tower to silence her when she demanded they cease their mining operations in Jasad's wilayahs. Jasadis worked in abysmal conditions, died in droves, and why? Because the king and queen wished for more gold and silver to furnish their palace. They hoarded magical artifacts and pitted the other courts against each other. No two more insidious royals have existed since them."

Arin had never spoken so much in a single sweep. My pulse drummed in my temples, the pressure in my cuffs shifting to my head. He had to be lying. Like Hanim and the Mufsid woman. They were all cut from the same Jasad-hating cloth.

"Stop," I repeated, more weakly. Somewhere, a lurking threat roused to life. I could feel its fingers tapping along my spine.

"Someone used magic to attack at the Blood Summit. Magic only a Jasadi could have wielded. Hundreds died. Magic inevitably leads to tyranny and abuse. It devours you at the core, and it cannot be allowed to flourish again. My father did not act alone in dismantling Jasad. Every kingdom sent soldiers to help ensure none could stake a legitimate claim to the Jasadi throne. Perceive his actions how you will, but I won't have you laboring under an illusion of Jasadi purity."

Agony scorched broad stripes in my head, fueled by my caged magic. Scrambling my vision in white. I could feel it, my body sending frantic pulses of warning. He mistook my silence and sighed.

"I understand your stance—"

"Arin," I gasped. The first time his name had ever passed my lips. "Please stop."

It worked. He tensed, tilting his head. His eyes went wide.

The creature blasted toward us, leaping directly for Arin. In the spare two seconds between its flight and landing, I assessed this new monster. Its body was beautiful, composed of sharp red crystals winking and gleaming in the dim light. A coat of rubies carved to deadly points covered it from the paws wider than my hips to its long ears. It was far too large to be a wolf.

The more important consideration, of course, was the teeth. They would sink through Arin and rip him apart.

Good! Hanim shouted.

I snapped my fingers, and the creature slowed.

It didn't freeze, but the air congealed around it, making movement heavy and cumbersome. I had less than a minute before it broke through. My mount bolted, following Arin's riderless, fleeing horse.

"Hold it as long as you can." Arin withdrew a circular object from his boot. A compass, maybe?

He removed his gloves. "If your magic fails, run. Do not look back or react to anything behind you. Get to the barrier above the tunnels. The Hound will not be able to cross."

"What about you?" I demanded. Ivory claws twitched in midair. Thirty seconds.

The object unclasped and extended, tiny metal spikes stabbing outward from each side of the two flat disks.

"This will hurt," Arin said, and clasped his bare hand with mine.

The reaction was immediate. My magic roared toward the surface of my skin, pounding against my cuffs. The agony of the Relic Room renewed. My magic stripped me to the bone from the inside out.

Arin's grip turned crushing, and if it weren't for the monster a foot away, a different fear might have taken priority.

My hold on the creature shattered.

Arin surged forward just as the creature's enormous claws swung, shoving his arm into its mouth. Had he lost his mind?

When I threw my magic out this time, it was stronger. I forced the creature's jaw open while Arin——who had clearly suffered a bout of insanity—pushed the object into the roof of the monster's mouth. Nearby, a boulder burst into flinty shards, and branches rained down on us from the quaking trees.

For once in your accursed life, behave! I shouted at my magic.

The creature swiped at Arin and snarled. "Move back!" I screeched.

My magic wavered. Arin snatched his arm just as the creature's teeth clamped together. The object seemed to have confused it. It shook its head hard. Trying to dislodge the obstruction.

I tried to hurl a faraway log at it. My magic nudged the log, uninterested, and chose to explode another boulder.

The creature's red eyes skipped past Arin and narrowed on me.

You should recognize when a creature has been sent after you by now, Hanim said. *This isn't random.*

I stared at the beast without blinking. "Wait," I told Arin. "Don't move."

He leapt to his feet, clearly intending to ignore me. Not this time. I pushed my magic toward him, and the Commander found himself stuck.

"Sylvia!" His eyes widened, fixed on the creature advancing toward me. "Go!"

If I was wrong, this was going to be an embarrassing way to die.

I reached for the creature's head, carefully framing its massive maw between my hands. Arin made a smothered noise, but the creature didn't dive for my flesh. It sat back on its haunches and panted.

Eyes made of the same bloodred jewels composing its jagged body held mine.

"Can you see me?" I whispered. A single Jasadi could not enchant a creature like this to carry their bidding, see through its eyes…this was the work of several Jasadis. Powerful ones.

"I don't understand. Are you trying to kill me or contact me?"

Steeling my nerves, I maneuvered my arm past its teeth and found Arin's object adhered to the roof of its mouth. I traced its edges. "Allow me to introduce myself properly," I murmured, audible to the creature and its masters only. "I am Sylvia, a village ward and chemist's apprentice. I cannot be recruited, and I will not be intimidated."

A clasp clicked, and the object tightened. Arin hadn't activated the switch. I almost felt sorry for the wretched creature. As soon as the magic keeping it alive extinguished, it would return to the dust from which it came.

"The time of our meeting is near, my friends, but here is a taste of what is to come."

I pressed the switch.

The creature howled, tearing a strip from my tunic. I stumbled back as it writhed, tossing its head from side to side. Its front legs buckled on another mournful howl.

When it stopped kicking, lying still and pitiful in the dirt, I dared to venture closer. Its paw twitched, and a flash of white drew my gaze. A piece of parchment had fallen from its kicking limbs.

"It's dead," Arin said, startling me. He crouched, pulling the object out of the creature's mouth. He twisted the sides in opposite directions, and the spikes disappeared. He stayed down, assessing its bejeweled corpse. I gave him my back and unfolded the note. It was written in Resar. I scanned the words, heart beating fast. There was no mention of my true name. I passed it to Arin.

He read it aloud. "We offer you here a display of our power. United, we can raise Jasad from the ashes and bring war to those who would see us exterminated. Do not trust the others. The enemies of Jasad begin from within." His thumb grazed the bottom of the parchment, where a kitmer's wings flared up on each side. "This is the Urabi's seal."

The enemies of Jasad begin from within. Did they mean Hanim or the Mufsids? How deep had the Mufsids infiltrated before the Blood Summit? Maybe all the awful events Arin described were perpetuated through the Mufsids. Incompetence was an easier crime to attach to my grandparents than corruption.

I craned my neck for our escaped horses. "We need to go."

Arin tucked the note into his pocket, examining the vast wilderness around us. "They must have found out a member of the Mufsids made contact with you and kept watch over the road to Mahair."

I cast a nervous glance around the woods. They could still be nearby.

Arin bent to retrieve his gloves and winced. Barely perceptible, and on most I would have ignored it, but Arin wincing was equivalent to a dozen soldiers screaming. He favored his right side, where the Hound had slashed at him.

"What did you say about martyrs, again?" I asked. "Are you angry because I used my magic on you? You passed through it in half a minute."

He put on his gloves, content to pretend I didn't exist. The fabric at his right side was matted, slightly darker than the rest.

I threw my arms up. "If you want to quietly bleed for the next hour, it is not my place to stop you. But don't expect me to drag you to the tunnels if you faint!"

He paused. "I wouldn't faint."

"I know you are the mighty immortal man, impervious to the woes of us commoners. If it would behoove Your Highness to allow me to dress your injury—why, I can't express how honored—"

"Fine." Arin scowled. "Unless your magic includes secret physician abilities, I am not confident you won't do more damage."

"You've injured me." I put a hand to my heart. "Somehow, I'll find the strength to live another day. You may not, and I have little desire to be implicated for the Nizahl Heir's murder without the actual pleasure of murdering you. Remove your vest, please. I promise to protect your virtue."

From his dark glare, it appeared he didn't appreciate my thoughtfulness. Arin tore the laces of his vest in a single yank. Heat pricked the back of my neck, and I studied my nailbeds.

He eased his coat, vest, and tunic off. I inhaled between my teeth. The creature had gouged scores into his side. A few were shallow enough to temporarily ignore, but four scratches were the size of my forearm. How was he still awake?

"Well?" He guided himself to a seat at the base of a tree, back straight and left arm angled away from his raw side. I crouched across from him and picked up the tunic.

The material was finer than anything I owned and did not tear easily. "My apprenticeship with Rory was not all chasing frogs." It mostly was, actually, but Arin did not need to know I had learned how to wrap my own wounds with the rag and cup of dirty water Hanim usually left for me to patch myself up with.

The sleeves finally tore. I stripped them into long pieces, avoiding his face. "You have neglected to tell me if you're angry."

"You neglected to mention a hidden ability to sense Ruby Hounds."

"Ruby Hounds, that's the name! Weren't those Baira's guard dogs?" I said. "I thought they were extinct."

After the entombment, magic had guttered like a dying candle across the kingdoms. Ruby Hounds took three centuries longer than Kapastra's rochelyas to die. In their time, the dazzling Hounds heeded Lukub's Sultanas alone. They had charged into battle alongside Lukub's fiercest steeds, prowled the Ivory Palace's grounds in the night. A century before the Battle of Zinish, the Ruby Hounds began to sicken, dying despite the Sultana's best efforts. Magic had already disappeared in Omal, and with Lukub's failing quickly, the Ruby Hounds rotted like fruit planted in tainted soil. Orban followed thirty years later.

"They are. To resurrect one is unheard of. The Urabi will be weakened after exerting such a large amount of magic." Arin's gaze, though shrouded with discomfort, was still keen on our surroundings. "They must truly wish to impress you."

I knotted the sleeve strips together. "This is going to hurt," I warned him, and placed the end of a strip between my teeth. The muscles in Arin's stomach tensed, but he didn't make a sound as I wrapped the makeshift bandage tightly around his torso. I had to press my knee into his hip to reach around his back. My knuckles grazed everywhere I wrapped the bandages. His chest, his waist, the small of his back. The effect on my magic was significantly duller than when he grasped my hand.

I made the mistake of glancing up and found my face inches from Arin's. Curiosity hooded the gaze fixed on mine, entirely too attentive for someone in his condition.

"Stop looking at me," I demanded. "I am not going to make a mistake."

A soft laugh escaped Arin. The sound reverberated beneath the palm I'd placed on his chest. It was the first time I'd heard him really laugh. Baira's blessed hair, how much blood had he lost?

"Are you aware you have five freckles under your jaw?" He offered this information to me with complete seriousness, as though it had escaped from a vault of secrets.

I resisted the impulse to touch my jaw. "They are called hasanas in Jasad, not freckles." I cursed the heat in my ears that meant they were turning the same shade as the dead Hound and quickly refocused on my task.

"You dangle yourself over a rocky riverbed, beat down my guards, wedge your arm into a Hound's mouth. Yet you blush at a bare chest."

Naturally, this encouraged the redness in my ears to spread to my cheeks. I tied the next strip with more force than intended, pulling a pained grunt from the Heir.

"I am not blushing. I'm afraid you have become delirious."

Arin tipped his head back against the tree. "Maybe."

My jest about dragging Arin to the tunnels might be closer to reality than I had imagined. I had forced him to fight past my magic. How much blood had he shed struggling against the barrier?

"I'm sorry," I said. "I should not have trapped you. It's just—you would have interfered and lost a limb unnecessarily. I knew it was here for me."

"Don't do it again." The fleeting humor vanished from his tone. He was completely somber. "If you had been wrong, I wouldn't have been released until you were dead and your magic's hold broken."

"You would have had time to run if it killed me first." I finished tightening the bandages. Though I wagered Arin would walk through a pool of his own blood rather than surrender to his body, tenacity did not grant any superhuman abilities, even to its most ardent disciples.

Arin's stare bored into the side of my face.

"Yes, I suppose I would have," he said, and looked away.

CHAPTER NINETEEN

The moment Marek introduced himself to me five years ago, all charm, lanky limbs, and sparkling teeth, I had instantly known him for what he was: trouble. Chaos with a pretty face. The impression was solidified within the first few weeks of his incessant flirting. Scowling and stalking away had failed to deter him. Knocking his eyeballs from his skull wasn't an option if I wanted to maintain my pretense of fragility. So I seized the next best option. I tattled to Sefa.

Now that hitting Marek was an option, I found it quite hard to resist smashing his head into the bedside table. I had been studiously avoiding him since the incident in the training center. Knowing how deeply he regretted his behavior didn't ease my own frustration. *Lovers' spat.* Two careless words could have ended Sefa's life.

The day after the Ruby Hound's attack, Marek cornered me in my chambers. "If we were in Mahair, I could earn your forgiveness with a stack of prickly pears or sesame-seed candies. I am at a loss here, Sylvia." He spread his arms.

I regarded Marek, once again wishing for Arin's talent for seeing through people. Cutting past the noise and into the heart of the beast. Whatever caused his outburst was linked to the same impulse that drove Marek to accept his back-breaking position with Yuli and his bristling hatred for Nizahl. In many ways, I understood Marek better than Sefa. Sefa's heart was the governing force behind her actions. She categorized every decision into uncomprosing columns of right and wrong. To properly burn, rage must be given room to grow, and Sefa had long decided she would never open herself up to becoming its kindling.

Not Marek and me. Whatever we felt, we felt in its full violence. But where I kept my feelings in a stranglehold, Marek felt—and expressed—his emotions to their fullest extent.

I needed to understand what was happening in his head. Another glib remark like that outside these tunnels could end in disaster. "Let us make truth our currency this time. What did you leave behind in Nizahl, Caleb?"

His contrition wavered into a grimace. Marek raised his knuckles to his temples, kneading his forehead. "Nothing good."

I crossed my arms. "If you want my forgiveness, earn it."

Marek dropped onto the bed. Resistance drained from him in a great sweep. "What do you want to hear? People like you and me keep our secrets for a reason."

"'People like you and me'?" I repeated with a disgust reserved for stepping in a bucket of fish heads. Did he want me to pat his hand and whine over our shared suffering? "Are you a Jasadi, too, Marek?"

"I did not mean—"

"I don't care."

He sighed.

"You want a story, Sylvia? I was born the youngest of five children to a family with an infamous military legacy. My father and mother had served in Supreme Munqal's army. My grandparents, Supreme Tairal. On and on it went. The Lazur family was synonymous with Nizahlan military excellence. We were expected to join as soon as we were old enough. My sister, Amira, died at twenty-one in a clash between Nizahl's lower villages. The grain stores had run low, and Nizahl's soil is hostile to all but a few crops. Supreme Rawain was Commander at the time, and he sent soldiers to quell the violence with more violence."

Marek raised his head to check that I was listening, then dropped it back on the bed. Golden hair fanned around his face. I perched at his side, keeping my expression carefully neutral. I considered this revelation of Marek's lineage with the scrutiny I would afford a cut on my palm. Prodding the edges, testing the sting.

"Darin died in the border battles with Orban. The khawaga cut him open and poured cheap ale onto his insides for the animals to smell. They left him in the sun for six days. My last brother, Binyar, rose in the ranks quickly under Supreme Rawain. He was among those chosen to lead the siege on Jasad's fortress after the Blood Summit. He never returned."

A tear trickled toward Marek's hair. He dashed it away.

Marek threw an arm over his face. "Hani was two years older than me. He wanted to enter Supreme Rawain's confidence, forge a place for our family at the highest tables in the kingdom. He spent years trying to earn invitations to the most exclusive parties and bend the ears of the kingdom's rich and powerful. What Hani did not grasp was that the inside of the Citadel was a thousand times more lethal than anything he might encounter on the battlefield. When I was thirteen, a prisoner was thrown into Nizahl's most heavily fortified dungeon. A high-risk Jasadi prisoner who had nearly killed the Heir. Hani and a dozen soldiers guarding the cells were slaughtered by a group of Jasadis later that night. The prisoner vanished, and we laid Hani to rest next to Binyar and Amira. When my turn for conscription arrived, I fled."

I sat up. "A Jasadi group killed your brother?"

Marek pushed himself upright. He tossed a half-formed smile in my direction. "I have no animosity toward Jasadis as a whole, if that is what you fear. The group that rescued the prisoner and killed my brother were skilled criminals."

A group of Jasadis breaking into a highly fortified Nizahlan prison should have been the news on everyone's tongue. Hanim, who regularly traveled into the kingdoms for supplies, would surely have heard about it. Not to mention a Jasadi almost killing the Nizahl Heir. Arin would have been…sixteen? Supreme Rawain must have expended great effort to bury the news.

An old conversation between Wes and Jeru surfaced.

I was appointed to his guard when he was sixteen.

I thought only Vaun was present for that.

How bad must the attack on Arin have been to still haunt his guards a decade later?

I tried to swallow past my dry throat. "Marek, do you remember what the group was called?"

Marek glanced at the door, lowering his voice to a whisper. "Yes, but you cannot speak of it to anyone. I only know because Hani mentioned them a few days before his murder, and he swore me to secrecy."

Foreboding tiptoed down the rungs of my spine. "I promise."

"I believe they called themselves the Mufsids."

As predicted, Arin came to the tunnels only to sleep and swap guards. We had mere days before we were due to leave for Lukub, but he had opted to spend at least one of them hunting the Urabi who sent the Hound. He left detailed instructions on what each training session needed to accomplish, but the guards could be creative about the methods.

Heavy footsteps approached the training mast while I stretched. *Please* let it be Jeru substituting today. Wes focused more on defensive strategies and avoided my magic altogether. Ren preferred having me run in the muddiest portion of the woods and throw spears at moving targets until I could scarcely move.

The person who entered the training mast wasn't any of them. It was Vaun.

"What are you doing here?" I asked, covering my unease with indignation. Loose training garments had replaced his uniform. "I don't train with you."

"Wrong. His Highness said you shouldn't train with me if there were any available alternatives," Vaun replied. "The others aren't here."

Alarm flared through me. Vaun and I hadn't ever been truly alone. His loathing for me had only increased with time, and I was hardly penning prose about him.

Vaun grew up with the Heir. Of all the guards, he was the best. Fast, strong, and brutally efficient. I wouldn't walk away undamaged.

If I objected, he'd back down. He had to.

"Afraid? I can always leave," Vaun taunted. He'd been waiting for this. Possibly orchestrated the errands keeping everyone occupied.

Our reckoning had dawned, and I wasn't turning away.

"Pick your weapon," I said. "Let's finish this."

Malice shone behind Vaun's wide grin. "Ah, there it is. So much pride for such a raggedy little orphan girl." He didn't spare the weapons lined on the chest a look. "Bare-fisted combat. There won't always be a weapon to save you, will there?"

"You talk too much for someone who's meant to be seen and not heard."

We circled each other. I bounced on the springy mats, glancing at Palia's and Niyar's shapes on the wall. The bird soared overhead, wings catching on the breeze as the magic reset, and the scene played anew.

"Conditions?"

"Try not to die." Vaun rolled his shoulders. "His Highness has plans hinging on your continued existence."

The people moving in the walls around us meant less than nothing to him. He had threatened my friends, terrorized me every spare moment he could. Countless Jasadis had died at his hateful sword.

"I'm going to enjoy this," I said.

I sprang first, aiming for his stomach. Getting him on the floor and disoriented was all I needed to end this victoriously. From there, it would be a simple matter of gouging out his eyes. Arin's training was for a Champion; Hanim's, for a survivor.

Vaun twisted out of reach, slamming his fist into the side of my head. I staggered, blinking back white sparks, and laughed.

"Is that it? Come now, Vaun. Where's your passion?" I attacked again. My blow met its mark, and he grimaced.

Vaun fought well. Almost too well. By the time I was wiping blood from my chin, I knew he'd been paying attention. Listening to the guards' conversations about my progress, memorizing my weaknesses. We fell into a violent pattern; I lunge, he swings, I either reel back or land my own blow. He was counting on my impatience swelling and causing a slip.

His strategy might have worked if my opponent had been anyone else. Vaun's patience rivaled mine in fragility. It was a matter of who broke first.

"All this for your precious Heir? I'll admit, he's not the sharpest spade in the armory, but he's not utterly useless. He can fight his own battles." The gibe came out garbled. He'd split my lip with his elbow a few rounds ago.

Vaun's nostrils flared. An insult to Arin always affected him in disproportionate amounts. I leapt forward. His nose cracked against my fist. He snapped my arm back hard enough to pop and kicked me in the chest, sending me sprawling.

I scrambled up. Gritting my teeth, I wrenched my arm back into its socket.

"Honestly, I find his incompetence thrilling. I'm here because he cannot manage to do his sole duty as Commander and capture Jasadis." This was too easy. Surely Vaun would see through these adolescent tricks.

He reddened. "Keep his name out of your filthy mouth."

I saw it, then. The fastest route to the finish. "But he likes my mouth," I purred.

The way Vaun reacted, one would think he'd swallowed a dozen vials of rochelya venom. A disturbing blankness washed over him. "I'm warning you—"

I spoke faster. "Your grand leader, debasing himself with an abomination. I tolerate his clumsy affections. What choice do I have? He's as incompetent in be—"

I never finished the sentence. Vaun tackled me. Rage hadn't made him ungainly. It simply removed his reservations. We grappled, but he held the superior position. In the grips of his frenzy, he hit me, over and over again. I grew slack beneath him. A piercing hum rang in my ears.

"Never again," he growled. He took a fistful of my hair, jerking my head back. "Lying whore. He wouldn't—no. Never again."

His forearm pressed down on my windpipe. I didn't need Niphran's specter to know he meant to kill me. I clawed at him, raking bloody lines down his cheek.

This would not be how my family ended.

"I should have run you through the first day," he spat. "Filth like you should never survive this long."

Behind him, the rabbit bounded in the air, out of the children's reach. The tree ruffled over Niyar's head, and from his seat at its base, he flipped the page of the book eternally open across his lap. Palia squinted on the palace steps, searching for Niyar. I'd seen this scene a million times since I arrived.

"You're right," I gasped. Black spots burst across my vision. My cuffs tightened. I should have died at the Blood Summit alongside everyone I loved. An honorable death, a worthy one. Never knowing the iron tang of blood filling my mouth, the crack of a whip as it sliced into my flesh. All my potential for greatness wouldn't have been tested. I wouldn't have failed Jasad so catastrophically.

But like a rat scrabbling in the dark, I'd lived.

On the wall, Palia put her hands on her hips, as though in wait.

Calling on every last vestige of strength, I unfurled my fingers.

We burst into flames.

They flared around me harmlessly, but Vaun bellowed and hurtled back. Tiny flames wound around my body, slithered in my braid.

I dragged myself to a stand, ignoring my shrieking body. Vaun retreated. I relished his fear, drank it in. I curled my fingers, and the curved sword on the chest flew, the pointed tip coming to a stop at his heart. I squeezed my fist, and it cut through his clothes. Vaun flung himself into the wall. The sword followed, pinning him in place.

Killing Vaun would solve so many problems. Letting him live would be letting more Jasadis die.

The hairs on the back of my neck rose.

"Drop the sword, Sylvia," Arin said, low and soothing. I had not heard him enter, but it didn't matter. I would sense him from miles away.

The words were hoarse from my mangled throat. "Why should I?"

Arin entered my line of sight, obscuring Vaun. Dust covered him from shoulder to waist, and a bruise bloomed high on his cheekbone.

"You are not a murderer."

"I am, actually," I chuckled. The fire jumped, preventing him from getting closer. "You don't make that distinction when killing Jasadis. Why shouldn't I behave as a killer if I'm to suffer the same fate regardless?"

Arin assessed my appearance, my wrecked face and the awkward angle of my broken bones. Comprehension washed over him, leaving grim resolution in its place.

He stepped aside.

The strangled noise Vaun made was almost enough to satisfy me. Almost.

I didn't care if this was another test. Vaun was a menace to me, to everyone I cared about. My cuffs pulsed. Blood beaded around the sword's tip.

I wanted to. So badly. My magic shook with it.

Again, my gaze found Niyar and Palia. The children ran past Niyar on the grass, chasing the bunny fleeing in midair. Just as the scene hitched, a leaf fluttered over Niyar's head. I had seen the leaf and the tree he sat against on countless occasions.

I followed the leaf up. At the top of the tree, a child's leg dangled. Her sandal was poorly fastened, hanging precariously off her toes. A few moments more and it would fall squarely onto Niyar's book.

Palia had those sandals made for my seventh birthday. She wasn't looking for Niyar—she was looking for me.

Hanim's prodigy would cut him through without hesitation. No one would fault me. No one living, anyhow.

The leaf drifted as the child's leg swung.

I snapped my fingers. Vaun's scream shook the room as the sword sliced neatly through his thigh and pinned him to the wall.

He was not worth what was left of my soul.

CHAPTER TWENTY

Arin came to my room a few hours later. I would rather have suffered my injuries than induce my already-roiling magic to the surface, but he stood in the door until I rolled out of bed. He took my arm—not my hand—until I no longer looked like I'd been thumped repeatedly into a wall. The disappearance of my wounds only served to heighten my disgust. The puppet must remain pristine for its master. The surge of magic at this touch felt more controlled, but I saw Arin's other hand tighten into a fist. Good. I hoped he suffered. I hoped the pull of my magic flayed him from the inside.

As soon as he removed his hand, I climbed into bed and gave him my back.

Sleep wouldn't come. My magic was active, its pressure against my cuffs unpleasant but bearable. It thought we were still fighting, but this kind of fight wasn't one where a sword would help. I couldn't close my eyes without seeing death: my family, Dawoud, Soraya, even Adel and Mervat Rayan.

Loss was an anchor I would always drag behind me. If I stopped moving, if I let the anchor catch, I would never summon the strength to keep going. I was not kind. I did not choose right over wrong or my heart over my head. But I was tenacious. I was spiteful. I had cultivated these lesser traits, fed them every morsel I could spare, because someone good would not have survived Hanim. Someone good would have died as miserably as Adel. But once I stopped needing to survive, what would be left? What if the worst parts of me had already cannibalized the best?

I slept poorly and woke a few hours before dawn feeling inclined to find Vaun and finish what I started. Perhaps the guards could predict my bloodlust, because it was Sefa and Marek at my door the next morning. They helped me pack the room while they chattered about nothing. I appreciated it—allowing me a signal to fix and focus on while I rebuilt the walls I'd damaged last night.

"Sylvia?" Marek reached for my shoulder and thought better of it. I hadn't moved in over ten minutes. "Do you want us to leave you alone?"

"No. No, stay." I swallowed and tentatively patted Marek's arm. He held himself stiller than a man luring a rare bird to his palm. Despite his hotheadedness, Marek always knew which moments demanded a gentler hand. Being raised by a Nizahlan military legacy family hadn't turned him into someone harsh and uncompromising, and I admired him for it.

As I stared at Marek, an intriguing prospect occurred to me. I'd allowed Arin's tirade about Jasad to quietly fester. I had nobody reliable to recount the events around the war, but here stood two people who had grown up close to the heart of Nizahlan politics. Two people I trusted as much as I could trust anyone.

"What did people say about Jasad before the war?" I asked Sefa.

Sefa finished packing her sewing materials under a protective layer of skirts. She didn't seem perturbed by the question. "About Jasad in general?"

I had to tread carefully. "The Malik and Malika, royal politics, the nature of their rule. That sort of talk." I glanced at Marek. "Either of you."

"I can't recall specific sayings, honestly. Most of what I remember is resentment," Sefa said. "So much resentment. One winter, the frost came too early and caused most of the farms to bloom before anyone was prepared for harvest. An unbelievable amount of food went to waste, rotted from disease or the cold. It was a lean winter. No kingdom was spared from struggling…except Jasad. The previous Sultana swallowed her pride and reached out to the Malik and Malika for help, and they refused her."

I had braced myself for such a conclusion, but it still brought a grimace to my face. I reminded myself that unkindness did not necessarily translate to corruption.

Sefa wasn't finished. "Ten days later, Lukub's northeast mountain borders were attacked. Jasadi forces raided the stores of Lukub's precious metals and stole their entire supply of silver and copper. The Sultana couldn't retaliate. Their armies were withering, and—"

"The fortress," Marek finished. "The fortress was a topic at our dinner table almost nightly."

A queasy unease had settled in my stomach. I was still caught on the raid on Lukub. Why would they do that? They had had plenty of silver and copper in Jasad; they hardly needed to steal it. Nothing in my life had ever been as stable as my notions of Jasad. So many cracks had begun to splinter through the image of Usr Jasad and my grandparents, and I could feel myself growing defensive in preparation for the shatter.

"Your family served the Supreme. Of course they spoke often of the biggest obstacle to invasion."

"Everyone talked about the fortress, Sylvia," Marek said, a little coldly. "It allowed Jasad to get away with doing whatever it wanted. I understand you hate what Nizahl has become. I do, too. But it is the only kingdom created at the will of three Awaleen. Its most basic function was to protect against the tyrannies of magic and power after Rovial's madness. Nobody could have replicated Jasad's fortress, not even when each kingdom still carried magic. They were insulated from the consequences of their actions, and Nizahl couldn't do anything about it."

My pulse pounded in my head. This was a mistake. I shouldn't have asked Nizahlans to refute the word of the Commander. They thought all magic was inherently unfair. "What a relief it must be for Nizahl to finally achieve their full purpose," I said, unable to prevent the hurt seeping into my tone. "They have certainly balanced the scales."

Sefa called out as I left the room, but the door was already closing behind me.

I calmed down after hiding in one of the empty rooms to eat. I had known there would be a risk I wouldn't like their answers, and I had asked anyway.

They stopped talking when I entered. I hated the guardedness that sprang to Marek's features. "Sorry," I said. "I was childish."

Sefa was already shaking her head. "No, we're sorry. We should have known the fortress meant something completely different to you. You were right to be upset."

"I was not upset."

Marek rolled his eyes and threw a bundle of tunics at my head. "Finish packing. We're going to be late."

Since most of my belongings would be sent back to Raya, I wasn't as prim about putting everything away as Sefa. As we passed the training center, I pressed a palm to the wall. "Forgive me," I whispered to my grandparents. Their flaws were many, probably more than I knew, but they had given everything for me. I could not say the same.

Sefa and Marek waited by their carriage, belongings already stowed away. We would be taking two carriages on our journey. Sefa and I watched Marek bustle around the horses, diligently checking over the gears, and exchanged a resentful glance. He had the energy of ten people.

"Not very ostentatious, are they?" Sefa remarked, nodding toward the carriages. Compared to the gilded contraption Felix rode into Mahair in, these boasted few adornments. Each wheel had a secondary support to help negotiate the unruly terrain, and the rectangular exteriors were painted a dull brown. If a vagrant caravan or enemy cabal happened upon us, they wouldn't give either carriage a second glance.

"Ego does not often defeat Arin's practicality," I said.

Sefa stared. I touched my chin, self-conscious. "What?"

"Arin?"

On cue, the tops of my cheeks reddened. With my hair pulled back, Sefa noticed instantly. She grabbed my elbow, yanking us away from the others. "What is your relationship with the Heir?"

Her accusatory clip raised my hackles. A sliver of rage raced along my jaw, cracked between my teeth. My eyes narrowed to slits. "I beg your pardon."

"You called him Arin."

"That is his name."

"Not to you!" she hissed. She stepped forward, either unaware or unbothered by the anger emanating off me. "To you, he is the Nizahl Heir. The Commander. The man who would cut you into more pieces than there are leaves in Essam if given half the chance. The way you two gravitate toward each other scares me. You are a Jasadi."

"There is nothing to concern yourself over."

From the tightness in her temples, she wasn't convinced. "I hope not."

We returned to where the others were climbing their horses. I waved away Marek's help, hauling myself into the carriage with a grunt. Though outwardly unremarkable, the carriage's interior had space to support two parallel benches, heavily cushioned and wide enough to lie down and sleep. Arin was already seated inside, a stack of parchment folded neatly beside him.

"Where is Vaun?" I managed not to make the question a snarl.

"Vaun has been dismissed from my service," Arin said, drawing a line under a sentence.

I gaped. Arin took Vaun on almost all his hunts. If the other guards were to be believed, the two had been together since boyhood.

"I have no use for easily provoked guardsmen."

Had I been a more charitable woman, I might have experienced a spark of sympathy for the devoted guard. What would Marek do if Sefa cast him aside so cruelly?

He would find a way back, Hanim warned.

With a mortified flush, I wondered if Vaun had relayed my taunts during our fight. "Did Vaun mention in detail what transpired between us?"

Arin's hands knit together over his stomach as he sat back. "I am open to any suggestions on how I can improve my clumsy affections—"

I hurled a folded quilt at him, boiling with embarrassment. He batted it aside. "Vaun had a weak point. You exploited it. Where we're going, you grapple for every advantage you can gain."

"The other Champions may not be as sensitive about insults to your virtue."

"This is the fourth time you've mentioned my virtue," Arin said, and I would swear to Sirauk he sounded amused. "Perhaps preoccupy yourself with a different matter."

"I don't—I have *not*—" Since I would rather have stuck my head under the carriage's wheels than continued this conversation, I shut my mouth.

Significantly more buoyed by the lack of Vaun in my future, I stretched my legs and tapped the other side of the carriage with my toes. Wes glared from his horse until I slid the window drape shut, pitching us in darkness. Arin's profile on the opposite bench disappeared. The carriage juddered into motion.

The rocking lulled some of my sharper nerves. I was contemplating the wisdom of dozing when Arin spoke, startling me. "After the Hound attacked me, you didn't run. If you had used your dagger to deepen the existing wounds, I would have lost consciousness and bled my last. You could have laid blame at the Hound's feet. The guards would have believed you. My body would have been borne to Nizahl, the Alcalah postponed, and you freed."

I'd become accustomed to the chilling labyrinth of his mind. Still, this one gave me pause. "You're right." The Hound's claws had raked deep. Cutting into them a bit more wouldn't have garnered notice. A few scratches and cuts on my person, and the authenticity of the encounter couldn't be doubted. "Jeru would sway Wes and Ren's doubts. The Mufsids would be held responsible—maybe Lukub, too, because of the Hound. In the melee, I'd be forgotten. It's a good plan."

I hadn't considered the enormous amount of trust Arin had shown by allowing me access to his wounds. He'd sat there, rigid, contemplating the methods of his own assassination. Though I couldn't confirm it in the gloom, the prickling on the back of my neck suggested he was watching me. I lifted a shoulder. "It didn't occur to me," I said truthfully. "I have to plan in advance for cold-blooded murder."

The carriage jolted, rocking to the left. Wes rapped on the window in apology.

"Peculiar woman," Arin mused. The carriage rattled on, carrying us into the heart of Essam Woods.

The trip to Lukub took three days. Three days of jumping at every noise, bathing in the river, and sleeping at the base of the tree with the least ants. Arin's eyes grew more bloodshot the closer to Lukub we rode. I doubted he had slept more than an hour. The open, uncontrolled environment must have been scraping his nerves raw.

The Nizahl brigade met up with us an hour away from the palace. Fifty soldiers, stiff in their Nizahl uniforms, knelt when Arin descended from the carriage. The sea of black and violet unsettled me to my core.

"My liege, if you will," Jeru said. He gestured at the carriage the soldiers brought. The new carriage resembled Felix's gilded nightmare more closely. Undeniably Nizahlan, it rose on massive black wheels, the body painted obsidian and outlined in violet. Sleek and menacing. Twin wings crested from the sides of the carriage, their iron feathers gleaming in the moonlight. Sefa, who possessed an unshakable need to verify her surroundings through contact, reached for a wing. Wes caught her wrist. "If you value your finger, think again."

The Nizahl royal emblem, a raven soaring between two crossed swords, had been meticulously painted across the side. The raven's beady gaze followed me.

I observed the new soldiers with contempt, following Arin into the carriage. Did we really need fifty soldiers for the Banquet?

Two panels in the window pushed outward, and Arin didn't stop me from throwing them open. I poked my head out.

"Greetings, traveler," I told Wes. He startled violently on his horse. His head bobbed level with mine, such was the carriage's ridiculous height. The tree line had thinned a few miles behind us, leaving greater room for the carriage to maneuver. The soldiers spilled behind us like rot trickling from a forgotten fruit, the beat of their horses reverberating around me.

"Get inside!" Wes ordered.

I glanced at Arin. "Can you command him to be nicer to me? Or at least less tightly wound?"

Arin unfurled a map of the Ivory Palace onto his lap. "No."

"I suppose that would be hypocritical, coming from you."

Wes groaned, long and loud. Luckily, everyone else was riding out of earshot.

"Sylvia, you're going to have to exercise some forethought before you speak," Arin said, uncorking a pocket-size vial of ink. He circled a spot on the map. "The other soldiers might take badly to your attempts at humor."

Outraged, I managed to say, "Attempts?" before I lost track of the rest. The carriage shook as the ground shifted from hard, packed earth to soft soil. To our left, the trees cleared to reveal six identical wells dug into the ground. A revolting stench assailed me as we rode past the wells. I glanced down—and promptly reared back.

"Why are there people in those wells?" I whispered.

Twenty feet deep and smooth on every side, all but one of the narrow wells had an occupant. An elderly man, beard matted with filth, turned to glare as we passed. A pool of foul water sloshed around his ankles. The others were emaciated, slumped in a fetal curl. The wells were too narrow for them to lie down. If they weren't already dead, they would be soon.

"Traitors," Arin said. We passed the last well, and I forced myself away from the window. "Sultana Vaida had them dug after her mother's murder. Traitors to Lukub are thrown in to starve and perish. Half her council died there."

"Nobody stops her?"

Torture was limited only by imagination. The forms it took were more than anyone could count. But I had thought at least one rule, one unassailable edict, united the hands of cruelty. Torture should be private. Torture was meant for dungeons and stone cells. The quiet of Essam. For the trees that watched you bleed and the silent earth you soaked in your tears.

"You should see what Orban does to traitors." Arin tapped his fingers against a knee. "Vaida prefers a more nuanced approach."

I hated that I understood the Sultana. Few weapons tormented as thoroughly and bloodlessly as fear. Lukubis walked past these wells, listening to the prisoners' mournful wails, and prayed they weren't next. People from all over the kingdoms escaped to Lukub for its glamor and style. They climbed Baira's Shoulders, the highest cliff in the kingdom, to gaze upon the beauty of a land founded by an Awala whose face could entrance an enemy to fall on their own sword.

Beauty dazzled. It drew the eye toward it...and away from the horrors hiding in its shadow.

"Malika Palia and Malik Niyar would have their soldiers lift thieves and traitors into the air." Arin set his neat stack of parchment aside. "Once they were suspended over the crowd, each soldier found a creative way to execute their prisoner. One soldier would drown their prisoner on dry land. Another would split the earth with a wave of a hand, burying their charge alive. I believe one particularly creative soldier decided to split his prisoner in half and shower the crowd in viscera."

My nails dug crescent moons into my palms. "Is magic a worse weapon than a well?"

"The well isn't promoted afterward."

The cuffs throbbed with my spiking magic. "Where was this compassion when your father pillaged our villages? When Nizahl soldiers destroyed centuries of custom and culture? When Lukub, Omal, and Orban helped strip our lands to bare parts? When Jasadis were raped, ripped apart, or sold?" Hot fury filled the carriage, blazing in the scant space between us. "Do not insult me by pretending invading Jasad was some mercy."

"Our." Arin cocked his head. "You said *our* lands. *Our* villages. Not 'the Jasadis'."

I glowered, searching for his trick. I always said *our*. What else would I say?

The carriage's momentum changed, sending me hurtling to the other end of the bench. Arin braced his elbow against the window, using his other arm to keep the parchment from scattering.

Jeru appeared in the window. "Apologies, my liege. We are on the palace grounds."

Eager for distance, I opened the carriage door and leaned out, throwing an arm over the roof as we sped ahead. The wind whipped my braid into my chin.

As magnificent as the Awala responsible for its birth, the Ivory Palace shone brightly against the night sky. Pillars rose in cerise spirals between towering ivory walls. Behind the gate, a ruby obelisk pierced the sky. White flowers grew in the seams of the walls, their petals sharper than the wings of our carriage. I followed the path of the precious jewels welded into the looming white gates that formed an enormous Ruby Hound snarling down at our approaching carriage. The Hound glistened a dark, sinister red under the waxing moon. Unlike Arin, I cared little for the sophistication of symmetry or the hidden meanings behind design. The Ivory Palace cast aside subtlety in favor of a message no one could misread.

Something beautiful waited behind these walls, and it was as likely to caress you as it was to eat you alive.

I returned to my seat when we pulled to a stop at the gate's head, letting the carriage door close. A pair of Lukubi guards approached Jeru and Wes. My heart thundered. I was going to enter Lukub as the Nizahl Champion. Sit among Heirs who had happily led their troops against Jasad, wetting their boots with Jasadi blood in exchange for Nizahl's approval.

What freedom is worth this? I thought, wild. *Can I cut into my own soul and sell away the Jasadi pieces?*

The carriage door opened. "Your Highness," the Lukubi guard said. "Sultana Vaida welcomes you and your Champion to the Ivory Palace."

Arin answered. I wasn't listening, focused on corralling my magic and my frantic breathing.

The gates parted with a groan.

"Loyalty rears its mutinous head," Arin said softly. "Mervat Rayan."

I looked into his wintry blue eyes, so like his father's. The air held itself still around us. The Nizahl and Jasad Heir. I would leave this carriage to deliver the Supreme the most complete victory over me. Over Jasad.

One day, I would stand trial before the spirits of my dead. One day, the bodies I never buried would call upon me to answer for my sins.

One day, but not today.

CHAPTER TWENTY-ONE

I was ushered into my room without fanfare. Three women arrived to attend me. Or they tried. I told them—quite emphatically—I could bathe and undress myself.

Sefa groaned when I closed the door on the baffled attendants.

"Lukub does not value hospitality as highly as Omal," I said, defensive. "The Sultana will not care."

After months of the tunnels' stark walls and dusty corridors, the chaotic rooms in the Ivory Palace shocked my nerves. Tapestries dyed in bright shades of red hung from the walls, their white tassels dangling over fox-fur rugs. Bundles of bukhoor mixed with resin hovered above the lanterns, saturating the air in a sweet, floral aroma. An ivory mask was propped in front of every candle. The light flickered behind its carved eyes.

"Lukubis may not care about hospitality, but they place great value on service," Sefa said. "Servicing the body and the spirit. Finding harmony between the two." She stepped over Marek, who had fallen asleep with a chunk of mushabak on his chest. The honey-soaked coil of fried dough shifted with the rise of his chest.

I squeezed the excess water from my drying hair. "Is it strange, visiting Lukub? You are a citizen here by blood."

Sadness tinged Sefa's smile. She removed the mushabak from Marek's chest and tossed it in the wastebasket. "I am not a citizen. Nizahlan law does not permit marriage outside its territories unless one of them renounces their kingdom of origin. My father gave up his right to Lukub's protections when he married my mother."

I drew the absurdly plush pillow against my chest. Sefa grew up caught between Nizahl and Lukub, but I had rarely given Omal a second thought. Though my father's Omalian blood ran in my veins, my grandparents had done their best to purge my interest in him. As though my worth as a Jasadi would decrease if I entertained any notion of my Omalian heritage.

"Let us not get distracted," Sefa said, stern. She flopped onto the enormous bed, running her dark fingers through the sheepskin covers. "Baira's kingdom is a land of illusion. They build lavish libraries and fill them with empty books, commission glorious paintings on the walls of deteriorating villages. My father told me a story about the feasts they host to celebrate the anniversary of the entombment. A tradition in the lower villages requires every family to leave an offering at Hirun's banks on the eve of the anniversary. These days, it's usually trinkets and what food they can spare. But in centuries past, the Sultanas encouraged the lower villages to throw the strongest child of every family into Hirun. If the child drowned, the family would say the river had blessed them by taking the child's strength for its own. If the child survived, the family would be barred from having more children."

"Let me guess," I said. "The lower villages were starving. The children most likely to survive the brutal winters were tossed into Hirun, leaving the weak ones to wither away."

"Fewer mouths for the former Sultanas to feed," Sefa confirmed. "Lukub's Sultanas are not women to be trifled with, Sylvia. Their skills of deception are parallel to none."

If they had managed to convince parents to drown their offspring with a smile, what sinister whispers could they weave into my own heart?

The rumble of Marek's snores and the amber glow of dawn behind the tapestry lulled me into a restless sleep. I dreamed of red-eyed masks grinning in the dark and children splashing into a boiling Hirun. When I careened to consciousness again, the sun hung much higher in the sky, and someone knocked insistently at the door.

"Sylvia?" It was Jeru. "Are you all right?"

Marek and Sefa were gone. I cursed, rolling to the wardrobe in a tangle of limbs. The women from earlier had arranged my belongings inside, and I yanked out the first article of clothing I touched.

"What time is it?" I flung the gowns to the floor.

Jeru's weary voice came through the door. How long had he been knocking? "It's past noon."

I hopped into the dress, staggering around the room. "No, no, no! How could you let me sleep so late?"

"Me?" Jeru returned, indignant. "Marek and Sefa tried to wake you up three times before they went to eat."

The dress slipped over me in a whisper of silk, settling over my curves. Sefa's painstaking work hadn't been in vain. The dress was long, swirling with hues of violet. Matching slits parted over each leg, and two tiny Nizahl pins held up the thin straps at my shoulders. Had I not been so terribly late, I would have found another dress. These slits hiked mid-thigh, showing miles of skin when I moved.

I scowled at myself in the mirror and rushed out the door.

Jeru stared. "Is that what you're wearing?"

"Yes. Maybe," I picked at the fabric. "The banquet isn't until tomorrow. Nobody will notice."

Jeru started to speak and reconsidered. He shook his head. "Sefa is certainly familiar with Lukub's fashions."

We sped past bustling servants and halls decorated in elaborate tapestries and delicate carvings. We took turn after turn, and I wondered if perhaps I should have asked Arin to share his map of the Ivory Palace. He had given me stacks of reading to complete the first three weeks, mostly layouts of buildings we'd enter, history texts, and instructions on following the customs expected of a Champion in each kingdom. I hadn't paid them much attention, since the only free time I had was the fifteen minutes between my bath and falling into a dead sleep. I regretted it—the grandeur of this palace ensured I would lose my way.

The walls changed from shades of red to pure ivory. The art on the walls tapered to a small collection of frames set inside the wall. I wanted to stop and study them, but Jeru urged me along. We had reached the Sultana's wing.

A heavy velvet curtain blocked the next hall. Jeru pulled it aside, unveiling parallel rows of guards lining the walls. Nizahl on one side, Lukub on the other.

"The Nizahl Champion," Jeru said. He prodded me forward.

The Lukub guards glared. The Nizahl ones smiled. I did not know which was worse.

Go, Jeru mouthed. I forced myself into motion.

A soldier on each side gripped a bar on the doors and heaved. They split, yawning open to reveal a receiving room even more lavish with decorations than the halls. Ribbons braided into spherical shapes dangled from the ceiling. Strips of gauzy curtain slanted around the ribbons and fluttered along the walls. A sleek bird with a white beak and riotously red feathers hopped in a cage shaped to resemble a Ruby Hound.

Arin and a stunningly beautiful woman sat across from each other, a tray of delicate desserts arranged between them. They both glanced up at my arrival.

Arin was the image of poise. Not a single strand of hair escaped from the tie at his nape, and he'd traded his usual uniform for more regal fare. The two of them together made for an arresting sight. I smoothed my hands along the dress, barely stopping myself from fidgeting with the fabric. I longed for the comfort of familiar clothes.

"Your Majesty." I dipped my head. "It is an honor."

When Sultana Vaida approached me, my jaw slackened. Lithe and graceful, she carried herself with the assurance of someone thrice her age. Her white gown glowed against smooth, dark skin. Dozens and dozens of intricate braids tumbled to her waist, tiny white and ruby flowers woven painstakingly through them. Slender and broad-shouldered, she regarded me with clever, dark brown eyes.

"Sylvia of Mahair. The honor is mine." Before I could react, she leaned forward to kiss my cheek. My eye twitched, but I successfully refrained from flinching at the contact. "Join us, won't you?"

"Forgive me my tardiness," I said, seating myself beside Arin on the curved settee. To my surprise, he didn't make room. Was he staying close in case he needed to intervene? I kept my hands in my lap, intensely aware of their proximity to Arin's thigh.

Vaida waved a heavily ringed hand. "I loathe overnight campaigns in those woods. I don't blame you one bit. I am forever attached to my creature comforts."

"We were discussing how rapidly you've progressed in your training," Arin said.

"I've had excellent help."

Vaida giggled, a musical sound. "Don't demur, darling, not in my company!"

Unbidden, Arin's warnings about Vaida rose to the forefront. He'd spent hours detailing what to expect from everyone we would encounter during the Alcalah. His description of the Sultana had puzzled me.

"Vaida must believe you are insignificant, a simple village orphan with aspirations of glory. Do not challenge her or distinguish yourself in any way," he had said. "The Sultana plays with people, bats them around for her own entertainment. But if she thinks you merit a second glance, she will make it her dying mission to eviscerate your secrets and reap your soul."

Arin was not a man prone to the melodramatic.

Vaida stirred a spoonful of sugar into her drink. "How magnificently your fortunes have changed, darling Sylvia. I could not believe the news. A chemist's apprentice from Omal's lower villages, chosen for the Alcalah? Handpicked by the Nizahl Heir, no less? I must confess, my kingdom spoke of little else for a time. My poor Champion was quite distraught at losing their attention." She pushed a chalice studded with rubies closer to me. I dared a glance at Arin, who gave me a small nod. I picked up the red drink and took a sip.

Karkade. The dry tang cut through the excess syrup she'd poured into the hibiscus tea. The drink was Jasadi in origin, but I wasn't alarmed. After Jasad's fall, the vultures had picked at Jasadi culture, tearing out the choicest bits for their own nests. I had seen the evidence in Mahair, watching bakers flip aish baladi into their ovens as though they had done it for generations. Then again, Adel probably *had*.

"I am grateful," I said when it became clear Vaida expected an answer.

"Ah, gratitude." Vaida wrinkled her nose. "Excise it with your sharpest knife and throw it away. Gratitude lowers women's necks for a chain far more than it raises them for a fight. You earned your place. Correct?"

"Correct." I would say anything if it meant she would stop talking to me.

"Tell me, Sylvia, does your husband wait anxiously at home for your safe return?"

I blinked. "My what?"

I sensed Arin's mounting unease. "Vaida—"

She talked over Arin, the first I met with the courage to do so. "A wife, then? Or a lover?" At my continued befuddlement, Vaida sat back. She looked genuinely upset. "It has been years since my last visit to Omal, but have all its citizens lost their appreciation for beauty?"

My veneer slipped a little, and I narrowed my eyes. "Don't fret, Your Highness. My life is not lacking in fulfillment."

Beside me, Arin was rigid and doing a fantastic job of concealing it. Vaida and I stared at each other. I thought of the people in the well, languishing in their filth. Suffering a slow, undignified death.

Disquieting, Arin had called her. I needed to break my stare, to flush and stumble with my words. To my consternation, a remnant of royal arrogance surfaced, howling to answer her challenge.

"Who fulfills it?" she asked, her voice husky. She slid her gaze meaningfully to Arin, and we both straightened as though struck.

"That's enough," Arin growled. Even his iron control bent against this woman. "Do not antagonize my Champion. We are guests in your home."

Instantly, the atmosphere shifted. Vaida picked up her plate. "Sylvia knows I'm teasing! Anyway, I already love her. Curiosity is a tempting mistress. No one knows that better than you, Arin."

Though Vaida's attention remained on Arin for the rest of the hour, I hadn't a doubt she was attuned to my every movement. Too nervous to reach for the sweets spread on the table, I stayed on my side of the couch until we left her receiving room. Arin led us past the palace courtyards to a thriving flower garden.

"One of Vaida's favorite patches," Arin said.

Guards in their various kingdoms' colors milled around. Servants rushed past us in frenzied preparation. "Crouch by the poppies and pretend to admire them." Arin lowered himself on a concrete bench.

I fought a prickle of embarrassment. "Which ones are the poppies?" Mahair didn't waste fertile soil for plants that couldn't be consumed or used for medicinal puposes. The only flowers I could recognize on sight were the ones Hanim warned could poison me.

Not a hint of scorn crossed Arin's expression as he pointed at a patch of red flowers with thin, parchment-like petals curling up around a fuzzy black center.

With a small smile of thanks, I slid to the ground, folding my legs under me. "I know what you're going to say."

"Oh?"

"I shouldn't have glared at her."

"You did well, Sylvia."

I pretended to keel sideways into the poppies. His mouth twisted ruefully. "I do wish you hadn't matched her gaze, since Vaida prides herself on provocation. She finds you interesting, but she won't bait you if you stay near me. She cannot afford to stir bad blood between Lukub and Nizahl."

The doll in the war room cabinet and its stained flag flashed through my mind. "The Battle of Zinish," I recalled. "She must honor the peace accords."

"Partly the peace accords, yes. With or without the treaty, Vaida would not cross me."

My dress caught on a thorn from a different patch of flowers. "She's afraid of you."

"She is not the only person capable of playing this game," he said, with a hint of aristocratic disdain. "I've known Vaida since we were children. Our minds are much the same."

"Well. That's terrifying." I adjusted my legs into a more comfortable sitting position. The slit bared my thigh, and I gave up trying to fix it. "Are we departing at twilight the day after tomorrow?"

It took Arin a second too long to respond. He seemed to be noticing my dress for the first time. His gaze trailed over me, a leisurely perusal that made my mouth dry. Arin's attention was usually as efficient as him—he didn't linger, and he certainly never perused. "Nizahl's colors suit you."

Something dangerous pulsed in the pit of my stomach. I couldn't help but mimic him, studying the change in his attire I'd noted earlier. The laces of his shirt stopped at his collarbones. It felt wrong to see the length of his throat so exposed. His hair had come loose sometime between leaving Vaida and entering the garden, falling like a silver cloud around his jaw. Arin of Nizahl was maddeningly elegant. I wanted to cut him open and compare our bones to understand why his gave him grace and mine gave me back pain.

I busied myself with the flowers. I'd spent too long inhaling tunnel dust—it had addled my head.

"Twilight. Yes," Arin answered belatedly. "Our route to Orban is longer than the others."

The others weren't traveling through the Meridian Pass.

The Meridian Pass was a narrow, flat canyon wedged between two reddish crags. Though it stretched a mere three miles, many riders met their doom there, crushed by falling boulders or chased by the vagrants and fugitives camped by the entrance.

The Pass was also the site of a massacre. Ten Jasadi families fleeing capture in Omal found themselves trapped inside the Meridian Pass by Omal guards on one side, Nizahl soldiers on the other. They had met a grisly end.

Most of the Champions leaving the Banquet would take the route merchants used to travel between Lukub and Orban. Arin did not want to chance the Urabi or Mufsids whisking me away in the crush of carriages, so we would be the lone contingent going through the Meridian Pass.

I was about to ask Arin whether we'd be riding in the same carriage again when an orange cat strolled over the hand I'd pressed against the ground. I recoiled, crushing three flowers in my haste. Stray cats were a common sight in Lukub, I'd heard. It seemed even the Ivory Palace could not keep them out. A kitten swatted at my dress, swishing its gray tail in a pile of ruby petals. A presumptious older cat plopped itself onto Arin's lap, glaring down at me from his knee. Idly scratching its ears, Arin said, "Allow the attendants to help you. The guards search anyone who enters your room, so the servants are secure. It reflects poorly on Vaida's service for your attendants to wander around."

We resumed our walk once the cats scurried away. "Do you allow your attendants to help *you* bathe and disrobe?" I challenged. I flushed as soon as I finished, already regretting the question. I couldn't imagine Arin permitting anyone to push his coat off his shoulders or undo the tight straps from his uniform. Would he level his steady gaze on them while their trembling fingers disrobed him?

Or stare at the far wall in blank indifference, unyielding in body and manner?

I turned a fierce scowl inward. The Sultana's nonsense about lovers had clearly scrambled my senses. Arin was attractive—it was as obvious and indisputable as the sun. But I had spent nearly twenty-one years capable of acknowledging attractiveness without being attracted myself. I had never wanted anyone, never yearned for the physical relationships Marek chased.

I finally empathized with the girls in the keep. Especially Gana. The fanciful ward used to dress in Raya's finest gowns every week, sing warbling ballads while dabbing fragrances on her wrists and behind her ear.

"There is power in conquering the unconquerable," Gana had said one year, after rejecting yet another fellow's advances. The keep had gone to Zeila's for celebratory tea and ahwa after a successful market. Zeila laid reed rugs on the floor, and we sat on beaded cushions, a wooden table wobbling at our feet.

I'd been a few cushions down with Sefa and Marek, sipping my bitter ahwa from a chipped cup. Gana's conversation with Daleel had reached my ears. "Men don't see women, dear Daleel. They see power. Which one of us has more of it, and how easily they can drain it out of her."

Apparently, this wasn't a trait reserved for men, because a dark thrill raced through me at the thought of conquering the Nizahl Heir. Stealing a piece of Arin's power in the surrender.

The breeze ruffled Arin's hair. He chuckled, drawing me back to the present. "No attendants are permitted in my quarters. Vaida has long resigned herself to my eccentricities."

Disturbed at the ghoulish direction of my thoughts, I moved away from him. "I should get ready for the banquet."

Without looking back, I walked through the shadow of a Ruby Hound protruding from the buttress and hurried into the palace.

CHAPTER TWENTY-TWO

Without the necessary exhaustion, my body rebelled against sleep in a strange place. I circled my room, opening drawers and laying out my gown for the Banquet. The night grew deeper, and still, sleep evaded me. I exchanged my bedgown for loose linen pants and a neat tunic. If I wanted any hope of sleeping tonight, I needed to walk.

Ren startled when I pulled open the door. He looked over my clothing and frowned. "No."

"I need the washroom," I said.

"I will accompany you."

"That hardly seems appropriate."

Bending Ren to my will was easier than I anticipated. His antipathy for me was the boring kind—not as powerful as Vaun's, nor as malleable as Wes's. After a few minutes of arguing how insulting Vaida would find it if I felt unsafe enough to take a guard to the bathroom, Ren stepped aside, his unhappiness clear in the rigid lines of his shoulders. "Make haste."

In the hush of darkness, the eyes of the Ivory Palace followed me as I walked across the hall. Usr Jasad had also been large, with separate wings and plenty of unexplored rooms to tantalize a bored child. But it had always been a home first, a palace second. Menace and magnificence beat as one in the Ivory Palace. Sultana Vaida's palace reflected a clear message: *beware beauty's embrace, for its guts are greedy and its teeth are sharp.*

Then again, perhaps Usr Jasad had represented the same. The only common ground I had unearthed between Nizahlans and Jasadis was their hatred for my grandparents.

I rounded the bend and paused at a tapestry of Baira. The Lukub Awala lounged in her throne, a scantily clad human male kneeling at her feet. Dozens of Ruby Hounds surrounded her. Baira had her hand on a snarling hound's head, her fingers luminescent with magic against its bloodred coat. I shuddered at the look of sheer desperation in the kneeling man's eyes. To be a mortal in the time of the Awaleen—I could not imagine a greater curse.

The scene unraveled along the hall. My footfalls were silent against the rug. The man kneeling at Baira's feet stood, shifting across the tapestry. He clutched his head, mouth falling open in a scream as a weeping woman reached for him. Their hands connected. The colors in the tapestry shifted as the man fell to the ground, dead, and the weeping woman dissipated in the air. An illusion.

The hall curved again, and this side revealed an ambush. Baira had her arms wrapped around Rovial's chest, restraining him. Dania drew runes on his forehead while Kapastra raised glowing palms in his direction. They stood on Sirauk Bridge. Clouds roiled beneath the bridge, reacting to the magic pouring from the Awaleen. Their power had collapsed the very sky.

"The entombment," came a dulcet voice. I whirled, reaching for a dagger I didn't have. Sultana Vaida raised her arms in a soothing gesture. "There, there. Did I startle you?"

It was a stupid question, so I gave a stupider answer. "No."

"Are you worried about Felix? The Omal contingent sleeps in the north wing." At my deadpan gaze, Vaida touched one of the red crystals dangling from her ears. She winked. "News travels quickly, darling. Drat Felix and his foul temper. Such a terrible fate he dealt that little girl."

"The entombment?" I repeated, electing not to satisfy her curiosity. I motioned toward the tapestry. An enormous amount of detail had gone into weaving Sirauk. The cursed bridge plunged into white mist behind the struggling siblings. Rovial's eyes were wide and wild. Magic-mad.

Vaida ran her fingertips over Baira's face. "All the Awaleen went willingly to their eternal sleep except for Rovial. Subduing the Jasad Awal made them weak enough to fall from Sirauk and into the waiting tombs below."

Hearing my kingdom's name from Vaida's mouth shocked me back to awareness. With Arin present, she had been a terror. I had no wish to discover where she would draw her limits in his absence.

"I apologize for disturbing you, Sultana." I started to move around her. A delicate press on my shoulder held me in place.

Sultana Vaida's eyes gleamed as dark as mine. Kitmer eyes, Niphran used to call them. We stood nose to nose; a fact I found unduly vexatious, having grown accustomed to being the tallest woman in a room. "My palace boasts much more than this tapestry. Let me show you." She dropped her hold on my shoulder, a dazzling smile belying the hardness of her gaze. "I insist."

She started walking without waiting for an answer. I toyed with the temptation to ignore her and jog directly to my room. I was not her subject, and she had no rights over me.

Arin's caution stalled my step. *Do not challenge her or distinguish yourself in any way.*

Vaida had already rounded the bend. Swearing under my breath, I hurried to follow. Lukub's Sultana strode to the east wing of the Ivory Palace. A row of Ruby Hounds' heads pushed out from the wall to our right. In place of their teeth were flickering candles, casting long shadows over the hall. Vaida's jewel-encrusted cerise gown cast patterns in its wake, its lace sleeves trailing behind her.

She turned right, and I nearly tripped over my feet. Dozens of guards lined each side of the corridor. They did not react to my appearance, their attention fixed straight ahead.

I stopped at the head of the hall. "The Heir's guards will worry at my absence."

She glanced over her shoulder. "Do they fault the security of my palace? The efficacy of my guards?"

"Of course not, but—"

"Then they should have no reason to worry."

Without turning around, she curled her fingers, beckoning me after her. By Sirauk's doomed depths, was I about to allow this woman to kill me out of a sense of decorum?

She might have information. Hanim's presence startled me. *She hates Nizahl. It might be useful.*

I grimaced. Why couldn't I have just asked Ren for a sleeping draught?

As soon as I crossed the threshold into the Sultana's private chambers, the doors closed with a mournful groan. Where Arin's chambers were an exercise in austerity, Vaida crowded hers with every color in the kingdoms. One wall was a vibrant indigo, another a demure emerald. Lanterns in every shape and size hung from the peaked ceiling, casting the massive room in a warm glow. Her bed stretched wider than Rory's shop, and quilts of various design and thickness were piled high at the foot. The bizarre blend of chaos and style I'd come to associate with Lukub's Sultana.

"Why am I here?" I asked, foregoing propriety. The vivacity of Vaida's chambers was unsettling, more so than if I had entered a room with bloodred drapes and rusted weapons.

"When I heard Arin had chosen an Omalian orphan from a lower village, I did not share in everyone's surprise," Vaida said. She picked up a glass doll, adjusting its limbs before setting it back on her bedside table. She tapped its nose with a polished nail. "Arin... he sees through people. Calculates potential and risk the way an architect evaluates promising land. He sees worth where others might see waste. Successfully, too—the Nizahl Champion has succeeded in the last three Alcalahs."

I pursed my lips, trying to figure out if I had just been insulted or praised.

From the bottom drawer of her bedside table, Vaida withdrew an ornate ring. She cupped it briefly, closing her eyes. "But you, Sylvia. There's more to why he selected you as Champion."

My voice could cut steel. "If you are implying I have some sort of amorous arrangement with His Highness—"

Vaida snorted. Her royal airs temporarily vanished, leaving a young woman only a few years my senior. "My dear, if Arin of Nizahl loves you, you can be sure the Alcalah is the least of your worries. Arin is not the kind of man who puts his heart before his head. His enemies are many, and he conceives of every way they can attack him. I'm sure you have seen how still he holds himself, how strong a hand he wields over his temperament. Even if he were capable of caring for someone else, I cannot imagine he would ever be so selfish as to let himself fall in love. He knows his own nature and all the dark places love could steer him."

The thought bothered me for reasons I couldn't explain. She had essentially described Arin as a beast with the capacity to become feral at any moment.

"He said you know him well. Clearly, he misspoke." It came out waspish. "He isn't... broken. He would love the same as any man."

"Oh, my sweet Sylvia." Vaida's smile was all teeth. "The way most men love is *so* boring. It is frequent and fickle and altogether unextraordinary. Arin would love to obsession. To madness. But do you want to know the real reason he would never allow himself to love another?" Vaida stepped close, her floral scent tickling my nose. "Arin is consumed by what he loves. If asked, he would get on his knees and let it kill him. He withholds his heart out of self-preservation."

The image rose before I could prevent it. Arin on his knees, steadfast and resolute. Chin tilted forward to accept the fate he would be dealt. Or maybe he would be wild for the first and last time in his life, eyes desperate and seeking. I bit the inside of my bottom lip until I tasted blood. I should have never followed her here and given her the chance to fill my head with her poison.

"Enough about the Heir. I have something to show you." Vaida slid the ring onto her finger and pressed it into the emerald wall. A hiss of released air blew dust into my nose as the center of the wall swung inward, revealing a stairwell leading into a void. I skidded away, my world ricocheting off its axis, searching for an item I could turn into a weapon.

"That was magic!"

"Not mine. Baira's magic still manipulates parts of the palace." She held up the ring. A Ruby Hound snarled on its surface. "Come along. You are safe with me."

She did not wait for my answer, stepping into the hole and descending into darkness. I yanked at the doors to her chambers. They were fastened shut. I braced my foot on the door and heaved. Nothing.

She is not going to kill Nizahl's Champion in her own palace, Hanim murmured. *Go. See what the Sultana has to show you.*

Cursing doors, guards, and royals, I gingerly stepped into the opening. The drifting scent of mold only grew stronger the lower I climbed into the void. I trailed my fingers across the damp wall, listening for Vaida. What if she killed me and sealed the evidence?

Your neck is thicker than both her arms. If she manages to best you, you deserve to die, Hanim said. I frowned, resisting the urge to check the circumference of my neck.

The stairs flattened into a small landing. A light flickered to life, revealing Vaida holding a candle. I could only see a few feet in either direction. The darkness at the edges *roiled.* Alive. Hungry. My skin crawled. I felt like an intruder, violating the sanctity of a space only meant to be occupied by the woman in front of me.

"This hideaway belonged to Baira. Every Sultana after her inherits this chamber, and the darkness shapes itself to the will of its new owner. If you think it's daunting now, you should have seen it when my mother commanded it." She raised the candle higher, and my attention fixed on her ring. A ring that essentially doubled as a key to the Sultana's most private hideaway. The seed of an idea took root in the back of my mind.

"Why am I here?"

The lights flickered over her smiling mouth. Behind her head, strips of parchment were stuck to the wall, dozens and dozens of them, names scrawled across each one with black ink.

"I need a favor from you, Sylvia." She spoke my name with a familiarity reserved for lifetime friendships. "You have to lose the Alcalah."

I paused. She lured me into a dungeon teeming with malice to ask if I would forfeit the Alcalah? I picked through possible replies, searching for the most respectful version of "I would rather choke on a muddy sandal."

"Can you read?" Vaida asked abruptly. She held the candle toward the wall, sending shadows over the pinned names.

I was fluent in every kingdom's native language, even the ones rarely used anymore. A skill Arin had discovered by tricking me into reading the scroll on his table. Our languages blended into uniformity a century ago, and only a few villages spoke anything else.

"No." A village orphan would have traded literacy for labor.

She glanced over her shoulder, assessing me for dishonesty. Apparently, it was only Arin whom my stoicism could not fool, because she turned back without arguing. "These are names. Members of Sultana Bisai's council. Palace staff. Everyone who played a role in murdering my mother is on this wall."

Sultana Vaida moved to the left, illuminating an entirely new set of names. "These are suspected Nizahl spies in Lukub. There are many I cannot locate. Spies sent under Supreme Munqual's reign have been in Lukub for decades. Supreme Rawain instituted a practice early in his power where Nizahl orphans were trained and sent into foreign kingdoms. They could grow older there, become part of the community. Supreme Rawain planted children in our kingdoms to spy on us, left those insidious seeds to take root and drain our resources."

The light shifted for an instant, outlining rows and rows of different names before Vaida spun around. "Do you think I killed my mother?" She sounded vaguely entertained, like a child asking their parent to guess a number.

"I saw the wells in Essam Woods," I said. "The people you left to rot within them. If you are asking me whether I believe you are capable of killing your mother, I am afraid you will not relish my response."

Vaida trilled a laugh. It echoed, bouncing off the cavernous borders. "Oh, but I see why Arin likes you. You have the boiling hate of a peasant, and the tongue of a royal."

The darkness crooned, crowding closer. The candle in Vaida's palm was the only barrier keeping the shadows from wrapping their fingers around us. I wanted to beat a speedy retreat, but even the stairs had been swallowed into gloom.

"I cannot lose the Alcalah, Sultana. I apologize if Nizahl has caused you trouble, but I owe a duty."

Sultana Vaida stepped closer. The cupped candle pressed between us, and in the emptiness behind her, rows upon rows of women materialized, the jeweled Lukub crown glinting on each head. They were gone between one heartbeat and the next, but the darkness teemed with their presence. Lukub's Sultanas. The will of Vaida manifested in Baira's dungeon.

"You owe Nizahl no fidelity. If you lose, Nizahl will forsake you. Felix's ego has deprived you of a haven in Omal. You won't be safe in Orban, either. Orban's trade relationship with Omal allows Felix the right to whisk any Omalian citizen back to their rightful kingdom for a tribunal. Or in your case, an execution."

The angular lines of Vaida's face sharpened in the dim light. Her chest swelled, pressing the candle between us.

"I can give you a home, Sylvia. Point at any building in Lukub, and I will make it yours. Felix's patrol can't touch you within my kingdom's borders. Any leadership position in my army will open to you before anyone else."

The casual treachery in her offer intrigued me. She would go against her fellow rulers, earn the ire of Omal and Nizahl combined, all for the sake of winning the Alcalah?

The darkness closed in around us, and I couldn't tell which danger to assess: the one at my back or the one smiling at me. I circled my wrists with thumb and finger, reassuring myself with the chilled metal of my cuffs.

"Why ask this of me? I could lose on my own, without any incentive."

Vaida flipped her wrist, brushing aside the question. "The three Champions Arin has chosen over the last nine years have emerged the Victor. Nizahl has not lost an Alcalah since Arin was a child. I am confident he has chosen another winner."

My breathing grew labored, fighting against the press of night on all sides. The darkness smelled like fruit forgotten in the heat, sweet and rotten. I pushed my knuckles against my mouth, suppressing a gag.

"Yes, Baira's chambers are inhospitable to those who don't possess the ring. I suffered the same reaction when my mother brought me here." The candle burned low, the wick reduced to a nub. We had moments until the light vanished. "Think carefully on your course of action, my darling. Think of your little chemist, hobbling around in his shop. That ramshackle keep and its disheveled orphans. The chatty girl and her chairs. If you become the Alcalah's Victor, I cannot harm you. But Arin is not the only one capable of visiting destruction on his enemies. Felix owes me a debt; he can be persuaded to forget a few tragic accidents in a lower village."

My cuffs warmed. Some of the darkness receded as my magic surged, responding to her threat. *Grief. Rage. Fear.*

"What benefit do you gain if I lose? Are you so determined to see your Champion triumph?"

The shadows skittered away, the hum of my magic ringing in the hollows. "Do not fret over my gain. Busy yourself with the thought of what you stand to lose. Consider your loved ones." Vaida stepped away, putting her back to the opposite wall. A chilling determination glinted in her gaze. She took another step backward. "Above all, consider yourself." One last step, and the dying candle cast its light over the wall behind her. Dozens of faces, mouths opened in soundless screams, protruded from the wall. Their skin was stretched and mottled, eyes a gaping hole in their bleached skulls.

In front of them, Vaida smiled, and the shadows extinguished the light.

I walked straight to Arin's room.

For all Vaida's threats, she had sprinted headfirst into the one error Arin had never made with me: she vastly overestimated my willingness to gamble.

What I stood to gain by accepting her offer was substantial. She had packaged her proposal with the right balance of persuasion, temptation, and coercion. Lose the Alcalah and you can call Lukub home. Lose the Alcalah or lose your village.

Unfortunately, I had no interest in redrawing the lines of my prison to match Lukub's borders. Assuming, of course, that Vaida did not sell me to the highest bidder as soon as Felix and Arin asserted their sincerest wishes to mount my head on their palace gates. Arin had won my trust—albeit after throwing several daggers into my limbs—and trust was not a resource I carried in duplicate.

Locating his room was laughably easy. It was the only one besides my own with its own set of guards.

Wes and Jeru did not look pleased to see me.

"Ren came by to tell us he couldn't find you," Wes said.

"I took a bath."

"Your hair is dry."

"I didn't wash it. Let me pass. I have a matter of urgency to discuss with the Heir."

Jeru glanced at Wes with a shrug. "He told us she could enter as she pleased."

My brows lifted. He did?

Wes knocked on the door twice. "Sire?"

"Enter," came Arin's distracted voice. Wes sighed and swung the door open for me. Arin didn't glance up when I slid inside. Wes closed the door with a resentful thud.

The Nizahl Heir had his back to me. He wore a pair of loose sleep pants, tied low at his waist, and nothing else. A dinner tray sat abandoned on the bed. Arin bent over a table, hip cocked to the side as he scribbled on some parchment. I studied the strong slope of his shoulders, the notches of his spine. I vaguely wondered if his back would be harder to break than the soldier's.

"Your room is bigger than mine," I remarked.

The muscles in Arin's back locked. I dropped to the bed, flicking around the items on his tray. I dipped a piece of his bread into the dark green molokhia. It had long since gone cold, and the skin on top stuck to my bread.

Arin turned. He sat back, bracing his hands on the table. "Do you want to trade?"

I swallowed the bite in my mouth with difficulty. My gaze lingered on his chest. The evidence of our encounter with the Ruby Hound hadn't fully healed. The bandage looked much cleaner than the sleeves I had haphazardly wrapped around it.

"No. Mine is closer to the stairs."

Dania's sacred skirt, but he was so *pale*. As though someone stretched a thin sheet of parchment over him and named it skin. On another, I'd call it sickly, but Arin's torso was long and lean. His body carried the kind of power gained from years of relentless combat. The elegance of his beauty shone in the sharp cut of his hips, the hollows of his collarbones.

Arin arched a brow, altogether too entertained for my taste. "Is anything the matter, Sylvia? You've grown pale."

I rolled my eyes. Of course he wasn't ignorant of his effect on others. His appeal was another weapon in his arsenal, honed to deadly perfection. "My natural complexion, I assure you." The echo of an exchange uttered a lifetime ago.

I carried the tray over to the table, giving him his privacy. Arin swiped a tunic from the wardrobe and tugged it over his head. I exhaled when he was clothed again, pressing my knuckles to over-warm cheeks. May Vaida be damned to the tombs.

It was strange. I had spent my formative years without more than a passing interest in the men of Mahair. Even if I could bear to be touched by them, I lacked the skills needed for true intimacy. A hand too near my throat, any sudden pressure—I was more likely to hurl a lover into the wall than wrap them close.

The Alcalah was not the time to entertain such absurdities. I snuck a glance as Arin deftly laced his vest and I immediately regretted it. If Arin's mind was a finely sharpened dagger, then his body was its armor. I couldn't imagine how anyone touched him and remained whole. Being with him would be honeyed annihilation, too much for a flesh-and-bone body to bear.

Enough. I rolled my shoulders. Too little sleep and too much near-death was my problem.

The Heir arranged himself on a wooden chair. "Is there a purpose to this late-night sojourn, or did you just want my dinner?"

"I would like to strike a bargain."

Arin settled back, gloved hands weaving over his stomach.

I told him everything. How Vaida lured me to her wing of the palace, the ring she pressed into the wall to unseal Baira's hideaway. Describing the sentient darkness proved harder, and I shied away from recounting the fear that slashed through me when the candle died. I had tripped over the stairs in my rush and fled past the stoic guards.

"There are names of people she's killed. Names of Nizahlan spies living in Lukub. Faces... cut-off faces that may belong to those same spies." Arin's expression didn't flicker until I talked about Vaida's threat. The offer she proposed if I lost the Alcalah.

"And you are telling me this with full knowledge I cannot stop you from acting on Vaida's offer, nor can I prevent her from sheltering you in Lukub. Not unless I expose you as a Jasadi, which would ruin me, stall the Alcalah, and give the Mufsids and Urabi an opportunity to target a new victim." Arin's eyes gleamed with approval. "Impressive."

I fluttered my hand in an imitation bow. "I have acquired quite the array of skills under your tutelage. After considering the benefits of Vaida's offer, I have decided they do not outweigh its hazards. Namely, living in a second kingdom torn apart by war with Nizahl."

At this, Arin broke out into a grin. My heart, which had done an excellent job of beating for my nearly twenty-one years of life, stuttered at the sight. The wonders of tonight would never cease.

"You were so concerned the royals would lay invisible traps for you. Here you are, seeing right through them."

Not as quickly as him, Hanim said. *He figured out Vaida's plan while you were still speaking.*

I raked lines into the chair's padded arm. I couldn't appreciate the compliment; I had hoped to be wrong. Had Vaida gone mad? "If she violates the Zinish peace accords, Lukub will be ravaged. Omal and Orban will join forces with Nizahl to uphold the treaty."

Arin lifted a shoulder. "Not if Nizahl violates the treaty first. After the Lukub Champion becomes the Victor, I imagine she will bribe a Nizahl soldier or struggling Nizahlan council person to murder him. The act of killing a kingdom's Victor is its own declaration of war, and Vaida's ready armies will move on Nizahl."

The insidious cruelty of Vaida's plan sent revulsion shivering through me. She would set in motion a devastating war...for what?

Arin remained unmoved. He had already witnessed Nizahl obliterate one kingdom out of existence. "She will never win a war with Nizahl," I said. "Not if she spends three lifetimes preparing."

"Something has convinced her she can."

"But why? Why risk it?"

"Perhaps she blames the Citadel for her mother's death. Perhaps she doesn't care if her soldiers die in droves. It matters little. The wisdom of Vaida's actions is not at issue." Arin tilted his head. "The wisdom of yours, on the other hand...What have you come to bargain for, Suraira?"

I had ruminated over this inevitable question the whole journey from Vaida's wing. There was only one answer. I had given a promise, and I intended to see it through.

"Marek and Sefa's release," I said promptly. "If you grant them leave to return to Omal after the second trial, I will stay our course."

Unlike Arin, my disposition did not lend well to long periods of stillness. I fidgeted with the tasseled cushion and tried to consider what he could be thinking.

When I was seven years old, one of my tutors fell ill. Soraya had attempted to lift my spirits by constructing a maze out of Niyar's thickest books. We sprinkled rice in the winding tunnels and folded bits of discarded fabric to create dead ends. After we finished, Soraya gathered crickets to race through our maze. Of the nearly two dozen competing, only one succeeded. It leapt to the top of the books and peered around, studying our haphazard creation. Instead of descending into the mass of sparring crickets below, it hopped on the books' spines, cutting straight through the maze.

"He cheated!" I had cried, cupping it in my skirt.

"Maybe so." Soraya picked up the cricket and balanced it on her finger. "To win a game, you must consider it from every angle, amari. Otherwise, you cannot rise above the commotion and secure victory."

Arin finally spoke. "I will suffer a forfeiture and gain nothing in return. Your duties are unchanged, regardless of your options."

Dread skittered along my bones. "Speak plainly. What do you want?"

"Kill the Lukub Champion during the first trial," Arin said. "If he dies, you eliminate the possibility Vaida will use him to instigate war."

He is a worthy adversary, Hanim said, reluctantly pleased. *An efficient conclusion to a potential problem.*

Efficient. Always *efficient.* I pushed from the chair, rounding to the window overlooking the courtyard. From this height, I could see past the bounds of the Ivory Palace, beyond the noble towns clustered around it. Snowcapped mountains studded the horizon like crooked teeth.

"If the Lukub Champion loses the first trial naturally, he will not become Victor. Why kill him and upset Vaida further?"

"Vaida will not know you killed him. No one enters Ayume except the Champions. The first three Champions to cross the forest and climb the bluff advance. The Lukub Champion will simply never reach the bluff. Tragic, but hardly unprecedented in the Alcalah." Arin appeared beside me, gazing out at Lukub. "Vaida will not have chosen a weak Champion. Without your interference, he will almost certainly advance. If you merely sabotage the Lukub Champion, he will inform Vaida upon arrival."

From the density of political pandemonium, Arin of Nizahl rose. He mapped every visible path to the finish, and he secured his victory.

I swallowed past the knot in my throat. "If I do this, Sefa and Marek will be assigned soldiers to escort them to Mahair."

"Plenty," Arin confirmed. I could sense his gaze on the side of my face. "The soldiers will be tasked with protecting Mahair in case Vaida seeks retribution."

I traced shapes into the fogged window. Lukubis did not have the constitution to be viciously exiled from their land, nor the magic to weave themselves into strange societies.

"Only *you* are capable of painting murder as the logical choice."

Arin's breath brushed the top of my head. If I turned around, I had a notion we'd be no more than a hairsbreadth apart. "Are we agreed?"

I tore my gaze from the glittering kingdom.

"We are."

CHAPTER TWENTY-THREE

Like a good little Champion, I allowed the attendants to help me dress for the banquet. Zizi, Mirna, and Ava chattered away while they untangled my hair and fussed with my gown. Comments about the meal, the guests, the wandering guards. They tried to rub sweet-smelling oils on my body, but I slapped their hands away. My politeness had its limits.

Since they were here as the Heir's staff, Sefa and Marek would be dining with the soldiers. After the attendants departed, I dug out Rory's golden gloves from my parcels. I needed an anchor to home, a line I could follow to shore in a sea of unknown.

I laid a palm on the mirror. The woman in the reflection cut an imposing figure in a billowing black gown. Thin violet lace criss-crossed from her hips to her breasts, exposing ribbons of her skin. The skirt fell shorter in the front, revealing her heeled boots, and trailed in a silky spill behind her. The Nizahl emblem hung from her pendant, displayed below her collarbones. Her hair fell in shiny ropes around her.

Regal. Striking. A false queen.

I clasped the pendant and shut my eyes. I let myself imagine ripping it from around my neck and grinding it beneath my boot. Tearing myself from this gown and setting it aflame, scouring the taint of Nizahl from my body in boiling water.

Standing in a Nizahlan gown, under a Lukubi roof, I felt more like the Jasad Heir than ever. Was it possible to miss someone you had almost been? Someone who but for a stumble in the sands of fate, I would have become.

Inexplicably, the watch guard frog hopped into my thoughts. Its frenzied croak averting its fellow frogs from my clutches at its own expense. What made the watch guard braver than the frogs who fled?

I opened my eyes. Rubbing the soft metal of my cuffs, I focused on why I was here. I would be almost-Essiya until the end of the Alcalah, when I would finally become Sylvia. I was my own most persistent ghost, and I had grown weary of her haunting.

I opened the door. Wes's brows nearly disappeared to the back of his head. "Huh."

Articulate. I walked at a fast clip down the crowded hall. We were to gather at the massive stairwell on the second floor. Each ruler but Vaida would descend with their Champion. If I wound up late twice and interrupted Vaida's grand entrance, Arin might just elect to push me down the stairs.

A group of guards, royals, and Champions had gathered at the head of the stairs, milling around in conversation. A hum of antici-pation vibrated in the air. I scanned for Arin and found him tucked into an alcove, arms crossed over his chest. The only color in his black ensemble was a violet belt around his trim waist and the matching detailing on his coat. He had brushed his hair back, but a renegade silver lock fell over his temple. Broad-shouldered and pol-ished, Arin observed the others with feigned boredom. A predator playing at docility, probably contemplating the creative ways some-one could try to kill him. He was the most achingly beautiful threat I'd ever seen.

Arin glanced up and froze. A myriad of emotions flashed over his features, too many and too complicated to name.

He straightened, gaze roaming over my gown. "Sefa did wonder-ful work on your dress." He sounded dazed. I had watched him bleed half to death without sounding anything but composed. "Although you are certainly not endearing yourself to Vaida."

"Oh?" I managed.

"It's customary for the hostess to outshine her guests." Arin's eyes swirled with humor and something quieter, more intimate. Just for me. "You've made that impossible."

I barely heard him. The most bizarre sensation trembled through me. A violence I didn't recognize. Violence...that wasn't the right word.

Against my own volition, I touched the loose hair at his temple. Arin held himself still as a statue while I swept the strand behind his ear. My fingers lingered against the strong line of his jaw. I had the most irrational wish for my gloves to dissolve into ash. But without them, he couldn't have allowed my touch to begin with.

What a reversal of fortunes, that I should seek a touch and be denied.

"There," I said, knotting my trembling hand into my skirt. It wanted to keep going, to taunt his relentless control, to push greedy hands into silken hair and watch the ice in his eyes melt to liquid flame. My control was fracturing beneath a pressure I did not recognize. I couldn't trust my own body. "Now she will hate us both."

The steady beat of a tubluh cut through the din. The crowd fell silent, turning to the bottom of the stairwell. Servants wearing gossamer red gowns or ivory tunics pushed open the looming doors to the banquet. Everyone gathered at the head of the wide stairwell, grasping the banisters or leaning forward. I remained in the rear with Arin. I had seen more than my share of Vaida's ostentatious displays.

"The ruby of Lukub. Champion of our shining Sultana Vaida. Raise your voices for the Alcalah's coming Victor, Timur of Lukub!"

The halls went dark as the lanterns behind us were extinguished. A red glow lit the walls, casting fiery shadows over us. The servants scattered a powder in the torches, and the guests squealed as the fire shot up in clouds of red and orange. The flames roared between the jaws of the Ruby Hounds protruding from the walls and carved into the balusters on each side of the stairwell. We were awash in red, the deafening crackle of fire mingling with the excited whispers.

"How do you think she would feel if she knew we saw a real Ruby Hound?" I murmured.

A flash of delicious spite flitted over Arin's face. "Murderous."

"Nothing new, then," I said, and Arin bit his lip. Trying not to smile.

"Are my attempts at humor improving?"

He smoothed his features almost instantly, but it was too late. He had revealed something entirely unintended, something I could not reconcile with my own understanding of him. Arin of Nizahl was a twenty-six-year-old man, filled with the ennui of one who thought most everyone in the room beneath him, struggling not to exchange a laugh with the girl on his arm.

Perhaps Arin was his own ghost, too.

The Omal Heir and his Champion stood to our left. Felix's glare bored into the side of my face. I waited for Arin to adjust his sleeves and winked at Felix. The brat reddened, his nostrils flaring wide. Nobody should reach Felix's age without experiencing a solid beating. It built character. I would love to be the one to pound humility into his skull. Was that not what cousins were for?

Arin offered his hand. "Shall we?"

My golden glove fit against his black one. In a burst of restless nerves, I said, "We match."

Instead of taking the excellent opportunity to mock my inane comment, Arin's eyes softened. "So we do."

We began our descent, perfectly tuned to the other pairs. The drama suited Vaida, who'd donned her crown for the occasion. She and her Champion took the steps first. When our turn came, a bizarre rift happened within me. As though the dusty, Omal half of me lingered at the top of the stairs, watching the decorated Jasadi half descend on the arm of the most powerful Heir in the kingdoms.

He is on the arm of the strongest Queen since the Awaleen, Hanim said. *Or the ghost of her, anyway.*

I resisted the urge to glance back. Hanim's voice had quieted lately, leaving more room for my own thoughts.

"Should I be watching my food? Felix is not happy to see me."

Arin tipped his head to speak into my ear. "Ren is in the kitchen watching the cooks. We already have serving boys tasting the food. Don't worry. Vaida would never allow anything as crass as an assassination attempt to ruin her banquet."

The dining hall took my breath away. Lanterns hung from white chains attached to the vaulted glass ceiling. They illuminated white petals flowering along the eastern wall and ivory vines weaving through the six Ruby Hounds. The Hounds circled in painted states of motion around the room. A more extravagant table could not exist in all the kingdoms. The servants pulled out high-backed chairs as we entered.

"Your kingdom's seal marks your seat," Vaida announced. She took her place at the head of the table, dangling her chalice over the clawed armrest. "My Lukubi guests, you may sit wherever is free."

I looked at Arin in a panic. I hadn't prepared for the possibility of sitting apart. I lacked his agility of speech and his even-keeled constitution. His gloved hand squeezed mine, once, before he went to the opposite side of the table. A servant led me farther down, where the Nizahl seal was embossed on the candle flickering in front of my plate.

I glanced around and swallowed a groan. The Orban Champion and the Lukub Champion took the seats on either side of me, leaving the Omal Champion across from us.

The arrangement could have been worse, I supposed. I could be

Arin, stuck between Vaida and Felix. The Champions were seated at one end of the table, the royals at the other. The twelve or so nobles Vaida had invited took their places in the center, their excited chatter echoing in the hall.

A few servants bustled around, filling our chalices with a floral wine. At the end of the table, Felix curled his lip in my direction. I lifted the dull knife from my plate and met his gaze as I slapped the flat of the knife against my palm. He flinched, and I hid a laugh against my wrist. The prospect of no longer needing to pretend was heady. Pretending to struggle to carry crates, because I needed to look weak. Pretending to smile when I wanted to scream, because a village girl should be grateful for any fate beyond a husband and six children.

Vaida's offer of freedom could never have given me this. Myself.

And who are you? Hanim asked, disparaging. *Do you think you can pluck yourself like a flower away from the garden that raised you, the roots that built you? The past is our sun, Essiya. Only by allowing it to shine can you bloom.*

"Hello," a deep voice said to my right, startling me back to my surroundings. The Lukub Champion smiled. He was an attractive man, his skin a few shades darker than Sefa's, with a twinkle in his eyes that dazzled several servants into overpouring his drink. He was tall, likely close to Arin's height, boasting a hard body familiar with years of labor. "Sylvia, is it?"

"Yes! Timur? Or was it Mehti? Forgive me, I have abstained from meals all day in preparation for the Banquet. I can hardly think," I reached for his arm, swallowing down my shudder at the contact. It was easier to bear a touch I had initiated. As predicted, the wariness smoothed from around Timur's eyes. I beamed, squeezing his arm once more before releasing it. "I loved your introduction! The red fire was just…" I gestured wildly, as though plucking the proper words from the storm of my appreciation proved too difficult.

Timur laughed. Good. The Champions would not be comfortable

around the Nizahl Champion if they thought I was anything like my host Heir. I needed them relaxed.

"Thank you," he said. "It is a pleasure to meet another Champion from the lower villages."

The Orban Champion, Diya, glanced over. I had fixed her in my periphery as soon as she sat. About her, Arin had had little to offer. A fact that bothered him to no end, I was sure. Diya of Orban possessed no distinguishing talents. She was short and curvaceous, holding her drink like someone might try to poison it. Arin told me Sorn's decision to choose her as his Champion had mystified Orban, and at first impression, I echoed their confusion.

"I believe the Orban Champion is also a lower villager in her kingdom," I said magnanimously.

"Interesting that you should recall such a detail but forget Timur's name," Diya said without looking at me. She scowled at the servant who tried to pour red wine into her chalice. Her hair was shorn to her scalp on both sides, the long strands in the center smoothed to the nape of her neck. She pushed her fingers into the wavy brown locks, sweeping them to the left.

Timur tapped his spoon against my plate. "Ignore her. She intends to win the Alcalah through sheer unpleasantness."

Sultana Vaida tapped her chalice, silencing the conversation. White lined her eyes, bright beneath her crown. Rubies sparkled on the tight bodice of her ivory gown. A cape of white flowers flowed behind her, the scent pungently sweet, on the cusp of cloying. Another two hours, and she would need to replace it. The Lukubi dignitaries gazed at their Sultana with a reverence I'd seen reserved for the Awaleen alone.

"Thousands of years ago, our Awaleen made the heartbreaking decision to save the kingdoms they had founded by purging the world of their magic. Baira, Kapastra, and Dania gathered at Sirauk to plan how they would stop their brother. The Awal of Jasad could not be imprisoned, nor could he be killed. The magic in his blood had eaten at his humanity, and what was left cared little for the wreckage he wrought. Our brave Awalas, fearing their magic might lead them down a similar path, resolved to lay themselves in the same trap that would contain Rovial. Rovial followed Dania to Sirauk, plotting to attack the Awala of Orban. But she had secret intentions. You see, the other sisters were lying in wait. Lukub's beloved Baira approached from behind and encircled Rovial in her unbreakable embrace. Dania drew the runes on his forehead that would guarantee an eternal slumber. Kapastra of Omal raised her hands and activated the magic they had woven around the bridge. Scholars believe Rovial screamed so loudly, he brought the skies themselves crashing to earth. Clouds and thunder enveloped the siblings as they plunged from the bridge, sealing themselves in the waiting tombs below."

Vaida raised her chalice. Around me, everyone lifted their glasses. Paying homage to the sordid little tale. Rovial's magic, Rovial's madness. Synonyms in their minds. The fate of Jasad began on that bridge, and I revolted at clicking a chalice in celebration of it.

My neck prickled. Arin was watching. I had a part to play, and dignity wasn't included in my performance. I raised the chalice. My cuffs glinted under the red lamplight.

This is the freedom you seek, Hanim said. *Not to taunt stupid Omalian Heirs or scream or be strong, but to be silent. Freedom is truth, and you have not the bravery to speak it.*

"To our Champions. The Alcalah will make foes of you all, but you must remember: the Awaleen whom you honor in these trials were once family, and it was by working hand in hand that they saved us all."

"To our Champions!" came the cries around the table. Timur clicked his chalice against mine. My smile strained like a branch beneath a knee, liable to snap at any moment.

"Your Sultana is an eloquent orator," I said.

"Oh, you should hear her speeches during Sedain. She need but point her finger, and the crowd would follow her anywhere."

Sedain was Lukub's annual realignment of the mind, body, and blood. They fasted for three days. The first spent in scholarly study, the second in physical pursuits, and the last day in bloodletting. Leeches, thorns, or animal teeth would drain the "bad blood," leaving them cleaner and clearer. The bad blood, of course, being any trace of magic. Ha! Vaida would probably prepare a broth of babies' heads if it meant her kingdom could have the ultimate advantage over Nizahl—magic and readiness for war. One of which Jasad had lacked.

When they brought out steaming soups, buttered breads, and platters overflowing with roast duck and lamb, I forgot my ire and heaped my plate full.

The Omal Champion glutted himself on duck and gossip. To the regret of everyone seated within spraying distance, Mehti enjoyed doing both simultaneously. Heavyset and tan, the Omal Champion resembled the workers on Yuli's farm.

I worried that perhaps Felix had instructed him to commit mischief toward me. As the meal progressed, it became readily apparent I needn't have worried. The sum of Mehti's intelligence could fit into Sefa's thimble. The fourth time he slapped the rear of a passing servant, I could hold my tongue no longer. "Mehti, is it?" I asked. I made a show of glancing over at Vaida. "I would be careful if I were you. I heard the Sultana took the arm of the last man who touched one of her palace girls without permission."

Mehti wiped his mouth on his sleeve, thick brows drawing together distrustfully. "True?" he asked Timur.

Timur was a model of sincerity. "Very true. She would have taken his head were he not a noble."

The greasy duck wing in Mehti's grip hit the plate. "She took the arm of a *noble?*"

I pressed my lips together, suppressing a snort. Even Diya paused her chewing to listen.

Timur snapped a carrot in half. "To the shoulder."

The Omal Champion did not bother hiding his dismay. "Aren't Lukubi women meant to be..." He gestured, a half-hearted attempt at propriety. "More adventurous?"

"Certainly, but they have this peculiar need to choose who they go on the adventure with." Timur shrugged. "I simply hope they do not feel the need to complain to Vaida."

Mehti's hands did not stray for the rest of the meal. Timur winked at me, eliciting a genuine smile.

Dania's bloody axe. I wasn't going to enjoy killing him.

Full bellies fostered a geniality among the group. After obliterating the shredded fiteer dipped in jam and honey, everyone ambled to the courtyard. I leaned against the doorframe, surveying the festivities. Felix appeared at my shoulder, a chalice in hand and a false smile at the ready. We both stared straight ahead.

"Enjoying yourself?"

"Immensely," I returned. "Push any little girls in front of horses lately?"

His grip on the chalice's stem tightened, though his tone remained light. "The night is young."

If Niyar and Palia had not assassinated my father, it would be Emre attending the Banquet as the Omal Heir. Felix, Emre's nephew, would be another forgotten royal in the palace.

"When you lose the Alcalah, do you have a preference for your method of execution? I find myself partial to dismemberment, although I am open to suggestions," my cousin said, leering at a passing serving girl.

"When I become the Victor, how lavish will the festival in my honor be? Perhaps a festival after Mehti's loss would be too embarrassing. The Nizahl Heir came to Omal and chose a worthy

Champion, while the Omal Heir himself failed to do the same. Do not think of my success as your humiliation, but as a sorely needed gift to Omal."

Felix drained the contents of the chalice and smacked his lips together. "I think mounting your head in my private garden will be the best part of the year."

My hand fluttered to my heart. Enraging the Omal Heir while the amnesty laws forbade him from laying a single finger on me was entirely too diverting.

"Oh, how sad. I hope the next year is more rewarding for you."

Sorn motioned Felix over. The Omal Heir's hate singed the night air, and too many teeth gleamed in his smile. "I hope you last the first trial. I cannot wait to host you and your village rats in the Omal palace." Ominous promise delivered, he threw the chalice at a servant's feet and joined Sorn on the other side.

The courtyard danced with song and light. The musician strummed his lute, the sweet sounds drifting in the nighttime breeze. A gorgeous woman sprawled in Sorn's lap, pressing his chalice to his lips and giggling.

"Courtesans," a voice said near my shoulder. Diya watched Mehti lounge in the grass, balancing a bowl of grapes and strawberries on his chest. "Do you know what they call a whorehouse in Lukub?"

The Orban Champion didn't pause for my reply. "A house."

I eyed her. "They have different customs. We should withhold judgment."

Diya snickered. She represented Orban's colors in her simple calf-length moss-green gown, belted at her waist by a brown leather buckskin. Dania's battle bracelets jangled around Diya's bronze wrists. "How diplomatic."

Arin would want me to politely engage with her, gather what I could on the mysterious Champion. "Orban has its fair share of odd traditions."

Information gathering could wait. Felix left me in the mood to incite.

She lifted her chin. "We are an honor culture founded on long-held traditions. Lukub is the place disobedient adolescents run off to for a taste of debauchery. Don't seek to compare the two."

Sorn's girl appeared to be excavating his mouth with her tongue while another pressed kisses along his shoulder. I wanted to ask whether she considered exhibitionism particularly honorable. On her Heir, she'd likely celebrate it as a display of virility.

"Your Heir is not immune," Diya said.

Arin and Vaida shared a bench, heads bent together. A clearly private conversation, and the way Vaida leaned toward him signaled intimacy. I knew Vaida wanted to destroy his kingdom, as surely as I knew Arin would snap her neck without a thought. And yet, a lump formed in my throat.

I tried to quell the unfamiliar anger brewing in my gut. "How did you come to be chosen as Champion?"

A servant extended a tray of diamond-shaped makroudh toward us. I lifted one of the date-filled sweets and nodded my thanks to him. Diya waved the tray away. Happiness bloomed on my tongue at the first buttery bite. After nearly two months of Nizahlan meals, I was ready to bury myself in good food.

"I stabbed my mother and father forty-three times each," Diya said conversationally. I choked on the second bite, sending crumbs flying. She continued, "His Highness Sorn saved me from hanging. I possessed a quality he wanted in Orban's Champion. There is date paste on your dress."

I patted my dress, assessing the diminutive Champion anew. "Eighty-six stabbings, and not a single wrist cramp? The Alcalah will be no trouble for you."

Diya sniffed, and her haughty aloofness reminded me strongly of Rory. "It was not a heavy knife."

Before I could fathom a response to such a statement, Timur loped over, blowing on the steaming surface of his mint tea. "This seems like the best corner of the Banquet," he said. "Mainly because it's missing Mehti."

The Omal Champion delighted a few courtesans by demonstrating how quickly he could crawl backward on his elbows.

"Crawling on one's elbows is a critical skill for a Champion," I said. "As well as a crab."

Diya seemingly reached her capacity for companionship. She darted to the swan pond without a goodbye. Timur leaned on the wall next to me, dipping the mint leaf in and out of his tea. "Did she tell you how she was chosen? You have the same expression I did when I found out."

"Should I be alarmed that I'm more intrigued than anything else?"

I popped the rest of the makroudh into my mouth. Conversation with Timur came too easily. Marek and Sefa would probably like the Lukub Champion.

"Absolutely."

"Damn." I clapped the traces of the dessert from my gown, slackening my muscles in fake disinterest. "How about yourself, Timur? Why did Sultana Vaida choose a lower villager as her Champion?"

"Ah, I fear my tale is not so compelling. I frequented festivals across Lukub for years and won all the sparring matches our towns hosted. Sultana Vaida's army general invited me to the Ivory Palace to meet with the Sultana. She asked me to be her Champion, and I said no."

I glanced at him askance, waiting for the guffaw and the knee-slapping. "Pardon?"

Timur drained the rest of his mint tea. "I said no the first time. My mother and two sisters are entirely dependent on my wages, and I did not have the luxury of working alongside the necessary training. The Sultana said she would pay them my wages herself. She offered more, but I did not want rumors to spread about the Lukub crown needing to buy its own Champion, not after Sultana Vaida's kindness. Once I am Victor, my family will have much more than what I made as a stonemason."

"Bit of an ego problem in Lukub, I see."

Timur slapped the wall behind his head as he pushed off. He bounced on his heels. "Are you saying you worry about losing the Alcalah?"

I matched his smile. His death would be gentle. An apology as much as a mercy. "Of course not."

The full weight of Mehti barreled into Timur, taking him to the ground. The Omal Champion straddled the Lukub Champion and lifted his arms to a swell of applause. "The key to a surprise attack—" Mehti began.

Timur planted a foot on Mehti's chest and shot the other Champion halfway across the courtyard. Mehti rolled down the slope, coming to a stop at Diya's feet. She stepped on his chest and kept walking.

"What is he like?" Timur asked, sitting cross-legged on the grass. I did not need to follow his gaze to know who he meant. There were not many men a Champion might revere.

"Efficient." I glanced over to see Vaida shifting closer to Arin, sealing their bodies together from shoulder to hip. She spoke to Sorn as her hand drifted toward Arin's knee. Arin reached for a chalice from a servant, subtly knocking her wandering hand aside.

Timur groaned. "You trained with Arin of Nizahl for months, and the best word you have is *efficient*?"

"What do you want to know, Timur?" I said, caught on Vaida's second attempt to reach Arin's knee. She was relishing his resistance. "He is brilliant. Cold, cunning. He eats too slowly, has an unnatural fixation with maps, and if you leave him near clutter long enough, he'll either kill you and organize it or organize it and kill you."

"Much better," Timur said. "I cannot comprehend how you managed to train with the Nizahl Commander. I can't hold a conversation with him without dissolving into a puddle of sweat." A servant circled with cups of muhallabia, snagging Timur's attention. The Lukub Champion rushed after him, sparing me a wave.

I didn't notice how long I'd been watching Arin and Vaida until Jeru appeared.

"Don't worry. She cannot play games with His Highness," he reassured me. "Stronger wills than hers have tried."

Arin posed an impossible challenge, and the Sultana savored nothing more than doomed effort. "Is it too early to go to my room, do you think?"

"I believe His Highness wanted you to—"

I swept past Jeru, lifting my skirts as I climbed the steps. "*His Highness* is preoccupied." Jeru made to follow. I twisted around, thrusting my hand between us. "I can find my room myself. The moment I shed this gown, I'll be asleep. We have a long journey ahead of us, and I am weary. Come guard my door only when the revelry has ended. Your disappearance would alert the others."

Though clearly conflicted, Jeru stayed behind. I weaved past the servants clearing the banquet hall. My boots clicked loudly up the staircase, empty of the bustling crowds. Closing the door between myself and the rest of the palace allowed the tension to drain from my shoulders.

Why should it bother me if Arin and Vaida chatted the night away? If she decided to touch his knee and whisper in his ear, was it any business of mine? The audacity of her, to keep making overtures and delighting in his careful ways of rejecting them.

A knock at the door interrupted my internal war. "Who is it?" I called.

"Ava, milady. They said you might require some assistance removing your gown." The young attendant's voice trembled, likely nervous to be caring for a Champion alone.

I'd forgotten the sheer volume of ties on this gown. Hooks criss-crossed in the back, covered by a panel of delicate lace. Bless Jeru, he must have realized I wouldn't be able to reach the hooks on my own. To be fair, I could just as easily cut myself out of the dress, since I never planned to wear it again.

I opened the door, ushering Ava inside. Her hair fell in long curtains over her face, and she kept her head down. The demurest Lukubi I had met yet.

"Shut the door, please. I won't need help with anything else tonight," I said. I gave her my back and tossed my gloves onto the bed. "Tell Zizi and Mirna not to trouble themselves."

At least I would be rested for tomorrow's journey. If Arin asked after my abrupt departure from the courtyard, I could fabricate an illness.

I held still, but Ava didn't reach for the ties. I glanced over. She had her back to me as she rifled through her bag. Calming herself before fumbling with my hooks?

Sighing, I turned to her. "I can do it my—"

A dagger plunged into my chest.

Time crawled to a stop. It took a deep breath, gathering itself, before everything exploded into chaos.

I acted without thought, instinct racing faster than sensation, and grabbed the hilt before Ava could withdraw it.

In the split second when she and I stood close enough to share our breath, I spotted the shifting contours of a glamor. I blinked, tugging at the corners, and the glamor shattered.

"Hello, amari," Soraya whispered.

No. No, no, no. It wasn't possible. This couldn't be real.

I stumbled away, holding the hilt steady. The world spun, and the dagger spearing my chest did not compare to the pandemonium breaking loose inside my heart.

"You're dead," I gasped.

Soraya's long curls were gone, replaced with a short, straight cut. The black waves framed a young face aged beyond its time. She would be twenty-seven years old now, maybe? Tiny scars littered my former attendant's fingers.

"Does it hurt? It shouldn't. I'm sorry. I had to do it quickly," Soraya said, staring at the dagger with concern, as though it appeared in my chest during a casual conversation. "If I hesitated, I would have lost my nerve." She dropped heavily onto the bed. "Killing you is the hardest task I have ever accomplished, and the worst."

This was too much. I couldn't set this aside. I couldn't think through it.

Soraya was here. She was *alive.*

And she had come here to kill me.

I rapidly ran through my options. Soraya's position intercepted my path to the door. Assuming the other attendants were innocent of this scheme, they wouldn't know to check for me this early in the evening.

"Your glamor must be excellent." I slapped my palm against the wall, resisting my knees' determination to crumple. Red-hot pain seared through my chest. "To sneak into the Sultana's personal staff."

Soraya's honeyed eyes gentled. How dare she? She had no right to look at me like she cared after—after—

"Not really. I kept out of sight, and the glamor distorted any flashes someone spotted."

We stared at each other, and the stinging betrayal won over the anger. My voice trembled. "Why did you do this to me?"

Immediately, Soraya's eyes filled with tears. "I did not want to, Essiya. I prayed you had died quickly at the Blood Summit. I never wanted you to know this." Soraya's face hardened, a terrifying rage flashing across her features. I had never seen her look anything other than patient or quietly amused. "I should have known Qayida Hanim would ruin everything."

"Ruin everything by not *murdering me?*" I choked out a laugh. "All these years I thought fate could not curse me with anyone worse than Hanim, and all along, you—"

Indignation yanked Soraya to her feet. "If she had done what she was meant to, none of this would be happening! Our entire effort would not be at risk because Jasad's rightful Queen still lived!" Soraya paced my chambers. "I should have suspected. She had already ruined our plans once."

The pain in my chest flared, maturing into an agony I could hardly think past. My stubborn mind raced, struggling to make sense of what Soraya said.

"It's you," I gasped. "You are the rogue Mufsid. You attacked me in the woods with Hanim's specter."

I coughed, spattering the bedsheets red. Blood soaked through the front of my dress, staining my fingers. Roughly guessing, ten minutes remained before the damage she had done became irreversible.

"Yes, and if Arin ever bothered to sleep, we could have avoided this entire Champion farce. The others are desperate to catch you before the Urabi and bring you into our fold. They have forgotten why we were founded in the first place. I have not." The woman staring at me was pitiless. Worse than Hanim, because at least the former Qayida wore her hatred on the outside. "There is no place for royals in the Jasad we plan to revive. Your grandparents brought destruction to our people, and I will not resurrect the system that failed us over and over. The Mufsids were forged to carve change, to reclaim Jasad's power and grind our boot on all kingdoms that sought to destroy us."

Her lips trembled, and she picked up Rory's gloves. "No matter how much I love you."

I groped behind me, searching for anything I could use as a weapon. My fingers slid along, bumping into a curved protrusion. The windowpane.

"Love?" I whispered. I thought of Sefa and Marek following me into Essam in the dead of night to bury a Nizahl soldier. Risking death to find me after the waleema, throwing aside their lives in Mahair to become fugitives once more. "I know now what love should feel like, and it is not this."

Soraya pressed the gloves to her chest. "Do you know why I called you amari? It doesn't just mean 'my beauty.' Amari means 'my moon.' That is what you were to me. Constant and true. All I wanted was to make you happy."

Tossing my gloves aside, Soraya blew out a determined breath. "But it is time for the sun to rise over Jasad, Essiya. We have dwelled in the night too long."

"You're killing Jasadis, yet I am the system bringing destruction to our people?"

A frustrated Soraya did not watch me as thoroughly as a woeful one. She kicked my chair into the wardrobe, and I took the opportunity to press my palm to the window. I angled my body over the glass. I would need my magic for only a split second, but faltering would doom me.

Grief. Rage. Fear.

So much of each whirled through me, but which would I need to rile my magic?

"We kill only the Jasadis too weak to join the movement for our recovered land. It is a blessing that they should die at our sword than at a Nizahl soldier's." Feverish energy entered Soraya as she spoke. "Think of it, Essiya. A Jasad built on equality, without royals or nobles. No lower villages. Jasad's rich resources made available to any citizen who seeks them. This is what the Mufsids will build. The Urabi couldn't care less about the kind of kingdom they renew, so long as it is theirs."

This made the third time someone maligned the honor of my grandparents' regime. *A Jasad built on equality* sounded eerily reminiscent of *corrupt walls of Usr Jasad* and *no two more insidious royals have existed since them*. Hanim had loathed the Malik and Malika with every fiber of her foul being, but I had always assumed her tales were just that—tales. If half the stories she told me about my grandparents or the Jasad throne were true...

Hanim told me the wilayahs tried to overthrow my grandparents. She recounted rebellions and uprisings from Janub Aya all the way to Laf il Rud. The upper wilayahs rallying behind the crown while the lower ones burned crops in protest. But the Mufsids belonged to the upper wilayahs, and the Mufsid woman I'd met had made it quite clear they wanted me for my magic and my name. Who had they lied to—me or Soraya?

"My grandparents employed you. They trusted you with their daughter's Heir. Why would you accept if you hated them?" My voice wobbled. Why would she pretend to care about me if she didn't?

Soraya took a step toward me. Her eyes were wet. I did not believe the softness for a second. She had already proven herself a phenomenal performer.

"I had my reasons. Essiya, I never planned to care about you. I tried so hard to hate you, to see the rot of royalty in your sweet face. But you would wrap your arms around my waist and plant your little feet on top of my own and ask to keep me company during errands. You were the most affectionate, clever thing."

I could barely conceive of a time when I could embrace someone without panic raking nails into my skin. And affectionate?

The words struggled through the ring of agony burning in my chest. I did not have long. "Stop distracting me. Why do the Mufsids think Jasad was corrupt when it benefited them most? Why do you hate the throne?"

Soraya's eyes hardened. "You know why."

"I *don't*."

Soraya grabbed the sides of my head before I could react. Her nails dug into my curls as she brought my face close to hers. "Why was the Summit called? Before it was the impetus for the Jasad War, before it was the Blood Summit—why did the kingdoms assemble? What were they discussing?"

I tried to shake her hands loose without moving my torso. "I was a child! I don't remember."

Her fingers tightened painfully. "Amari, do you know why I let the Urabi find out you existed, though I despise those spineless brats? Why I broke from the Mufsids, a group I have led for half my life, when they elected to recruit you instead of bury you?" The rings of Soraya's eyes were flecked with gold. They burned into mine. "You have the potential and power to be worse than any who have come before you. You can reshape yourself to survive any conditions you are placed in. Who we are is where we were. Where we come from. The generations of our blood and our roots. But you… you broke a girl's arm for not climbing a tree with you and forgot about it the next day. You set Dawoud's most precious quilt on fire because he would not allow you to play with it in the courtyard, and then you asked him about the quilt not two hours later. Your mind is a maze of mirrors, reflecting only the memories you choose to save. The best thing Malik Niyar and Malika Palia did for Jasad was putting you in those cuffs."

My breath shuddered onto her forehead. What was she talking about? They put the cuffs on me at six years old. Before Soraya. How did she know about them?

"I asked her twice. If she was not going to use her arms to climb with me, then she didn't need both of them to work." The empty words came from somewhere far away, and *oh, oh, I remembered, Mervat Rayan and her red face, her grating screams, the bone peeking out of her sleeve.*

But no, Essiya was good. Wasn't she? Essiya was kind and compassionate, nothing like the girl Hanim made. How could she do such a thing?

Soraya released me with a dry laugh. "You will remember what your grandparents did when your mind reflects on the correct mirror."

She sighed, playing with the jewelry left out on the table. "I'm sorry it took so long to find you. You were extremely well warded after the Blood Summit, and no one searched very hard. We thought you were dead until a new recruit suggested we try searching for Hanim again. That time, the spell led us right to her grave. As soon as I saw it, I knew you were alive. I believed. We searched for you, even when the others called us fools. Your cuffs resisted the strongest tracking spells, and it took years before I found that ugly Omalian village."

How many Jasadis did she slaughter in her pursuit of me? How much more of our people's blood had her hands spilled?

My cuffs tightened. How many had *mine* spilled?

"You led the Commander to Mahair."

"Oh, yes. We were so concerned he'd kill you first. But of course, Arin can't turn away an opportunity." She said his name with familiarity, an exasperated fondness. "Is he still angry, I wonder?"

Before she turns around, Essiya, Hanim said. *Now!*

I still had so many questions, but Soraya would not kill another Jasadi tonight.

"Who are you to decide which Jasadis should live or die?" I snarled. "You are no better than the Supreme."

My magic pulsed lazily. I yanked at the thread, spreading my fingers wider against the thick glass.

Soraya's head whipped toward me, but it was too late. The glass exploded, raining shards around us.

I hurled myself from the window.

The fall didn't take long. A whistle of air, and I landed hard in a bed of flowers. The impact left me vibrating, limbs feeling drawn and quartered. My slippery hold on the knife's hilt went slack. Blood trickled leisurely toward my throat from the shifted position.

Distantly, I became aware of the shrill screams ringing around me.

I fixed on Soraya. She sneered from my window, framed in broken glass. She turned, vanishing into the room.

She'll escape. She's going to escape.

I'd landed in the patch of poppies from this afternoon. To my distress, blood dripped onto the crushed petals. Black spots danced across my vision, mingling with the stars overhead. If I died, at least the Ivory Palace was an enchanting last sight.

A crowd formed around me. Why were they milling about? They needed to find Soraya!

At last, Arin shoved past them. Relief washed over me. Arin would find her. He wouldn't let Soraya escape. At the sight of me, Arin went ashen and rounded on the crowd. "Get a medic!" he roared. Jeru and Wes ushered the onlookers away.

He dropped to his knees next to me. "Stay with me, Sylvia. Help is coming."

"She's escaping," I whispered. Arin pushed my hair from my face, bending closer. I turned my face into his hand, temporarily trading thought for comfort.

"What?" His worry bothered me. Why should he be upset? The Mufsid rogue lurked nearby. A person he had hunted almost every other day of our trainings.

"She's near. The Mufsids—*Soraya*. Go."

My meaning was unmistakable. Arin reeled back, shaking his head. "No. No, I'll help you myself," he growled. He started yanking at his glove. Jeru and Wes balked behind him. I sent them an invisible signal to intervene, to stop him.

"Arin!" With the last vestige of my strength, I snatched his sleeve. The action sent more blood spurting down my front.

I mouthed it over and over. *She's escaping.*

If he healed me in the vicinity of all these witnesses, we were finished. My secret exposed, and his plans ruined. But if he caught her, if I held on long enough for his return. If, if, if. It might be over.

A rough sound tore from Arin's mouth, a look of singular devastation shattering his lovely features.

I relaxed. He had decided.

With a low oath, the Nizahl Heir leapt to his feet. "Keep her *alive*," he snarled, with such blistering menace that Jeru and Wes shrank back.

He disappeared, several arms reached for me, and I gratefully relinquished my hold on consciousness.

ARIN

I t was her.

The name Sylvia had uttered was different from the name that had been given to Arin ten years ago, but he knew.

She had tricked him once. It would not happen again.

The horse beneath Arin leapt. They sailed over a water trough, scattering a penned herd of sheep. She was weaving, trying to dissipate the traces of her magic. But he could feel it gliding over his skin like the thinnest blade. She would not escape him this time.

Arin leaned forward, spurring his horse to dangerous speeds. She would find somewhere noisy to hide. There were plenty of options to choose from. The upper towns of Lukub were celebrating the Alcalah alongside the Ivory Palace. Crowds in red and white were strewn in the streets. Performers twirled on raised platforms, bare feet moving lithely to the beat of the tubluh. Everywhere, chaos.

A horse appeared next to his. "Your Highness, I came to help," Wes said. He was out of breath.

"Why are you here?" Alarm locked the muscles in Arin's body. "Is she—"

"No, no. The Champion is alive. Jeru and Ren are with her and the medics. I cannot be of service to anyone there, so I left."

Arin stared at Wes. He could feel the trail of Soraya's magic fading. If he had any hope of catching her, he needed to move. To cut her off at the alleyway behind the festival and win the game she had started when he was sixteen.

If he went after Soraya, Sylvia would die.

It was a fact. Her wound was deep. She had likely broken several bones in her fall.

Arin needed Sylvia to capture the Mufsids and Urabi. Apprehending Soraya would satisfy his ego, but not his mission.

A reasonable voice reminded Arin he could simply torture the necessary information out of Soraya. She had been with the Mufsids for many years; with pain's incentivizing persuasion, Arin could wring their location out of her. The Urabi's, too, he suspected.

All he had to do was spur his horse forward.

"Why shouldn't I behave as a killer if I'm to suffer the same fate regardless?" Fire danced in her hair. Vaun groaned. Her dark eyes, which should have been lit with the silver and gold of Jasadi magic, brimmed with pain. Pain so severe, Arin suspected she had stopped seeing it for what it was. She would have recast it as anger, as an inborn quality of her character. Incomprehensibly volatile, he had thought. Lack of emotional mastery. She probably thought the same. She was bleeding, right there in front of him, and the fatal wound wasn't the one either of them could see.

"If Sylvia survives, she will return," he told Wes. His loyal guard's eyes widened.

"Sire, you cannot mean to let her go. You have chased her since—"

Arin turned his horse toward the Ivory Palace and snapped the reins.

CHAPTER TWENTY-FOUR

I sank through clouds of mist and ash, grappling for purchase.

We were in a nursery, me and two other shadows. An infant slept in the corner.

"You cannot do this to him!" a frail woman gasped. Recognition rippled through my flickering body. Isra of Nizahl. Arin's mother. "He won't survive it. Please, Rawain, you have to wait."

The second shadow took shape. I stumbled back, hitting the baby's bassinet. The Supreme did not react, oblivious to my presence. Supreme Rawain regarded his weeping wife with disdain. "What do you care what happens to my son?"

"He is mine just as he is yours. Please, I beg you. Two years old, three. He'll withstand it then. Imagine the power of your ascension with a healthy Heir at your side. Your father had you. See how he prospers! When you become Supreme, Arin will be your Heir. Your legacy."

Rawain palmed the jeweled glass orb at the head of his scepter. The sight of it had his wife reaching for the infant, bundling him in her arms.

"Two years, not three," Rawain grunted. "He cannot remember the loss."

She rocked the child in her arms, stroking tufts of black hair.

Black hair?

Voices floated in the nothingness, calling my name. My false name.

The voices argued loudly. One of them, melodic even in fury, sent awareness trickling through the fog.

I was so cold.

The voice changed, coming closer. The lilting one spoke in gentle Nizahlan. I glanced at the place where my hand used to be, startled by a phantom pressure.

I landed in a void of darkness. Water lapped at my legs.

The darkness writhed, coalescing into four thrones before me. I stumbled back. My foot caught on the edge of a sheer stone. If I had a body, I might have bled.

Each throne save one held an occupant. They glittered with the glory of the stars and sun, the only light in a barren wasteland. They were time and life and death made magic, existing beyond the realms of earthly souls.

Reverent tears dripped from my chin, joining the shallow waters moving beneath the Awaleen.

"An eternity of sleep does not guarantee their safety," said Kapastra, beloved mother of Omal. "What if we wake?"

"What if we do not?" whispered Baira. Her beauty seared me so thoroughly I could not lift my gaze a second time. "What if we dwell between the bounds of life and death forever?"

"We cannot remain aboveground any longer," Dania boomed. "Our children need peace."

"Rovial ruined them. Why should we punish ourselves with him?" Baira rasped. "Especially since he is not even—"

"Fortify your faith in my prophecy, sister," Dania said. The Orban Awala's gaze lingered over the vacant throne, a grief older than the fabric of our world swimming across her features. "Infinite slumber is not our destiny. When—"

Dania paused. Her head turned slowly.

The darkness pulsed, and she took shape directly in front of me.

"You should not be here." Her power undulated the void around us. "Not yet."

She pressed two fingers to my temples. Warmth replaced the

encroaching cold, chasing it to the fringes. Colors filled the shadowy outline of my body. The mist whirled.

"Soon, Essiya," Dania promised.

I woke choking on a scream.

Eventually, my racing heart slowed. I blinked up at the roof of a tent, far bigger than the one I'd slept in during the trip to Lukub.

I sat up gingerly, waiting for the tearing pain from my wound. Nothing happened. I palpated my chest. Smooth skin met my touch.

A stirring to my right distracted me from my complete bewilderment. Arin slept soundly, an arm's length away from my makeshift cot. He hadn't woken. Crescent shadows circled his eyes, deep enough to bruise.

Pushing myself tentatively to a stand, I staggered under a spurt of dizziness and glanced down at myself. They must have cut me out of the gown. I had on a long woolen frock that fit too snugly around my hips. I'd been lying on several stacked bedrolls, yet Arin only had a thin quilt beneath him.

I eased myself through the flap in the tent.

Dawn hadn't yet breached the horizon. The air was warm. Far warmer than Lukub. The soles of my feet brushed cracked earth, unsettling tiny pebbles of dry sand. This was an Orbanian landscape. Had we crossed the border?

I soaked in these little marvels, grateful to be alive for them. Nine smaller tents clustered near Arin's. A mighty procession of horses whinnied, clomping their hooves against the ground.

How long had I slept?

The guards on sentry duty came into view. I ducked into the tent, not ready to be seen or spoken to.

Arin jerked to his feet, blade aloft before he'd fully roused from his slumber. I raised my arms.

"You're awake," he said. The blade fell to the ground.

"Yes, and you shouldn't be." I frowned. "A rambunctious leaf could knock you over. Come, take my cot."

Rendered inanimate by exhaustion, the Nizahl Heir simply stared at me. I gestured for the cot, and he followed the command without argument. Rovial's burning beard, how much had healing me cost him?

We sat across from each other.

"You have an unpleasant habit of nearly dying," Arin said.

"Twice does not a habit make." I tapped the newly repaired place where Soraya ran me through. "I suppose I have you to thank for this?"

Arin exhaled. "I could heal the wound only in increments. I had to wait until you roused enough for your magic to respond. Two days, pressing your hand and waiting."

Two days? A chill traveled along my arms. Soraya had almost succeeded.

I raised my brows. "How? Weren't you moved to finish me off?"

"Every second I touched you," he said flatly. "It was...much harder than I anticipated. She did significant damage."

Shivering, I thrust aside the reality of how close I'd come to tasting death. "I suppose I owe you my gratitude. Thank you."

"Don't—" Arin cut himself short, more agitated than I'd ever seen him. "Keep your gratitude. Fortune alone saved you."

Fortune hadn't healed the hole in my chest, but I let it pass. I asked the most important question. "Did you catch her?"

Arin fixed his gaze on a spot over my shoulder. "She escaped."

I clenched my teeth, suppressing a slew of curses. The small part of me that loosened in relief went unacknowledged. Soraya was as dead to me as she was before the Banquet.

"We'll catch her at the Alcalah. We'll catch Soraya and the rest of the Mufsids."

"Why aren't you angry?" Arin snapped. "You nearly died to give me time to catch her, and I failed."

On a good day, I could eke out one or two visible emotions from the Nizahl Heir. A small smile, an eye roll. He was always tightly wound, a coil without a spring. The bruises under his eyes weren't the only markers of his fatigue.

"I imagine you've punished yourself enough. If anyone is at fault, it's me. I allowed an attendant to plant her dagger in my chest. She hid her glamor well, and I didn't think to check."

"Just to be clear," Arin said, heavy with disbelief, "your frustration stems from somehow not reading the intentions of a random servant, who you allowed into your chambers only after I asked you to?"

Halfway to opening my mouth to correct him, I paused. I would have to tread with extreme care in divulging information about Soraya. A single insignificant detail could be the key for Arin to piece together the truth of my identity.

I changed the subject. "She wanted to know whether you were still angry. Angry over what?"

Arin leaned back, once again averting his gaze. Dismay pushed me to my feet. "What are you hiding?"

The warning in his scowl was clear. "Leave it."

Leave it?

I paced the tent, willing my magic to settle. I didn't understand my reaction. Nothing had changed, not in essence. Arin kept secrets. Two Jasadi groups sought to reestablish Jasad. I worked with Arin to stop them. He had never pretended to be anyone other than himself. It was me who lacked any sense of self. Hanim, Arin—they knew my weakness, knew I could be shaped into a weapon and aimed in the right hands.

"I did not know her as Soraya," Arin said.

His ploy—and it was definitely a ploy, because Arin didn't tend to bandy about free information—worked. I stopped pacing, the panic ebbing in favor of curiosity. I crossed my arms over my chest.

Arin's features were carved from stone. "I met her in our academy when I was sixteen. She claimed to be the daughter of a traveling noblewoman. Her wealth and charm opened doors in Nizahl. In a few weeks, she gained my friendship and confidence. I admired her in every way."

Shock reverberated to the farthest corners of my body. How many ways could he mean "admire"?

His eyes chilled. "We became intimate. I didn't sense her magic— I suspect she was draining it regularly. She had designs beyond seduction, of course, and sought to fulfill them after I fell asleep one night. We had shared a bed for weeks. I still don't know why she chose to try her luck with my guardsmen right outside the door. I woke to her blade at my throat."

"Your scar," I whispered. My stomach churned. She'd come so close to success.

He nodded. "I disarmed her, but I don't know how I survived. I shouldn't have."

I shivered with a rush of loathing. At least I was not the only one on the receiving end of Soraya's dishonesty.

"I have the blood of everyone Soraya has harmed on my hands," he said. "Allowing her to escape the Citadel was my greatest mistake."

Thinking Arin wore his scar as a barrier between him and the world underestimated the Heir. He had plenty of barriers already. His scar served as a reminder. A debt to settle. His relationship with Soraya explained a few discrepancies. Vaun's rabid animosity toward me, Arin's visceral reaction to Marek's snide comment about a lovers' spat. The conversation between Jeru and Wes a lifetime ago.

"How did she escape?" I couldn't imagine such a deadly attack on the Nizahl Heir was treated carelessly.

Arin slid to his feet. "How do you think? Someone slaughtered the soldiers guarding her cell. Highly trained soldiers, barely older than you. They didn't have a mark on them, and I doubt they were given a chance to scream." Wrath tightened the Nizahl Heir's jaw, answering the question I hadn't dared ask. Any fondness he entertained for Soraya died with his soldiers.

An old conversation floated forward. My voice emerged in a wash of horror. "Wait. Hani. Kapastra's bloody hands, please do not say Soraya killed Marek's brother."

I grabbed the dresser to steady myself. Accepting that the girl who rescued me from a lonely childhood wanted to kill me? Fine. She was in good company. But this? What had my grandparents done to break Soraya so completely?

"Caleb's brother was among the slain," Arin confirmed. "It signifies nothing good that Soraya has gone against the Mufsids to kill you."

I hadn't realized the Mufsids had been operating for so long. I wasn't shedding tears over any Nizahl soldiers, but the number of Jasadis they must have hurt in all those years…I couldn't comprehend it. Hadn't we been through enough? The Mufsids and Soraya had no right to demand allegiance, no right to take what was not freely given. Someone should have noticed. Someone should have cared.

Dark threads of guilt spread inside me. Panic, the ever-present companion to it, crawled up my throat. I knew this feeling. Like I had failed a test designed for me to pass. This guilt had strangled me every day I lived with Hanim, and I had worked incredibly hard to leave it behind.

Nizahl ruined our kingdom, but you stole its dignity, Hanim said. *Do not pretend to care now.*

"Soraya will not survive the Alcalah," I vowed. I had not given my people much, but I would give them my promise. I dug my nails into my palm. "I swear it."

It took less than an hour to pack and prepare the horses. Arin left the tent while I changed clothes. Sefa and Marek entered halfway through, and I reassured them I was all right.

Since the brigade of soldiers accompanying us made anonymity

impossible, Arin chose not to board us up in the carriages. The
assembly formed a sprawling formation. Our horses ambled at a
steady pace over the desert stretching between Lukub and Orban.
Cracked yellow earth surrounded us, unraveling for miles on every
side, broken only by the white-capped mountains in the horizon. A
most bizarre landscape of seasons. I preferred the arid environment
to the wet chill of Essam, but I hated how exposed we were.

Up ahead, two soldiers spoke to Arin. Or tried to, anyway. The
skinnier one seemed unable to drag his gaze higher than Arin's chin.

Why would Soraya try to kill the Nizahl Heir instead of the
Supreme?

*"Stay away! I won't let you touch her," Niphran shouted. She swung my small
frame into her arms, backing away. I twisted my neck to see Dawoud approach my
mother with both hands raised.*

*"The Malik and Malika want the second Heir to join them for supper. No harm
will come to her. I promise you."*

*Sweat dripped onto the arms I'd wrapped around my mother's neck. Her whisper
was visceral with fear. "I know what they want to do to her."*

Wes snapped his fingers inches from my face, startling me. "Sylvia?"

Kapastra's horned beasts, what was that? A memory or a dream?

Soraya's words echoed in my ears. *Your mind is a maze of mirrors,
reflecting only the memories you choose to save.*

A headache threatened at my temples. "How much longer?" I
asked Wes.

"Not much," he said. "How do you feel?"

"Hungry. I'm expecting a feast to rival all feasts upon our arrival."

Wes smirked. "The Champions do not gather after the Banquet.
They'll deliver trays to your accommodations."

I groaned. "Who knew I would long for your tooth-chipping
bread, Wes?"

"You can chew on your horse's harness. It's probably softer."

We rode in companionable silence. The soldiers near Arin strayed to the fringe of the assembly, leaving him solitary in the center. Surrounded by those who would die for their Heir, and yet few who could muster the nerve to speak to him. His hair shone near-white in the sun's glare, tied neatly behind his head.

"He went back," Wes murmured, so quietly I almost missed it. I tugged on the reins, slowing my horse's pace to match his. Putting distance between us and Arin's keen ears.

"Went back to what?"

"After His Highness set off to chase the rogue, I left you with Ren and Jeru and followed him," Wes said. "He pursued her through the upper town and ran right into a festival. She vanished in the melee.

"But see, Sylvia, His Highness has memorized every map for every kingdom in existence. He has succeeded in trapping offenders under far more complicated conditions. He could have found a path around the festival and cut her off."

He paused. I made an impatient noise. "What stopped him?"

The glance Wes shot me held enough fresh insolence to put Vaun to shame. "He made a calculation in that moment between the time it would take to capture the girl and the time you had left. He made his choice."

I was at the waleema, facing down Felix's guards.

I choose her.

"I don't understand," I said. Desperation colored my voice. "Why would he go back for me? He's a practical man. He's been after her for years." What did it matter if my death was a possibility? My death was a possibility in the Alcalah, too.

"It wasn't a choice based on practicality," Wes replied, his tone implying I had exceeded every limit of naïveté.

Ren steered his horse to us. "We're here. Sylvia, you'll go through alongside the Commander."

I pursed my lips, relieved at the disruption. This was too much information for someone who had spent the last two days asleep.

The soldiers spread into formation as I galloped ahead. The Meridian Pass loomed before us, a gigantic reddish-brown rock formation sloping into a steep gorge. In the otherwise barren land, the Meridian Pass blotted the sun. The canyon splitting the center of the Pass couldn't fit more than two riders side by side. Half the cavalcade went in front of Arin in the narrow canyon, and the other half lagged with the guards.

Moss grew in bold swaths over the sheer red crags. A brewing sense of *wrong* slipping along my spine intensified as we neared the foreboding crevice.

"I remember the massacre," Arin said. I jumped. The first fleet disappeared into the Pass. I patted my skittish mare's head. "I was seventeen and just appointed Commander."

We approached the narrow opening. The horses spooked easily, and I tucked my knees tight in case mine tried to buck me off.

"I didn't authorize it," Arin continued quietly. "There were children. The soldiers acted the way the former Commander taught them."

The former Commander, his father. The crags cast a long shadow over us. An impenetrable silence hung in the canyon, broken by the sound of hooves clicking against rock. Dust swirled lazily in the gloom, and I struggled to see the soldiers ahead of us.

"What would you have done differently?"

It dealt him a hard blow, my question. Arin's breathing changed, coming in harsh bursts. His knuckles whitened around the reins. "I am not—"

He inhaled sharply, bowing forward under a sudden pressure. I finally turned to him. "What's wrong?" I demanded. I searched for a secret assailant. "What's happening to you?"

His gaze emptied. Bluish veins strained under his skin. I doubted he could hear me.

"I am not my father," he whispered.

Ren rode forward from the brigade forming the rear, pulling his horse alongside Arin's. "Sire, our scouts have not reported in. I think we may have lost con—"

An arrow speared through Ren's eye.

Screams split the air around us. Arrows rained into the canyon. Ren's body slid from his horse.

A gasp died on my lips. I caught the reins of my horse to keep it from lurching over Ren. Sefa and Marek! Where were Sefa and Marek?

I couldn't leave Arin in this condition. His gaze was glassy, unaware of anything outside his head. Magic. It had to be. But why only him?

The amount of power necessary to trap Arin in this state was staggering. It should have passed through him quickly, through whatever breach in his biology allowed him to sense magic in the first place.

An arrow flew into the throat of the soldier ahead of us. The Meridian Pass flickered, and suddenly, it was my father on the horse ahead. His features slackening in death as blood poured in an inverted V around the arrow cleaving his throat.

"Wake up!" I shouted, shaking Arin's arm. "Please!"

My magic slammed around my cuffs, agitated. I had to stop the arrows. This was a Jasadi attack, and I did not need to venture a guess what they wanted. How could Arin allow us to risk the Meridian Pass? We were waiting targets down here.

The soldiers would protect their Heir. Sefa and Marek only had me.

Grief. Rage. Fear. I had no doubts as to which was motivating my magic this time.

When I pushed my magic toward him, it complied. I could only hope it wouldn't hurt him more. I had neither the skill nor the time to form a proper shield.

With great difficulty, I turned my horse away from him and spurred it on. If anyone was going to kill Arin of Nizahl, it would be me.

Dust and pebbles churned over the canyon, obscuring my vision. A boon. The soldiers wouldn't see me toss my horse's reins to the side and leap onto the side of the Meridian Pass. The smooth rock face slid beneath my boots, but I had climbed worse. With a push from my magic, I scaled it quickly.

I hauled myself to the top of the canyon. Arms grabbed me. A dozen bows took aim at my face.

"You need to stop," I panted. "Do what you will to the soldiers, but I have friends down there."

"It is you." A man lowered his bow in disbelief. He studied me as though I might disappear at any moment. "Malika Essiya."

The group on the opposite side of the canyon was still shooting arrows. Every muscle in my body was tensed for a scream I recognized.

"Are you...the Urabi?"

He nodded, pressing a palm to his heart. One by one, the other archers lowered their bows. "My name is Efra, Mawlati. We have come to rescue you."

The next time I saw Soraya, I would make her gargle with all the teeth I planned to knock from her mouth for leaking the news of my existence to the Urabi. They were looking at me with a reverence I didn't deserve, calling me by a title I left in the ash with my grandparents' bodies.

She had plucked my nightmare into reality. My heart pounded in a familiar song: *run, run, run.* I was watching Niphran burn on a lake. The kitmer pacing around me, waiting. My knees buckling beneath the weight of the crowd of shadows on shore.

"He is using me to lure you to the Alcalah," I said. "You have to run."

Efra stared at me. "The Nizahl Heir knows you are a Jasadi?" And then, with blistering accusation, "And you agreed to help the silver serpent lure us to our deaths?"

"Will someone grab her? We need to move!" cried a bowman on the opposite side.

Efra's disgust filled me with shame, and shame was an old friend. My heart slowed.

The Meridian Pass vibrated. New shouts alerted the Urabi. Some lifted their bows; others, their hands. Rotating through the finite supply of magic at their disposal.

Like a black cloud rolling over the horizon, hundreds of Nizahl soldiers marched onto the Meridian Pass. An object with three sharp spearheads landed next to my foot. The rope on the other end tightened, dragging the three-headed hook to the edge of the cliff and catching.

My lips parted. Arin had not led us into a vulnerable position by choosing the Meridian Pass. This was a calculated trap. A moving piece on his game board. He knew an attack at the Meridian Pass would be impossible for an enemy to resist.

"They're climbing!"

We had seconds before they were upon us. These Jasadis would be slaughtered. They had committed crimes against other Jasadis, yes, but they were not for Nizahl to punish. My magic brimmed against my cuffs, eager to assist.

Clouds of dust still swirled around the canyon, granting me the perfect cover. I raised my hands, twisting them in the air as one might squeeze a wet rag. My magic pulled taut. Waiting for my command.

"It's a trap!" I shouted. I shot a desperate glance at Efra. "They will kill you!"

Knowing Arin intended to capture these Jasadis did not mitigate my horror at seeing it before my eyes. The first soldier's head appeared over the cliff. The Urabi were out of time.

I couldn't watch a Jasadi die again. I hadn't felt responsible for Adel, but the Urabi were here for me. Because of me.

You said our lands. Our villages. Not "the Jasadis'."

I threw my arms open. A high-pitched whine reverberated in my ears. Magic poured from me in waves, each stronger than the last. The ground beneath us quaked. Dust exploded as rocks cascaded down the shaking slope.

Through the haze, I spotted Efra. Shock had frozen him in place, and the Urabi yanking at his arm seemed unable to dislodge him.

The ground shifted. With a roar of detritus and dust, each side of the Meridian Pass moved apart. I touched my cuffs. They singed my fingers. My magic…it was splitting the canyon wider.

When I glanced back, Efra was gone. The Nizahl soldiers in the canyon were tripping over the bodies of their fallen fellows, stumbling in the force of the shaking earth.

Relief poured through me. The Urabi had escaped.

I scanned the fallen bodies, heart in my throat. I did not see a head of bright blond hair or black curls.

The Meridian Pass finally stopped moving. I grabbed the rope the soldier had thrown and fixed the sharp end to the earth. My feet glided down the side of the canyon.

"Sylvia!" came Sefa's shout. She and Marek were far ahead, barely visible at the other end of the canyon. Jeru waved from Marek's right. He must have whisked them to safety.

Oh, thank the tombs. I exhaled, pressing the heel of my hand to my forehead. They were alive.

I found Arin immediately. Instead of being surrounded by his soldiers, he was utterly alone on his horse. Bowed forward in the same position of agony I had left him in. How? The Urabi had departed and taken their magic with them.

It must be another force. Magic in the crags itself, undetectable to all but Arin. He had mentioned his father. What if it was remnant magic from the massacre? Remnant magic was rare, but the violence of the deaths here might have been enough to leave a trace.

Wes rode right past Arin, neck craned in search. "Where is the Commander?" he boomed.

He couldn't see him. Kapastra's crooked horns, I told my magic to shield him, and it rendered him invisible.

A whisper of alarm snaked through me. I had expended more magic than all the Urabi attackers combined. I should have felt exhausted. Half-dead.

I sprinted toward Arin without a hint of fatigue. I grabbed his coat and pulled myself onto the horse. Wresting the reins from his slackened grip, I snapped the horse into a trot. Arin didn't react, trapped in his torment.

"Leave him alone," I growled to the nothingness. My magic pulsed. I did not know how to repel the crags, but I had an acceptable grasp on how to block their influence. My cuffs burned as my magic cut off the insidious power assailing Arin.

His muscles loosened fractionally. I hadn't blocked everything.

I slid one arm over Arin's midsection. The other went across his chest, crooked so I could clasp my hands together at his shoulder. A diagonal, backward embrace. His heart raced beneath my wrist. "One, two," I counted. "You're alive." I tightened my hold as his shallow breaths came faster. "Three, four. You're safe."

I didn't know if he could hear me. Would a distraction help? The tools at my disposal were few, so I employed the quickest. "I was a mean child and an eternal nuisance to my caregivers. In Jasad, our fig and date trees sometimes grew into one. The gardeners would weave these hybrid trees into creations you cannot even imagine. A labyrinth of branches almost as tall as the obelisk in Vaida's palace. I used to find the highest spot in those trees and draw for hours. I'd enchant the cicadas to swarm groups of children or create leaf monsters to skulk behind the fruit merchants and scare their customers. A boy once told me the black spots on strawberries are dead spider eggs, and I have not eaten a strawberry since."

The rise and fall of his chest started to even. Encouraged, I continued, "The woman who raised me after Jasad fell is why I cannot tolerate touch." The words stuck in my throat, unwilling to budge. Ashamed. "I miss her, sometimes. I hear her voice, scolding or taunting me, guiding me in danger. I hear her more than my own mother. Five years of terror and pain, and I have the nerve to *miss her.*"

A gloved hand slid over mine. I startled, rushing to withdraw my arms. Arin's grip tightened. "Don't."

After a few minutes, I relaxed. I rested my cheek against his coat. It carried his scent, a wonderful amalgam of ink and rain. My eyelids dropped.

Ah, the exhaustion. I was not immune to it, after all. It pleased me, sharing such a small but universal Jasadi experience.

I must have dozed against Arin's back. When I opened my eyes, we had cleared the canyon, and dozens of soldiers surrounded us. Arin's expression was carefully blank. Dread turned my stomach. Nothing good ever accompanied Arin's detachment.

He flicked his wrist without turning away from me. The soldiers rode away, fanning out like ants in the desert. We dismounted.

"The attackers' magic moved the canyon. Pushed it farther apart and knocked my soldiers loose, allowing the Urabi to escape." His voice was flat. "Might you know anything about it?"

"If you plan to dangle your hook in the water," I said hotly, "you would do well to inform your bait."

"We have an agreement." His threat was almost obscured by the condescension of its delivery.

"I am still here, aren't I?" I spread my arms wide. "If I had wanted to leave with them, I would have. I said I would compete for you, not help you catch them."

I had foolishly lowered my guard, forgetting how suddenly and deeply Arin's icy demeanor could cut. It yanked the tail of my hurt and snapped it into a frenzy. I took a step, bringing myself close to the Heir.

"You are right. You are not your father. Rawain is cruel by nature, but you?" I lifted my chin, spearing him with the full force of my wrath. "You are cruel by choice."

CHAPTER TWENTY-FIVE

The soldiers carried the bodies of their fallen into Orban after dusk.

Wes and Jeru took me straight to the Champions' Pavilion. Five homes built a quarter of a mile from one another formed a loose semicircle. Every home had a kitchen, a washroom, and two sleeping quarters. The royals stayed in King Murib's castle. The Pavilion was prepared for the Champions every three years and housed Orban's grain stores the rest of the time.

Unlike Lukubis, Orbanians rejected all extravagance. Early in the Alcalah's history, they had tried to force the Champions to stay in tents.

Moss had completely obscured the fifth house. Vines draped around the former dwelling of the Jasadi Champion. The home was a blight upon the Champion's Pavilion to some, an uncomfortable reminder for others.

Guards from Omal and Lukub swarmed in the tight circle around the Pavilion. The Nizahl soldiers split from us, joining the ranks. Soraya's attempt to kill me during the Banquet had clearly motivated Arin to restructure my protections. I passed no fewer than twenty soldiers plastered to the front of the house. Soraya and the others would need to evade layers of security to get to me.

Inside the Nizahl Champion's home, I hung up the garments I would need for the next few days. Sefa had created a spectacular gown for the Victor's Ball. The elite celebration for the winning Champion took place the evening after the third trial.

Would I have the chance to wear this gown? Any one of these trials could be my last. Though they claimed death was not the standard in the Alcalah, previous years indicated otherwise.

Something shattered outside. Before I could think, I was putting the wall at my back and crouching behind the wardrobe. My hand found my heart.

One, two. I'm alive. *Three, four.* I'm safe. *Five, six.* I won't let them catch me.

"Sorry!" came Jeru's faraway shout. I exhaled roughly, collapsing from my crouch. The Mufsid woman, Soraya, the Urabi. The slew of near-death encounters was finally catching up to me. Was I destined to spend my life waiting for the next net to sweep me away?

I counted my heartbeats, finally moving from behind the wardrobe by number sixty-seven. Sefa and Marek entered shortly after with trays for supper. They were stationed with the rest of the Champions' traveling staff, so I wouldn't see them again until after the first trial. Assuming I survived, of course.

I could barely listen to their conversation. "I think I should sleep," I said, interrupting Marek's tirade about Jeru's lack of hand-eye coordination. Apparently the shatter had been Marek's favorite cup.

Sefa's forehead puckered. "Marek, give us a moment."

I settled back against the hard mattress. I already missed the Ivory Palace's luxuriously soft pillows and bed of feathers. "Sefa, if you are going to give me another speech about adventure——"

"It isn't by choice."

I stopped fussing with the atrocity Orban called a pillow. Sefa spoke with uncharacteristic solemnity. "What isn't?"

"I overheard you at the Meridian Pass. You told Arin he was cruel by choice, but Sylvia, it isn't choice."

How Nizahlan of her to say.

My thoughts must have revealed themselves in my scowl. She huffed. "I went to school with the Heir. We were years apart, and

I rarely saw him. But everyone at the school had a key parent in the Citadel, and children listen. The Heir was never uninjured. His mother was a nervous woman, obsessed with protecting her son, so none of us understood how he managed to keep breaking bones. I heard from a friend of a friend's brother that at ten years old, Arin had recovered from his very first stab wound."

"*First* stab wound?" I asked faintly. Rovial's blessed beard, what was happening in the walls of the Citadel? "Who?"

"Assassins, maybe? We could only speculate." Sefa sighed. "A painful past is no excuse. I would never defend the Nizahl Heir to you. But I wanted you to know, because...the way he looks at you sometimes. Like you are a cliff with a fatal fall, and each day you move him closer to its edge."

"He believes in magic-madness. Jasadis will never be people to him. He will always think it is only a matter of time."

But as I said it, a different conversation rose to my memory.

We build our reality on the foundation our world sets for us.

Sefa patted the spot next to my hand and left. I lay on the slab of torture King Murib saw fit to call a bed and gave myself to thought, an activity I generally took great lengths to avoid. My mind was not a place to stop for the sights, but Soraya's speech about mirrors and memories continued to plague me. She had lied about so much. I should know better than to believe anything she said.

A rap came at my door. I recognized the cautious knock and sat up.

"Enter."

I waved Arin inside when he lingered at the threshold, and he closed the door behind him. We regarded one another for an endless beat, each gauging the atmosphere. I pushed what Sefa had told me out of my head. I wished it mattered, but it didn't. I could not judge an Arin I had never met. This version was the sole Arin at my disposal, and it alone would stand trial in my eyes.

He spoke first. "I should have told you I was expecting the ambush. I knew the lines of your loyalty, and I chose to push them anyway."

I narrowed my eyes. Was he apologizing? To *me*?

"My soldiers would not have killed them. They are instructed to take them to Nizahl for trial."

"Please," I said. "I respect you too much to think you could ever be so foolish as to believe those are two separate fates."

I couldn't bring myself to stoke the same flames of fury back to life. This night might very well be my last, and I didn't want to spend it as angry as I spent the rest of my days. An apology was more than I could have expected. "I'm sorry about Ren." Despite my dislike of the guardsman, he had been loyal to Arin.

"Me too." Arin shut his eyes for a second. I wondered if he was seeing the other soldiers Soraya had killed. Adding Ren to the tally of his failures.

"I am not sorry about interfering. You cannot ask me to actively assist you in capturing Jasadis. My only part in this is to compete in the Alcalah."

Arin's brow furrowed. "I didn't ask you to assist. It was meant to proceed without your involvement."

My lips parted, winded from the blow. He had expected me to do what I did best: stand idly by. Maybe I would have, had the arrows not put Marek and Sefa at risk. Most people feared what they were capable of doing, but I...I was starting to fear what I was capable of ignoring.

"So you aren't angry anymore?"

He lifted a shoulder. "The power you displayed will encourage the Urabi to utilize every resource to capture you. When they come again, I'll be ready."

He didn't elaborate, and I did not ask him to. No matter what the voice inside me urged, this was not my battle. I wouldn't let it be.

"Sylvia." There was a strange note in the way he said my name. "You helped me in the Pass. The magic might have driven me from my mind if you had not stopped it."

"Arin." I said his name the same. "You are more miserly with your gratitude than with your praise. Just say thank you."

Arin gifted me one of his rare smiles. My stomach clenched, and it took an inordinate amount of time to tear my gaze from his mouth. He should know better than to share his smiles with me. I should know better than to crave them.

"Thank you," he said softly.

Rarely did fortune place me in an advantageous position, and I would not see the opportunity wasted. I hadn't forgotten Arin's agonized state in the Pass.

"How can you sense magic?"

In Arin's world, information was a transaction. He did not gift it freely, and he certainly never wasted it. The price for this information was prohibitively high. I had nothing to barter for it. I hadn't possessed an ulterior motive for helping him in the Pass, but Arin would sleep better if he thought I helped in anticipation of this moment. Just another material exchange removed from the vagaries of emotion.

He nodded to himself, as though he had been prepared for my question. "I will satisfy your curiosity, Suraira."

He lowered himself to the chair across the bed. With the moon casting half his face in shadow, his back straight and gloved hands curled over the arms of the chair, he was an artist's dream.

"As Heirs, we inherit the enemies and debts of our father. I am my father's sole child. I represented an invaluable emotional currency for his enemies. The Citadel was well protected, and my mother rarely left my side." Arin turned his cheek to the window. His eyes dissolved in the moonlight, swirling in its colors. "When I was two years old, my father executed a Jasadi merchant found guilty of enchanting the weapons of Nizahlan dissidents in the lower villages. There was an outcry from Malik Niyar and Malika Palia. They had wanted him punished in Jasad. Two weeks later, a musrira misted past our guards and into my bedroom."

I frowned, tempted to interrupt. I had begged Dawoud to introduce me to a musrira when I was a child. Most Jasadi magic did not show a preference in how it was expressed or exhibit an affinity toward a particular use. Musriras were one of the rare exceptions. These Jasadis possessed the ability to move through space in spirit. They could vacate their physical forms in a safe place and spirit themselves anywhere they wanted to go. Usr Jasad had been warded to the teeth, but even our most powerful security barriers could not keep out a musrira.

"She cursed me. We believe she intended the curse to kill me, but my mother interrupted halfway through. The curse took only half effect. I woke up three days later with a new attunement to magic. I could sense it, feel it." He turned away from the window. A strand of silver hair came loose at his temple. "Temporarily drain it."

"You said…you once told me my magic felt strong. If it pains you to touch me now, when I can barely use a fraction of it, what would happen if my magic were free?"

Arin raised his chin, unmoved by the question. It must have occurred to him soon after the events in the Relic Room.

"I can't know for certain what would happen if your full magic was accessible. I might be able to drain it normally. Maybe I'd never reach the bottom of your magic's well, so to speak, and could only temporarily drain portions of it," Arin said. "But if you want my strongest theory, I suspect touching you while you can fully express your magic would kill me."

He offered it calmly, as one might report the presence of rain in the clouds. It took me a minute to gather myself and collect the jaw I'd dropped. "That is quite a theory." One I doubted had any shred of likelihood. My magic was powerful, but not to the extent that draining it would kill him. That *touching me* would kill him.

"Anything else?" Arin braced his hands against the arms of his chair, clearly ready to conclude the conversation.

The dreams I had plummeted through after Soraya's attack. They were only dreams, but in one of them…

"Was your hair black before the curse?"

I might have asked if he licked muddy horse hooves from the shock flickering over his expression. Kapastra's horned beasts, could there have been a measure of truth to those dreams?

I thought quickly. Arin would want to know how I knew, and "I saw it in my dreams" would not serve me well.

"Sefa told me she heard a rumor at the school you attended together."

The tension relaxed fractionally. He was still suspicious, but my answer must have been acceptable enough for the time being. "I see." He stood abruptly, straightening the lines of his coat. "You should sleep. I will come escort you to the trial tomorrow."

A resounding end to the conversation, then. My questions about the full scope of his curse lingered, but he had given me plenty to consider.

"Of course. Yes. I will see you in the morning." A wave of inexplicable sorrow crested over me. For better or worse, tomorrow would usher in the beginning of the end. End of Essiya, and maybe the true start of Sylvia. I covered by dipping into an exaggerated bow. "Good night."

Arin studied me. My smirk faded. I had worn a thousand faces in my twenty years. Fooled friends and enemies with my false names and empty smiles. But sometimes, like now, Arin gazed at me a certain way, and I thought he saw it. My true face, hidden beneath the debris.

I wondered what it looked like.

I wondered why in a world ripe with monsters and magic, only he could see me so clearly.

"Good night, Suraira."

They summoned the Champions at midday. We had two hours from then to reach the cliffside on the other end of the forest. The first three Champions to cross Ayume Forest and climb to the top of the bluff would move to the second trial. I followed the rest of the Champions down the damp, winding tunnel. Each step added a fresh wave of anxiety. The tunnel would take us to the edge of Ayume.

Slightly ahead, Diya walked with her shoulders pulled back. Water droplets clung to her shorn hair. Timur and Mehti spoke in low tones, and I stared at the back of Timur's head until he glanced over. He waved, pointing at Mehti with a coconspiratorial eye roll. I smiled back.

The Lukub Champion would die today.

Someone cleared their throat pointedly. Diya slowed to match my pace. "Do you think they have an alliance?" She nodded at Timur and Mehti.

It seemed more likely Mehti had trapped Timur in conversation, and the Lukub Champion's politeness kept him captive. "Why? Are you suggesting you and I form one?"

Diya scoffed. "What value could an alliance with *you* provide?"

"Now, Diya. How did you know insults were the way to my heart?"

Instead of a snide retort, Diya pinched her nose. "Do you smell that?" She glared at Timur. "It's coming from the Lukubi."

I snorted. Her antipathy for everything Lukub had no bounds. From the gloom ahead, five narrow sets of steps ended the tunnel. Five steps for five Champions. Everywhere we went, Jasad followed.

Diya took the steps to my right, Mehti to my left.

"May we share the Awaleen's fortitude and see each other again in joy," Timur said. I prodded around the thin canvas covering the opening, rising to the top step. The other Champions copied my position, palms pressed to the canvas.

"For Baira!" Timur bellowed, and leapt through the canvas. A beam of sunlight poured into the tunnel from the new opening.

"For Kapastra!" Mehti shouted, vanishing after him.

Dania and I glanced at each other in silent understanding. I peeled a corner of the canvas back and peeked around. When I couldn't find any animals or waiting threats, I nodded at Diya. "Would you like to dramatically fling yourself first, or shall I?"

"I hope Ayume has a taste for empty air," she said. "It will find plenty between their ears." Diya pulled her knees to her chest and drew herself through the opening.

I tightened my stomach and vaulted up. The sun blazed overhead, stinging my cheeks. The cheerful conditions clashed with the smell assaulting my nose. Sweet decay with a rotten edge. I had doused many a cloth with an identical-smelling substance during my route, including the one I used to put Zeinab's mother to sleep.

Ayume's assault began with its very air.

We were permitted to bring only a small dagger with us. Holding my breath, I pulled mine free and cut a large triangle from the bottom of my tunic. I tied two of the ends behind my head, covering my nose and mouth with the makeshift mask. The protection it afforded would dwindle the longer I remained in the forest. Rationing my breaths was critical.

The landscape was identical to the drawings I'd looked through my first week. The hill sloped into a lake running along the perimeter of the trees. The forest stretched like a roll of darkness, dense and lethally quiet. Beyond it, the clouds cut around our ultimate goal: the cliff.

I took a step down and nearly lost my footing. The hill was steep, covered in loose dirt and sediment. I tried to squint past the sun's glare to study the dimensions of the lake. If it stretched too widely at this juncture, I'd need to double back. Any error would waste precious time and put me closer to traipsing Ayume in the dark, the effects of the sour-smelling air dulling my senses.

Stabbing my dagger into the soil for leverage, I hiked down the slope in stops and starts. The sun cast dazzling white diamonds on the lake's surface. Spiderlike eddies traveled into the main body of water, the lake's glittering surface disappearing between the trees.

My reflection stared nervously up at me. After the Urabi's attack in Essam, I had practiced climbing the rope against the river's current for a week. Forced my body to push forward despite Hirun's indomitable insistence to the contrary. I heard Arin's stern warning as if told in the present. *Dark magic is embedded in Ayume, and nowhere more so than in its lake. The lake is a void, with water more viscous than sand. Under no circumstance should you allow the water to submerge you completely. Keep your head aloft. Let yourself sink, and the lake will never release you.*

If not for the scarcity of daylight, I could circle the lake and forgo crossing it completely. The Alcalah tested more than an ability to finish; a Champion's physical prowess came second to their ability to balance choices. Discernment, Arin called it. Filling my chest with the tainted air, I sealed my lips shut and waded into the lake. The water was shockingly cold, and it sucked at my legs, coaxing me deeper. I twined my hands behind my neck and lifted my chin. The water hugged my waist, lapping higher with each step.

When the water reached my shoulders, the ground disappeared below me. I lowered my arms and kicked, paddling through the tar-like water. The weight of the lake was a rebellion against logic, and my lungs burned for air before I was halfway across. Something long and slippery wrapped itself around my thigh, winding around my leg. It flitted away, but not before terror filled the limited capacity of my chest.

Have you forgotten our first lesson? Panic erases all skill, any training. Keep your head and do what needs to be done, Hanim commanded.

I tipped my chin back, keeping my face pointed to the sun as the water swallowed my neck. The water hardened. My legs slogged uselessly against the resistance. The lake caressed my cheeks, sliding at my lower lip.

Is this how Fairel had woken up after the horses trampled her legs? Fairel, who had only wanted to protect Nadia's chairs. She would never join the young women balancing pots on their heads as they ambled through Mahair. She would never chase the ducks escaping Yuli's farm or scale Essam's trees. Fairel would lead a full life, because her spirit demanded nothing less, but it was not the life she would have had if not for Felix of Omal.

Pain pricked in my deadened arms. Magic flooded my body, and I gasped as sensation returned to my limbs. The water loosened around me, becoming malleable again. I swam, relishing the sharp discomfort of the cuffs, and nearly wept when I made contact with solid ground. I staggered from the lake. Any attempts to save my breath flew away as I panted like a dog in an Orbanian summer.

I needed to find Timur. The sun sank lower in the sky, casting long shadows from the trees. It had passed like minutes, but I must have been in the lake close to an hour.

As soon as I got to my feet, a shrieking bird dove toward me. I shielded my face as it tore into my sleeve, clawing my arm. I slashed my dagger at it and ran into the trees, leaping over bushes with vines writhing like serpents. Leaves sharper than glass rained around me. Timur should have finished crossing the lake already, unless he tried to cross at a wider juncture of the lake. If Mehti and Diya reached the bluff before me, Timur would lose his chance at the second trial.

Without my interference, he could not cry sabotage to Vaida. He would not die in Ayume.

I tore away a branch clinging to my vest, straining to hear the other Champions. A flock of birds screamed as they flew into the bladed leaves. Bloody feathers floated into my field of vision, and I stumbled over an eddy of water divorced from the lake. A rabbit lay sideways in the shallow pool, enveloped in the void but for a single, open eye.

The battle of Ayume had warped this territory into a sick mimicry of nature. Dania's twisted magic saturated the very pores of Ayume. The Orbanian forest survived as a relic, a living massacre, kept sentient by the blood of Kapastra's fallen soldiers surging through the forest's veins.

I lost track of time as I cut through the forest. When the trees thinned, I unfurled my clenched fingers from around my dagger and panted. The white cliffside loomed ahead, its edge a crooked line along the sky. Sunset threatened on the horizon. Had any of the other Champions already reached it? Had they climbed the bluff?

I pressed the cloth closer to my mouth, sipping the air and running my gaze over the vast line of Ayume. Where were they?

"You finished first."

I wheeled around. Timur tossed a rock from hand to hand. Sweat shimmered on his forehead, and his words came sluggishly. He had inhaled too much of the toxic air.

"I wish you hadn't. I wish Her Majesty had been wrong, just this one time."

Essiya, back away, Hanim said suddenly, urgent. *Get away from him.*

"What do you mean?" I asked. Behind my back, I pulled my dagger free and planted my thumb on the base. "Are you all right, Timur?"

I already understood. Had I not been embroiled in the muck of my conscience, the possibility would have been glaringly obvious.

Vaida needed her Champion to win. I remained her biggest obstacle. If I would not concede defeat, I would be stopped.

"What did she offer you?" The sky clung to the vanishing sun as twilight painted orange streaks over the horizon. "Wealth? Protection?" I recalled our conversation in the courtyard. "Is she threatening your family?"

Timur's brawny arms trembled. He coughed, spitting a bloody wad to the ground. "My sister is dying. The supplies the chemists need to make the cure are limited, and we do not have the means to pay them ourselves. Sultana Vaida—she promised, she said if I made certain you lost the Alcalah, Maram would be taken care of."

"What about the riches awarded to the Victor? Surely such wealth could produce a cure for your sister."

Timur was already shaking his head. "There isn't time. There is one vial of the cure available now, and if you do not continue to the second trial, my sister will have it by this evening."

I wanted to throw the leaves of Ayume at Vaida, slice her layers of artifice and manipulation bare and toss what remained for the carrion-eaters.

"She created the problem, and now she bargains to fix it! Royals weave traps for the likes of us. They watch while we squirm and expect gratitude when they deign to release a select few from their web. I was a chemist's apprentice in Omal. The foremost chemist in the entire kingdom. I can help your sister, Timur. We will make more vials. You do not have to carry out Vaida's will."

"Knowing you are in a trap does not make it any easier to escape." Timur's eyes brightened with unshed tears. He shifted to the side, revealing a cavity in the gray boulders behind him. He hurled the rock into the cave. "Forgive me, Sylvia."

Three sets of indigo eyes materialized from the cave, and a guttural growl shook the earth.

At one point in time, the three nightmares emerging from the cave were probably average mutts. The mangy dogs Fairel loved, the ones most often covered in soot, found nosing through Mahair's smoldering garbage. Ayume had layered its evil over these dogs. Black drool dripped from jaws the size of boulders. Claws protruded from misshapen paws, and long, pointed teeth mashed together. They did not spare Timur a glance, but fixated on me.

"Diya smelled it," I realized. The dogs fanned into a semicircle around me. I hadn't thought much of it, reducing her comment to another dig against Lukubis. "You doused yourself in an odor before we entered the tunnels. It's keeping them away from you."

I ripped my gaze from the dogs long enough to snarl at Timur. "Follow me, Timur. Guarantee your mission is done, because if I survive, I will see your sister dead before any illness can."

The dogs howled, leaping. I tore into the trees. The lake's eddies extended into the forest. If I could find a branch of the lake deep enough to drown three dogs, I would be safe.

Timur crashed through the bushes behind me. The sun kissed the sky goodbye, the last fingers of light vanishing in the rush of evening.

The instincts I honed from the blindfolded runs in Essam sharpened with my spite. Arin prepared me to succeed when every condition demanded otherwise. I would not be ended by a pack of dogs in Orban.

My muscles became lethargic as I drew in gulps of air. The dogs nipped at my heels, their shrill barking grating against my ears.

"Essiya, come down from there! You'll hurt yourself!"

I barely kept from tripping over an overgrown root. "Dawoud?" I cried out.

The voices echoed around me. Ayume or my magic? *Why do you do that? Always pull away?* the wind asked in Fairel's voice.

Every limb in my body burned. I wanted to collapse, to rest for just one moment in the soft soil. I hooked to the right. Behind a cluster of abandoned nests, a leg of the lake appeared.

A few moments more and I would have reached it. But in my eagerness, I ventured too close to an emaciated bush. A branch wrapped around my ankle, nearly sending me to the ground. I yanked, and the branch tightened. I tried to climb the tree behind the bush and cut my palm open against the spiked bark. I was caught fast.

The dogs burst from the right, Timur close behind. Their muzzles opened in a macabre grin, and Timur turned his head. "Goodbye, Sylvia."

My cuffs heated. "If you are going to kill me," I seethed, "have the decency to look me in the eye."

I snapped my fingers.

The dogs froze mid-leap, their hateful indigo eyes leveled on mine. My magic ripped the branch from my ankle, but my body's suffering affected my magic, too. I stumbled with the release and caught myself on the tree.

"Y-you," Timur panted. He collapsed to his knees, the effect of chasing me apparent in his drooping features. The air would put him to sleep long before he could reach the cliffside, let alone climb it. "Jasadi."

Part of me insisted I leave Timur to sleep. The scent repelling the dogs could not last long, and they would eat him alive. The same grisly fate he reserved for me. With my magic warm inside my failing body, I forced the images of Sefa and Marek to replace the dogs. I ignored the evil roiling in this forest and surrounded myself with the meticulous jars of Rory's shop and the warmth of Raya's keep. These were the exceptions to my *grief, rage, fear* rule, but their effect on my magic was the same.

"I will grant you a kinder end than the one you planned for me."

I snapped my fingers. A boulder cracked against the side of Timur's head, and his wide eyes went blank. One of the dogs' paws quivered. I would not be able to hold my magic for long.

Skirting the dogs, I groped for a pulse at Timur's throat and groaned when one fluttered against my fingers. A dog's forked tail swished.

I stripped Timur's coat from his shoulders and put it on. There should have been enough of the scent left to keep the dogs from following me. I summoned the last traces of my receding magic and pushed my palm outward.

Timur's unconscious form floated, drifting past the dogs and over the bush. My arm shook with the effort of holding my magic. He needed to be lowered at the correct angle, or this endeavor was a wasted mercy.

The heat left my cuffs, and Timur's body dropped like a stone. He did not splash on impact. The water crept over him hungrily, inch by inch. The lake swallowed the Lukub Champion with a sigh. The rippling surface went smooth. Another life digested in the belly of Ayume.

Stumbling in the direction of the cliff, the world tilted and spun. I clenched my fists and whimpered at the resulting stab of pain from my right palm. A sticky wetness ran down my sleeve. I lifted my arm, narrowly avoiding another snaking branch.

Amber-colored sludge was stuck to the center of my palm, trickling over my cuff. The skin beneath bubbled with pink drops of blood.

Arin's warning. *In the future, avoid touching the trees while you run. Even the sap in Ayume can kill you.*

"May you fester eternally in your tomb, Dania," I spat.

Apprenticing under Rory did not come without its cursed knowledge. Though Rory created cures in areas where few solutions existed, even he rarely bothered with venom. From the pain radiating up my arm, I judged I had less than twenty minutes before the sap immobilized my entire body.

A rope dangled from the bluff, the frayed end brushing my

shoulder. The sheer rock face sneered down at me. The cliff cut into the night sky like a blade of darkness. I pressed my forehead to the crumbling stone and closed my eyes. Already, the fingers of my right hand hurt to fold. If my arm quit halfway up the climb, I might be able to dangle from the rope long enough for the air to finish its task and send me to sleep. At least then I would not be conscious when I plummeted to my death.

I tossed off Timur's coat and hoisted myself onto the rope. Bending my legs, I pushed off the cliff and used the swing's momentum to begin the climb. I clutched the rope with one hand at the bottom, one on top. I wrapped the knuckles of my bottom hand in the rope for leverage while the top one pulled me upward—an old trick of Hanim's to prevent sliding. The pattern held; I pushed off the side of the cliff and climbed a foot, swapping the bottom hand every few minutes. I tried to think of Fairel or Rory, Sefa or Marek. Anything to invigorate my magic. But my arms ached, and my eyes struggled to stay open. The sap pumped its poison through me, competing with the fatigue to see which could kill me first.

Instead of anyone dear to me, I thought of Soraya.

I had adored her so completely. Wept over her death long after the tears for my grandparents dried. She had loved me, too. But the hate...the hate that poisoned worse than any sap, that rotted Soraya and left behind the woman who stabbed me in Lukub.

A sudden wind batted me to the side. The rope catapulted me into the bluff. I hit the rocks and lost my grip, sliding down for a dizzying few seconds before I caught myself again. The friction from the rope tore my palms open, coating my forearms in blood.

Swaying gently, I tried to gauge how much left there was to climb.

"You're not even halfway there," a little girl said from my right. I jolted, the rope fibers digging into my raw hands. The little girl dangled from a second rope, peering at me with distaste.

It's not real, Hanim said. *It's the forest's magic.*

"I am not the forest's magic. I'm yours," she griped. "Hurry. You have moments left."

"Essiya," I breathed.

"Essiya," she returned. "Or Sylvia, I suppose, which is not the name I would have chosen. You named us after Soraya's mother. Little odd, isn't it?" The girl spun around on the rope. "Why are you keeping me trapped? We are going to die."

"I'm not keeping you—" I coughed, clenching my knees around the rope to keep from sliding farther down. "There are cuffs blocking my magic."

Essiya snorted. She twisted, hanging upside down. "Would you use me without the cuffs? You never do in your dreams. We just watch our mother and everyone burn."

"Of course I would."

"I think," Essiya barreled on, and Rovial's tainted tomb, had I really been such a nuisance as a child? "I think even if your magic was free, and you had every advantage to reclaim our kingdom, you still wouldn't save Jasad. You are content to live on the outskirts of other people's land, a vagrant in all but name. You blame Hanim for hardening your heart, but she is dead. Your heart belongs to you again, and you refuse to give it over to Jasad. That is why Soraya wants us dead."

I noticed belatedly my cuffs were vises around my wrists. My magic spread over my skin, numbing the worst of the poison's effects. I resumed my climb.

"You are bold for a hallucination," I snapped. "There are others capable of leading Jasad better than I could. What do I have other than a royal name?"

Essiya kept pace, climbing as I did. My hands were little more than raw meat, but the tingle of my magic prevented the agony from stalling my ascent.

"What else do you need?" Essiya countered. "The Mufsids and

Urabi combined do not have a tenth of the power you have. Yet they fight. The Jasadis hiding in Lukub, Orban, Omal, even Nizahl—they fight. Power is a choice, Sylvia. When you choose who you are willing to fight for, you choose who you are."

"Even if I do not win? Even if I am an insignificant wave in an ocean of resistance? There is every chance I can live a peaceful, mundane life as Sylvia. Nothing is guaranteed for Essiya. Not a good life, not victory, nothing." The jutting lip of the cliff's peak came into view. I grunted, tightening my stomach as I swung toward the cliffside. I kicked the hard surface, sending rocks tumbling below. "I should give up certainty, give up Sylvia, for a legion of faceless Jasadis?"

I reached for the edge of the cliff, missing by inches. One more swing, one more pull. A light touch at my wrist startled me from my destination. Essiya materialized in front of me, and we clung to the same rope. Kitmer-black eyes bored into mine. "All your choices require sacrifice. The question is, what are you willing to lose?"

Essiya released the rope, falling into the gloom. My magic slowed with her disappearance, and a cry tumbled from my lips at the renewed sensation in my palms. With a guttural shout, I hauled myself up the last foot, hooking my arm over the cliff's edge. I plunged the dagger into the dirt and dragged myself onto solid land. As soon as my knees were on the earth, I crawled away from the sheer drop and discarded the dagger. My blood left smears on the hilt.

A beat. I exhaled, tearing the cloth from behind my head. My magic receded more, exposing me to a riot of agony.

Countless lanterns seared into my eyes. Thousands of faces moved in my periphery, but none the one I wanted. The gathered masses gaped at me.

"The Nizahl Champion joins the Orban and Omal Champions in the second trial!" the announcer boomed.

The crowd exploded.

The cheering was muted, the spectators' colors reduced to moving dots on a rapidly darkening landscape. A tall figure appeared from the frenzied dots. "Sylvia?" Arin called. His low voice was the best sound I had ever heard. The Commander swore. "Get the canvas!"

I stitched together the words I needed and held up my palm. "Sap," I croaked. "For twenty minutes."

The last of my magic dissipated, and I sagged into Arin's chest. The Nizahl Heir's arms went around me, and I distantly registered that he was shouting, but I had ceased to care. He was warm and strong, and he smelled like the rain that never fell in Ayume.

I breathed Arin in, my head slumping over the crook of his arm as Ayume's air finally put me to sleep.

CHAPTER TWENTY-SIX

I would very much appreciate it if you could stop trying to kill me," Sefa said when I woke up. The physician jerked in the chair, then rushed to my side. My palms were wrapped tightly, but the worst sensation was the foul taste in my mouth. I was still in my quarters in the pavilion, so I couldn't have slept long. A day at most. I curled my toes and stretched, relieved when my muscles complied. I must have bled out the poison faster than my body absorbed it.

"You know, I expressed the same sentiment to Ayume," I said, slapping aside the physician's hands and sitting upright. Affronted, the medic stomped to his bag and bustled from the room. "Where's Marek?"

"He went patrolling with some of the soldiers," Sefa replied. "For someone who hates the Nizahl army as vigorously as Marek does, he certainly is capable of endearing himself to soldiers."

I grinned at Sefa until distress crawled across the other girl's expression. She probably thought I had suffered some mental affliction.

"You and Marek will not enter Nizahl. I made certain of it," I said. "Vaida will be displeased, but I have an idea to make sure she doesn't retaliate."

"Made certain of it how?" On cue, her brows pinched, forming Sefa's six columns of stress in her forehead.

"I did not slaughter any squalling babes, Sefa," I said. Timur was a fully grown adult when I drowned him. "What matters now is you and Marek can stay in Omal after the second trial without needing to accompany us to Nizahl."

Sefa, piecing together the Lukub Champion's death and her new-found freedom from Nizahl, did not share in my excitement. "And how exactly do you plan to keep Vaida from following through on her threat? Forgiveness is not a virtue shared among many royals."

"Her seal," I said. Seeing Vaida's ring open the doors to her disturbing underground room had planted the seed. My deal with Arin was well and good, but no plan was complete without a contingency. "I will need your and Marek's help to steal the Sultana's seal at the Omal palace. We can use it to negotiate our safety."

A knock at the door interrupted Sefa's response. She straightened, her petrified gaze colliding with mine.

"Enter!" I shouted. "Sefa, what is it?"

The door swung open, and my neck pricked. Eerie foreboding arrived seconds before I heard his voice.

"Our Champion wakes at last," Supreme Rawain said.

The axis of my world ground to a scraping halt. A quiet shatter echoed in my head.

A man with a raven-headed stick sits near a woman drowning in her Nizahlan garb. An older lady with soft brown eyes keeps glancing at me and then away. Teta Palia said she was the Queen of Omal, and I wasn't to speak to her. At the other end of the oak table, Gedo Niyar hands me a sesame-seed candy. Teta puts her hand onto my knee to stop my restless legs from kicking. I want to go home. Dawoud said he would take me to Har Adiween so I can climb the dancing trees. I glance around the table. Something important is being discussed, probably. I go back to staring at the raven-headed stick. I wonder if I would be allowed to hold it.

The man in violet and black catches my eye. He winks.

The table explodes.

Dangling from the rope in Ayume was nothing, *nothing* compared to the war waging inside me. My cuffs became shackles of fire around my wrists, damming the magic baying for violence in my blood. Furious tears gathered at the corners of my eyes. Iron filled my mouth as I bit my bottom lip. I wasn't ready.

I turned my head.

Thousands of Jasadis shadowed the Supreme. Their murky outlines warped, mournful, and folded into the scepter at his side.

My memory had done Supreme Rawain a disservice. Age had laid a conservative touch on his handsome features and powerful build. He was shorter than his son, but taller than me. Gray streaked the hair at his temple.

His eyes. The same unnatural shade that met mine the day I lost everything. The day he stole my world. As unblemished by the trappings of compassion or kindness as they had been at the Summit.

My bedridden state had one advantage; he would not question why I would not kneel, and I didn't need to explain that I would sever my legs before I knelt to him.

Supreme Rawain strode into the room. Framed in the door, Arin's indecipherable gaze followed his father.

"Well? How is she doing?" the Supreme asked.

The physician slunk back, clearing his throat. "Superbly, Your Highness. The venom has passed without ill effects, and the worst damage was to her palms."

Rawain clapped his hands. "Wonderful. You gave us a fright, Sylvia. I'll admit, I had reservations about Arin's choice of a Champion, but you have certainly lived up to his vision." He laughed, the sound sliding like viscous oil over my skin. "My son has been reluctant to introduce us. Worried I would intimidate you." He raised his brows at an impassive Arin. "See? She's of hardier stock."

I shook with the effort of crushing my magic back. It struck over and over, lightning charring its fragile vessel. Sweat beaded on my forehead. I needed to speak. My teeth were stuck together, and I had the most terrible notion that they were protecting me from what might fly out of my mouth if I unhinged my jaw.

Rawain did not seem concerned with my silence or inability to lift my gaze from his chest. "Since you're feeling better, I insist you join Arin and me for supper this evening."

"We leave for Omal at dawn," Arin said, speaking at last. "She should rest."

"And rest she shall," Supreme Rawain said. "After supper."

My cuffs seized, tightening desperately against my magic's assault. In a flash, Arin was between us. "I will have the guards bring her. We should go; King Murib is expecting us."

I wanted to shove Arin aside and lunge. Rip out the throat spewing poison, crush the head that molded its crown on the scorched remains of my kingdom. How dare he come in here and speak to me? To praise my efforts for him?

Grief. Rage. Fear. A pit of darkness fed my magic, and it chose which hand to help—and which to ignore. It cared for Jasad and for the ones I loved, but it would happily watch me scream beneath a beast's gaping maw or Hanim's whip without once stirring.

No wonder my magic never helped me. It hated me as much as I hated myself.

"Then let us be on our way. I can't tolerate another tour of his banal little weapons cellar," the Supreme said. He lifted his chin in disdain. "Who would steal from Orbanian huts and hovels?"

Rawain's voice moved to the door. I had both hands fisted in the quilt.

"Heal quickly, Sylvia. I look forward to acquainting myself with such a worthy Champion."

As soon as the door closed behind them, I keeled off the bed. I doubled over, wrapping my arms around my middle. The hurricane of my magic roared. Charring me to ash like the rest of my kingdom.

Isn't this what you wanted? Niphran's gentle but stern voice replaced Hanim's. *You wanted to be forgotten. Unknown, unrecognizable. You have succeeded. You are nothing more than Sylvia, Nizahl's Champion.*

"Sylvia?" Sefa laid a tentative hand between my shoulder blades.

"Don't touch me!" Every inch of my skin pulsed, as though it could shed itself for a new, better me beneath.

Several sets of footsteps approached. The guards' murmuring washed over me. The physician—or maybe Jeru—reached for me, only to stop short at my shuddering recoil. "I said don't *touch me!*"

"Leave her." Marek.

"Now," Sefa added.

The noise receded, and the door scraped shut behind them. I tore the wrappings around my hands, revealing perfectly healed palms. I hadn't needed Arin's touch to bring my magic to the surface this time.

Good. Rawain likes his property in faultless condition, Hanim sneered.

I wrapped my arms around my middle and rocked.

At the root of all chaos is reason. It was a comfort Dawoud would share with me when I was especially afraid or angry. He was raised in Ahr il Uboor, a wilayah with a population of seven hundred and, according to him, more fanciful stories than sense.

But the error of my existence was a chaos my mind couldn't reason. Four kingdoms living in harmony with Jasad for thousands of years had elected to invade and reduce us to rubble. We must have done something to deserve it. We must have earned the fate that befell us. Right?

I quaked in the corner and pressed my forehead to the wall.

For hundreds of years, Jasad has bled its glory from the lives it ruined.

Everyone talked about the fortress, Sylvia. It allowed Jasad to get away with doing whatever it wanted.

. . . it is time for the sun to rise over Jasad, Essiya.

Because if we did not deserve our fate, I could not bear the alternative much longer.

The next time the door opened, I stood in front of a row of gowns. My neck tingled as I adjusted the towel around my body.

"Which dress would the Supreme prefer for his Champion?" My voice sounded as empty as I felt. "I would not want to displease him."

When the silence lengthened, I glanced over my shoulder. Arin had stalled a mere foot away, staring at my back. I clicked my mouth shut. I had forgotten to cover the evidence of Hanim's favorite hobby. Until now, Rory and Raya were the only two with the misfortune of seeing my graveyard of scars.

"Who did this to you?"

I moved to face him. A glove to my shoulder kept me turned.

"That's none of your concern."

"These are old," he murmured. "Layered."

When his hand ghosted over my skin, I couldn't stop a shiver. He traced the gnarled path of flesh along my back. Assessing the defective condition of his Champion. I dropped my forehead against the wardrobe, forcing my ragged breathing to stabilize. I was not in a sane enough state to handle the Heir.

"These are from a jalda whip," he guessed. The pressure moved to my right side. "A switch."

I eased the towel's knot enough to reveal my lower back, morbidly curious. Could he put a name to every instrument Hanim had used against me? I couldn't.

"Is this an arakin?" he gasped, sprawling his palm against the base of my spine. I jumped.

"A what?"

"These were banned decades ago. Your scars—they can't be more than six or seven years old." He sounded furious. "Those crops do real damage. You might have died."

I tightened my towel and turned.

"Is an arakin the one with the poisoned metal spikes? Yes, those were quite inspired. Tipped with just enough venom to scream yourself hoarse for a week or so, but not enough to put an end to your misery."

"What—" He stopped. Closed his eyes briefly, gathering the words. The most articulate man in the kingdoms rendered speechless by Hanim's handiwork. "What happened to you, Sylvia?"

I laughed. It was alarmingly choked.

"You are not the first to use me for your own ends. I have a legacy of disappointing people, you see."

I kept my attention fixed over Arin's shoulder as he reached past me. He pressed a black gown with buttoned sleeves and a violet neckline into my arms.

"I am still waiting," Arin said.

"Waiting?"

I had learned to defend myself against every version of Arin. Devised strategies to safeguard against his ever-twisting mind and sharp tongue. But no one taught me how to protect myself from the Nizahl Heir when he looked at me like this—gentle, human, with his steadfast gaze pinning my own. Grounding me.

"To be disappointed."

Unlike the Ivory Palace, the Orban castle made for a modest sight. Painted an unappealing tan, it rose a mere three stories and stretched from the end of the Champion's Pavilion to the border of Essam Woods. What it lacked in luster, the castle doubled in protection. Orbanian khawaga were a deadlier, less disciplined version of the Omalian patrol. They settled disputes by their own exacting standards, and the stories of their abuse in the lower villages had circulated far. Fifty of them surrounded the palace, their curved janbiya daggers hanging from their belted waists.

At the main entrance, a khawaga held a snapping, growling dog by its scruff. I stared at it while Wes walked up to the khawaga. Would Ayume's dogs have sniffed around the lake's edge, pawing for Timur's corpse? Timur, who had loved his family enough to kill for them.

The sole adornment to the drab castle was on the double doors leading inside. A green-horned bull glowered as we approached, towering over us. My whole body could fit inside one of its flared nostrils. The bull's three tails stretched from one door to the other.

Three khawaga hurled their weight against the door, and it reluctantly yawned open to admit us. "The Supreme stays on the second floor," the khawaga grunted, eyeing the guards. "Do not wander."

Reed carpets crunched beneath us as we headed to the stairs. King Murib certainly adhered to Orban's spirit of frugality. Not a single tapestry or jewel decorated the walls. The stairs groaned under our feet.

Jeru and Wes took their stations on either side of the door. Inside the room, twelve chairs circled a rectangular table. The lanterns were shaped into Orban's bull, half its body coming out of the wall while a candle flickered in its gaping mouth. The servants lit the candles sitting along the table, bathing the room in an orange glow.

"Champion," a servant called. He pointed at a chair three seats away from the head of the table. "For you."

I took my seat and stayed still while the servants buzzed around me, laying out platters of rolled grape leaves, seasoned oxtail, and greasy ox hooves. Orbanian culture did not center around creative agriculture like in Omal. They ate what their soil produced, mainly dense grains and spring vegetables. Meat in Orban was a delicacy few could afford.

"Sylvia." I flicked my gaze from the empty plate. Arin had slid into the seat across from me. The door opened before the Nizahl Heir could speak.

"Excellent. You are both already here," Supreme Rawain said.

Violet ribbons weaved a complicated pattern on the front of his billowing robes, and each sleeve ended with Nizahl's royal seal emblazoned across the cuff. His ringed fingers closed around his scepter. The ensemble did not suit Orban's humble setting in the least. He took a seat at the head of the table. A servant went to close the door.

"Leave it. I am expecting another guest," Rawain ordered. "What a day. Murib speaks far too much for someone with little worth saying. Vaida could sing him off a cliff with two notes." The servant left a miswak next to each of our plates. Supreme Rawain tapped the tooth-cleaning stick against the table. "In the event a Champion does not escape Ayume during the first trial, Murib usually keeps a khawaga waiting on the cliff through the night. If the rope is untouched by dawn, the khawaga finds a better use of their time than waiting on a dead Champion. Did you see the Lukub Champion in Ayume at all, Sylvia?"

"No, my liege." I focused on a point past Supreme Rawain's shoulder.

My liege, Hanim repeated in disgust.

Rawain shook his head, leaning his scepter against the chair. "Vaida is insisting Murib leave a khawaga at the cliff another day. Murib is bowing to her will. Asinine. Anything crawling over that cliff's edge will be slain on sight."

A rapping at the door drew a smile from Rawain. "Ah, the last member of our company has arrived."

The door opened, and I glimpsed the identical alarm on Wes and Jeru's faces seconds before Vaun entered the room.

The Nizahl guardsman bowed deeply. "Your Highness. Commander."

A quick glance at Arin confirmed he was as surprised to see his former guardsman here as Wes and Jeru were.

"Vaun, sit. You and Sylvia are well acquainted already, yes?"

A pronounced limp slowed Vaun's gait, and he eased himself into a chair between Arin and the Supreme with a wince. "Yes, sire. We are." The Nizahl guardsman finally looked at me. Instead of the loathing I expected, vindictive glee animated Vaun.

This isn't right, Hanim said. *Rawain does not remember the names of guardsmen. He does not invite them to a private supper two kingdoms away.*

"Sylvia was going to tell us how she finished the first trial," Rawain said. He peered into his chalice, taking an experimental sip. He grimaced. "I am especially curious to hear how you climbed a rope with poisoned sap clotted on your palm."

Arin's plate remained untouched. I held his gaze as my cuffs tightened, my magic chasing the emptiness back to its dark corner. Only one possible piece of information could compel Rawain to invite Vaun against Arin's wishes.

Rawain suspected I was a Jasadi. Why else ask such a pointed question about the first trial?

Strangely, I found the prospect thrilling. Let him suspect I was his enemy. Let Vaun's accusation cut a place in his head and carve my name into his skull. I had lived in the maw of discovery almost my entire life, simply waiting for its teeth to close. But now... fear had spent its currency, and a more dangerous power paved the road ahead.

I smiled brightly at Supreme Rawain. "I climbed it the same way I would have without poisoned sap, just with more screaming. Sire."

Ah, I had missed Vaun's furious glare. His reliably terrible presence undid some of the damage I had wrought unto myself after Rawain's visit.

Rawain laughed, causing Arin and Vaun's heads to whip toward him. "My apologies for a silly question." He unrolled a grape leaf, evaluating the seasoned rice inside. He tried to rewrap it. "You were in a distressing state when you reached us. My son reduced several medics to tears."

"His Highness has been diligent in preparing me for the Alcalah."

I could play at pleasant if it would prove Vaun a liar. "I would have hated to waste his efforts in the very first trial."

"Yes, he is quite particular about such matters. Too particular, sometimes. But I could not have hoped for a more accomplished Commander."

Arin inclined his head in acknowledgment. His unease was obvious, at least to me—he'd carved the tip of the miswak into a point.

"How did the sap adhere to you?" Vaun said. "I expressly recall His Highness cautioning you against leaning on the trees."

I lifted a shoulder. Vaun wanted some incriminating answer he could pounce on.

"Fear renders memory obsolete. I reacted on instinct and suffered for the error."

"You were the last Champion to emerge, a full hour after the Omal Champion. How is it the air did not send you to sleep?" Vaun pressed.

Arin slowly turned his head to stare at his guard. Vaun quailed, shrinking in his seat like a reprimanded child.

"I tied a cloth around my mouth and nose to slow its progress. I am a chemist's apprentice," I informed Rawain. "I recognized the odor."

"Absolutely astonishing." Rawain leaned back in his seat. He cupped the scepter, running his thumb over the delicate glass orb at the center. "It reminds me of the Alcalah twelve years ago. The Jasad Champion bewitched the rope into lifting him over the bluff. The other Champions were furious at the injustice, of course. The Alcalah has been vastly more interesting with four competitors, since strength decides the Victor instead of happenstance of birth."

My cuffs became vises the moment "Jasad" left his lips. I clenched my teeth, barricading against the excess magic.

"I would have shared in the other Champions' fury," I said. "The honor of the Alcalah is not found in shortcuts."

"Precisely," Rawain said. "There is only treachery in magic."

If we pulled at this thread for much longer, my leashed magic would surge past the cuffs and send the table careening into Rawain. His scepter shimmered under the candlelight, diamonds of white sparking from the glass orb.

"The glass is impervious to breakage," Rawain said, following my gaze. "It cannot crack or splinter. It was a gift from my darling late wife after Arin's birth."

Pain pricked my head, and the memory bloomed like a drop of crimson blood. Isra of Nizahl seated beside Rawain at the Blood Summit, her hands knotted together on her lap. She had had the look of a woman always braced for the worst, and I'd met her gaze only briefly before she fixed it on some distant point. *Nizahlan women are so shy*, I'd thought, and preoccupied myself with the tassels on Teta Palia's sleeve.

She knew what was coming. She knew he was going to kill her along with everyone else, Hanim said.

"It is lovely." The scepter exuded malice. Steel claws closed around the glass orb, and a violet raven glared from the iron helm. Why my ten-year-old self had wanted to touch it was beyond me.

Every minute of the meal stretched into a millennium, and by the time the servants cleared away the dessert platters, I felt strung tighter than a lute string. Rawain's interrogation tactics varied in almost every way from Arin's. Rawain masked his careful maneuvering with good humor and charm.

At the meal's conclusion, Supreme Rawain approached me. My fingers twitched, longing for the dagger in my cloak's pocket. My cuffs were heated rings around my wrists, and if I released my hold on my boiling magic, I could drive Rawain's scepter into his throat without budging from my spot.

"I look forward to your success in the second trial, Sylvia," he said. I went stock still as he gripped my chin, pressing a light kiss to my forehead. "I have a sense you will be a merit to Nizahl."

CHAPTER TWENTY-SEVEN

In the five years I spent in Omal, I never once ventured into the palace town. Omal's palace was built in the center of the kingdom, a solid presence around which the coursing life in Omal flowed. Sefa and I craned our necks from the carriage window, ignoring Marek's teasing. Painted in the light blue of a spring sky, the palace dazzled at the heart of the upper town. Gates constructed from white agate circled the palace, opaque in the sunlight. The gates swung open for our procession. Compared to the khawaga and their mutts, the Omalian patrol was a welcome sight.

Four long pillars rose in the corners of the palace, capped with a sparkling sapphire cone. Glimmering domes separated each story of the palace. Seven rounded archways composed of alternating blue and white glossy tiles led past a gushing fountain to the front steps. The limestone above the arches was decorated with interlocking geometric patterns.

"No wonder the villages are starving," Marek muttered.

"I just want to sit somewhere and stare at it," Sefa said dreamily.

Stunning ceramic tiles composed the path to the entrance. I momentarily forgot we were entering the home of a man who had expressed interest in mounting my head in his garden.

The entrance to the palace nearly sent Sefa to the floor. Stretching higher than the archway, a rochelya composed of shimmering blue and white glass peered down at us. Kapastra's prized pet and Omal's symbol. The lizard-like creature's scaled tail curled around clawed feet. Sefa tapped the flat curve of its ear. "For good luck," she explained.

The doors were already open, a set of servants in Omalian livery waiting to receive us. We had arrived later than anticipated, and neither Felix nor the Queen was present to welcome us.

"Queen Hanan and her Heir look forward to your presence at dinner tonight," the head servant said, bowing. Arin's soldiers streamed around us, taking our belongings before the servants could.

Our footsteps echoed in the entrance hall. Sefa's elbow dug into my side, and she pointed above our heads.

Winding circles and diagonal lines rippled in tapering tiers from the peak of the palace over the decorated banisters and ornate walls below. The light refracted from each triangle was an opulence rivaling the open skies. "It looks like a honeycomb," Sefa said.

"They are called muqarnas," Arin said. "Omal is not their original place of conception."

"Jasad is," I said. Half the Omal palace possessed aspects of Jasad's architecture. "The only part that originates from Omal is the audacity. Muqarnas date back to Jasad's Awal. Rovial designed them for his kingdom. Each muqarna is meant to hold a small focal point of magic shining down on Jasad's vulnerable. The dying came to heal under muqarnas, and the heartsick found peace."

At Arin's narrowed gaze, I innocently added, "There was one in my villa at Ahr il Uboor." Mervat Rayan's villa could have been full of them, for all I knew. I still wasn't sure if Arin believed the Mervat story, but his attention seemed to have been temporarily rerouted thanks to Soraya and Vaun.

The sprawling halls were reminiscent of the twisting tapestries weaving through Lukub's Ivory Palace. Personally, I found Orban's economy of space more suited for safety, but at least here the Nizahl assembly had an entire floor to themselves. Chairs were placed next to doors, a thoughtful nod to the guards stationed outside our quarters. Sefa and Marek had shared a room in each kingdom we visited, and Omal was no exception. The head servant motioned at a door to the right, and Sefa bounded inside with glee, Marek following with their luggage. Jeru drew their door shut and set himself in front of it, ignoring the chair.

Arin's chambers opened in the very center of the hall, where an assailant would have to pass a sea of guards, but not so far that a shout couldn't be heard from the stairwell. Arin did not enter, but walked with me to the very last room.

"These will be the quarters for the Nizahl Champion," the head servant said. His stern civility reminded me of Dawoud. "There are attendants available to assist with preparations for tonight's meal or guide you through the palace. Please do not hesitate to call upon Omal's servants, and I thank you again for the honor of your stay."

Arin gestured at Wes. "Her door needs supervision every minute she is inside. Two soldiers may serve as a replacement for you or Jeru, but I prefer one of you be present at all times."

Wes moved in front of my door. He did not mention that this setup left Arin without a single guardsman at his own door. Apparently, it was more likely Felix had designs against me or my companions than the Nizahl Heir.

"We cannot leave any window for her or the others to move on you, not without losing the opportunity to capture them," Arin had said.

One benefit of having innumerable people trying to trap or murder me? No more attendants.

Arin strode down the hall, a retinue of soldiers falling into step behind him. He went past his quarters, and several soldiers broke off to stand outside the door. They shooed away attendants offering to unpack the Heir's belongings.

"I guess Felix is not as familiar with Arin's 'eccentricities' as Vaida is." At Wes's frown, I raised my hands in surrender. "His phrase. If you want to come inside and rest your feet, you are welcome. I do not see how Felix could attack me in a hall teeming with Nizahl soldiers."

"You do not see it," Wes said. "I don't. But the Commander does, and we will minimize the risk accordingly."

I rolled my eyes, kicking the door shut behind me. After the sparseness of the Champion's Pavilion in Orban, these rooms dripped with extravagance. Light streamed in from open windows shaped like crescents and triangles. A tiered chandelier held dozens of candles above a round table. A sculpted rochelya's long neck wrapped around the table, its stone tail winding up the table's leg. The bed could fit every girl in the keep, piled with frilled pillows and fitted with a patterned white headboard. I stood on the plush blue divan and peered out the window, leaning my elbows on the vaulted pane. The sky opened in a light rain.

We were in my father's home. Had he read his books by the fountain? Charmed a girl to round the gardens with him under the stars?

Queen Hanan was my grandmother, Felix her nephew. Rumor said Queen Hanan rarely left her wing of the palace anymore, not since losing her son in Jasad and her husband at the Blood Summit. Felix controlled Omal in all but name, and the evidence of his incompetence was everywhere.

The Omal palace had leeched its kingdom's wealth for its own. Lukub was the wealthiest kingdom because every citizen had a home to call their own, food in their bellies, and a trade to practice. Orban rejected the concept of hierarchical villages and towns, and one could only gain a title or a noble status from earning distinction in Orban's army. Their southern villages still fared worse than the rest, and I wondered if Orban's determination to claim equality in their kingdom kept them from seeing all the places where it crumbled. Meanwhile, Omal had the largest population, the wealthiest nobles, the most profitable markets, and yet its lower villages slipped closer to starvation each winter.

I flopped onto the bed, pitching the unnecessary pillows to the side. One of them sailed past the bedside table, sending an object clattering to the ground.

Kicking aside the overstuffed pillow, I picked up a gray clay doll. The toy spanned the length from my wrist to the tip of my tallest finger. Stiff black twine wrapped around it from head to foot.

The twine. The twine should have been unwrapped. Why was it there? The doll needed to breathe. It couldn't breathe with the twine around it.

Dreamily, I slid my nail under a strand of the twine and plucked. The doll slid from my grasp, slipping across my wrists before I caught it.

In a blink, my mind cleared. As soon as I separated the doll from my cuffs, the haze settled over me again, and I frowned at the twine. It should not have been there. The doll couldn't breathe. I had to give it back its air.

I dropped the doll and scrambled away. "Ghaiba," I gasped.

There weren't many people who would leave such a thing in my quarters. I used a discarded tunic to pick up the doll. Hesitantly, I pressed its head against my left cuff and braced myself.

Nothing.

Soraya had said my cuffs resisted the strongest tracking spells. I assumed the spells simply couldn't find any of my magic to track. What if my cuffs deflected some types of spells? If the runes kept my magic in, it was possible they also kept magic out.

Felix must have hoped I wouldn't recognize this terrible doll. Said to come from Lukub during Baira's rule, the ghaiba was an ancient entity that manifested as a shapeless, vicious cloud. Once inside a victim, it tore into their minds, distorting reality and showing them visions of every regret, agony, or secret doubt they kept hidden. If left inside too long, the ghaiba could leave its host catatonic or dead. After the entombment, Lukubis found a way to trap the ghaiba in these dolls and seal it with black twine. Hanim spent months trying to find one and test whether my magic could expel the ghaiba once it sank into me.

Why would he leave one in my quarters? If he was trying to intimidate me without alerting Arin, the easiest targets were—

I hurried from my room and shoved past Wes, breaking into a run. The hall stretched endlessly, and I nearly wept with relief at the sight of Jeru. A symphony of terror exploded in my chest when I threw open their door.

Jeru and Wes crashed into me from behind. Wes uttered a low oath.

"Get the Commander," Jeru croaked. "Now!"

Jeru tried to enter after me, but I shoved him back. "The ghaiba can split itself among multiple people. Do not enter."

I slammed the door shut.

Sefa and Marek floated in the middle of the room, their dilated eyes roving wildly, chasing the nightmares in their own heads. Their limbs dangled forward, twitching. The scent of spoiled eggs assaulted my nose. On the floor below them lay a doll identical to mine. Black twine hung limply from Marek's fingers.

Sefa's eyes rolled back in her head. She jerked violently. Marek's arm twisted to an unnatural position, and a guttural moan leaked from his open mouth.

The door burst open. Arin blew in, rain clinging to his coat and darkening his hair. He took in the gruesome sight and shoved the door shut when his guards attempted to follow.

He picked up the doll. "How long?"

"I don't know, I found mine five minutes ago." Marek's shoulder snapped back, and I shrieked. "How do we get it out?!"

He snatched the twine from Marek's grip. "Tie this around the doll."

Tying the cursed twine around the doll would flip the doll's compulsion, drawing the ghaiba out of its host. I wrapped the twine from the top to bottom of the doll. "Each of them has absorbed half the ghaiba. It'll take hours for the doll to pull it out of them!"

"I am aware," Arin said. He pulled off his gloves and shed his coat. "It might be to your benefit to wait outside." At my scowl, he clenched his teeth. "Then be prepared to catch them."

"What are you going to do?" I had an inkling, but it couldn't be right. He could not possibly be considering—

The Commander moved with the swiftness of a serpent's strike, grabbing Marek's exposed wrist in one hand, Sefa's in the other. Marek's deadweight fell onto the bed, and I rushed forward as Sefa tumbled. We collided in a heap next to Marek. I checked their breathing; shallow, but steady.

A loud crash spurred me to my feet. The doors of the wardrobe smashed to the floor, and the muscles in Arin's back went rigid as the ghaiba attacked the Heir. He doubled over, gripping a shelf in the wardrobe as his face contorted with agony.

A great shudder went through him. His knuckles whitened around the shelf. What doubts did Arin have that the ghaiba could feed on? What regrets?

I gripped his forearm, squeezing the stiff tendons. Touching him in this state was foolish, but I couldn't stand how helpless I felt. Another endless moment crawled past, and Arin exhaled, eyes flying open.

He tore his arm from me, the white sheen on his face dissolving with anger. "Have your limited senses forsaken you? I can scarcely bear your touch under the best circumstances. It only takes seconds to lose control, seconds to snap your neck."

"*My* limited senses? I am not the one absorbing ghaibas into myself! How did you even know your maneuver would succeed?"

Arin swept his hair from his forehead, pointedly ignoring my question.

I threw my arms up. "It was a theory, wasn't it? You calculated the likelihood your ability to sense magic would attract the ghaiba enough to leave Marek and Sefa."

"Close," Arin said, and offered no clarification. He sat with his back to the wardrobe. "The stronger the mind, the greater the ghaiba's challenge. I suppose it found me tempting."

"Do not do it again." The harshness of my tone took us both by surprise. I was still kneeling next to him, a persistent tremble working through me. The sight of Arin bowed in pain was not one I wanted to witness twice. "One day, you will miscalculate. You can't test a theory using yourself, do you understand? You are an Heir, there are risks you simply cannot take! It is sheer madness, irresponsible—"

"Breathe." With a wince, he reached for his abandoned gloves and put them on. His gloved hand covered the one latched to my knee.

"No."

Birds had practiced their sweet songs for generations, but even their music did not compare to the sound of Arin's laugh.

We stared at each other until the shadows in the room lengthened.

"Why do you keep trying to save me?" he said, and if I hadn't been inches from him, I wouldn't have heard it.

"Why do you keep needing to be saved?"

Oh, you foolish, foolish girl, Hanim groaned.

Arin seemed to realize his hand was still on top of mine. He straightened, clearing his throat. "You said there was a doll in your room?" Arin asked.

I shook myself, fumbling to withdraw the wrapped monstrosity from my cloak's pocket. I passed it over, avoiding Arin's eyes. He eased himself to his feet. I followed at a distance, moving to hover over Sefa and Marek.

"They haven't stirred," I said.

"They likely won't wake until morning." He nodded to their

discarded bags. "The boy unwrapped the doll soon after entering the room."

"He hates it when you call him the boy," I said.

"Yes, he does," Arin agreed. I rolled my eyes, tugging a quilt over the sleeping pair. Let it never be said the Commander was beyond pettiness.

"Felix will try again," I said. "We cannot accuse him of sabotage outright, and he is a conniving little rat."

Arin's smile was a figment sprung from nightmares. "Leave that to me."

The Omalian dining hall stole my breath as much as the rest of the opulent palace. A row of chandeliers twinkled along the middle of the ceiling, illuminating the long, luxurious dining table heaped with food. My mouth watered at the roasted ducks, the stuffed squash, the steaming bissara. Food meant to feed twenty here would have nourished the whole of Mahair.

Servants lined the walls around the lengthy table. I sat between Diya and Mehti in the middle. Queen Hanan dined at the head of the table, Felix to her left and Arin to her right.

She did not glance up from her food, and I took the opportunity to study my paternal grandmother. Though she and Palia were both queens, they differed in every respect. Long brown hair framed Queen Hanan's thin face, curtaining her darting eyes. She did not command the room with a word like Palia had. Quite the opposite. The Omal ruler seemed determined to fold herself into the smallest pocket of space, unobtrusive and unnoticed. What might she say if she knew she shared a table with Emre's daughter?

Diya elbowed me, nodding at Mehti when I glanced over. The Omal Champion chomped on yet another ring of golden mumbar.

The fried intestine stuffed with rice, onion, and chickpeas was an Omalian favorite. "How many of those have you had?" I asked.

Mehti paused, regarding me with the uncertainty of one whose household cat begins to bark. "Do you want one?"

I made a face. "I helped prepare mumbar at my keep once. Cutting a hole in thin bags of flesh and stuffing them to bursting tends to ruin an appetite."

The Omal Champion shrugged, unaffected by the description. "I have cut holes in humans without losing my appetite for battle."

While no one understood why Diya was chosen as Orban's Champion, the same could not be said for Mehti. Though born to wealth, Mehti lacked noble status, and his parents had rejected the crown's offers to draw them into the fold. Arin had explained that choosing Mehti was a way to force the title of noble onto the recalcitrant family through a mask of a Champion's honor. Should Mehti become Victor, he would be elevated to nobility, and his family with him.

"Have you had much practice cutting holes into humans?" Diya drawled.

Mehti snorted, lifting a bowl of soup to his lips and glugging. Omalian nobles at the end of the table watched him with bewilderment. "Not as much as you," he said when he came up for breath. He wiped his greasy mouth.

Diya shrugged modestly. "I cut many holes into two people. Is it the quantity of holes or quantity of people we measure?"

"All right," I interrupted loudly. "I would like to enjoy my meal, please."

"No one is stopping you," Diya said.

"I have been meaning to ask." Mehti rested his elbow on the table and angled toward me. "Why did it take you so long to escape Ayume? I was at the far end of the lake from you. You did not see me, but we crossed at the same time."

I clipped the bud of alarm before it could bloom. No one was near when I killed Timur. Mehti moved like a boar; I would have heard him miles away.

"A bush snagged my ankle," I said. "It knocked my dagger out of reach."

I blew on my chicken-and-orzo soup. They called it bird's tongue soup in Mahair, which had alarmed me until Raya explained that it referred to the shape of the orzo, not the content of the soup. Marek, in his infinite maturity, spent months pointing at every bird we passed and asking if I was hungry.

The two Champions winced sympathetically at the lie. "One of the trees tried to sweep me up while I ran," Diya offered. She rolled up her sleeve, exposing a thin, red scratch from wrist to elbow.

"I dodged one of those branches and slipped into an eddy of the lake. Took everything I had to pull myself out," Mehti said. "Do you think the Awaleen appreciate what we do for them?"

"The Awaleen are asleep in their tombs, and they hear no prayers and care for no honors," Diya said. "The Alcalah is a boasting contest for the royals, with our lives as the trading cards."

A low hum pulled my attention from Mehti's reply. No one else seemed to hear it. I followed the source to a servant leaning against the wall behind Sorn. She halted her conversation with another servant abruptly, gaze dulling. She reached into her pocket with the same dreamy expression I had worn a few hours ago. Sorn's head blocked my view of her hand, but the mystery of what she held disappeared when black twine fell from her fingers.

Screams erupted around us as a white, writhing cloud surged over the table. Some, including Mehti, tried to hide under the table, but slivers of white broke off from the ghaiba and slipped into their noses. The ghaiba split into small masses, each attacking a different person at the table. The screams vanished as the ghaiba took root inside them. Diya slumped back in her chair; Mehti's head landed in the mumbar.

A shot of white raced toward me, and a pure burning sensation filled my nose. I coughed, and the ghaiba spilled from my open mouth in gray wafts, dissipating mournfully. Foiled by my cuffs.

At the end of the table, the royals lay facedown, whimpering into the linen. Except Arin, who closed his eyes and pinched the bridge of his nose, as though the ghaiba were nothing more than a pesky migraine. While it would not render him unconscious, even he could not avoid the ghaiba's effects entirely.

I glanced at the unresponsive table and pushed my chair back. This was the opportunity I had been hoping for. During the journey to Omal, I had conspired with Sefa and Marek to break into Vaida's room before the second trial and take her seal. We needed assurance in the event she came after Mahair for the loss of Timur.

If she wore the ring now, I could pry it from her unresisting finger and return to my seat in seconds. And it could only be seconds, because Arin would push through the sliver of ghaiba inside him and reclaim awareness faster than the others. I hadn't shared our plan to steal the ring with him, though Sefa wanted to. There were instances where my friend forgot the strategic Commander was also the ever-maneuvering Nizahl Heir. While the seal would be a useful piece of leverage in my hands, it would be a lethal weapon in Arin's.

None of the many rings on Vaida's fingers were the one she had pressed to the wall in Lukub. I searched her pockets, checked her jangling necklace, but the ring wasn't on her person.

Vaida lurched to the side, knocking a bowl of bissara into Felix's lap. They were fighting past the minuscule amount of ghaiba inside them. Waking up, which meant Arin would open his eyes at any second.

I launched myself into my seat as Arin's gaze flickered toward me, questioning. He had seen me return to my seat, but not from where.

Arin retrieved the doll from the moaning servant, winding the black twine around it once more. Without a concentration of the ghaiba in one place, the doll's compulsion worked quickly on the individual pieces, and white plumes shot from limp mouths and noses. Arin wrapped the doll in a white cloth and placed it in the servant's hand, reclaiming his chair as the table roused to life.

Murmurs broke out. Guards carried a sobbing Queen Hanan from the room. A few prodded the weeping servant toward Vaida. She deposited the doll on the table.

"Sultana, it was in my pocket, I do not know how it came to be there, please, I am so sorry." Disconsolate, she covered her face.

My lips parted. I had taken the girl for an Omalian servant, but she was Lukubi. Arin had slipped Felix's doll into the pocket of one of the servants traveling with Vaida.

At the sight of the doll, Felix purpled. Rage blossomed on Vaida's face, and both royals shot to their feet. The aftereffects of the ghaiba had left them scattered, less vigilant of their audience.

"You *idiot*," Vaida snarled. "I delivered them to you in a fortified stone box, and you tossed them for a servant to find?"

"I left them exactly where I said I would! My servants are competent enough to avoid objects they do not recognize!"

"If she had untwined that doll anywhere else, we would both be dead!" Vaida snapped.

A voice cut through their squabble, smooth and measured. "I did not realize magic had become such a problem in your kingdoms," Arin said.

His gloved hand closed around the doll. A deathlike pallor whitened Felix's face as the reality of their mistake hit. Vaida's white-lined eyes widened. The table caged its breath. He had spoken the word few dared utter. *Magic.* He tossed the doll in front of Vaida. Those of us outside the eye of the storm stayed still and silent.

"Nizahl will gladly assist Omal and Lukub in sweeping out the scourge of magic. My armies are ready at a moment's notice."

Arin rose. The silver-tongued Nizahl Heir transformed before us. Ice encased his hardened features, and danger whispered in every movement of his poised body. The Commander's stare was death's cold caress, robbing Vaida and Felix of their breath.

I imagined what scene unfolded in the royals' minds. Soldiers in black and violet swarming their kingdoms like locusts, sundering villages and raiding towns in search of magic. Troublesome youth would be labeled potential magic users and detained. Any trapped Jasadis would use offensive magic to avoid capture, sending towns crashing down around them. The Commander would glide through the destruction, the conductor of chaos.

Nizahl did not enter a kingdom it intended to leave whole.

Arin's bone-chilling smile would unnerve even Sirauk's deadly depths. The message was clear: an attack on his Champion would not go unanswered a second time.

"Will that be necessary?"

"No, no," Felix said, tripping over his words in the rush. "There is a misunderstanding at play here. We did not—Vaida brought the dolls to—"

Vaida spoke over the bumbling Omal Heir, clear and firm. "It will not be necessary."

She lowered her chin, tumbling her flower-woven braids over her shoulders. The specter of unspeakable horror retreated, leaving the Nizahl Heir to incline his head in acceptance. The room drew its first full breath.

In the following havoc of guards and servants, Arin slipped away. I followed, hesitating at the door. Vaida spoke quietly to her guardswoman. Felix aimed a crooked sneer in my direction. I waved, luxuriating in his loathing.

He'd swiped his paw at the wrong beast. I would suffer the consequences done to his pride if I failed at the Alcalah, but it did not matter. Watching the Sultana and Omal Heir experience for a moment what my people endured every day under the graveyard of Nizahl's shadow was worth whatever Felix might do.

I chased Arin, speeding up two flights of stairs. I skidded to a halt in front of him before he could turn into our hall. He raised a brow when I stood there mutely. "Yes?"

How easy was it for him to slip the doll into Vaida's servant's pocket? She would have been flustered, overwhelmed at his proximity. The doll's weight in her pocket wouldn't even register. Vaida's servant, not Felix's, because blame needed to be thrown in both directions. He knew how many people would be in the dining hall. How many times the ghaiba would divide itself to attack everyone. How long it would take for him to fight off his allotment, how long it would take for the others. He knew the ghaiba's influence would disorient Vaida and Felix into a children's squabble, one he could use to condemn them.

"If I were a sensible woman, I would slit your throat while you slept."

Pale blue eyes glinted in the gloom. "Is that a threat?"

The same vicious hunger I had struggled against at the Ivory Palace bloomed in my veins. Baying for action. A hunger that demanded I *take*, forge a claim to him in flesh and blood and power. Etch my name into his bones for the world to see.

Arin's gaze darkened. We were two swords meeting on a bloodied battlefield. Inevitable. Wreathed in violence.

"I haven't decided yet," I whispered.

CHAPTER TWENTY-EIGHT

The night before the second trial, I slipped away from the palace town's festival, Sefa and Marek at my heels. The royals had their own section of the festival, surrounded by guards on the ground and observed by ones on the roofs. I maintained a wide berth from Supreme Rawain and Vaun, who watched the boisterous celebration with matching distaste. The merchants setting up booths around the large wooden platform painted what they were selling on the front of their booths. None of the royals ate from them, of course, but I spotted Mehti thrusting a bag of coins at a merchant standing behind a booth with a painted chicken.

Sparring matches like the one Mahair hosted took place on the raised platform, interspersed with groups of dancers and actors. They reenacted the Awaleen's conversation around the oak table as our predecessors debated whether to entomb themselves with Rovial. They played out the final battle between the siblings, their fall from Sirauk into the waiting tombs below. Kapastra shone as the hero, the courageous sibling in the Omalians' performance.

Since the festival took place over the entire town, different music played the farther along one wandered. I had already heard the sweet tones of a zither and a fast-paced Omalian lullaby on the lute, watched men wave sticks around as they danced to the beat of a drumming tubluh. The Omalian merchants coming from middle towns were relegated to the outskirts of the festival. I sipped my

sugarcane juice, dodging the spinning rainbow skirt of a man dancing the tannoura. An old merchant waved from the ground, his
knobby knees folded beneath his slim frame. He'd laid out his wares
on a quilt, and the bright colors drew me.

"Do you have any money?" I asked Wes. When he nodded, I knelt
to inspect the items closer.

Beaded bracelets and woven anklets mixed with rings of every
size and design. At the corner of the quilt, dusty from where it hung
into the dirt, a braided rope necklace caught my attention. Dyed a
patchy black, the thin rope supported a dangling pendant. I turned
the pendant over, revealing the inside of a halved fig. The seeds were
tiny gold beads, the veins connecting them embroidered violet and
pink. The outside of the fig was violet and outlined in gold. I ran my
thumb across the fuzzy front.

"How much for this?"

I gave him twice what he requested. I wasn't stingy with Nizahlan
money, and Arin would compensate Wes. I slipped the necklace into
my pocket.

"Your taste is terrible," Jeru said.

The road curved downhill suddenly, sending pebbles skidding
to the sides. My heart pounded as a woman with curly black hair
disappeared into the crowd. Everywhere I looked, flashes of Soraya
stole across the exuberant town. Any of the Urabi or Mufsids could
be at the festival. They circled me, predators around a bleeding stag,
waiting to see who would be closest when my legs collapsed.

I tried to ease my restlessness by focusing on the task at hand.
We returned to the main stage and its crush of revelers. The dancers
taking the stage wore gossamer gowns shaped to resemble rochelyas. A strap of fabric wound around their breasts and their hips,
representing the rochelya's long neck. A short skirt flared out at the
waist. They kept their hair pinned up to expose the rochelya's teeth
clasped behind their necks, holding up the salacious ensemble. Bare

except for the parts the rochelyas covered, the dancers' appearance on the stage distracted the royals and guards equally.

Sefa, Marek, and I took our leave as they began their sinuous belly dance. The Omalian guards at the palace recognized me, allowing us free entry. If we had attempted this venture in Orban, I had a feeling the khawaga would have rendered our mission obsolete.

"Do you know where Vaida's room is?" I asked Marek.

Servants streamed up and down the stairs, preparing the rooms for the drunken royals and nobles who would be stumbling into them.

"Third floor, east wing. I will recognize her door by the guard in front of it."

Marek and Sefa had woken up in the morning with a headache, but none the worse for wear. They refused to speak of what the ghaiba had shown them, and they'd relished my description of Arin's retaliation at the dinner.

While I had wasted the day walking the gardens with the other Champions and dressing for the festival, they had prepared for tonight.

So far, the plan was moving forward with shocking success. Sefa had asked an Omalian guard where she could deliver the Sultana's gown for the evening, and he pointed her in the right direction. Marek would be charged with distracting the single guard on duty while Sefa and I rifled through Vaida's room.

As for what would be done with the ring after we stole it, Sefa offered an unanticipated resolution. It seemed she and Marek had not been idly waiting in Orban while I completed the first trial. They had returned from their trip into Orban's villages with a scribbled spell from a small apothecary. Three slashes marked the spell, which Sefa explained as the amount of magic a Jasadi would expend using it. I had asked, "Three out of what?" and received a dumbfounded silence in response.

Once we stole the seal and used it to barter for our protection, the spell should theoretically prevent Vaida from reneging on her promise. She would not know it had been cast unless she sought to harm us, in which case she would find herself losing track of the thought.

The servants paid us little attention as we approached, and only a few guards remained in Vaida's wing, peering enviously from the window at the end of the hall. When we reached the hall with the Sultana's room, Sefa and I hid around the corner. A Lukubi guard leaned against Vaida's door, idly adjusting the strings on her vest. Marek rumpled his hair, undid the top laces of his tunic, and swaggered past us.

Her face brightened at Marek's approach. She recognized him from the Ivory Palace. He aimed a mischievous grin at her, bracing an arm above the guard's head as he murmured in her ear. She trilled a laugh. Watching Marek wield the appeal that came so naturally to him, I couldn't help my swell of envy. My personality did not lend itself to romantic musings, even the fleeting kind. Or so I had thought. Recent events seemed to indicate otherwise. But where Marek could be dying from six stab wounds and still find the energy to charm the nearest living creature, I had nearly broken my ankle trying to avoid Arin this morning. I didn't understand the reactions I was experiencing, so I did what I do best in times of inner turmoil: I ignored it.

A gleeful shriek snapped me back to attention. The guard was swatting at Marek's chest with her free hand while he kissed her fingers one by one. From Sefa's exasperated sigh, this was far from her first encounter with Marek's weaponized allure.

The guard hooked her fingers into Marek's waistband, yanking his hips flush to hers. He captured her lips in a filthy kiss. Broad hands lifted her against the wall. The guard wrapped her legs around Marek's waist, mussing his golden hair and nibbling at his ear. Marek gripped her thick thighs and carried her backward, sparing a wink in our direction before kicking a random door open and disappearing inside.

I straightened, following Sefa to Vaida's abandoned door. "Should we…interfere?"

Sefa closed the door behind us. "Seducing beautiful women is not a hardship for Marek. Let them have their fun."

Vaida's quarters were twice as large as mine, and I suppressed my groan. There were countless places she could have hidden a ring. The breeze from her open window carried a faint note of the festival's music.

"I will take the right side, you take the left." I yanked the drawer of her dressing bureau. A mountain of red undergarments burst free. "Did Marek do this often while you two were bouncing between villages?"

Sefa rummaged through Vaida's bedside table, sweeping each drawer. "Constantly. He couldn't seem to help drawing attention everywhere we went."

"Does it bother you?" I threw open the wardrobe doors, searching for any hidden jewelry chests.

"Why would it?" Sefa moved to the opposite bedside table. "Just because I have no interest in such affairs does not mean I expect the same from Marek."

My curiosity chose this inopportune moment to demand satisfaction. I flipped the cushions on Vaida's chairs, digging into the corners of the divan. "Was there ever a time when Marek wanted more than friendship?"

Sefa pursed her lips before groping under the pillows piled on Vaida's cavern of a bed. "Yes, and then that time passed. I have encouraged him to find someone in Mahair, to build a life with a partner who welcomes his passion and devotion." She crawled under the bed, and I went through the washroom. When we emerged, she continued. "He refuses."

"Where you go, he will follow. A relationship with another person will falter under his commitment to you," I pointed out.

Sefa heaved a sigh, opening the doors to the second wardrobe adjacent to the bed. A dozen ivory gowns hung inside.

"We have depended on each other for too long. He thinks letting himself love someone will break his attachment to me. I don't know how to prove to him he doesn't owe me his life." Sefa admired the stitching on the hem of a delicate silk gown. She glanced over as I slit open a cushion and stuffed my arm inside. "Are these questions new to you?"

I flipped the cushion to its good side and shoved it back to the seat. "It was not my place to ask before."

"But it is now?" Sefa asked, smiling. She parsed the items on Vaida's beauty table, knocking perfumes and powders together. "If it means anything, it has always been your place to ask."

I stopped slashing Vaida's cushions. Sefa always did this. Casually offered her heart to me. I had thought it was a personal failing, the ease with which she gave it away. But Sefa—Sefa was stingy with her confidences. She simply chose to trust me, in particular, over and over again.

"Sylvia? What is it?" Sefa abandoned the table, perching on the divan beside me.

Essiya, Hanim warned.

I swallowed past my dry throat. "You were right."

"Right about what?" Sefa frowned. She scrutinized my downcast gaze. Understanding flashed across her features, and her jaw dropped. "Oh, Sylvia, no."

The words spilled with the force of blood bursting from a severed artery. "The Heir—he enrages me, Sefa. I have never encountered a more paranoid man in my life. He lives from one theory to the next, manipulating people with utter detachment, and I can never guess what horrors his mind will concoct. Did you know he eats with his right hand when he is in a good mood and his left when he isn't? Why do I even remember that? And if he touches me, it does not—I don't—" I shoved the dagger into the cushion, tearing a diagonal line across the velvet surface. I could not bear to look at Sefa. "He is Nizahl's Commander. I should burn with hatred every second spent in his presence."

"Do not tell me what you should feel," Sefa said. Brown eyes met mine without a trace of judgment. "Tell me what is true."

How could I tell her I did not have the words? Words...those were the least of my troubles. They were not my eyes, fastening to him as soon as he entered a room. My heart, beating in double at his nearness. But worst of all, I could not admit to Sefa that the Nizahl Heir made me feel most like myself—and myself was not someone I had the luxury of learning.

Vaida's voice echoed from outside. "She's coming!" Sefa panicked.

"Into the red wardrobe. Go!" I shoved her from the divan, waiting until she pulled the doors shut over herself to catapult over the bed. I closed the doors of the white wardrobe, immersing myself in darkness just as the door rattled.

I peered through the narrow slats in the wardrobe. The door burst open, and I had a surprisingly clear view of Vaida reeling into the room.

"This beggarly kingdom may lack in every other respect, but Omalian festivals"—she hiccupped—"do not disappoint."

By her unsteady gait, the Sultana had not been conservative in her consumption of Omal's wines. A second figure stepped forward, and I recognized the line of his broad shoulders before he spoke. "Watch your step," Arin said.

Vaida tripped over a chair leg, careening into the Heir. She caught herself on Arin's chest and seemed baffled to find her wrists clasped in a gloved grip and held away. Vaida frowned.

"Is this about yesterday? It was a misunderstanding. Don't you believe me?" She arched up on her toes. I squinted, balanced precariously against the wardrobe doors.

"Have you never wondered what we would be like, Arin?" she murmured. "Don't you ever do anything for the pure pleasure of it? You must; no control is so perfect."

I could only see Arin's profile, and I caught a glimpse of his implacable features. Unmoved by the most beautiful woman in all the kingdoms, the descendent of Baira herself.

"My control is far from perfect," he said. "But it is better than yours."

In a single motion, Arin pressed his fingers to a point on the Sultana's neck and jerked her head to the side. Vaida's eyes rolled back. I covered my mouth with both hands as he caught the Sultana's limp body, depositing her on the bed. I let myself breathe when Vaida's chest moved. He had only put her to sleep.

Arin drew Vaida's bedside dresser forward. He swept his hand over the back, pausing halfway down. Angled out of my sight, I saw him straighten and extract a small box from his pocket.

He accomplished in a moment what you and your useless companion could not do in twenty, Hanim said.

He found the seal. What was he doing to it?

I mentioned the seal passingly the day I described Vaida's offer to him. It should not have shocked me that even a brief mention served as a catalyst for Arin's next plan.

He tucked the box into his pocket again, returning the seal to the back of the dresser. Arin paused on his way to the door, tilting his chin.

His hearing, you fool! Hanim reprimanded.

I smothered Vaida's gown over my nose and mouth. Arin skimmed over the wardrobe, lingering for a beat that sent panic coursing through me. I exhaled when he turned away and opened the chamber's doors.

"The Sultana took a tumble while removing her shoes and hit her head on the descent," he said.

"Oh no! Shall I fetch the palace physician?" the guard gasped.

"The damage will only be a headache and a distorted memory of the evening," Arin said. "I recommend you fetch ice. Immediately."

"Of course," the guard fretted. The door slammed shut behind them. I counted to ten before bursting through the wardrobe doors. Sefa followed suit, slapping aside the clinging gowns.

"Did you see what he did to the seal?"

"He rolled it in some sort of molding material," Sefa answered. "How did he know where Vaida hid it?" She yanked the table forward. I glanced at Vaida, checking that she slumbered deeply.

"They have known one other since childhood," I grunted, crouching behind the dresser. "It appears Vaida maintains her routines."

The ring dangled from a nail Vaida had driven into the back of the dresser. Victorious, I picked it up—only to drop the ring as blistering heat scalded my fingers.

"What is it?" Sefa reached for the ring, and no sooner had she made contact with the metal object than she was withdrawing with a squeal. "It is warded against us."

"How did he press it into the mold?"

Sefa tried to pick it up with the bottom of her gown. The fabric singed and blackened. "Perhaps his gloves afforded a measure of protection?"

I ground my teeth, the irrepressible urge to strangle him taking hold. "Or he did exactly what he did with the ghaiba. Magic passes him like a sieve, and he must have guessed he could tolerate the agony long enough to mold the seal and return it."

"Quite a guess." Sefa scowled at where the ring lay on the thick rug.

"Not a guess," I growled. "A theory. Well, he is not the only one who can have them." The doll's compulsion over me broke when it fell onto my cuffs. If Soraya was to be believed, and my cuffs resisted the strongest tracking spells, it was possible they would negate the seal's magic long enough for us to carry it to our wing.

"Hurry, the guard will not be long in the kitchens," Sefa said.

Getting the ring to balance on my wrists without touching it proved a trickier feat than expected. Sefa clearly thought I had forsaken my wits, if her wary frown was any indication. Sefa could only see the ring sitting on the inside of my wrist, with no explanation as to why it did not char my flesh. With my hand facing upward and fingers pointed to the ground, I precariously balanced the ring on my right cuff.

"Good, good," Sefa breathed. "I will go ahead and clear the path to our wing. Marek is probably waiting around the corner." Checking again to reassure herself the ring hadn't seared open my wrist, Sefa slipped outside the door, leaving it cracked for my foot to kick open.

I took a careful step toward the door, then another. The ring wobbled. I tried to keep my wrist as flat as possible. I had almost reached the door when I heard the voice.

"I would advise you against taking another step," it said.

I nearly dropped the ring. Turning around without sliding it off the cuff took agonizing seconds.

The Sultana sat up, and twin white orbs stared at me in place of her eyes. Not a singular doubt existed in my rebelling stomach that the thing upright and smiling in bed was not the Sultana.

"Are you...Baira?" I choked.

The thing laughed, tossing Vaida's head back. "Oh dear, no. But it was she who fused me to her seal, and I am afraid I must insist you return it to its rightful inheritor."

I had not endured this venture only to be thwarted by a formless ghoul. Keeping my gaze trained on it, I shuffled back.

Between one breath and the next, the thing wearing Vaida

materialized in front of me. The ring clattered from my wrist, falling somewhere between our bodies. It lingered too close, sharing my air. Its milky eyes brightened.

"Nearly there," it sang. "They tried again and again, but your choices never changed. Who knew this one would meet with success?"

Its childish curiosity vanished, and I shrank from the ruthless threat in Vaida's manipulated face. The rich Omalian quarters disappeared around us, and the thing's voice echoed in a dark, ravenous cavern. Ancient magic pressed in against my sides, raking nails over my skin. With the certainty of the damned at the executioner's axe, I knew this was not a magic mere mortals were meant to see. This was the cry of the first bird ever pushed from its nest, tentative wings stretching for flight. The first thunder of a restless sky. The waters moving under the Awaleen as they rested on their thrones beneath Sirauk, kept alive by their magic and trapped by it, too. I was a gnat fluttering toward the surface of the sun, burning from the mere flight.

"Baira's seal is for her Sultanas alone. Do not breach her commandment again."

The thing primly returned to its former position, and with a last smile at me, its eyes rolled forward. Vaida collapsed into the same position from which she had risen.

There were footsteps at the door, and I heard Marek's teasing voice trying to cajole the guard away. At a loss, I kicked the ring under the dresser and prayed Vaida would think she knocked it from its nail during her drunken stupor.

I squeezed outside. Marek framed the guard's face in his hands, blocking her periphery as I snuck down the hall.

"Where is it?" Sefa exclaimed when I rounded the corner. "Did it start to burn?"

I massaged my wrists, rattled by the echo of power waiting to devour me in the cavernous empty. "Yes, it did."

CHAPTER TWENTY-NINE

For the second trial, we had the privilege of an escort by carriage to the starting location. Diya pressed her forehead to the window, counting each tree we passed under her breath. Mehti handled stress the same way he seemed to handle everything: in excess. He maintained a steady stream of chatter about the dancers from yesterday's festivals, then dove into a detailed description about the basturma he'd eaten wrapped around a roasted chicken.

Mehti tossed his feet up between us, huffing when Diya shoved them off the bench. "The children in our town tell stories about Dar al Mansi. A boy offered to trade me his rock when we were in school if I stepped inside its bounds."

"Did you?" Diya asked grudgingly. Mehti was entertaining in his own odd way, and I enjoyed the distraction from listening to the carriage wheels rumble.

"It was a very nice rock." He sniffed, crossing his arms over his chest. "The other boys were impressed."

"What does it matter?" Diya returned to the window. "Dar al Mansi is only dangerous during the Alcalah. The captured creatures stay in Nizahlan prisons the rest of the time."

Unlike Ayume Forest, Dar al Mansi lacked any corruption at its core. Called "home of the forgotten" after the village buried within it, Dar al Mansi was a new addition to the Alcalah. Preparing for this trial caused Arin no small amount of tension.

Two years after the Blood Summit, groups of Jasadis fleeing

Rawain's siege stumbled across the lonely Omalian village. On Arin's map, Dar al Mansi was linked to Omal proper in a warped hourglass shape. Dar al Mansi sat at the bottom, shrouded in Essam Woods, and Omal at the top. The village was already abandoned when the Jasadis happened upon it, left to the wilderness by its previous occupants. The sketches Arin gave me at the start of training had one image of the Jasadis living happily, disturbing no one, their magic reviving the land around them. The next charcoal sketch showed Nizahl and Omal forces creeping through Essam, surrounding the village from every side.

The Jasadis in Dar al Mansi sensed the encroachment and pooled their magic to draw Essam Woods into the village. Trees sprouted inside homes, munban nests replaced shop floors, and muddy soil rippled over the rocky terrain. Their magic drained from such a surge of power, the Jasadis were helpless to defend themselves. Scholars believed they ordered Essam Woods to cover their village in hopes of confusing the soldiers. I had studied the sketches Arin gave me for hours; the Jasadis knew their fate when they spent their magic. It was acceptable to them. Allowing Nizahl and Omal to destroy a second home was not.

A grove of trees over a wooded hillside kept Dar al Mansi separated from the other Omal towns. Any creatures the Champions failed to exterminate would be left to the soldiers.

"What are the three trophies you want?" Mehti asked. "The last Alcalah, a Champion emerged with the head of a nisnas, a feather from Al Anqa'a, and a viroli's tail. I want to try to slice a piece off a zulal, if they have one."

"I want a trophy from the three easiest things to kill," Diya said. "As though crossing the village alive is not its own challenge. A zulal? You are going to anger a worm wider than Hirun and tall as Essam's trees in hopes that the audience will cheer louder when you emerge? We're only required to bring three pieces of evidence of our kills, and that is all I will do."

"Where is your sportsmanship?" Mehti pouted. "The battle vigor of Orban's Awala should be reflected in her Champion."

The carriage bounced, rocking from side to side. Diya looked down her nose at Mehti—quite the achievement, considering she was half his size. "This trial celebrates your demented Awala, not mine. Dania did not keep company with savage creatures."

"What do you call the khawaga, then?"

I traced the handle of the carriage door. I dreaded the second trial most of all. It was harder to ignore the reality of my betrayal while walking through a graveyard of my people as Nizahl's Champion.

"The Omalian patrol is waiting in Essam Woods to slay any creatures escaping Dar al Mansi," I said, silencing the pair. I hadn't spoken since the carriage left the palace grounds. "I wonder if the soldiers would attack *us*."

"Why on earth would they? We aren't monsters," Mehti said, appalled.

Neither were the Jasadis, I almost said.

"What makes us any different? We are entering this village to kill and maim. In the measure of monster or man, what tips the scales?"

Mehti only looked further scandalized at the question. Diya's lips pursed. Contemplative.

The carriage juddered to a halt. "Omal Champion, descend!" the driver called. Unlike Ayume, we were dropped off at different starting points for the second trial. Mehti puffed his chest, rubbing his hands together eagerly. "A good hunt is just what I need to revive me from this bore of a conversation. For Kapastra!" He bounded from the carriage, rapping his fist against the side of the carriage. Diya and I watched him excitedly sift through the weapons provided for him.

"Choice," Diya said. At my quizzical frown, she crossed her arms over her chest. "The ability to choose is what tips the scales. Monsters have no choice in their evil, but humans choose it deliberately. My parents chose to sell my younger sister to the khawaga. They convinced themselves they had no choice; how could they leave their prosperous town for a village overrun by vagrants? They traded my gentle sister for a taller roof and nicer walls. The khawaga returned my sister in pieces. I punished my mother and father for each part of her I buried."

"Forty-three stab wounds each," I remembered. "I hope they lived long enough to feel every single one."

Diya smiled faintly. "I can make choices, too."

The carriage rumbled to a stop. "Orban Champion, descend!"

Diya paused at the door. "Do try not to die. I would hate to listen to Mehti yammer on a third time."

I fluttered my lashes. "Why, Diya. Is this your formal offer of friendship?"

She considered the distance between herself and the ground. "Die, then." She leapt.

I shook with laughter. I ignored the driver's grumbling and stuck my head out the window as the carriage forged on. "But I accept!"

The driver snapped the reins, and Diya disappeared between the trees. I tipped my chin up, searching for the sun in the cloudy skies. I'd missed the feel of it in the tunnels more than I realized.

"Nizahl Champion, descend!"

Taking a deep breath, I jumped from the carriage. The driver did not spare me a glance, urging the horses in the opposite direction of Dar al Mansi. A layer of dew covered the weapons left at the bottom of the tree. Omalian winters were not an ideal setting for a trial that depended on the acuity of sight and sound.

A pale fog hovered around us. Thin shafts of sunlight peeked from the gray sky. I listened for movement and encountered silence too complete to be natural.

I evaluated the weapons. Arin's instructions were clear. Two weapons I could tuck into my clothing and one I would carry. I chose a rounded dagger with its scabbard, tucking it between my breasts. I had wrapped a tight undergarment around my breasts and ribs for this precise purpose. Poor Wes turned the color of a plum during training when I refused to tuck the dagger into my waist and reached into my tunic instead. I slid the second, shorter blade into my boot.

I chewed my bottom lip, deliberating between the axe and the spear. I practiced almost exclusively with the spear. Its weight would be familiar, and it was Arin's weapon of choice.

I ran my nail along the sharp line of the axe. Too much comfort in battle was its own danger.

A piercing shriek rang from above me. I threw myself to the ground, curling below the nearest tree. Through the blanket of skeletal branches, I watched with breathless awe as Al Anqa'a was released over Dar al Mansi. Wings the size of a carriage unfurled. The limited light reflected off glass feathers fading into the colors of a sunset, a gradient of magnificent oranges and pinks blending along its wings, ending with gray-tipped feathers. Talons long as a man and sharper than any sword curved forward.

Al Anqa'a was the only creature they did not kill at the conclusion of the trial. They had clipped its wings to ensure it could fly only in a low loop, and its beady eyes scanned the village below for movement. I exhaled when it flapped its wings, circling to the left. I darted between the trees, leery of any open space. Once Al Anqa'a fixed on its prey, there was no escaping its clutches.

Rounding a cluster of thistles, I came upon Dar al Mansi in all its eerie glory. Thick green vines covered the earth like bulging veins, creeping up the sides of crumbling shops and over the rubble. Fully grown trees sprouted from low buildings, their bases pulverizing the outer walls. Human life reclaimed by the savage wood.

The space between trees lengthened from here, which meant I would need to keep pressed to the walls to stay hidden from Al Anqa'a.

I dashed from the tree to an overturned carriage in the middle of the road. My nausea grew with each step into Dar al Mansi. I could not tell whether my cuffs were reacting to the residue of magic left here, or if my stomach simply couldn't handle the suffocating smell of decay.

Crouching behind the carriage's wheel, I assessed the distance I would need to cover to reach the nearest shop. Al Anqa'a circled over the square. I curled into a tight ball.

A guttural smacking sound erupted from my left. Limping from what might have been an apothecary, the unmistakable shape of a nisnas emerged. I'd heard tales of the ghoulish creatures, yet they paled in comparison to the reality. A nisnas was what might have become of Timur if I had left him lying on Ayume's forest floor, vulnerable to the forest's sinister magic. One arm dragged behind the nisnas, longer than the rest of its misshapen body. Where the other arm should have been hung a translucent sack of blood, swishing with its slow crawl toward me. Half a leg bulged from the center of its torso, and the single yellow eye in its bulbous head blinked at me. Stubby fingers formed a spiked collar around its throat. Yellow skin grew over its mouth, leaving it incapable of anything beyond a stifled gurgling.

Wes's description of the thing did it the most justice.

"A nisnas is what happens if you put a rotting mortal body into an iron bowl and smash it with a pestle," he'd said.

The nisnas dragged itself forward with surprising speed. Al Anqa'a circled the square once, twice, disregarding the nisnas. I begged the bird to take its flight elsewhere before I had to choose between risking an open space or the nisnas. When the nisnas's foul stench reached my nostrils, and I could see the shriveled skin of its face, Al Anqa'a swerved past the square with a rush of wind.

I hurled myself away just as the nisnas's dangling arm whipped out from the side. Rolling to my feet, I swung the axe, cleaving its liquid arm sack. A gurgling moan that might have been a scream erupted as blood and pus poured into the soil. The nisnas skittered toward me on pointed nubs of bone. The axe connected with the line of its swollen head, cutting through the fingers growing from its neck. Though only a strip of brown tendon kept its head attached, the nisnas did not slow. Its arm thrashed around my legs, sending me crashing to the ground.

"Get off me!" I grunted, hacking at the thing. I tried to conjure thoughts to provoke my magic. It seemed disinclined to participate.

Eventually, I chopped enough of the nisnas to wiggle from its grip. The pieces trembled on the ground, and right before my eyes, began to knit back together. I grabbed a wiggling finger and stuck it into one of the knots in my braid to hold it still.

Ichor trailed from the axe as I ran. The places on my clothes where the nisnas touched me were singed, the sludge coating its body eating through the thin fabric. I quickly stopped to scrub dirt on all the places the sludge had touched my skin.

I scuttled like a roach for the next mile, weaving between crumbling buildings and overgrown thickets. The shadow Al Anqa'a cast gave sufficient warning of its approach, and I made myself small every time it circled.

When it came around again, I ducked into an open doorway. The remnants of a family home crunched under me. An enormous tree towered in the center of the house, thriving in the ruin. An infant's rattle dangled from a branch, and a matching crib lay smashed around the tree's roots, which rippled over the floor like a stone dropped in still water.

What must Nizahl and the other kingdoms have done to Jasad for the villagers here to prefer this death to another invasion? What horrors had been inflicted upon Jasadis' homes for consumption by the woods to be the merciful alternative? They hadn't pooled their magic together to repel the soldiers, but to destroy their village on their own terms.

Glass crunched as I walked deeper into the monument of death. What did Jasad look like, if this was the aftermath in a random village?

Running was not a choice for them, Hanim said. *Nizahl had led the charge against their land once already, and they would not be chased from another home.*

I picked up a patch torn from a colorful quilt. They had embroidered the kitmer's agile, catlike body, its golden wings, even its feathered head. Clinging to Jasad, even after it was long gone.

"I apologize for the mess," said the man leaning against the tree. "I wasn't expecting visitors."

I dropped the patch. Surprise morphed to alarm, and I lifted the axe, checking for the nearest hole in the wall I could fit through. I cursed myself for wandering in so deep.

The man approaching me looked utterly unremarkable. He could have been a fast-talking merchant, a lecherous royal, a vagrant. His features were too bland, as though an artist had outlined the basics of a human man's face and forgotten to fill in the rest.

"There's no need for that," he said amiably, gesturing at my axe. "Not with all the delicious magic you can use instead."

I paused, and he chuckled at my expression. "Did you think I wouldn't smell it? Oh, but I haven't had a good taste of magic in so long. I have been searching for a morsel, and here a feast has presented itself to me."

"What are you?" I held the axe between us as I maneuvered away.

"Hungry," he said. "Starving, actually. You understand. I can feel your hunger, too." He moved toward me, unperturbed when I slashed the axe in warning. He sighed. "I much preferred eating Lukubi magic, back when they had it. Jasadis are too much trouble."

"I do not have any magic for you to eat. Whatever you are smelling is from this room." I glanced at the door. A few more steps. Fighting in an enclosed home with a tree plunging through the middle was not a recipe for success.

"Nonsense. Your magic is ripe. Fragrant." He inhaled deeply. "Much better than anything these pitiful fools ever possessed."

I was being goaded. Fully aware of this, I let my temper flare anyway.

"For a hungry man, you seem to have energy for quite the abundance of stupidity."

His features vanished for a second, as though his face had blinked from existence. When they returned, he wore a sneer. "I glutted myself on Jasad as it burned. Nothing compares to the flavor of magic used in desperation. I sated myself on the ruins of the kingdom, and no one bothered to stop me." He took another step toward me. "I fed on the Jasad Heir's magic before it left her cooling body. Hers was bitter, left behind a terrible taste. Like Niphran herself."

My hold on the axe wavered. "Y-you killed her?"

"Me? Darling, my kind could not even enter Jasad until the fortress collapsed. Poor Niphran was already slain in her lonely little tower when I arrived."

"Be quiet!" I shouted. The door pressed against my back, yet I could not make my legs carry me away. "You will not malign the Jasad Heir in this village."

"But this is Dar al Mansi, isn't it?" he purred. "And who was more forgotten than Niphran?"

My cuffs were burning vises, magic pulsing to the tune of my rage. His nostrils flared, reptilian gaze widening. "*Oh*," he murmured, and licked his lips.

I had had my fill of his chattering. The axe caught him in the stomach, slicing a thick gash across his belly. It should have emptied his innards onto the floor. He didn't even flinch.

"I would have liked to feed on the Malik and Malika. Even Niphran's little bastard daughter. Instead, I had to settle for the likes of these." He waved at the destroyed home. "Such a shame, that the weakest kingdom retained magic the longest."

My magic roared, and my arms moved with preternatural speed in cleaving the axe into his throat. I yanked it from the clench of sinew and muscle.

The man's features melted as his body began to warp. Hairy,

elongated bovine legs replaced human ones, and six long, curved spider limbs erupted from his stretching torso. Three heads burst from his expanding neck, then joined together with a head at the top and two at the bottom.

"Dulhath." The one creature even Hanim had not dared summon. I dodged the pointed tips of its many spider legs and brought my foot down on the nearest tip. It cracked, and the dulhath's shriek pierced my ears. I hacked the limb swooping from the right.

Another leg swiped my feet out from under me. The world spun, and I knocked my head against the tree. Blinding pain exploded in my temple as a pile of shattered glass broke my fall. Viscous sludge dripped from teeth sharper than knives, gnashing in my face. I flipped to my feet, tearing open the sleeves of my tunic on the glass.

The dulhath surged toward me. I raised my hand, finally relenting to the battering demand of my magic. It wailed as its heads began to unwind from each other, white goo strung between each slab of head as it moved. I snapped my fingers, and the heads tore in separate directions, ripping its massive body into three.

I severed the bottom of a spidery leg and roped it around my thigh with a strip of the abandoned quilt. I sneered at the dulhath's quivering heads, tossing the infant's rattle onto where I hoped its face was.

"The only weak thing to die in this house is you."

After checking the gloomy sky for Al Anqa'a, I sprinted at full speed past the bracket of shops, leaping over craters teeming with munban nests and tarnished pots. At the looming silhouette of Al Anqa'a, I rushed through the narrow crevice separating a butcher's shop from a cluster of sapling trees. I glanced over my shoulder as I rounded the edge.

A springy wall slammed me to the ground, sending my axe flying. I squinted, adjusting my sight in the shade. A strangled cry slipped from my lips before I could stop myself.

A zulal undulated around Mehti's body. Only his head was visible from the massive worm's winding embrace. Death clouded eyes that hours ago had danced with mischief. The zulal throbbed around the Omal Champion, suckling the moisture from his body in its deadly coil. When the worm finished, it would leave behind his desiccated, shriveled carcass and slither away to lie in wait for its next meal.

My axe had fallen partially under the zulal. I crawled toward it, extending my fingers as far as they could go. When the handle eluded me, I crawled a little closer.

The zulal abruptly stopped rippling around Mehti's corpse. Damn it to the tombs! Abandoning the axe, I sprinted away as the top half of the white worm unraveled with a wet sucking noise. I did not glance back to see if it was slithering after me. I pulled out the dagger hidden in my tunic, its lightness an unpleasant contrast to the axe's satisfying heft.

When Al Anqa'a finished its next circuit, I pushed off the building. Not far ahead, the trees reverted to their natural clusters as Dar al Mansi ended and Essam Woods began. From there, it would be a fifteen-minute hike to where the masses waited to greet the returning Champions.

I weaved through a flower garden, the bottom of my boot collecting mud and moldering petals. By the time I reached the border, I hadn't encountered another creature. The prospect of doubling back for the zulal and looking into Mehti's sallow face appalled my common sense. There had to be another creature this close to the border, right?

A rustle from the right spun me around. I lifted the dagger, flexing my arm in preparation. One clean strike, and I would be done with the second trial forever. A man stumbled from over the tree line, disheveled and limping. My fingers tensed on the handle. Another dulhath?

The man lifted his chin, giving our surroundings a glazed glance. I didn't recognize him at first.

The years hadn't treated him gently. The strong brown arms that swung me out of trees and lifted me onto his shoulders were withered. Lines burrowed in his proud forehead, and it seemed to take everything at his disposal to raise his head.

I stumbled back when his weary gaze met mine.

Dawoud, head of Niyar's staff, the man who would sneak me cakes from the kitchen, who spent his rare free moments listening to me babble about my day, who taught me the best way to climb a fig tree, stood in Dar al Mansi.

Tears filled his eyes. He recognized me, too.

If they had spilled me into a ravine of filth, burned the sins of fifty lifetimes into my skin, I could not have felt dirtier than I did right then.

"Are you real?" I demanded. My grip on the dagger shook.

"Essiya," he whispered, and the sound that left my mouth was not human.

Dawoud rushed to me, the instinct to comfort defeating his physical deterioration. I wilted away from him.

"How are you here?" I choked out. "How are you alive?" The most terrible of notions occurred to me, and bile burned in my throat. "Tell me you are not with them, Dawoud. Tell me the Mufsids or Urabi have not sent you."

"Of course not!" An echo of his former self rang in his affronted tone. "I have not crossed paths with either group in a year."

"Then *how?*"

Dawoud sighed. "I was captured in Orban three months ago by a group of Nizahl soldiers. Rawain's High Counselor knew the role I held in Jasad, and he found innovative methods to pull information from me."

The realization swept over me like ice rain. I clapped my hand over my mouth, whirling away from Dawoud as my stomach heaved. He was Supreme Rawain's prisoner. They released him into Essam Woods, toward Dar al Mansi, despite knowing he was a Jasadi.

I was right all along. Vaun planted the seeds of doubt in Supreme Rawain's head. I let the guards persuade me that Rawain would not trust another over his son. And in most matters, Rawain wouldn't.

But Jasadis were not most matters.

Dawoud's brow pinched, resurrecting the ghost of a once-brilliant analyst. "If you don't kill me, the Supreme will think you are a Jasadi," Dawoud said. "I wonder how he knew to send me. I'm not the only prisoner."

When I stood there dumbly, Dawoud's voice gentled. "I thought of you every night. When I heard what had happened, what they'd done, I couldn't think of anything but you. The argument we'd had over your dress; would that be our last? You were so angry with me, stomping your little feet and hiding in your tree."

"I didn't like the gold ruffles." I couldn't breathe.

"I thought, not Essiya. Not her, too. Anyone else."

Grief burned in my chest. "I'm sorry, Dawoud. I'm so sorry."

He was never meant to see me like this.

"They called you Sylvia," he said. "The guards. They said you are the Nizahl Champion."

The shame blistering through me burned hotter than Vaida's seal, searing more than a hand thrust into crackling flames. He said it plainly, not a hint of judgment in his voice, but the words whipped me to tatters.

Sylvia. Nizahl's Champion, Hanim murmured. *That was your choice.*

"I had to. It was the reasonable—it was the logical choice," I babbled, fully aware of the concern gathering on Dawoud's face. What must I look like, mumbling to myself, covered in dust and gore, bearing trophies from monsters? Niphran's daughter besieged with a new madness. "I couldn't help them! I cannot. I have nothing to offer. Look around us. How could I have stopped this? I didn't know you were alive—how could I have known?"

You could possess all the magic in the world, and you would still give Jasad your back, Hanim said. I fisted my hands in my hair, shaking my head like a dog trying to unseat a persistent fly.

Before Dawoud could respond to my ravings, a shriek shook the earth. Too late, I registered the long shadow over us. Al Anqa'a dove, and I hurled myself into Dawoud as its claws curled over the place where he had stood.

"Here, take this." I shoved the dagger's handle into his hand, pulling out the one in my boot as I leapt to my feet. "Go, stay close to the buildings!"

Dawoud glanced at the dagger, uncomprehending. "You think I am going to leave you to fight alone?"

Al Anqa'a screeched, and I fervently hoped the crowds waiting beyond Dar al Mansi could hear it. That they knew Dar al Mansi, for all that it was forgotten, would never stop demanding to be heard.

I flipped the dagger, keeping Al Anqa'a fixed on me as it folded its wings to dive again. "I am more than capable of fighting alone."

Glass wings chimed with the wind as Al Anqa'a swept toward me. I dropped in a long slide as it approached, pointing my dagger up. I braced my arms, keeping the dagger firm and high. Al Anqa'a wailed as the dagger pierced its featherless underside, and its talons caught me in the shoulder and swung. I crashed into the side of a crumbling house.

Al Anqa'a shook itself, and the dagger fell to the ground. Its beady gaze narrowed. I pushed myself from the crevice of rubble. A sharp claw pierced my calf, dragging me out of the narrow alley. I tried to grab hold of an anchor, tearing out roots and scrabbling at boulders.

Al Anqa'a unhinged its beak, its wings unfolding over me. A breathtaking tableau of color unspooled, more brilliant than every dawn and dusk I'd witnessed.

I writhed under its unyielding talons, trailing blood behind me.

Suddenly, Al Anqa'a bellowed again, releasing me to arch into the air. Behind it stood Dawoud, his hands raised and his lips moving. His eyes glowed gold and silver. Al Anqa'a teetered in the sky, a powerful gust of wind from its wings sending Dawoud stumbling.

"Dawoud, stop!" I cried out. He would need every ounce of magic he had to escape the patrol surrounding Dar al Mansi. He couldn't waste it all on Al Anqa'a.

Sweat beaded on his forehead, gathering in its deep grooves. "Essiya, end this," Dawoud said. I limped to my dagger and wiped it against my thigh. "You know what Rawain wants."

It was my turn to stare uncomprehendingly. "I am *not* going to kill you," I snarled.

The sensible part of me knew failing Rawain's test would mean an end to all my plans. An end to Arin's designs. But I had lasted this long by recognizing the burdens I could bear, and killing Dawoud was not among them.

Al Anqa'a knocked a wall from a shop, sending bricks blasting around us. Dawoud's magic couldn't hold it much longer. My cuffs tightened, swelling with my fear.

He couldn't hold it, but I could.

I stared at my cuffs as they grew tighter than they ever had.

Al Anqa'a swiped at Dawoud, missing him by inches. I threw my arms into the air, my cuffs throbbing as my magic hurtled into Al Anqa'a. The creature screamed, its sunset glass wings clinking. An opaque mist blanketed the sky.

Dawoud regarded the shrieking bird with no small amount of awe. But when he glanced at me, shock swept over his features. "What's wrong with your eyes?"

I frowned, blinking rapidly. My arms quaked with the strain of holding Al Anqa'a away.

"They're—they have not changed. Not a hint of gold or silver." He peered closer. "Where is the magic in your darling kitmer eyes?"

"The cuffs," I spat. "My magic flows through the cuffs, not my body. Dawoud, you have to run. Please. I cannot hold it much longer, and the patrol will be closing in on Dar al Mansi."

Dawoud went deathly white. He staggered away, looking at my wrists with more terror than he spared Al Anqa'a. Had the effects of expending so much magic caught up with him?

"How can they still be there? How?" he gasped. "Oh, my dear Essiya, oh no. What has happened to you?"

You have the potential and power to be worse than any who have come before you.

"Dawoud," I set my feet as Al Anqa'a bashed itself against the barrier. I slid backward with each blow to my magic. "Did I ever burn your favorite quilt?"

A peculiar look flashed over Usr Jasad's head of staff. It was the look of someone who believed one wrong pull of the ropes would bring the sky crashing down. A look I recognized from my childhood. His thick brows furrowed. "I should have let you take it to the courtyard," he said.

Soraya was right.

Mirrors. My memories were fragments, reflections of what I needed them to be to survive. Dawoud's pained admission cracked open the day I burned his quilt. The shatter echoed into my body, ringing in my bones.

Essiya was no better than Sylvia. I had always been this broken. This selfish.

Sylvia was just a reflection of the worst parts of a girl I had buried.

In a burst of fury, Al Anqa'a surged past the barrier of my magic. Sparks fell like gold rain from the breached barrier. Its talons closed around my body, and I swore as my feet left the ground.

Its grip faltered when I kicked out. A single talon pierced the back of my tunic like a hook. I dangled downward, the fabric of my tunic slowly ripping. Al Anqa'a's wings thrashed, struggling to lift us against my magic's wall.

On the ground, Dawoud picked up the dagger. He stared at me, tears tracking down the face that had once been more beloved to me than my own mother's.

Dawoud's mouth moved, and I realized what he meant to do a split second before he plunged the dagger into his heart.

"No!" I screamed. Al Anqa'a cried out as the barrier broke in a sky-shaking tremor. Gold sparks shot through the air like falling stars. Dawoud crumpled, and I lifted my arms, sliding out of my tunic and crashing to the ground. The dagger had slid into Dawoud in the same place Soraya stabbed me. Al Anqa'a flapped to the east, abandoning prey that had become more trouble than it was worth.

"Your Gedo Niyar would be so proud of you," Dawoud said when I skidded to my knees next to him. I pressed my trembling hands to his wound, and he groaned. "I should have believed them when they said you were alive. I didn't dare to. The thought of you alone for so long, while we—" He coughed, red droplets splattering on his chin. "Your cuffs were never meant to last this long. No one is meant to be alone for so long."

"Then don't leave me." Desperation turned the words into a plea.

Blood gushed between my fingers, and my cuffs heated as I called on every ounce of magic I had. My magic had to act somehow. Dawoud would not die in the dirt in Dar al Mansi. He would not be another Jasadi claimed by this village.

"I should have never stopped searching for you." His hand came to rest over mine, his calloused palm cool over my knuckles. I flinched at the touch, and Dawoud's sharp eyes narrowed. "What happened to you, Essiya? Where were you?"

My magic tore uselessly around us. "Hanim," I ground out. I would speak, if only to keep the stubborn man from doing so himself. "She kept me in Essam for five years."

My goal to talk him into relaxation failed miserably, because he tried to lurch upward. Blood poured down his front. "Qayida

Hanim?" The remaining color leached from his face, leaving him gray and aghast. "That miserable traitor. She took you? She—she ruined us all. Soraya, Essiya, do you know about Soraya?"

"Dawoud, please, stay still," I begged.

"Hanim brought her into the palace. Into our home. Hanim recommended her to your grandparents, because—" It seemed sheer spite kept Dawoud awake. His eyes rolled wildly. "They planned it all. But Hanim…" He shuddered in what might have been a laugh. "Soraya should have known better than to rely on the fidelity of traitors."

"I don't care about them," I urged. "Lie *still*."

Dawoud's smiled with white lips. "My determined little Essiya," he breathed. "To die knowing you are alive is all I could have wished for."

I lost the battle against my heart. "Please stay. Please. I have so much to tell you. I apprenticed with a man named Rory. A chemist. I could hardly tolerate the subject with my tutors, remember? But he taught me about how to heal the body from the inside and out. He took me to a woman named Raya. She reminded me of you, except more rigid. I became her ward, and she treated me kindly." My teeth were chattering, shaking along with the rest of my body. Dawoud's breaths slowed beneath me. My magic's assault on Dar al Mansi evaporated.

Dawoud was dying.

Wiping the blood from my hands, I slid behind him, pulling his head into my lap. I combed my fingers through his hair, raking them into his scalp the way he used to do for me after a nightmare. "I am here. I won't go," I said, and I repeated the words long after Dawoud's chest stilled and his body went cold.

CHAPTER THIRTY

Night loomed over Dar al Mansi. I eased out from beneath Dawoud's body. Once night fell, hordes of patrolling guards would attack the remaining creatures in Dar al Mansi.

I stared down at Dawoud's still face. Supreme Rawain did this. He threw Dawoud into Dar al Mansi for me to slaughter. We were animals to him, playthings to use and dispose of.

And I was his Champion.

The rage cooled the howling grief in my chest. I bent down, and even without months of training, I wouldn't have struggled to lift Dawoud in my arms. Though starved and tortured, Dawoud never bowed to Nizahl. Proud until his end, dying like every Jasadi in Dar al Mansi.

But unlike them, he would not dwell in the home of the forgotten.

I carried Dawoud through the stretch of Essam Woods separating Dar al Mansi from the rest of Omal. Lantern light and movement flickered between the trees. The marching patrol.

Essam cleared, and a commotion greeted my entry. The audience seethed on two opposite slopes, craning for a view of the narrow landing between them. They cheered as I walked onto the path, although the ones at the bottom quieted at the sight of the dead man in my arms.

The announcer's expression scrunched with confusion as I approached. I glanced behind him. Supreme Rawain and the other royals lounged at the front, ringed with guards. I carefully kept my gaze away from Supreme Rawain or his son.

Jeru and Wes broke from the outskirts as the announcer peered down at Dawoud and my state of undress. Al Anqa'a had taken my tunic in its talon, and a large white band covered my breasts, keeping my stomach and shoulders exposed. He cleared his throat. "Do you—uh—"

I gently laid Dawoud in Jeru and Wes's arms without meeting either of their eyes. They would care for him. See he was taken somewhere the scavengers could not reach.

I tossed the nisnas's finger to the ground and pulled the dulhath's spidery limb from its binding around my thigh.

"A nisnas finger. A dulhath leg. A Jasadi. Three monsters. Three trophies." I smiled, and the announcer took a step back. "Go ahead. Declare me."

"Sylvia," Jeru tried, voice hoarse. I looked at him, and the Nizahl soldier blanched.

The announcer whirled to the gathered masses. "The Nizahl Champion joins the Orban Champion to proceed to the third trial!"

I walked past him, past Jeru and Wes and the dead man in their arms, past the applauding royals. I did not stop to see the satisfaction in Rawain's gaze or the irritation in Vaun's. I entered the Champions' carriage with Diya, and the wheels groaned as the carriage jerked into motion.

We stayed silent until we reached the palace. Diya pulled the quilt from around her shoulders and tossed it into my lap. "Give them nothing to see but the look in your eyes," she said.

Numb, I pulled the quilt around my shoulders. No servant intercepted me as I entered the palace, and no guard asked questions. I floated up the stairs in a haze. In the stillness of my quarters, I let the quilt spill to the ground.

Does it hurt more when your failures have names? Hanim whispered. *Does it hurt more to put a face to the people you have let down?*

The drawers rattled in the bedside table, shooting into the

opposite wall. My cuffs pulsed around raw wrists, but I did not feel the pain.

You could be faced with not a single obstacle and still find an excuse to turn away from your people, she said. *Dawoud is dead, your family is dead. Soraya was never yours. Who do you have left?*

The wardrobe flew into the divan, upending cases of meticulously packed gowns. Blankets tore, and the bedframe snapped, taking the bed to the ground. Flames danced over the rug, trailing up the wall.

Dawoud mouthed my name before he drove the dagger into his chest. A name I gagged and buried deep inside me, a name that should have burned to ash with the rest of Jasad.

For so long, I thought Essiya's name brought death wherever it went. But hearing Dawoud speak it...I had forgotten what it meant to be real to someone. I had felt more whole in those few minutes than I had in eleven years. Even if I no longer knew who Essiya was.

The door opened as several pillows exploded, raining feathers on the dancing fire.

My neck prickled, and I turned to see the Nizahl Heir closing the door.

The fire licked over the mattress, casting the room in an orange glow. Something wet had been steadily dripping from my chin since I entered the palace, and I wiped my cheeks with detached wonder.

"Do you know that I can't remember the last time I cried? Maybe six, seven years ago." Cracks spidered in the mirror. The glass burst, raining shards over the destroyed wardrobe. I caught a tear from the corner of my eye and examined it thoughtfully. "They just keep coming."

"Do you intend to bring down the Omal palace, then?" Arin asked conversationally, as though the objects hurtling around the room were nothing more consequential than overexcited dust motes.

"Oh, I'm not greedy. Just this half of it will do." The triangular head of the window toppled in a rupture of white concrete.

An advantage of living with the Nizahl Heir for months was how familiar I had become with the tiniest shifts in his inscrutable expression. "What was his name?"

Everything on my side of the room rose into the air and hurled into the opposite wall.

"Be quiet," I growled.

Arin could not anchor me this time. I would not let him break the blessed emptiness again.

Arin dusted wooden shards from his coat. His boots extinguished the flames beneath them as he approached. "Who was he to you?"

"I'm warning you." Instead of flourishing with my outrage, my magic started to splutter.

Arin trapped me against the wall, his arms bracketing the sides of my head. All I could see was pale blue, steady and unwavering. "He will be taken to Jasad," Arin said. I clutched my chest, shaking my head. "They will prepare him for burial in the Jasadi custom."

"Stop, stop," I cried out. I shoved at his shoulders.

"He will be buried in a spot where the grass still grows." Arin's voice filtered into my head. A firm, cauterizing force cutting a path through the wound. "A fig tree will be planted to mark his memory."

My cuffs slackened even as the chasm inside me yawned wider. I tried to block the sight, but it unfolded before me anyway. Dawoud washed by gentle hands and wrapped in white linens. The death rites gently whispered in Resar. A fig tree blooming beside him every spring.

Arin caught me as I slid down the wall. The Nizahl Heir pulled me into his chest as sobs racked my body, easing us to the ground. I sobbed like I hadn't since the Blood Summit, when my first life ended. Pressed against the son of the man who had taken everything.

"I am not a butcher." I wept into Arin's throat. "I am not an axe to be swung in any direction I am pointed. He deserved better than this. He deserved better than me."

Everyone in that village deserved better. Supreme Rawain

harming Jasadis came as no surprise, but their own Heir? I killed and buried Hanim to avoid this fate.

Arin didn't reply. Solid arms tightened around me. He was real. Arin was real, Dawoud was real, and I was nothing more than a ghost inside the body of a coward.

Gloved hands framed my face, drawing me back. Arin's ironclad composure faltered as he searched my tearstained face. There was a wildness to him I had never seen before. "Look at me, Suraira." A fierce defiance radiated from the Nizahl Heir. "You don't have to do this. Run. Take a horse and get as far away as you can."

I blinked. "Wh-what?"

"I won't come after you. I have hidden holdings in every kingdom. Throughout Essam Woods. They're yours. Take them. Be free." Arin's grip was tight enough to hurt, belying his words.

I searched his face. Which one of us had lost their mind?

"A donkey kicked in the head six times wouldn't suggest such an unreasonable course of action. Are you mocking me?"

Arin looked at me until it started to hurt. A covered thumb slid across my cheekbone. "What appeal can reason have in the face of your tears?"

I stared at him. The silky locks of silver hair falling around his ears. His death-defying scar. The shape of his mouth. A mouth I had watched speak terror in the eyes of men and spin the axis of destiny to his unyielding will. A lethal, poisonous mouth. One that curved upward under my heavy gaze.

Why was the Summit called? Before it was the impetus for the Jasad War, before it was the Blood Summit—why did the kingdoms assemble?

"The Malik and Malika of Jasad were magic miners."

We both froze. I pressed the tips of my fingers to my lips, not daring to believe they had shaped themselves around such horrible words. Words that could get me gagged and imprisoned almost as fast as my magic.

"Your magic is powerful, Essiya. Gedo Niyar and Teta Palia might try to take some of it. Tell them no. Fight them if you must." Niphran smoothed my curls away from my face, heaving with the effort of being out of bed. *"I am going to tell you a long-lost story, but you cannot ever share it with anyone. Not Dawoud. Not Soraya."*

Magic mining was a myth. A story so dangerous, so potent with the potential to unleash chaos, that even uttering the words was once cause for punishment. Time had washed it from importance, made it so the only ones who recalled the myth were long dead and forgotten. Or insane women locked in Bakir Tower.

My nails cut into my palms. The mirrors in my head were shattering. Unlocking my memories in pieces, disjointed shards I would bloody myself putting together. Fairel broke the first one, and they had not stopped since. How many more were left?

I muffled my gasp as Arin yanked me into him. My arms went around his back. He was shaking.

"You little liar," he whispered. Choked and low. "You maddening Jasadi girl, I cherish your tongue too much to see it cut out of your head. Never speak those words to me or anyone else again. Do you understand?"

He pulled me away and shook my arms. My teeth clacked together. Urgency hardened in his voice. "Tell me you understand!"

My eyes were wide. I had singlehandedly sent the least reactive man in the kingdoms into a panic.

"I understand."

He released me. I sat back on my heels, putting distance between us. Dawoud hung over my thoughts like a black shroud. I couldn't think past him long enough to study the pieces of the mirror that had propelled Arin into such a state.

We stared at each other for a charged moment. I wanted to press for answers, but the vehemence of his reaction had rattled me. What did Arin know?

I had a fondness for my tongue, so my investigation would be done far away from the Nizahl Heir.

I spoke too loudly, eager to scrub the shaken look off Arin's face. "They haven't attacked yet. The Mufsids or Urabi, even Soraya. What if they bide their time until after the Alcalah, after your soldiers are gone?"

Arin closed his eyes for the briefest second. When he opened them, any evidence of uncertainty or tension was gone. "About that." Arin helped me to my feet, and I glanced around the wreckage of the room. No mortal strength alone could have wrought such damage, and everything was too fractured to be put together again. It reeked of magic.

Arin came to the same conclusion. He kicked a merrily flaming splinter of the wardrobe into the fallen pillows. They ignited, fire leaping to the mattress. He would probably alert the Omalian servants after the ash clouds hid the debris. He might say a lantern or candle fell over, and the servants would believe him, because he was Arin of Nizahl, and the Commander did not set fires in foreign rooms.

"Another theory?"

"Better." Arin found a salvageable tunic from the wardrobe and passed it to me. "A plan."

A fleet of carriages painted in a spectrum of colors surrounded the Omal palace in the new morning's dawn. The exodus to Nizahl for the third trial had begun, with several contingents leaving directly after the second trial. Among them Vaun and Supreme Rawain, the latter of whom needed to greet the Citadel's guests as they entered Nizahl.

In the spiteful cold, I hopped from foot to foot beside two tan carriages. Sorn, the Orban Heir, had patted his vivid green and brown carriage and asked Arin if Nizahl's colors did not suit his taste. To which Arin had responded, "If I am to be ambushed on the road, it will not be because of the paint on my carriage." Even Diya had suppressed a smirk at Sorn's embarrassment.

"There is a market coming up soon," I said. My breath puffed out in wisps of white. I drew my cloak closer. Sefa scowled at the moth-eaten collar. I had been given dozens of luxurious cloaks to wear, and she did not like how I still clung to my raggedy one. "Help Rory set up a booth. Make sure it's by the fountain, or he will pitch a fit."

"Ah." Sefa glanced at Marek.

He sighed. "Sylvia, we are coming with you."

I squinted, waiting for his expression to fracture with humor. "What a peculiar jest."

"It is not a jest. We're coming. His Highness caught us outside yesterday, before we had even entered the palace," Sefa said. "We waited for you to ask us to go with you. Why haven't you?"

"Why?" I sputtered. "Dania's sacred skirts, have your wits tumbled free of your heads? The High Counselor is in Nizahl. Marek is wanted for assault and avoiding conscription. Under no circumstances are you entering Nizahl!"

"Actually," Marek said. "We are."

I spun around, checking we were in front of the Omal palace and not in some bizarre dream. "Marek, you have been fighting this since the beginning! I know His Highness can be extremely persuasive, but we can accomplish what we need without you. If this is about last night's...episode, it is unlikely to repeat itself, and you needn't—"

"Damn it to the tombs, Sylvia, you do not need to bear everything alone!" Marek ran a hand through his hair. "Why is it so unbelievable that we would come without being dragged by the ear?"

"You reckless fools. We can execute Arin's plan without you! I will be all right."

"We go back to Mahair with you or not at all," Sefa snapped. She lowered her voice, glancing around surreptitiously. "We bought glamors from a vagrant in Orban who says he paid a Jasadi to enchant them."

I threw my arms up. "Glamors will not hold long against people closely acquainted with your true faces." The High Counselor, for example.

"Which is why the Commander's instructions are to send us into the lower villages. Marek is from the military towns and my mother is a noble, so there will not be a risk of recognition in Nizahl's southern provinces."

Arin exited the palace, his guards in tow. He nodded at Felix and exchanged a few words with Queen Hanan. My cousin and paternal grandmother watched him walk toward us. Felix's dark glare delighted me. He had been effectively neutered. He would not attack me in Arin's own kingdom, and after the debacle with the dolls, Vaida would not trust Felix to pour water into a cup. All his hopes for retribution rested on the outcome of the third trial.

My gaze crossed Queen Hanan's. I searched for the features of a father I had never known in the older woman's face. The perpetually weary look in the Omal Queen's eyes flickered. Her brows furrowed. I quickly looked away.

Reaching the carriage, Arin took in my thunderous expression and glanced at my companions.

"I did not force them," he said, guessing the source of my ire. "Jeru, ready the horses. We will take the southern route. Tell the soldiers to keep within our radius, but not to converge on the path. Sefa and Marek, your carriage will go ahead of us."

"Wait, I have—" My objections were drowned out by the flurry of activity as riders leapt to their horses, and the thirty Nizahl soldiers began a procession from the palace.

"He didn't call you the boy!" Sefa said in a loud whisper, hopping into the carriage. Marek followed her with an eye roll.

Swearing, I shoved into the carriage. I wouldn't have an opportunity to speak to Marek and Sefa until we stopped at the first cabin. By then, it would be too late to change anything.

The sun rose in the east, a palm of blushing light unfurling behind the Omal palace. We rode past the crystalline gates. Their contours gleamed in the nascent morning.

"You knew they would come if you said it was for me," I accused an hour into the ride. We had finally rumbled into Essam Woods. The sight of gnarled trees threatened to catapult me into reliving last night's hike with Dawoud in my arms. I swallowed, fighting the instinct to shove the memory aside. An instinct as natural to me as breathing. He deserved to be remembered, even if it made me wish I had died with him.

We are who we come from. Dawoud was Jasad to me. He was love and warmth and free compassion. I anchored his memory, fixing it to the inhospitable soil of my mind, and some piece of me sighed in relief.

"I did not ask." Arin had spread his parchment around as soon as the carriage lurched out of the palace, making meticulous marks every here and there. "I relayed my intention to draw out the groups and told them they were free to decide their course."

The plan had formed in the madness of our last evening in Omal.

Instead of waiting for the Mufsids, Urabi, or Soraya to move first, Arin intended to lure them out during the third trial. The guards would spread rumors about the Orban Champion's declining health, which would spread among the soldiers, who would spread it through the upper towns. Sefa and Marek would ride into the lower villages with a few disguised soldiers, pretending to be beleaguered organizers for the Alcalah. They would drink in various taverns, and under the guise of inebriation, complain about the weak security the third trial offered compared to Omal and Orban.

With Diya's supposedly failing health increasing my likelihood of becoming Victor, and therefore being assigned personal guards for the rest of my days, the groups would see their window of opportunity closing. Sefa and Marek maligning the protections around the third trial would provide further incentive to attack.

"Wouldn't the groups suspect something was amiss? If they have managed to evade you this long, I struggle to believe a hefty amount of trickery is what will move them to act," I had said.

"Oh, they will almost certainly see through the ploy." Arin had deftly buttoned his coat, observing the servants rushing between the fountain and my burning room. "But none of them will be willing to risk that another might take the bait and succeed in catching you first."

The trip to Nizahl passed in a blur of arguments and cold cabin rooms. Sefa hummed every time I tried to talk sense into her. Marek would dip his hands in mud and chase me around the cabin. Idiots, both of them.

We were due in Nizahl today. To distract from my churning dread, I plucked one of Arin's maps and smoothed it open on my legs. I studied the map for long moments, trying to decipher the unintelligible markings.

"Have you started doodling in your spare time?" I asked, squinting at the downward V shapes and scribbled names. I traced a bridge that might have been Sirauk.

Arin didn't ask to see the map. "The mountains."

My forehead furrowed. The carriage's motion jostled me into the window. "Which ones?" Hundreds of mountains bordered the kingdoms, theoretically overlooking seas and deserted lands. Theoretically, because fewer than five had completed the journey to and from the mountains. Vast as they were, the most attention the mountains were given on maps was a quick scribble of their general locations.

"All of them," Arin said. He crossed his ankle over his knee and separated the papers over his triangled lap. Met with my silence, he glanced up.

"You have a map of the mountains?" I asked faintly. "A detailed map?"

Arin's expression strongly suggested he thought I had knocked my head against the carriage door one too many times. "I have several, but they're far from finished."

The fist around my heart squeezed. Acknowledging the Heir's brilliance came naturally, but at some unidentifiable point, I had grown to admire it. Forgetting his peerless mind was in service to a pitiless kingdom. "We never stood a chance against you, did we? Rawain's siege never really ended, because he has you to see it through to the very last Jasadi. Given a thousand fortresses, Jasad would still be doomed."

Arin's gaze shuttered. A chilly guardedness that had been gone long enough to make its return startling descended over the Heir.

"I can circumvent much," Arin said. "But even I might falter at a thousand fortresses."

A few miles from the Citadel, Ren steered Sefa and Marek's carriage south. Only the Champions and the royal guests were permitted to enter the Citadel grounds, and of that exclusive few, none could spend the night inside the Citadel. The royals would lodge in the upper towns for the night, and the trial would be held in the morning. At the conclusion of the Victor's Ball the following evening, everyone would be required to show a purpose for remaining in the kingdom.

Hospitality did not rank among Nizahl's limited virtues.

Sefa and Marek would begin their portion of the plan tonight. After donning their disguises, the pair would sow rumors about the third trial's security throughout the lower villages. I wanted Sefa and Marek to spend tonight in the Champions' suites with me, but the rooms were wedged between the second and third gates to the Citadel. Too close to the Nizahl royals and people who might recognize them.

I wouldn't see them until after the trial. They would wait for me in the carriage during the Victor's Ball. We would ride out with a brigade of Nizahl soldiers and, if I won, the Victor's appointed guards.

"We know how to take care of ourselves," Sefa assured me.

I allowed Marek to pull me into a light hug, pushing my uncooperative arms to pat him on the back. "Trust yourself," he murmured. When I nudged him loose, his gaze was on Arin's carriage. "No one else."

My worry remained long after their carriage disappeared. I reminded myself that they had been crooks and vagrants before coming to Mahair—they would manage a single night. So long as Sefa didn't stop to help any whimpering puppies and get herself thrown into the back of a wagon, anyway.

One of Arin's maps flew onto my foot as the carriage heaved to the right. I peered out the window, watching the wilderness of Essam disappear into smooth land.

The soldiers fanned out around us. The first of three looming black gates appeared. They were impossibly tall, disappearing into the hazy mist rolling beneath the moon. A raven forged from glinting steel took flight from between two clashing swords at the helm of the entrance. Nizahl's symbol split in two as the gate yawned open. My trepidation spiked as we went through the next two gates, and I held my breath as our carriage glided forward.

The Citadel rose ahead of us in a cylindrical spiral of twisting iron and steel. The blade-like peak impaled the sky, as though punishing the clouds for daring to dwell higher. Several metal legs extended from the middle of the main spire, each connecting to one of the Citadel's seven menacing wings. A spider of destruction poised to spring. Massive violet and black crests shone at the peak of every wing, the seven ravens' sinister gazes tracking the reckless as they ventured into the maw of the beast.

"Welcome to Nizahl," Arin said.

CHAPTER THIRTY-ONE

I would give Nizahl this: they were much quieter than the other kingdoms.

Since they were the youngest kingdom, and the only one not to have an Awal or Awala to honor, Nizahl's customs diverged sharply from the others. There were no festivals, no markets, no celebrations. Once a year, Nizahlans gathered to watch the young soldiers advance into the Commander's army in a special ceremony. They ate game, grains, and bread. They were a strictly hierarchical society, placing a high premium on respect to those above you.

To Nizahlans, Lukubis were depraved, Orbanians animals, and Omalians loud swindlers. They did not see that their kingdom's sterility was its own danger. Nizahl lived like a predator poised in wait, holding its breath for the right moment to strike.

Jeru accompanied me to Diya's rooms for supper. Arin had been whisked through the other gates as soon as I left the carriage. "It might interest you to know His Highness the Supreme didn't invite Vaun into his carriage when he departed from Omal."

I knocked on Diya's door. I did not want to think of Dawoud while I stood in his killer's kingdom. "Good." I was not foolish enough to believe Supreme Rawain's suspicion fully laid to rest, but Dawoud's death had at least cast doubt on the merits of Vaun's claims.

Our meal was quiet. Diya inspected each bite of food before eating it and stared out the window while she chewed. "I hate birds," she said. She sliced into the boiled pigeon on her plate. "But I do love to eat them."

I had grown almost fond of Diya's belligerent nature. She was a cactus I enjoyed pricking my finger against. I had a notion that Orbanian Fairel would take a great liking to Diya. The young ward had terrible taste in people. "Is that why you keep glaring at the Nizahl crest? Worried one of the ravens will fly down to gobble you up?"

The Orban Champion snapped the pigeon's wing in two, unamused. "Laugh as you wish. I know you can feel the dark pulse in this land. Those ravens terrify me." Diya shuddered, pushing aside her plate. "You should beware symbols of power. They have a tendency to create lives of their own."

Diya evicted me as soon as we finished eating. I walked back to my room between the second and third gates that bracketed the Champions' suites. A compromise for not allowing Champions to spend the night in the Supreme's home; we were still protected within the scope of the Citadel's grounds. I passed khawaga dressed in galabiyas, the brown-and-green garments falling to their sandaled feet. Nizahl soldiers circled my suite, their starched livery at odds with the neighboring Orbanian garb.

Meanwhile, my perennial inability to sleep in new places was in top form tonight.

"I want to go for a walk around the grounds," I whined. "Who could possibly attack me in the Citadel? I can't sleep, Jeru."

A hassled Jeru yanked at the ends of his curly hair. I'd been nagging him for the better part of an hour. "Would it help if I knocked your skull against the door a few times?"

My neck prickled. The soldiers at Jeru's back bowed, clearing the way for a tall figure to climb the steps.

"That seems ill-advised," Arin said, startling Jeru so badly the guard choked on his own saliva.

"Sire, I—" Jeru turned the shade of a ripe pomegranate, but Arin waved the guard's mortification away.

"Get your cloak," Arin said to me. "I'm going to take the Nizahl Champion for a walk around the Citadel's grounds."

Shock flitted across Jeru's face before he schooled his features. I supposed Arin didn't make a habit of personally escorting guests around the premises. "Of course, my lord. I'll alert the soldiers to open the third gate."

"I assumed you would barricade yourself in your quarters until tomorrow," I said, pulling on my cloak. Damn it, where had I tossed my boots?

Arin tracked my frenetic movements around the room with vague amusement. There weren't many places the boots could be. The only decoration in the room was a painting of Supreme Rawain, placed opposite the bed to ensure nightmares all night long. He was depicted leaning on his scepter in one of the Citadel's chambers.

"You've heard the rumors," Arin sighed.

"That you're a recluse? Everyone has." Ah, I'd buried them beneath my bags. If I had a fraction of Arin's instinct for tidiness, I would lead an entirely different life. "You can admit it. I won't think less of you. You wish you were alone with your maps and a glass of that horrendous lavender drink, don't you?"

I turned, boots firmly tied, to find Arin in the middle of carefully folding the only set of clothes I'd unpacked: my outfit for the trial. Something in my chest swelled at the sight. The rumple in his brow as he smoothed the sleeves, the way he angled the stack so I couldn't miss it. Handling my belongings with the thoughtfulness and care I'd originally confused for severity and uncompromising perfectionism.

When he saw me looking, a red tinge brightened the top of his cheeks. I blinked, and it was gone—a trick of the light, maybe.

"No," Arin said.

"No?"

"No, I don't wish I was alone with my maps and my talwith. I am where I want to be."

Before I could open my mouth, he walked out of the suite. I bundled my cloak tighter against the seasonably cold night and hurried to catch up. I waved at Jeru, who grunted and stomped away. "I am going to miss antagonizing your guards." The third gate yawned open ahead of us, lined with soldiers on either side. They bowed as we passed.

Despite the tension of tomorrow's trial, Arin's demeanor was lighter than usual.

"You're glad to be home."

A strand of hair caught on the edge of his smile. "I am."

This close to the Citadel, I understood what Diya meant about the dark pulse. The halls connecting the main spire to the wings were rectangular and narrow, running high over our heads like open-air tunnels. Even the wind rustling through the grass seemed to whisper warnings I couldn't make out. Every facet of the Citadel's grounds was petrifying.

"The Victor's Ball will be held in this wing." Arin pointed. "The one behind it is for assemblies with the Supreme's counselors."

I struggled to suppress my laugh. Though not readily apparent to most, Arin was in a good mood. He was speaking easily, and the tight line between his shoulders and neck had fractionally loosened. It was a shame what brought him comfort had the opposite effect on me.

"What about that one?" I pointed to the wing behind the Citadel. The only one without a raven rising from between the two swords.

"The war wing," Arin answered. Some of the tension returned to his features. "It has not been entered since the siege. When we need to intervene to settle disputes between the kingdoms, we use the third wing."

I frowned, a question on the tip of my tongue. Wouldn't it be more prudent to use the war wing for regional disputes if the goal was to efficiently arbitrate? What faster motivator could there be for squabbling kingdoms to settle than the prospect of war?

"Your nimwa system," I realized. We walked past the Citadel, and I was glad to have the Supreme's home out of my sight. Identical rows of short, square metal buildings studded the road ahead. The soldiers milling around bowed deeply at the sight of their Commander. "If Nizahl enters a state of active war, mandatory conscription takes effect again. The lower villages will need to send their children to the Citadel."

Arin looked at me sharply. "How do you know about the nimwa system?"

I bit the inside of my cheek. "Why does it matter how I know? I think it is a wonderful system you've created."

To my unadulterated delight, Arin scowled at the praise. By Sirauk's cursed depths, the Nizahl Heir was *flustered*. "It can hardly be called a system."

I counted on my fingers. "You give every family in the lower villages an allotment of grains, oats, potatoes, and rice. The more members of a family, the higher the allotment. A youth supporting their family is exempted from conscription, and if there are several eligible children in a single household, the age to join is raised to twenty. Which, of course, essentially means everyone in the lower villages is exempt."

Arin pursed his lips. "Wes."

I brushed his arm as we walked past the first of the metal buildings. "You care about your people, Arin. That is not a quality to be embarrassed about." The statement felt like a confession, meant for whispering in the lonely dark. "You will be an excellent Supreme one day."

At Arin's silence, I glanced up to find him staring at me, an indecipherable look in his eyes. My fingers curled in the pockets of my cloak, fighting the asinine urge to reach for him. I wanted to laugh, avert my gaze, anything to defuse the pressure. If I let it settle, if I looked at it too closely, the fragile stage upon which we circled might crumble.

"I am glad to hear you speak my name outside of imminent danger," Arin said softly, and the battle was lost.

Idiot! Hanim howled. *How many ways can you betray us, Essiya?*

It didn't feel like betrayal. It felt like wandering through the woods for an endless night and finally stumbling into the dawn.

It was the feeling I had at the sight of Mahair after hours of catching frogs by the moonlight. The rush of Hirun around me. Fairel's giggle and the click of Rory's cane. Anchors, real and solid, pinning me to earth.

I smiled shakily. "I will make frequent use of it, then."

After a lifetime of running, he was my homecoming.

Rings formed in the pond to my right as the ground rumbled. Arin grinned, gloved hand closing around mine as he tugged me forward. A slew of soldiers stumbled from one of the metal buildings—military compounds—and sprinted to the south. We were behind them, out of view. The sight of so many bedraggled Nizahl soldiers, devoid of the rigid discipline training would bring, brought a chuckle to my lips. The Supreme wouldn't be pleased I was witnessing this. The Commander had taken an Omalian villager deep into the Citadel's ground, to the compounds housing Nizahl's newest recruits.

"The midnight runs," I said. "Is anyone holding a mop?"

Arin groaned, releasing my hand. My fingers curled around the absence. "You are not to be left alone with my guardsmen anymore."

We resumed our walk. The sight of his soldiers seemed to have invigorated Arin; he spoke more freely than he ever had. He described the trades the soldiers needed to learn, because their duties extended beyond surveillance and fighting. The recruits rotated between the compounds, and only when they were deemed to have performed with exceptional skill in their trainings and trades were they advanced into the army.

"Do you train the new recruits yourself?"

"Rarely. They are too frightened of me." He sounded unhappy about a fact most would find pleasing. "They will simply obey."

I lost track of the number of soldiers who bowed to Arin as we walked. "Is obedience not what a Commander should seek?"

"Obedience should be conscious, not instinctual."

We turned around, beginning our return to my suites. Another soldier bowed, and I huffed. "Have you considered coloring your hair? You might be able to walk an entire ten feet without being recognized."

Arin raised a brow. His silver hair was luminescent, a crown in its own right. "Why would I avoid recognition? The only people who do not wish to be known are the ones with something to be ashamed of."

The Citadel's silhouette took shape ahead. The heart and soul of Nizahl. Inside, Rawain would be toasting to his Champion's success in the trials. Anticipating the glory I would bring to his kingdom.

"Yes," I said. "I suppose you are right."

The ride to the arena passed in tense silence. Sprawled in the center of massive brown fields, the arena loomed ahead like a blight on the land. To prevent a crush of spectators, carriages were stopped half a mile from the arena. My stomach hadn't ceased its anxious gnawing since leaving the suites an hour ago. "I can walk the rest of the way."

"It's raining," Jeru said.

I deliberately blinked the water from my lashes to communicate my thoughts on his astute observation.

"I will go with her." Arin stepped smoothly from the carriage.

Wes and Jeru gaped. "But Your Highness, you'll be on foot while the other royals are entering by carriage."

"The Heir is due a bit of impropriety," I said. Jeru looked as though he could not tell whether I had gone mad, or if he had. Resignation loosened Wes's shoulders, and the older guard even seemed a little amused.

Arin adopted a brisk pace. The soldiers lined the path on either side of us, far away enough to afford us a modicum of privacy. "My soldiers are set up in every corner of the arena. They are stationed at every entry, every exit, every possible location an intruder could exploit. They are dressed in the colors of other kingdoms, and I have instructed them to carry no weapons that could identify them as Nizahl soldiers."

"I'm sure you're ready," I said.

"I do not want you distracted by security concerns during the trial. Your only goal today is to defeat the Orban Champion, and the rest is mine."

I lifted a shoulder. "It might be better for the Mufsids or Urabi to get close. Easier for your soldiers to identify the assailants in the crowd if they're actively attempting to reach me."

It was the wrong thing to say. Arin whirled, blocking my path. Incandescent anger lit his lovely features. "Not this again! Sylvia—" He cut himself short and glared at the soldiers. "Turn!" he ordered.

They hastily took several steps away and gave us their backs.

Rain dripped from the bottom of his hair, dampening his coat collar. "You will walk out of this trial whole and become the Alcalah's next Victor. There is no other acceptable result." The wind carried away the ashes of his anger, revealing a fear that stole my breath away. "Don't ask me to abide your death at my hands."

Swallowing past the dryness of my throat, I said, "I spoke poorly. I have every intention of walking out of that trial as an insufferable winner."

Arin punctuated his words with a glare. "Trust your instincts. Your magic will sense the threat, even if you do not. You're stronger than them. You'll be fine." It sounded like he was talking to himself as much as me.

I fluttered my hand, infusing my voice with a confidence I didn't feel. "Save me a dance at the Victor's Ball, Your Highness."

His smile was small and fleeting. "I would have to learn first."

I gasped, clutching my heart. "Have I stumbled across a fault? In the magnificent Commander, the lofty Nizahl Heir? Impossible. I cannot believe it."

Arin sighed. "That's quite enough."

The arena curved high on the sides and lower in the center, shaped like a high-sided bowl. Black and violet columns encircled the arena, and a stone statue of Nizahl's raven and swords towered over the arriving guests.

I motioned to where Diya disappeared beneath a violet awning. "I have to go alone from here." I swept a dramatic bow to Arin, gratified when exasperation broke across his tense face.

Every step away from him weighed heavier than the last. This trial posed a double-edged threat. Though Diya seemed to like me and might hesitate to deliver a killing strike, she was the deadliest Champion of the lot. Meanwhile, Soraya lurked somewhere, preparing to kill me before the Mufsids and Urabi could whisk me away.

There was a real chance I would not see him again.

I spun around. Arin cut an imposing figure against the frothing clouds, boots glistening from the rain and coat lifting against the wind. He stood there, watching me leave, even though the storm raged around us. "Tell your guard to turn again," I called. It barely carried.

Arin raised two fingers and slashed them to the side. The guards gave us their backs a second time. I trotted to him, stripping off my cloak. I held it out. "Would you take care of this for me?"

An agonizing beat wherein I was certain he'd refuse, and I'd have to impale myself on Diya's sword from the humiliation.

He took the cloak, folding it carefully over his arm. "I'll treat it like my own."

"Better," I said. Without hatred's spool at the center, the fondness in his eyes was unraveling me. "Wool—"

"—is a difficult material to launder," Arin finished. "I remember."

"Good." Now would be an excellent time to jog away. My feet stayed rooted.

It was just. He remembered.

A raindrop slid along his jaw. "Is there anything else?"

"I am going to try something." I squared my shoulders. "Don't stab me."

I meant to approach precisely, place my arms at preapproved locations and angle my head just so. We were both wary, and Arin seemed to relish touch about as much as I did.

Instead, I launched myself at the Nizahl Heir. He caught me with a surprised grunt, arms winding around my waist. He was too tall, leaving my feet dangling in the air. I wrapped my arms around his shoulders.

Arin exhaled, warm against my neck, and held me fast.

"I have a joke about an Heir and an orphan. It's so ridiculous, even your mighty stoicism will crack," I whispered. I buried my face in his collar. "Would you like to hear it?"

His breath ghosted across my skin. "Probably not."

"That's all right. It's funnier in my head."

I wanted to stay there. I wanted to tell him that I had not easily embraced anyone since Soraya bid me farewell the morning of the Blood Summit. That with him, every aversion was a craving. That even though one day I would kneel before Jasad's judges in the afterlife to account for it, I would not renounce a single moment of loving the Nizahl Heir.

I pulled away reluctantly. I patted the cloak, avoiding looking at Arin. I had looked my lot at him, and the beating creature in my chest could not withstand another indulgence. "You should start practicing your steps. I'm a wonderful dancer."

The arena in Nizahl took three thousand men to build. The oval-shaped structure stood two stories tall at its peak, each tier moving farther back, like levels in a staircase to the sky. The bottom of the arena, where the competitors emerged, was roughly a thousand feet. The lowest seats rose above the long walls surrounding the competitiors, shielded from any stray arrows or knives by a thick glass divider. Each kingdom had its own section, marked by a pillar at the very top level, and their unique crests were carved into the pillar's front. The section to the right belonged solely to the royal families. The Supreme, Sultana Vaida, King Murib and his Queen, and Queen Hanan sat in the front. Behind them were their Heirs, and behind the Heirs were younger siblings, cousins, and their assorted spouses. I glanced past the empty seat next to the Supreme and focused on the task at hand. One more trial.

The announcer's booming voice shook the arena. Diya and I stayed in the tunnels, waiting for our introductions. He talked of the first Alcalah, of unity and peace, of joining with one's neighbor in celebrating the best of our kingdoms. Utter nonsense, and eerily identical to the speeches delivered at the Blood Summit.

"This is the sort of honor-of-Awaleen, glory-of-kingdom nonsense Mehti devoured," Diya murmured. Water dripped in the damp tunnel as the announcer prepared to call us in. "If he had made it to the third trial, he would still never become Victor. What hope would he have of seeing through fabricated illusions when he cannot see through these?"

The announcer called our names, and we emerged into a cacophony of cheers and exuberant faces. A table laden with weapons took up space on each side of the pit. A black line had been drawn in the sand, demarcating Diya's side from mine. We walked to our sections.

The announcer pranced around a slab of concrete, keeping away from the shifting sand. As soon as he finished speaking, he'd dart back into one of the doors beneath the arena to hide. "The day we have waited for has finally arrived. We thank the Awaleen for the act of entombing themselves with their wicked brother, Rovial. They loved humanity enough to sacrifice themselves for it, and in return, we present to you the strongest Champions the kingdoms have to offer. Our Awala Baira believed in the potential of our imagination and the depths of the human mind. In celebration of Baira, our Champions will be given an elixir to induce vivid hallucinations. They'll see themselves fighting lions in Orban's desert flats, evading hunters in Essam's wilderness. Can they battle through the elixir's challenges before the sand below them sinks or the other Champion wakes up?" The presenter raised his arms. "But wait! Do you see the four tunnels around our Champions? From one of them will emerge a beast more fearsome than any illusion. If a Champion does not break themselves from Baira's illusion in time to fight the beast, the sand will be the least of their concerns. Our Victor will be able to cut through the fabricated threat to the real one!"

The announcer picked up a tray. Emerald liquid sloshed within two glass vials. He took the tray's long handle and extended the vials to hover between us.

"If our Champions cross the black line you see before you, the nature of the fight will change. Instead of success by simply overpowering their opponent, victory will only be won through a fight to the death."

I would bet every hair on Marek's yellow head they engineered these elixirs to make the hallucinations such that keeping to our sides of the pit would be near impossible. If we were outrunning hunters and lions in our head, our feet would naturally carry us forward. Rory had talked about these elixirs, about the light poisons they infused to give the body the impression of death and the roots they mixed in to scramble our senses.

Diya and I raised our vials. *Good luck*, she mouthed.

The elixir wasn't nearly as sweet as the color suggested. I wrinkled my nose, tossing the empty vial into the sand. Diya wiped her mouth with a grimace.

"Do you feel elevated yet?" Diya asked.

"It's hard to tell, since I'm already so much taller than you."

She rolled her eyes, and the action reminded me so strongly of Sefa that I had to look away. Diya hooked an arrow into her bow. "I need to practice aiming. You have a big head, and I would prefer to avoid killing you if I can help it."

Nausea descended between one insult and the next. It wasn't unlike the sensations I had experienced at the very start of practicing my magic, when any minute display had me lunging for a bucket.

"Something's wrong," I mumbled. My magic hadn't moved, yet the sickness expanded, surging through me.

Three events came to pass in quick succession.

First, Diya's eyes rolled to the back of her head. She collapsed in the sand.

Next, a glowing barrier closed around the pit, blocking Diya and me off from the tunnels and the rest of the arena. Screams erupted, but I couldn't see anything behind the barrier. Which meant they couldn't see us, either.

My stomach cramped. I crashed into the table, scattering weapons everywhere. The arena spun.

The elixirs. There was magic in the elixirs.

"Soraya," I ground out.

Soraya knew a direct magical attack would be repelled by the same force distorting her warding spells, so she found a new way to shove her magic past my cuffs: having me ingest it.

Finally, the sickness unhinged its maw and consumed me whole.

My last thought before I hit the sand was a triumphant one. Arin had done it. He had lured them into a trap of his own design. The Mufsids and Urabi would be frenzied, trying to breach the barrier before Soraya succeeded in killing me.

It would be their final act.

She had taken me into a dream. Maybe a memory.

I stood in Bakir Tower. Unlike the opulence of Usr Jasad, the tower's limestone and mud brick leached away color and light. In the center of the narrow room, Niphran paced. Not the wispy Niphran in my dreams, but the woman herself. She looked strong, her long shoulders straight, cascading hair tied behind her head. Most surprising of all were her eyes—clear and lucid like they had not been in years. Black kitmer eyes.

"Mama?" I whispered.

She didn't hear me. I moved closer. Niphran's circuit around the room didn't slow. She braced her hands at the window and gasped.

Outside Bakir Tower, the palace bells rang, and a stream of people marched into Jasad's upper town. I couldn't appreciate the heartrending tableau of Jasad as it once was. Screams rang out from the palace.

We were under attack.

Niphran's door opened, and we both whirled around. A teenage Soraya stood on the other side.

"Where's my daughter? Where's Dawoud? The palace is under attack!" Niphran shouted.

From her waistband, Soraya withdrew a wavy dagger. "The palace is finally in the right hands."

Through the window, I saw people climbing onto the palace's roof, shouting from the minarets. The palace servants were led out on the ends of spears, cowing to their polished conquerors.

The Mufsids.

Niphran touched her temple, glancing around the barren room for anything she could use to protect herself. "The bedpost! Snap it from the middle of the hourglass curve," I urged. She did not react. When I tried to reach for it, the wood passed harmlessly through me.

"My head feels clear for the first time in years," Niphran breathed. "I can think again."

Cruel amusement flashed across my young attendant's face. "I would think so. It's the first day you have been free from your *special beverages* in six years. I wanted you to see the true Jasad being born without an addled mind. You are the only royal left who can."

Niphran and I latched on to different parts of Soraya's declaration.

Special beverages? "Her madness…was just poison?" But how? Soraya came under the palace's service two years before the Blood Summit, and Niphran deteriorated years before then. Niyar had waited to appoint Niphran as Qayida until she regained her health, and in the meantime—

In the meantime, Hanim had been chosen to lead Jasad's armies.

My heart staggered to a stop. Niphran's madness was Hanim's doing?

"Only royal? Where are the Malik and Malika?" Niphran started forward, halting when Soraya raised the dagger. "Where is my daughter?"

The boredom on Soraya's face wavered, just for an instant. Niphran went white. "No, no, don't say—"

"She's not dead yet," Soraya snapped. "He plans to attack on the last day of the Summit, after the messenger carries news of your death."

He. She could only mean Rawain. I'd known the true culprit of the Blood Summit all along, but the confirmation still cut the knees out from under me. My memories were true. I wasn't crazy. But how had he done it?

I was watching my worst suspicions unfold into reality. The Mufsids had been working against Usr Jasad before the siege. It was they who'd slaughtered everyone in the palace, days before Nizahl even reached the kingdom. But why? The Mufsids belonged to wealthy wilayahs, profiting from Jasad's gains long before the other wilayahs did. They had the least reason to hate the Usr.

Niphran covered her heart with both hands. "Essiya loves you. She had so few people left to love, and she chose you."

"Shut up!" It echoed in the lonely caverns of Bakir Tower. "If I could have—" Soraya turned away, and to my utter disbelief, tears glistened in her eyes. "I want the rotten lot of you to fester under the earth. If I could have spared Essiya, do you think I wouldn't have? No one can inherit Jasad! There can be no blood claim to the throne."

Niphran wasn't deterred. For someone resurfacing from years of lethargy, my mother was certainly thinking fast. "Then hide her. Give her a new name. Send her to live with Emre's family in Omal. She is only a child, Soraya."

"I have worked too long and too hard to rescue Jasad from the plague of royals. Essiya's death is on the Jasad crown's hands, not mine." Soraya sighed. "She will join you soon."

"Do your coconspirators know you intend to kill her?" Niphran pointed out the window, where flames had begun to burn in the palace gardens. I watched fire leap onto the same fig and date tree illustrated on the wall of the training center and wanted to weep. "I can't imagine they'd go along with your scheme if they did. This is all for her magic, isn't it? They want it more than anything. They want it enough to light a match over our entire kingdom."

Uncertainty passed over Soraya. "They will come to understand why Essiya had to die. They'll see the potential of her magic is not worth the cost it will exact."

"I won't let you take her." Gold and silver flickered weakly in Niphran's eyes, her magic sluggish after years of disuse.

The dagger plunged into Niphran's chest. My mother grabbed Soraya's shoulder, and the attendant's ruthless stare was the last thing she saw before her eyes fluttered shut. The dagger slid free, sending Niphran crumpling to the floor.

Her hair spilled around her in a pool of black. Blood wept from her wound as Soraya's footsteps faded, leaving only Bakir Tower's unforgiving silence.

The sinister plot unraveled as my mother breathed her last. Hanim poisoned the Jasad Heir for years. Kept her too disoriented and unstable to assume her rightful role as Jasad's Qayida. When Hanim found herself banished, Soraya was already positioned in the palace to take over Hanim's duties and keep the Heir docile.

I reached for Niphran's cheek. Most of my short time with my mother was spent resenting her shortcomings. What kind of parents were Niyar and Palia to witness their mighty daughter's downfall and not question its source?

An enormous crash shook the ground. When I glanced up, I stood beside Soraya and a swarm of people in one of the palace's balconies. The fortress ran as far as the eye could see, winding around our kingdom. Colored in the amber of tree resin, the ethereal barrier soared higher than the Citadel itself. Gold and silver streaked across the surface like the shimmering trail of a shooting star.

"It'll hold," Soraya said tersely. The people around her— Mufsids—stared at the fortress as the earth quaked with another crash. "We used all our magic to cast the enchantment."

"What if we said it wrong?" the woman beside her asked. The reason why fully grown adults were deferring to a girl of sixteen was made clear when Soraya replied in a cutting tone, "I read the enchantment exactly as Hanim wrote it."

A man shoved to the front, rounding on Soraya. A deep gouge split his cheek from nose to ear. "Did you consider maybe she wanted the enchantment to fail? She asked us to attack before she was banished, and we refused her. What if this is her revenge?"

"She would never let Jasad fall to Supreme Rawain!"

"Why not?" he bellowed. Another reverberating thud shook the air, and a crack splintered over the fortress's facade. "We betrayed her. With Jasad under his control, she stands to regain her power. Hanim has no loyalties, no principles. She wants the throne, and she thinks the Supreme means to rule Jasad. By the time she realizes his true intentions, the entire kingdom will be destroyed!"

"How could she think Supreme Rawain would ever let her take Jasad's throne?" Soraya balked. With a deafening smash, the multiplying cracks in the fortress fractured. The Mufsids threw themselves to the ground as a million gold and silver rays engulfed them. Like a rupture of the sun, the light swathed Jasad in warmth, the result of centuries of magic and enchantments fed to the unassailable fortress.

The thunder of thousands of hooves rocked Jasad as horses appeared through the broken fortress. Black-and-violet uniforms stretched as far as the eye could see. On the crests draped over their horses, a raven rose between two clashing swords. The crest fluttered as the riders pounded over the scorched ground where the fortress had stood. The flame from their torches dotted the horizon like a starlit night.

Nizahl descended on Jasad in a swarm of darkness.

The Mufsids were already fleeing, but Soraya remained beside me. We watched the soldiers gallop into the towns. We listened as the screams began.

"It wasn't supposed to be this way," said Soraya. When she turned, she was older. The Soraya from the Banquet.

Jasad melted around us. White walls replacing its verdant fields.

Around us, flickers of Jasad seeped onto the walls. Hooves pounding down the street. Flames licking up the side of a lower village's school.

"Hanim deceived me. She ruined us," Soraya said. "I wanted to show you I would never have sent you to the Blood Summit if I suspected the fortress would fall."

"Do not patronize me. You have lied since the moment I met you."

"Not about this! I was barely more than a child myself when Hanim recruited me to the palace. You clung to me, and I held you right back. I had no choice, Essiya. My love for you could not outweigh what needed to be done."

"There is always a choice," I snarled. "What I don't understand is why. I wouldn't have challenged your claim to power if you had united our people and secured their trust and safety. I was content in Mahair, with my life in the village. My magic is trapped! It can't harm anyone."

Bitterness laced Soraya's laugh. "I have a long memory, Mawlati. Many have forgiven your grandparents' sins, caught in the nostalgia of a lost age. But I remember. You would have grown into the image of every royal who had come before you."

The room vanished. We were in the eastern province of Jasad, in a tiny, ramshackle village. Thatch and moldering wood held up the tiny hovels, and rank-smelling liquid muddied the potholed dirt road. Flies buzzed around a dead munban. Children wearing clothes three sizes too small threw rocks into the pools of filthy water.

Three Jasadi soldiers marched past in gold-and-silver uniforms, scattering the swarming flies. The children receded, eyes widening in their haggard faces. Two of the soldiers carried a stretched canvas similar to the one the Alcalah's medics used. A large, shrouded figure lay still on top.

The Jasadi soldier knocked on one of the doors. A scowling woman stuck her head out. She batted away the three small girls peeking around her skirts. The soldier held out a thick letter, sealed with a soaring kitmer. Jasad's royal crest.

Her gaze flew to the body.

Soraya stood near the children while the woman dropped to her knees, tearing at the shroud. The soldiers tried to yank her back. "I remember my father's mangled, charred carcass. The smell of it."

One of the girls who'd been throwing rocks ran over. She was no older than ten or eleven, but the weeping little girls tugged on her sleeve, mouthing a name. *Soraya.*

The girl picked up the letter her mother had dropped. The adult Soraya moved to read over her shoulder. "'Malika Palia and Malik Niyar offer their sincerest regrets for the *tragic* accident.' Almost every house in our village had received one of those letters. They fed us to their greed and pretended to care when it chewed."

"The magic mining," I realized. My hand flew to my mouth. The memory I'd uncovered in Omal... "The other rulers were accusing my grandparents during the Blood Summit. But I thought... I thought magic mining was impossible."

"It is impossible to mine magic from the land." Soraya's mother threw off the shroud covering her husband, and my stomach heaved. The corpse of Soraya's father did not resemble any creature that had once walked the earth. His bones were crushed into fragments and rearranged. The sharp edges of his bones were clear and glassy. His skeleton—because he had no mass or flesh—was covered in soot and ichor.

"But not people. No one had ever thought to mine magic from blood until your grandparents. When they realized Jasad's magic was weakening, and our children were born with less power each generation, the Malik and Malika drained the magic from the people in the poorest wilayahs, one by one. Taking our magic for Usr Jasad or feeding it back to their favorite wilayahs. Do you have any idea what it feels like to have the very source of your magic stripped from your body? My father believed in the importance of respecting the throne, and they *consumed him*."

Your magic is powerful, Essiya. Gedo Niyar and Teta Palia might try to take some of it.

If my grandparents were cruel enough to mine magic from their own people, how terrified of my magic must they have been to put it behind cuffs?

"Then why would you work with the Mufsids? They're as complicit as my grandparents!"

"The Mufsids have resources, connections. They saw to it that Hanim was appointed as Qayida. They placed me as your attendant. And when it came time to wipe the throne of Jasad free of your family's scum, they were primed to strike. The only point of disagreement was you. Their goals were entirely centered on your magic, but once the fortress fell and you were declared dead at the Blood Summit, I had no problem cementing my control."

"Why my magic?" I demanded, at a complete loss. I knew it was powerful, but how could it merit all this chaos? "What do they want to do with it?" They couldn't mean to simply mine my magic like they'd mined it from Soraya's father. They could have accomplished that at any point before the siege, especially if they had unfettered access to me through Soraya.

Suddenly, Soraya stumbled, agony ricocheting across her face. "He found me," she spat. "Damn it to the tombs, how?"

The walls shifted again, and I didn't waste the chance. I hurled myself at Soraya, taking us both to the ground. In an instant, she disappeared from beneath me, and I landed in a massive bedroom.

A different Soraya sat in front of an oval mirror. Without the dirt caked into her hair and the rage lining her features, this younger version of my attendant was easier to recognize. She ran a brush through the pin-straight hair falling to her shoulders. My Soraya, sweating with the effort of remaining upright, grunted, "I hated ruining my curls. But I already had too much marking me as a Jasadi."

I walked past the young version, coming to a halt at the foot of a wide bed. I caged my breath. Beneath the covers, a teenage Arin slept. I watched him breathe, shaken by the vulnerability in his youthful features.

"He likes to think I'm the one who made him so cold," Soraya said, climbing beside him. Her fingers passed through his cheek, and I wanted to break them one by one. "He was already such a *challenge*. Paranoid, distrustful. Constantly looking for a reason to doubt. He didn't trust kind gestures, and he interacted with life at arm's length."

She grinned at me with a spark of the mischief that earned my devotion in the first place. "If anybody was going to bring a mountain to its knees, it would be you, amari. Arin of Nizahl falls in love with the Jasad Heir. Ha! And he thought my deceit was bad. No wonder he has shuttered his heart so tightly: the damned thing keeps leading him astray."

"I did not deceive him," I said. "When we met, I was not the Jasad Heir. I was an Omalian villager, barely even a Jasadi. I didn't intend to become—to start—"

The other Soraya finished brushing her hair. She put the brush on the vanity.

"To start caring?" Soraya finished. "Yes, Hanim does an excellent job of excising that particular failing. It doesn't matter. Arin doesn't consider betrayal the way we do. To him, it is the fury of being outmaneuvered. Of miscalculating." The other Soraya straddled Arin over the covers, gazing down at his peaceful face. His unscarred face.

Meanwhile, Soraya's magic was weakening. The room's colors faded in and out, and her skin had a sallow cast.

On the bed, a blade materialized in the other Soraya's grip. With a shaky breath, she slashed down, toward Arin's throat. The Nizahl Heir's eyes flew open. He twisted, changing the dagger's trajectory. Blood curved up his jaw, forming the line of the Commander's infamous scar.

Arin flung Soraya into the wall. She collapsed into a heap on the floor. Arin staggered to the door as a young Wes burst in with a flurry of guards, alerted by the thud. Wes moved just in time to catch Arin as he dropped to the ground.

Among them was Vaun. He held a thick cloth to Arin's profusely bleeding gash, eyes swinging to the door as a writhing Soraya was dragged out. The Supreme ran in, and just as the room warped, I could have sworn the colors in his scepter began to swirl.

We slammed into the white room. Soraya doubled over. "I suppose this is goodbye. I need to preserve enough magic to fight him off." Her eyes glimmered a faint gold and silver. "I love you, amari. I hope you remember that when death joins us again someday."

I lunged, and this time, I succeeded in tackling her to the ground. She shoved me off, and I chuckled as the gold and silver in her eyes whirled faster. Trying to whisk herself away, was she?

"You can't leave, Soraya. My magic may not work out there, but we are in its domain now," I said. Her grand scheme to thwart my cuff's protections by pouring her magic into the trial's elixirs had forgotten that putting magic into my body wasn't the problem. I stood up, baring my teeth in a deranged smile. "My cuffs, you see, have this vexing habit of trapping magic inside me."

Soraya's doe-eyed regret vanished. The walls around us crumpled like a fragile autumn leaf, scattering us in a million directions.

Depositing us on the frozen surface of a lake.

Shadow figures swayed on the distant shore. Watching me. Waiting. I'd been here before.

"Not if you die before my magic does." She flickered in and out, the struggle of holding me to the dream and battling Arin's effects apparent.

I skimmed the top of my head, probing along the edges of my crown. My silver gown rippled onto the lake. The embroidery on my skirt came alive, and the caged kitmer paced in the folds of fabric, its catlike body stretching in agitation.

Soraya had sent me into my most recurrent nightmare.

"I wanted more time for you," Niphran said. Regal and melancholy, the heart of Jasad made flesh. "More peace. More love. A chance to thrive in the world before it collapsed around you.

"Then again," she continued, donning an expression of bemused awe, "I suppose you have, haven't you? Oh, if my mother and father could see us now. The daughter in love with the shy, bookish Omal Heir, and the granddaughter in love with the Nizahl Commander. Which do you think is worse?" Her trilling laughter didn't reach her eyes. Fire licked at her dress, orange tendrils climbing up her immobilized form.

I turned in a circle. There had to be a way out. Every spell had seams, corners you could slip your fingers beneath and yank. Better yet, where was Soraya? I'd use her head to break the ice. "I am not in love with the Nizahl Heir."

"Don't lie to me, Essiya," Niphran said, stern. The flames danced around her waist.

"Can we focus?" On the shore, the shadow figures swayed faster. Straining to hear our ludicrous conversation? "The fire—"

Gold and silver churned in her eyes. "He's very handsome. Before I met your father, I was infatuated with boys like him. All the ice and sharp edges. The Nizahl Heir, though! I don't think I could have ever been so audacious, even in my youth. I am impressed."

The kitmer clawed, unable to escape its silk prison.

The flames gleefully consumed my mother. The moment she

disappeared from view, she shrieked. Shrill, ear-piercing shrieks. "Help me!"

I beat my fists against the ice. Ripped my crown from my hair and scraped it against the thick layer of frozen lake. Why wouldn't the ice break?

Smoke stung my eyes. I scrubbed them, Niphran's harrowing screams intensifying. It happened as it had in a hundred dreams. I glanced down to see smooth, bare skin where my cuffs had been.

I knew how it would go. The fire would burst. Eat the shadow people and then feast on me. I couldn't watch it happen again. If my freed magic wasn't the solution, what was?

Hanim's old taunt. *You could possess all the magic in the world, and you would still give Jasad your back.*

"Essiya!"

I had already watched my mother die once today. I threw myself into the fire and collided with Niphran, wrapping my arms around her. The shadow creatures rushed forward. Instead of consuming us, the fire shot up, crawling over the night sky. Bringing dawn to the shadows. Not shadows—Dawoud, Niyar, Palia. Countless Jasadis, given faces and names at last.

Niphran's eyes shone. "You saved me."

My arms closed around empty air as my mother vanished, taking the lake and the Jasadis with her. It was just Soraya and me, standing in my old palace bedroom.

Soraya fell, clutching her stomach as my magic rippled around us. I sat on the ground beside her, and sadness swelled in my chest. The best memories of my childhood were in this room with her and Dawoud. "I'm sorry Hanim betrayed you, Soraya. She trained us to be pawns in her game." I touched the crown of Soraya's bent head. *Grief. Rage. Fear.* I had let them lead me, but Soraya had let herself become them. "If I had never gone to Mahair, I would have become as empty and lost as you. Treating love like a disease to be purged."

I took her face in my hands. Her gaze was pained and panic-stricken. "Goodbye, Soraya," I whispered.

My magic surged around the attendant, gales of gold and silver whirling around her faster and faster. She threw her head back as my magic flowed into her, lighting under her skin.

Soraya screamed, and I threw my arm over my face as magic painted the bedroom white.

CHAPTER THIRTY-TWO

I prepared for the Victor's Ball alone.

They had placed my belongings in a room in the Citadel's main spire. My plum-colored gown spilled over the cushioned bench in a whisper of silk while I practiced different expressions in the gilded mirror. Proud, humbled, delighted. My cheeks hurt.

There wasn't much to be done about my eyes. A dead and pitiless black, they couldn't be coaxed to mimic any form of life. I lined them in finely powdered blue kohl and glanced away.

A knock sounded at the door. Time to perform one more time.

The mirror reflected Arin's entrance. He closed the door behind him, and I slipped on my gloves from Rory. "How long do I have to stay?"

He leaned against the door. I could count on one hand the number of times I'd seen Arin *lean*. The man came out of his mother's womb stiff and unimpressed. It was a telling sign. "Two hours. Once they're well and truly inebriated, no one will notice if you take your leave."

I pinned my hair from my face. The tight curls draped over my back.

"The Victor's carriages have been readied. Sefa and the boy will meet you there. I've assigned a retinue of my most qualified soldiers to accompany you. They will take you wherever you would like to go, and once you have reached your destination, you may select any ten of them to become your permanent guard. Your winnings will be delivered separately and discreetly to a location of your choosing." Arin spoke without inflection. I wondered if he had practiced his expressions for tonight, too.

I swiveled on the bench. The full sight of him momentarily knocked all other thoughts askew.

A tunic dyed in the most vivid shade of violet framed his broad shoulders and the flat, hard panes of his torso. Stitched over his heart was Nizahl's symbol. Trim black pants hung from his narrow waist, tucked into clean, light boots. An amethyst circlet rested in a cloud of silver hair. He had replaced his heavy coat with a form-fitting black tailcoat that tapered behind his knees. Five shiny purple buttons lined the left side of the coat, with tiny ravens on the opposing side.

"Don't stand anywhere near me," I managed. "I'll never be able to slip out with everyone's eyes on you."

"I can assure you I will not be the subject of interest tonight," he said wryly, but a small smile touched the corners of his lips. A shy Arin—now I had seen it all.

I sighed, bracing my elbows on my knees and covering my face. "Any changes?"

Arin's pause answered for itself. "No."

When I woke in the pit, anarchy ran rampant in the arena. Nizahl soldiers had trapped the visitors from the outside, and the soldiers hidden in the crowd captured anyone whose eyes reflected the slightest gold or silver. Sorn and Arin had rushed from the tunnels the moment the emerald barrier fell.

The sand had nearly submerged the top of an unconscious Diya's head. It took the Orban Heir and six khawaga to pull her out of the sand's grip. I had watched helplessly as Sorn dragged Diya's limp form into his arms and shook her shoulders, bellowing for a medic. I was significantly taller than Diya and had sunk only halfway when Arin reached me. Once he was assured I was awake and coherent, the Nizahl Heir removed his gloves and opened a single exit for the arena. The guests lined up at the door, and he pressed fingers to the forehead of everyone walking out. Those who resisted were detained.

Fifty Mufsids were seized. Any feelings I might have indulged at their capture had been extinguished by watching the Mufsids slaughter the staff at Usr Jasad and bring down the fortress.

I learned later that Arin had discovered a glamored Soraya slumbering beneath a carriage, an empty vial in her grip. "Her magic was already fading when I touched her," Arin had said. "In moments, she was dead."

Avoiding details, I had explained how she chased me through her memories. The magic she infused the elixir with made it possible for me to die within my own dreams, but it also made it possible for her to die in mine. If my memories were mirrors, then Soraya's were a vengeful void.

Soraya was dead, a band of Mufsids were caught, and I was Victor. The Orbanian Champion, the casualty of our victory, sank into a slumber from which nothing could rouse her. Sorn had arranged for a carriage to transport her to Orban and scattered messengers to every corner of the kingdoms in search of a cure.

"Diya is alive. Sorn is a bullheaded man. If there is a cure, he'll find it. She knew the risks the third trial presented. It could have been far worse," Arin said.

"How?" I stalked to the wardrobe. "She drank a poisoned elixir. Do you think Sorn trained her for that?"

I stomped on the ember of anger sparking in my chest. Anger opened the doors for everything else to come flooding through.

"You caught your Jasadis," I murmured. "Our bargain is fulfilled."

A muscle jumped in Arin's jaw. "So it is. Freedom is yours."

My laugh rang hollow to my own ears. The dream of taking over Rory's shop and funding another keep for Raya's wards, of buying Yuli's old carriage for Marek and taking Sefa on adventures. Tainted now, rotted by inescapable, infernal knowledge.

My grandparents had betrayed our people in the most treacherous manner imaginable. Usr Jasad was an illusion, a beautiful story hiding the rotted roots beneath. My magic had driven the Mufsids to inadvertently pave the way for the siege. Everything I thought I knew was a lie.

Somewhere between Soraya and Dawoud, my last illusion of freedom had shattered.

"Here." Arin held out my cloak. "I didn't want to leave it in the carriage."

I took the bundle and flipped it over. To my disbelief, the moth-eaten collar had been repaired. I thumbed along the new stitching. "Thank you."

"Sylvia." Arin's voice was strained. "Don't do this to yourself."

"Do what?" There was a lump in the cloak's right pocket. Odd; my dagger was in my boot.

Arin moved, standing close enough that I nearly dropped the cloak. He slid his index finger under my chin, drawing my reluctant gaze up. Agitation colored Arin's voice, drawing out his faint accent. "I want to help you. Tell me what I can say—"

I covered Arin's mouth with my hand. He gripped my wrist in the blink of an eye. His gaze bored into mine, and when my hand wasn't thrown off, I let myself speak.

"Soraya tried to kill me. For years, she led the Mufsids in murdering Jasadis. Diya may never wake because of her. Her death should have left me effervescent with glee."

My words came out in a burst, as most unpleasant truths tend to, clamoring to be heard. The heaviness burst in its wake. "But all I feel is grief, Arin, because another Jasadi is dead." My grandparents had as heavy a hand as Hanim in who Soraya had become. In the entitlement that led the Mufsids to turn against their own people.

I had worked so hard to block myself from this pain. To turn guilt into anger, sorrow into scorn. Hanim shamed and burdened me beyond what I could bear, and when killing her didn't stop the noise, I built barriers taller than the gates of the Citadel. "All I wanted was to exist for myself alone, but I—I don't really exist, do I?" I whispered, and they were the truest words I had spoken.

I retracted my hand, scrubbing my wet eyes. "What did you call it? An 'infantile mastery of my emotions'?"

Arin looked at me. Not his calculating, considering glances, or his wary stare. He just looked at me, almost helplessly.

"Anyway." I coughed, groping in the cloak's pocket. A stream of inane chatter flowed past the brambles of my discomfort. I had shared too much. "Unfortunately for you, if I am not brooding, I'm complaining, and I plan to do plenty of both this evening."

I drew from my pocket the fig necklace I purchased from the Omalian street merchant. Oh. I'd forgotten about this.

Arin's brow arched. The motion was unfairly attractive. "You're turning red."

"I don't turn red," I argued, but this might very well have been the exception. Every drop of blood was rushing to my cheeks. I had endured a tainted elixir, poisoned sap, the talons of Al Anqa'a. They paled in comparison with the sheer effort it took to extend the fig necklace in the Nizahl Heir's direction. "I bought this for you," I said in a shower of syllables. "You don't have to wear it, of course, I just thought. If you wanted. The violet color reminded me of the ravens on your coat." I didn't say that figs reminded me of safety and comfort. Two things that—in a painfully ironic twist of fate—I had come to associate with Arin.

Arin stared at the necklace. Two more seconds and I would pretend to faint, or maybe hurl myself on a wandering soldier's sword. Anything to keep him from reviving me to this fervor of mortification. What was I thinking? The Commander didn't wear jewelry, and certainly not a cheap Omalian necklace with *fruit* on it—

A gloved hand closed around the necklace. He tied it around his neck without looking away from me, patting the spot where it settled. "As though I would turn away a gift from Suraira herself," he mused. A shake of his head, as though the very concept thwarted rationality. "From the Alcalah's Victor."

The redness spread from my cheeks to my scalp. I laughed, fumbling with the cloak. "Consider me flattered. The great and mighty Commander accepting my humble offering! The true victory to celebrate."

Arin's fingers convulsed around the fig. "Stop."

Did he think I could control this burgeoning panic? Stem the epiphany that I wanted more of Arin, more of his life, his time, his rare smiles? I wanted to be known by him. To lay my shame and regret in his confidence and trust he would hold them firm.

"Come now, my liege, modesty doesn't become you." My limbs had a separate agency from my mind, gesturing at nothing and everything. "I'm only rejoicing in the honor and high dignity of such a gesture from—"

"Enough!" Arin shouted.

I dropped the cloak. He advanced, a complex array of desperation and anger warring across his features.

"I am not immortal, lofty, mighty, or magnificent. I cannot be, because I am just a man." Every word was bitten off, drawn from a place that simmered in neglect for too long. Ice-blue eyes, eyes that saw too much, saw through my careful pretenses, searched my own. "I am only a man."

Later, I wouldn't recall who reached first. Those details faded to make space for the rest.

We met in a collision that should have rocked the very foundations of the Citadel. Arin's mouth slanted over mine, arms weaving steel bands around my waist to pull me tight against his chest. I buried my hands in his soft hair, dislodging his circlet.

A tightness inside me went slack, and a thousand coils of tension sprung to take its place. Coils of blind need, of pure demand.

Arin tasted like nothing I could name. I had made a vow against intoxication, but I would recant immediately for the chance to savor the decadence of him. I barely registered my back hitting the wardrobe. My legs wrapped around his waist, and I tore one of Rory's gloves in my hurry to take them off. I traced Arin's scar, the shadows under his eyes, yanked at his collar. Ravenous to touch him, to spell my name in his skin, leave him as thoroughly and irrevocably marked as he would leave me.

Arin kissed me with the same singular attention and skill he displayed in every facet of his life. He took me apart with each drag of his lips against mine. His clever hands found their way beneath my skirt, the leather press of his fingertips against my thighs hard enough to bruise.

And I wanted it. I wanted to press my fingers against the evidence of him and thrill in the throb of pain.

An echo accompanied every beat of my pounding heart, a hollow sound in the cacophony. We had done something terrible to each other. Unraveled the core of a shared monster.

Cursed knowledge, Raya would say. How could I walk away after knowing how he felt in my arms? My name whispered in his wrecked voice—how could I allow anyone else to say my name after him?

I scrambled at the lacings of Arin's vest, cursing against his lips. I finally managed to loosen the laces and shove up his tunic. I traced the ridges of his stomach, digging my nails into his hip when he shuddered. Heat spiraled through me at the strangeness of him. This unreadable man, who never reacted to my insults or my temper, yet so responsive under my touch. I needed more of him. More of *this*. Needed to drive the unshakeable Commander to madness under my fingers and lips and skin. To stop picking through the debris in my head and lose myself in him.

"Do you have the faintest clue how you frustrate me?" His mouth found the pulse jumping at my throat. The solid contours of his body pressed me to the wardrobe, pinning me in place. "How you fascinate me?"

My magic thrilled when leather palms skimmed higher up my thighs, tumbling alongside the heat bolting in my veins. "Bed. Now."

The feral glint in Arin's smile sent anticipation shuddering through me. I would never feel fully secure with him. He would never be completely safe with me. "Is that an order, Suraira?"

I tightened my legs around his waist in response.

The world flipped as Arin wrapped an arm around my waist and turned. I hit the bed with an *oomph*. Arin braced a knee against the bed. He gazed down at me with hunger and something quieter. A far more dangerous emotion.

The way he looks you at sometimes. Like you are a cliff with a fatal fall, and each day you move him closer to its edge.

I reached for Arin and drew him down to the bed. I cradled his face between my hands. I ensured I had his full attention before brushing my lips over his forehead. He caught my wrists, holding tight. He didn't pull away.

I wanted to peel him open and memorize him from the inside out. I'd had it so wrong. Arin was not a coil without a spring. Pressure had compressed Arin into the sharpest, coldest parts of himself. The parts most likely to withstand the pressure. Under an identical force, I broke. I tore myself to pieces to avoid it, knowing I might never be able to build myself back the same way again. But I wanted to hope what we'd lost could still be saved. That despite what we'd become, we could learn to be soft again.

I kissed his left eye, then his right. The corner of his mouth. The bolt of his jaw. Arin began to shake. "Sylvia." It was half plea, half pain.

Vaida's voice found its way through the fog of want. *He withholds his heart out of self-preservation.*

"I despise you." I brushed my fingers over his hair, relishing the weight of his body against mine. He was holding himself carefully, as though he might crush me if he lost focus. Silly man. I kicked his ankle out and huffed a laugh as he caught himself, rolling me on top.

I followed the sharp line of his nose. "I dream of killing you."

Arin pulled my fingers away. Worry lashed me. Had I gone too far?

Eyes dark with amusement searched mine. He smoothed the furrow forming in my brow with his thumb. "My demented Suraira, we have much to discuss about seduction."

A knock against the door startled a yelp out of me. Arin covered my mouth.

"Victor Sylvia? Are you in need of any assistance?"

I bit his glove. He withdrew with a smirk. "No, thank you!"

His lips sealed over mine in a sensual slide. I cupped the back of his neck, winding myself around him like a snake trapping its hunt. I hooked my thumb into his waistband, tracing the curve of his hip.

The sudden loss of Arin's heat whipped me to awareness. He had turned his head to the side, jaw tight.

"I need a moment," he forced out. "Your magic…"

"What does it feel like?"

"I can't trust my own hands. It feels like I might reach to caress your lovely neck and snap it instead."

I should have been afraid. I was, in truth, but I was always afraid. The emotion formed a central cornerstone of our relationship.

He was telling the truth about the musrira—or the truth as he believed it to be. A thwarted curse had rendered him so sensitive to magic that my very touch could pain him. It was as good an explanation as any other.

But I wondered.

I gently, deliberately, rested my palm against Arin's cheek.

If you want my strongest theory, I suspect touching you while you can fully express your magic would kill me.

He snatched my hand in a tight grip. His gloved fingers flexed around my bare wrist, but he didn't throw my hand aside.

"Arin." I laid my cheek on his hair. "Am I hurting you?"

He dropped a feather-light kiss to my chin. "Constantly." But it was wistful, content.

I stroked the length of his face. The rhapsodies of poets and the lovelorn melodies. I understood them now. I lacked the talent for composition, so I traced the veins at the underside of his wrist, pressed kisses along the hard line of his jaw, memorized the shape of his smile. Maybe it would translate.

"We should go," Arin murmured against my lips. "They'll be done with the speeches. Most of the guests are deep into the talwith."

"Ugh, talwith." He helped me off the bed. "What if we say the Nizahl Heir was expressing his personal congratulations to his Champion?" I waggled my brows.

Arin adjusted his circlet on his head, mumbling under his breath. Imploring a higher power for patience, probably. I unpinned my hair, letting it bounce around my heated cheeks.

When I tried to reach for the door, Arin grabbed my wrist. "I can handle one more." He reeled me back for a hard kiss. He tangled a hand in my freed curls, tilting my head with his thumb on my chin to keep me still. I'd seen him hold lethal weapons similarly, wielding them just so. If Arin was as fastidious with his lovers as he was with everything else, I didn't see how anyone could survive him. He had barely touched me, and already I felt wholly charred.

When Arin drew back, a wicked promise bloomed in his eyes.

"You are not what I was expecting," he whispered.

"You've said that to me before," I said, embarrassingly breathless.

The narrow hall connecting the spire to the wing hosting the

Victor's Ball clinked with our footsteps. Glass panels ran from the top to the bottom of each wall, and I was poignantly aware of just how high from the ground we were, with only the thin floor supporting us.

The distressing hall ended, and we maneuvered down a spiral staircase. At the bottom, an archway in the shape of a raven unfurling its wings led into the ballroom. Two swords formed the top of the arch.

Arin pulled aside the curtain. "After you." Steeling my nerves, I passed the archway into a ballroom of pure splendor. Lanterns hung from vaulted ceilings and lined the walls. A platform was set up in the center and draped in a silky black sheet for the royal tables. Nizahl had certainly not spared any expense. Liquor flowed liberally. The musicians played Omalian instruments in a nod to my home kingdom. Hundreds of well-dressed guests twirled throughout the ballroom, their chatter splashing over me in a wave of sound.

Diya had not been unacknowledged. The banquet table boasted a broad variety of salted meats and thick za'atar bread, sugared pomegranate seeds in carved wooden bowls, sweetened bread soaked and baked in fresh milk. Three other tables were dedicated to ales and bottles of lavender talwith, the Orbanian specialty.

The royals sat on high-backed cushioned chairs on the platform, watching the buoyant dancers and conversing. One royal remained notably absent from the Orbanian table. Sorn lingered in the shadows, a cup dangling from his fingertips.

"I'll be back," I murmured. Arin frowned, but he didn't attempt to stop me.

The Orban Heir tracked my approach with a mixture of scorn and ennui. "Well, if it isn't the Victor. Come to gloat?" Sorn drained his glass. I could barely hear him over all the noise.

Though I figured Sorn's intelligence was roughly equivalent to that of an unshelled walnut, he had cared for his Champion. It was more than what could be said for Vaida and Felix. "I'm sorry about what happened to Diya. She didn't deserve to lose in such a deceptive and dishonorable manner. I am confident she'll wake."

From nowhere, Sorn produced a bottle, upending its remains into his glass. My nose wrinkled at the cloying scent. Talwith. How much had he consumed? "You're confident? My, the village orphan is confident Diya will wake. Quick, summon the heralds! We must share this marvelous news!"

What else had I expected? I turned on my heel, leaving Sorn to make a further spectacle of himself. I wished Diya was here, if only so I could ask her what on earth endeared the boorish Heir to the caustic, quick-witted warrior.

Traditionally, the Victor took a coveted seat at the royal platform. Supreme Rawain lounged in his chair, his scepter tucked under his arm as he rolled a grape between his fingers. He wore Nizahl's traditional black robes and a violet cape pinned at his collar. Sitting in a bucket of broken glass was preferable to sitting anywhere near Rawain.

Arin offered his hand. "I believe we have an agreement."

"Have you learned your steps?"

Arin swept me in a turn, hooking me under his arm and spinning me out. A few people around us clapped. He reeled me in with a grin that I wanted to pocket. "At the age of nine."

"Liar." I shook my head with mock outrage. Arin was pulling significantly more attention than I was. "Everyone and their uncle is staring at you."

He hummed. "I don't typically participate in these affairs. They're surprised."

I scanned the gathered royals. "Which one is the High Counselor?"

"He went after a servant a few moments ago," Arin said. "Why?"

"Sharing a room with the abusive milksop is grating on my nerves." I leaned in, sliding my hand higher up his shoulder.

Arin's eyes narrowed. "Abusive?"

I debated whether or not to share Sefa's story. I had withheld it this long because it wasn't mine to tell, and knowing the real reason Sefa and Marek were wanted by the High Counselor was unlikely to have altered Arin's original threat against them. Sefa had shared the truth with me the day after Marek did, but she hadn't spoken of it since then.

But if Arin could possibly rid Nizahl of the High Counselor's influence, it was worth telling him. I relayed the tale as succinctly as possible, including Marek's involvement in their escape. When I finished, the shoulders beneath my palms were strung tighter than a bow..

"Cease your self-flagellation," I murmured. "You couldn't have known." Disbelief twinged at how easily he had believed me. Since when did Arin take anyone's word at face value?

"I would have offered Sefa to a tribunal of the High Counselor's allies. Brought her to *justice*," Arin snapped. "He's lingering near the banquet table to harass the servants."

A cursory glance found an average-size man drifting purposely into the young serving girl's space. He had a small mouth and a long forehead. Utterly ordinary. Nothing to indicate he nurtured an appetite for helpless young girls.

Arin's gaze skidded past me. He swore, missing a step and bumping against the couple behind us.

Nothing alarmed me faster than a visibly alarmed Arin.

"The guards are dragging in a man and a woman wearing a glamor."

I whirled around. Sure enough, Sefa in the glamor of an old woman and Marek glamored to resemble a black-haired laborer struggled between two Nizahl soldiers. One of them broke off to whisper in Supreme Rawain's ear.

I tried to rush forward, but Arin's grip on my elbow was crushing. "Wait."

On the platform, Supreme Rawain heaved a sigh. "Arin?" He inclined his head toward Sefa and Marek. Arin nodded, cutting through the crowd. He did not release his hold on my arm.

Relief flooded Sefa's face at the sight of me. "You're all right," she exhaled. "Sylvia, someone raided the Victor's carriages. The soldiers think it was us. We told them we were waiting to travel back to Omal with you, that the carriages had been ransacked before our arrival."

"They do not believe us," Marek growled, resistant in the soldier's grasp.

I winced as pain bloomed where Arin still held me. Urgency underscored the Heir's brusque voice. "Release them. Alert the soldiers to close the gates. I want my personal guardsmen at the carriages. Every soldier on the Citadel's grounds needs to comb for the raiders, so wake the recruits."

Marek and Sefa were freed as the soldiers scattered to obey. I covered Arin's hand on my elbow with my own, and he finally glanced at me.

"The Urabi," he explained, stony. "We didn't catch any of them leaving the trial, and I assumed they had not taken the bait. They must have snuck onto the Citadel's grounds while the soldiers were detaining the crowd. The third trial is not the end of the Alcalah: the Victor's Ball is."

I didn't have a chance to react. The High Counselor, who had forgotten the serving girl in favor of squinting at Sefa while she spoke, suddenly reared back. "Sayali," he gasped. "It's you."

Sefa spat at his feet.

Three guards surged forward to hold Marek down as he lunged. "Your Highness!" the High Counselor yelled. He went ruddy, his spilled drink trickling down the front of his tunic. More guards converged, swarming them. "These are the animals who robbed me and left me for dead."

Supreme Rawain glanced over again, almost reluctantly, and roamed over the mayhem. He stood, gesturing with his scepter. "Arrest them," he called, as one might absently call for a glass of water. "They can await trial in the dungeons."

My heart stopped.

"Sylvia!" Sefa gasped as the soldiers bent her arms behind her back. They forced Marek's head to the ground.

I was on a frozen lake as my mother burned. Collecting frogs while the world screamed around me. I was at the Blood Summit, and Niyar was shouting, *"Run!"*

Arin stopped the guards from dragging Sefa and Marek from the ballroom, but only his father could order them released. Pulse pounding in my neck, I ran through the possibilities. Even if I bided my time and devised a brilliant plan to rescue them from Nizahl's highly secure prisons, I could fail. The minute Sefa and Marek were taken from this ballroom, their fate would be out of my hands.

I couldn't lose anyone else. I wouldn't.

Essiya, don't be foolish. You have everything you want, Hanim purred. *All the wealth you will ever need. Safety from Nizahl persecution. Your precious Heir. Why lose it all for a pair of foolish Nizahlans?*

But it wasn't Hanim's voice speaking anymore. It was mine. My own voice whispering in my head, haunting me more effectively than Hanim's memory ever could.

And for the first time, I answered. I snatched the voice and shoved it somewhere leagues deeper than the hole I'd used for Hanim's mortal body.

I am not yours to plague anymore, I snarled. Love was not submission. It was not testing how far I could bend before I broke. Love was Sefa's hand finding mine in the dark to reassure herself of my presence. Love was Marek entering the kingdom of his nightmares to help me. Raya's squash soup on my birthday, Rory's gruff smile when I named an herb correctly, Fairel's giddy laugh. Dawoud turning the dagger onto himself. A table exploding in the Blood Summit. Love was Arin cradling my face in a burning room and telling me to run.

I looked at Marek and Sefa, and I made my choice.

"Your Highness." I climbed the platform to Supreme Rawain. The steps groaned beneath me. "I am here to plead for their lives."

Rawain tilted his head. I'd piqued his curiosity.

"Who are a pair of thieves to the Victor?" Rawain asked. Arin appeared at Rawain's shoulder, muscles coiled with apprehension. I couldn't look at him.

He would never forgive me.

"They are my companions. They are innocent of this crime."

The scepter thudded against the floor. He looked bored again. "The trial will decide their innocence. I'm afraid I cannot grant you this request, dear Sylvia."

I thought of a wink across an ancient oak table. A serene smile as the sky crashed around us, raining ruin onto the Blood Summit. He wouldn't be satisfied until he took everything from me.

When you choose who you are willing to fight for, you choose who you are.

I knelt at the Supreme's feet.

Every line in Arin's body went taut. I gathered fistfuls of my dress, bowing my head. "Please, Your Majesty. I beg you to spare them."

Supreme Rawain had the same thoughtful calculation I adored in his son. In the former, it sent revulsion pulsing in my gut. "Why should I?"

A bargain would have to be struck. Nothing less would ensure Sefa and Marek's safety.

"I offer myself in their place."

Sefa and Marek weren't Jasadis, but there wasn't a doubt in my body they were mine. I would not suppress them. I would not let myself forget everything good to safeguard myself from the bad.

My magic cascaded, gathering hungrily at my cuffs.

Rawain laughed. He shared a commiserative glance with a puzzled King Murib. "I don't want to punish my own Champion. Especially one who's given us so much pride!" he exclaimed, drawing a few nervous chuckles.

He wouldn't embarrass Nizahl by arresting his own Champion. Not for a few common thieves. Supreme Rawain was no different than Hanim. One thing joined them together years before my birth. One immutable, depraved need, and it was what I called upon now.

I allowed myself to look up at Arin. Like a dying woman at an oasis, I drank my fill of the beautiful Heir. Horror twisted across his features. As hard as he tried to plan every conceivable outcome, even the Nizahl Heir could not prepare for the hidden shadows of a broken mind—nor what might happen if light was turned upon them.

In the measure of monster or man, what tips the scales?

I rose to my feet. "You knew me before I was your Champion." My voice rang loud and clear. My magic howled for release. There was no tightness. No pain.

If it was power he wanted, it was power he would get.

"We met across a sacred oak table many years ago. At a site of peace and prosperity. You knew me by another name. Look closely, Rawain. Don't you remember me?" I leaned over the table between me and the Supreme. "I certainly remember you."

I gazed into pale, reptilian eyes, and I winked.

Shock swept Supreme Rawain's expression clean. "Niphran's daughter." His grip on the scepter convulsed. "It cannot be. You're dead."

My smile brightened. "Not anymore."

"*Guards!*" Rawain bellowed. He leveled the crystalline head of his scepter at my chest as soldiers poured into the ballroom. Sefa and Marek were forgotten in the fray. "An abomination masquerading as our Champion. You will pay for what you've done, Sylvia of Mahair."

I tutted. "Let me refresh your memory." My wrists ached with the pressure on my cuffs. "My name is Essiya. Malika of Jasad."

Arin saw them first. "Cuffs," he said, in a dawn of wonder.

The cuffs glowed, alight with molten magic. Except, this time, it didn't stop. This time, the glow flooded every corner.

You should beware symbols of power, Diya had said. Like the power of a true name suppressed for too long.

Essiya went beyond queen, beyond Jasad. Essiya was a symbol, and she had taken a life of her own. *Who we are is where we come from.* Who we were.

My silver cuffs clattered to the floor. Iridescent cracks raced across my body, the glowing streaks breaking open over my skin. I saw my reflection in Queen Hanan's chalice just as silver and gold rolled over my eyes.

"Retreat!" Arin roared. He shoved his father away from me and twisted, throwing his arm over his head.

My magic ruptured in a tidal wave of gold and silver. Screams filled the ballroom as the ceiling exploded. My magic whipped the raining glass in every direction. The guests stampeded through the archway, knocking the Nizahl crest into the wall. A kitmer took shape in the center of the ballroom. The feline rose from its haunches, gold feathered head glimmering. Golden wings fanned out, crashing into the walls penning it in. Its roar shook the ground as the roof caved around its head.

Lanterns smashed between me and the rest of the royals, the flames catching on the spilled tablecloths. Dust floated from the falling stones, swirling lazily above the chaos.

I stumbled past the kitmer's paws to where Sefa and Marek hid behind a shaking pillar. The guards converged around the royals, scuttling them from the ballroom rapidly collapsing around us.

"Run!" I shouted. Stones crashed into the tables. "I cannot control it!"

Sylvia— Sefa mouthed. She squinted, struggling against the wind's tide. Dust sprayed into her hair, seconds before a boulder tumbled from the wall to our right. She reached for me.

I snapped my fingers. Sefa and Marek disappeared, and the boulder smashed into her vacated spot.

The kitmer's wings broke against the Citadel's walls, and I laughed, spinning in the destruction.

This was freedom. I finally understood why Rawain tried so hard to wipe magic from the lands. Imagine never knowing this kind of euphoria. Never feeling magic streaming through you, whistling through the air at your command. A purity of power, purging away the hurt and mischief of mortality.

I understood why my grandparents would kill for this.

Something sharp lodged into my shoulder. Then another and another. Arrows flew through the storming kitmer and into me, dozens of them, covering my body in pinpricks of pain. The wind shrieked, and the platform flattened under the collapsing ceiling.

Normal arrows could not fly in these conditions.

I stumbled into a table and yanked an arrow out from my thigh. The tip dissolved into sepia specks.

Sim siya. A Jasadi paralyzing agent. I seized, crumpling onto the spilled pomegranate rubies. Fog descended over my mind.

A circle formed around me. Hands linked over my body, and voices chanted in melodic Resar. Though my vision swam, I could distinguish one face above the rest.

"I know you," I slurred. The man at the Meridian Pass. Efra.

The Urabi had found their moment to strike.

The woman next to the grim Efra smiled. "This will only hurt for a moment, Mawlati."

The chanting accelerated as the wing of the Citadel imploded. The kitmer soared above the destruction, wings painting the night sky in the blazing colors of Jasad. A renewal. A deadly vow.

My hand had fallen over my heart. I counted the slowing beats as the Urabi's chants grew louder and the world lost its colors.

One, two. I was alive. *Three, four.* I would never be safe again.

Somewhere, Arin would be reeling at my betrayal. His eyes would go icy and unforgiving, and a scar to match the one on his jaw would gouge into his soul. Perhaps he'd hunt me as he hunted Soraya.

Five, six. "I choose her," he'd said.

In a different life, I thought, *I would have chosen you, too.*

The hands separated, and we disappeared.

EPILOGUE

ARIN

In the following madness, Arin of Nizahl stood still in a sea of movement.

The guests teemed on the Citadel's lawn. Soldiers steered carriages stacked with barrels of water to the burning wing and ran inside.

"She died. I thought she died," Queen Hanan repeated. The Queen of Omal sank into an unseemly heap on the ground. Felix hovered over her, trying to pull his grandmother to her feet. "Emre's daughter is *alive*?"

Accusations flew between the royals. She had stayed under each of their roofs, eaten at their tables. "Find her!" Rawain slammed his scepter into the earth. "Close the gates! Send sentries into the woods!"

Arin knew he should speak. He should tell his father the soldiers would find nothing on the Citadel's grounds. Instruct them to barricade the roads instead. If the news reached Nizahl's upper towns, it would spread through the kingdom in days. Panic would catch like dry kindling, and the lower villages would begin hoarding food and hiding children eligible for conscription.

But there was a different chaos breaking loose inside the Heir. Gaining speed, preparing to detonate. He searched for control in the seething mass, but it evaded him.

The Nizahl Heir did not know what would come out of his

mouth if he tried to speak. Though the fire raged in the Citadel's wing, expelling soldiers covered in soot and ash, Arin was the greatest threat to the people around him.

For the first time in his life, Arin could not think.

Vaida's voice danced by his ear. "The Jasad Queen, really? Poor darling, how terrible you must feel. To have had your greatest enemy so close for so long, only to lose her now." The Sultana moved around to face him, a smug smile on her ruby mouth. She leaned into him. "And you certainly kept her *close*, didn't—" The Sultana's words died on her lips as Arin's gloved hand struck out, closing around her throat.

He became distantly aware of the dispersed Lukubi guards shouting and running for them. Of his father bringing his scepter down on the stiff line of Arin's arm as he lifted a kicking Vaida into the air.

"Arin," Sylvia whispered. She pressed her cheek to his hair. "Am I hurting you?"

Vaida scrabbled at his inflexible fingers, struggling in his grip. She looked into his eyes, and whatever the Sultana saw had her writhing like a cat in water. Nizahl soldiers collided with the Lukubi guards in a clash of swords.

Two bodies slammed into him from the side, taking him and Vaida to the ground. Lukubi guards snatched the heaving Sultana away as she started to cry, whisking her toward the Lukub carriages.

The horrified faces of his personal guardsmen stared down at him. Supreme Rawain switched from rage to charm in an instant, placating the aghast royals. "We all know my son is not prone to such terrible displays of temper. The effects of a Champion's betrayal, you understand. He will apologize to the Sultana as soon as Her Highness has a moment to collect herself."

If he wished to, Arin could fight off his guardsmen. He could slaughter every Lukubi intercepting his path to Vaida, reach into the carriage, and snap the neck he had already spared twice.

"Sire," Jeru murmured, audible only to Arin's ears. "We found sim siya arrows near the banquet table. She did not leave on her own." Ash floated in the air above Jeru.

"The Urabi have taken her," Wes finished. "My liege, you must return to yourself. The Urabi have claimed the Jasad Queen for their cause."

His steadfast guardsmen, trained at his hand, subject to the most harrowing journeys in his service, were frightened for him.

Arin stared at the black sky and let ice trickle into his veins, encasing the seething darkness, halting its progression.

He could not rein the storm forever. Just long enough.

"Get off," Arin clipped.

The guards lurched to their feet, and the guests skittered back as Arin stood.

To Wes, he said, "Bring back any soldiers entering the upper towns. If they have caused a commotion, say a thief has made away with the treasures in the Orbanian carriages. If King Murib is willing, take ten khawaga with you."

Finally, he stepped toward Jeru. The curly-haired guard stiffened.

Arin's voice was silky. "Find Sefa and Marek."

Jeru's nostrils flared, but he gave a short nod.

With his guards disappearing to carry out his will, Arin turned to the assembled guests. He avoided his father's shrewd gaze. "Only those on the royal platform were close enough to hear exactly what transpired before the wing collapsed. The other guests merely witnessed the Nizahl Champion use magic. It cannot spread that the Jasad Queen is alive. There are Jasadis hidden in each of your kingdoms, burrowed deep into the fabric of our society. Should they learn their Queen is calling them, your lands will unravel. It only takes a single servant overhearing one conversation. Her identity must be kept secret at all costs." He moved his gaze over their faces. "The Nizahl Champion revealed herself as a Jasadi and attacked the Citadel tonight. No more, no less. Do you understand?"

One by one, the royals nodded their assent. Felix trembled with anger, but he dipped his head. It would have to be enough.

At the top of the Citadel, Arin stared out of his wrought-iron balcony. He ran his thumb over the cuffs he'd retrieved from the ballroom's smoldering ruins. The first rays of sunlight gleamed over Nizahl. The ushering of a new day.

The longer Essiya of Jasad lived, the more likely the news of her return would spread. Without a royal to rally behind, the siege against Jasad had cost thousands of lives. A Jasadi uprising with Niphran's daughter at the helm would plunge the kingdoms into a war from which they would never recover.

The Malik and Malika of Jasad were magic miners.

If she continued the profane practices of her lineage, war would be just the beginning. Her magic was beyond anything Arin had ever felt. Beyond any power that should still exist.

"Your Highness? You summoned me?" Vaun's voice was subdued behind him. Arin's gaze did not leave the blush of dawn tinting the distant corners of his kingdom. She was out there somewhere.

"Tell the council to gather," Arin said. Around and around, his thumb tracked the cuffs. They couldn't hide her from him forever.

Confusion delayed Vaun's response. "The council is already gathered, my liege."

"Gather them in the war wing."

Vaun inhaled sharply. "Yes, sire." Arin did not hear the guard's footsteps disappear or the door closing behind him.

The Nizahl Heir traced Essiya's cuffs, and he started to plan.

The story continues in...

Book TWO of The Scorched Throne

ACKNOWLEDGMENTS

The true terror of sitting here and writing these acknowledgments is knowing how impossible it is to record every person whose support and kind words took this book from a badly titled Word doc to the book it is today. I'll give it my best go.

My eternal and profound thanks to my agent, Jennifer Azantian, for listening to my (many) voice memos, fiercely championing me and my work, and always knowing what to say when I spin out. To my editor, Nivia Evans, for seeing the potential in this story in its earliest phases. You sent me the Twitter DM on October 27, 2020, that changed my life, and I'm so grateful to have your editorial talent and sharp eye on my side. A giant thank you to the rest of the passionate, brilliant team at Orbit for their enthusiasm and support in bringing *The Jasad Heir* to life—Angelica Chong, Rachel Goldstein, Angela Man, Laura Blackwell, and Ellen Wright. To my wonderful Orbit UK editor, Jenni Hill, for seeing something special in *The Jasad Heir*, and editorial assistant Rose Ferrao for sending emails I'm excited to open. Lisa Marie Pompilio and Mike Heath, please know I'm never going to stop screaming about the beautiful cover you created. Thank you to the #DVPit organizers who created the amazing event that connected me and my editor. Koren Enright and Kalyn Josephson, I'm still so relieved you read the pure chaos that was this book's first iterations and said, "Yeah, I'll take this one." Your mentorship during Pitch Wars kept me sane while I dove into the world of publishing. I don't know where I (or this book) would be without your incredible wisdom, insight, and Arin jokes. Team Void Cats forever!

Every author knows how scary it is to send their baby WIP into someone else's hands, but Destiny, Janae, and Abby—you guys made it so much less terrifying. I can't believe you didn't block my number the seventieth time I asked if you were still reading. Hannah Sawyerr, our sprints and Facetimes and overlapping deadlines have meant the world to me, and I'm so blessed to have you and your endless cheer in my life. Olesya Lyuzna, my first critique partner and co-podcaster, one of these days we'll meet and the world will never be the same. Jess Parra, one of the funniest and most fiercely supportive women I know—thank you for always telling it to me straight and being the coolest honorary aunt on the planet. Carolina Flórez-Cerchiaro, Brittney Arena, Ream Shukairy, and Maeeda Khan, I'm so grateful for your enthusiasm and kindness.

My family probably skipped directly to this section as soon as they opened the book (as if I would ever forget you). Mama, you've been telling people I was a writer since I was in the third grade, and I'm sorry I spent years begging you to stop. Baba, who always listens and always knew I'd get here. I'm so grateful you ignored my whining and made sure I learned Arabic and fell in love with Egypt. To Yusuf, for having endless ideas for promoting the book, despite your general disinterest in fiction. Hend, who started reading my half-formed stories when she was ten and never stopped asking for more. And Hanan, who didn't originally read much but happily read this book three times—I adore you and your willingness to let me talk your ear off about my ideas.

To every reader and bookseller who picked up this book, ordered it to their library, added it to their TBR—your kind words and support have been an unending source of joy for me throughout this journey. I'm forever thankful to you for taking a chance on a debut author.

Finally, to my elementary school librarian, even though you may never see this. You saw me reading alone every day at recess and took me under your wing. You let me check out five books at a time instead of the school-sanctioned two, and you asked about every single one I read. You put a chair just for me behind the counter, so I could scan books with you if the world became too overwhelming. Because of you, the library was more than just a place to read—it was my haven. I will never be able to thank you enough for reminding me the real world can sometimes be as magical as fictional ones.

ٱلْحَمْدُ لِلَّٰهِ

extras

orbit

meet the author

Sara Hashem

SARA HASHEM is an American Egyptian writer from Southern California, where she spent many sunny days holed up indoors with a book. Sara's love for fantasy and magical realms emerged during the two years her family lived in Egypt. When she isn't busy naming stray cats in her neighborhood after her favorite authors, Sara can be found buried under coffee-ringed notebooks.

Find out more about Sara Hashem and other Orbit authors by registering for the free monthly newsletter at orbitbooks.net.

interview

What was the first book that made you fall in love with the fantasy genre?

I'd say the major players for binding my heart to fantasy were the Magic Treehouse and Charlie Bone series. The itch to travel for me started young, and those books took me places a plane never could. I will never get over how fortunate I am to share a world of my own in hopes it whisks a reader away.

Where did the initial idea for *The Jasad Heir* come from and how did the story begin to take shape?

A story typically takes shape for me around a central question. For *The Jasad Heir*, I wanted to know: What do you owe to a place and a people you've barely known, but without whom you wouldn't exist? I'm not the biggest fan of revenge story lines, so I was stymied with her character for a while. I kept thinking, what should she do? How should she fight for her kingdom and her people?

And then eventually, why should she want to?

I wanted Sylvia to feel familiar to eldest daughters of immigrant families in particular, who feel the weight of duty and obligation far earlier than most. But we usually carry it out of love, even when it wears us down. Sylvia was missing love. Responsibilities were stacked so high on her shoulders that she broke, severing herself from any kind of tie or duty so thoroughly that she stopped associating herself with Jasad. In the first half of the book, she refers to them as "they" or "the Jasadis." There's the other her, Essiya, who represents an idealized version of herself.

Once I had Sylvia's arc (sort of) nailed down, the rest came easier. I love scheming and court machinations, magical mayhem, book versions of the *Rocky* training montage, and a villain who doesn't realize he's a villain.

What was the most challenging moment of writing The Jasad Heir*?*

The most challenging moment was after Soraya stabs Sylvia. Sylvia is vowing to take down Soraya, but her motivations when she makes the declaration are incredibly tricky to balance. She's torn between her burgeoning sense of community and duty toward Jasad, her own lone-wolf brand of self-preservation, and a very personal pain at discovering a relationship she'd cherished was a lie. Especially since she realized trauma has rendered her own mind and memories unreliable. The guilt, the defensiveness, the stubborn hurt and anger are emotions Sylvia grapples with throughout the novel.

The Jasad Heir *is partially inspired by protests and uprisings of the Arab Spring. What was your approach to incorporating those ideas into your work? Did you do any specific research to build the world?*

I completely avoided researching Arab Spring. I was living in Egypt during the uprisings, but I was barely a teenager. My sharpest memories are of people. The fear, the wonder, the hope. My aunt complaining about the curfew and insane increase in the cost of fruit. Distracting my siblings while tanks rolled down the street (followed by my sister begging us to take a photo of her inside the wheel of a tank, because she was ten and thought they were cool). I remember standing outside with my father in bitterly cold weather and asking how anyone could bear to sleep in a tent in Tahrir Square in this temperature. I was amazed any passion or rage could survive in such conditions. Sylvia is a child when Jasad falls. She sees it happen only from a distance. She grows up feeling like she owes a debt to a place she barely remembers, that her connection to Jasad has only ever brought her trouble. To truly risk herself for something, to essentially sleep in a freezing tent with danger surrounding her on all sides, Sylvia had to feel like she belonged in that fight.

As for research about the Egyptian influence, a solid shout-out to my parents! The way Sylvia learns about Jasad as she grows is how most children from immigrant families do—through stories our family and community share with us. So if I couldn't find the answer through my own experiences or a good research dive, I called my parents and asked them a million questions they were excited to answer.

The characters in The Jasad Heir *are complex and often find themselves torn between different loyalties. If you had to pick, who would you say is your favorite? Who did you find the most difficult to write?*

Oh, this one's easy. Arin was my favorite to write, and Sylvia was the most difficult. The way Arin perceives the world in *The Jasad Heir* is clear-cut and exacting. He faces very little of the inner conflict Sylvia endures, because his sense of self is firm. The way he feels for Sylvia throws a wrench in it, of course, but it's still an external deviation he can isolate and examine without implicating his entire identity. Whereas the incongruence between the way Sylvia behaves, the way she views herself, and the way the rest of the world views her (as Essiya) constantly clash.

I'll add writing scenes with both of them was incredibly fun for these same exact reasons.

Who are some of your favorite authors and how have they influenced your writing?

Oh my gosh, this is so hard. Childhood faves include Richelle Mead, Kristin Cashore, and Stephenie Meyer (fun fact: I went to my very first book festival shortly after moving to Egypt and bought *The Host* because it was the biggest book there). Nonexhaustive list of current favorite authors includes Tracy Deonn, Talia Hibbert, Tasha Suri, S. A. Chakraborty, and Ilona Andrews. These authors belong to different genres and age categories, but they share an ability to create transporting stories driven by complex characters and immersive settings. I wanted to write characters who resonated with readers even if they didn't understand why, and a world they kept coming back to until they did.

Without giving too much away, could you share what readers can expect in the sequel?

More immersion into the different kingdoms! Scheming and subterfuge in settings we grazed in *The Jasad Heir*.

Angst. Longing. New betrayals.

And the above-mentioned character with a firm sense of self and little inner conflict aside from Sylvia? Well...let's just say nothing stays untouchable forever.

And, finally, if you could visit one kingdom from The Jasad Heir, **which would you choose?**

Lukub! Good hikes, fun festivals, and the ever-present possibility of being thrown into a well for espionage. What's not to love?

if you enjoyed
THE JASAD HEIR

look out for

THE PHOENIX KING

Book One of
the Ravence Trilogy

by

Aparna Verma

Yassen Knight was the Arohassin's most notorious assassin until a horrible accident. Now he's hunted by the authorities and his former employer, both of whom want him dead. But when he seeks refuge with an old friend, he's offered an irresistible deal: defend the heir of Ravence from the Arohassin and earn his freedom once and for all.

Elena Ravence is preparing to ascend the throne. Trained since birth in statecraft, warfare, and the desert ways, Elena knows she is ready. She only lacks one thing: the ability to hold fire, the magic that is meant to run in her family's blood. And with her coronation only weeks away, she must learn quickly or lose her kingdom.

Leo Ravence is not ready to give up the crown. There's still too much work to be done, too many battles to be won. But when an ancient prophecy threatens to undo his lifetime of work, Leo wages war on the heavens themselves to protect his legacy.

CHAPTER 1:

Yassen

The king said to his people, "We are the chosen."
And the people responded, "Chosen by whom?"

—from chapter 37 of *The Great History of Sayon*

To be forgiven, one must be burned. That's what the Ravani said. They were fanatics and fire worshippers, but they were his people. And he would finally be returning home.

Yassen held on to the railing of the hoverboat as it skimmed over the waves. He held on with his left arm, his right limp by his side. Around him, the world was dark, but the horizon began to purple with the faint glimmers of dawn. Soon, the sun would rise, and the twin moons of Sayon would lie down to rest. Soon, he would arrive at Rysanti, the Brass City. And soon, he would find his way back to the desert that had forsaken him.

Yassen withdrew a holopod from his jacket and pressed it open with his thumb. A small holo materialized with a message:

Look for the bull.

He closed the holo, the smell of salt and brine filling his lungs.

The bull. It was nothing close to the Phoenix of Ravence, but then again, Samson liked to be subtle. Yassen wondered if he would be at the port to greet him.

A large wave tossed the boat, but Yassen did not lose his balance. Weeks at sea and suns of combat had taught him how to keep his ground. A cool wind licked his sleeve, and he felt a whisper of pain skitter down his right wrist. He grimaced. His skin was already beginning to redden.

After the Arohassin had pulled him half-conscious from the sea, Yassen had thought, in the delirium of pain, that he would be free. If not in this life, then in death. But the Arohassin had yanked him back from the brink. Treated his burns and saved his arm. Said that he was lucky to be alive while whispering among themselves when they thought he could not hear: "Yassen Knight is no longer of use."

Yassen pulled down his sleeve. It was no matter. He was used to running.

As the hoverboat neared the harbor, the fog along the coastline began to evaporate. Slowly, Yassen saw the tall spires of the Brass City cut through the grey heavens. Skyscrapers of slate and steel from the mines of Sona glimmered in the early dawn as hovertrains weaved through the air, carrying the day laborers. Neon lights flickered within the metal jungle, and a silver bridge snaked through the entire city, connecting the outer rings to the wealthy, affluent center. Yassen squinted as the sun crested the horizon. Suddenly, its light hit the harbor, and the Brass City shone with a blinding intensity.

Yassen quickly clipped on his visor, a fiber sheath that covered his entire face. He closed his eyes for a moment, allowing them to readjust before opening them again. The city stared back at him in subdued colors.

Queen Rydia, one of the first queens of Jantar, had wanted to ward off Enuu, the evil eye, so she had fashioned her port city out of unforgiving metal. If Yassen wasn't careful, the brass could blind him.

The other passengers came up to deck, pulling on half visors that covered their eyes. Yassen tightened his visor and wrapped a scarf around his neck. Most people could not recognize him—none of the passengers even knew of his name—but he could not take any chances. Samson had made it clear that he wanted no one to know of this meeting.

The hoverboat came to rest beside the platform, and Yassen disembarked with the rest of the passengers. Even in the early hours, the port was busy. On the other dock, soldiers barked out orders as fresh immigrants stumbled off a colony boat. Judging from the coiled silver bracelets on their wrists, Yassen guessed they were

Sesharian refugees. They shuffled forward on the adjoining dock toward military buses. Some carried luggage; others had nothing save the clothes they wore. They all donned half visors and walked with a resigned grace of a people weary of their fate.

Native Jantari, in their lightning suits and golden bracelets, kept a healthy distance from the immigrants. They stayed on the brass homeland and receiving docks where merchants stationed their carts. Unlike most of the city, the carts were made of pale driftwood, but the vendors still wore half visors as they handled their wares. Yassen could already hear a merchant hawking satchels of vermilion tea while another shouted about a new delivery of mirrors from Cyleon that had a 90 percent accuracy of predicting one's romantic future. Yassen shook his head. Only in Jantar.

Floating lanterns guided Yassen and the passengers to the glass-encased immigration office. Yassen slid his holopod into the port while a grim-faced attendant flicked something from his purple nails.

"Name?" he intoned.

"Cassian Newman," Yassen said.

"Country of residence?"

"Nbru."

The attendant waved his hand. "Take off your visor, please."

Yassen unclipped his visor and saw shock register across the attendant's face as he took in Yassen's white, colorless eyes.

"Are you Jantari?" the attendant asked, surprised.

"No," Yassen responded gruffly and clipped his visor back on. "My father was."

"Hmph." The attendant looked at his holopod and then back at him. "Purpose of your visit?"

Yassen paused. The attendant peered at him, and for one wild moment, Yassen wondered if he should turn away, jump back on the boat, and go wherever the sea pushed him. But then a coldness slithered down his right elbow, and he gripped his arm.

"To visit some old friends," Yassen said.

The attendant snorted, but when the holopod slid back out, Yassen saw the burning insignia of a mohanti, a winged ox, on its surface.

"Welcome to the Kingdom of Jantar," the attendant said and waved him through.

Yassen stepped through the glass immigration office and into Rysanti. He breathed in the sharp salt air, intermingled with spices both foreign and familiar. A storm had passed through recently, leaving puddles in its wake. A woman ahead of Yassen slipped on a wet plank and a merchant reached out to steady her. Yassen pushed past them, keeping his head down. Out of the corner of his eye, he saw the merchant swipe the woman's holopod and hide it in his jacket. Yassen smothered a laugh.

As he wandered toward the homeland dock, he scanned the faces in the crowd. The time was nearly two past the sun's breath. Samson and his men should have been here by now.

He came to the bridge connecting the receiving and homeland docks. At the other end of the bridge was a lonely tea stall, held together by worn planks—but the large holosign snagged his attention.

WARM YOUR TIRED BONES FROM YOUR PASSAGE AT SEA! FRESH HOT LEMON CAKES AND RAVANI TEA SERVED DAILY! it read.

It was the word *Ravani* that sent a jolt through Yassen. Home— the one he longed for but knew he was no longer welcome in.

Yassen drew up to the tea stall. Three large hourglasses hissed and steamed. Tea leaves floated along their bottoms, slowly steeping, as a heavyset Sesharian woman flipped them in timed intervals. On her hand, Yassen spotted a tattoo of a bull.

The same mark Samson had asked him to look for.

When the woman met Yassen's eyes, she twirled the hourglass once more before drying her hands on the towel around her wide waist.

"Whatcha want?" she asked in a river-hoarse voice.

"One tea and cake, please," Yassen said.

"You're lucky. I just got a fresh batch of leaves from my connect. Straight from the canyons of Ravence."

"Exactly why I want one," he said and placed his holopod in the counter insert. Yassen tapped it twice.

"Keep the change," he added.

She nodded and turned back to the giant hourglasses.

The brass beneath Yassen's feet grew warmer in the yawning day. Across the docks, more boats pulled in, carrying immigrant laborers and tourists. Yassen adjusted his visor, making sure it was fully in place, as the woman simultaneously flipped the hourglass and slid off its cap. In one fluid motion, the hot tea arced through the air and fell into the cup in her hand. She slid it across the counter.

"Mind the sleeve, the tea's hot," she said. "And here's your cake."

Yassen grabbed the cake box and lifted his cup in thanks. As he moved away from the stall, he scratched the plastic sleeve around the cup.

Slowly, a message burned through:

Look underneath the dock of fortunes.

He almost smiled. Clearly, Samson had not forgotten Yassen's love of tea.

Yassen looked within the box and saw that there was no cake but something sharp, metallic. He reached inside and held it up. Made of silver, the insignia was smaller than his palm and etched in what seemed to be the shape of a teardrop. Yassen held it closer. No, it was more feather than teardrop.

He threw the sleeve and box into a bin, slid the silver into his pocket, and continued down the dock. The commerce section stretched on, a mile of storefronts welcoming him into the great nation of Jantar. Yassen sipped his tea, watching. A few paces down was a stall marketing tales of ruin and fortune. Like the tea stall, it too was old and decrepit, with a painting of a woman reading palms painted across its front. He was beginning to recognize a pattern—and patterns were dangerous. Samson was getting lazy in his mansion.

Three guards stood along the edge of the platform beside the stall. One was dressed in a captain's royal blue, the other two in the plain black of officers. All three wore helmet visors, their pulse guns strapped to their sides. They were laughing at some joke when the captain looked up and frowned at Yassen.

"You there," he said imperiously.

Yassen slowly lowered his cup. The dock was full of carts and merchants. If he ran now, the guards could catch him.

"Yes, you, with the full face," the captain called out, tapping his visor. "Come here!"

"Is there a problem?" Yassen asked as he approached.

"No full visors allowed on the dock, except for the guard," the captain said.

"I didn't know it was a crime to wear a full visor," Yassen said. His voice was cool, perhaps a bit too nonchalant because the captain slapped the cup out of Yassen's hand. The spilled tea hissed against the metal planks.

"New rules," the captain said. "Only guards can wear full visors. Everybody else has to go half."

His subordinates snickered. "Looks like he's fresh off the boat, Cap. You got to cut it up for him," one said.

Behind his visor, Yassen frowned. He glanced at the merchant leaning against the fortunes stall. The man wore a bored expression, as if the interaction before him was nothing new. But then the merchant bent forward, pressing his hands to the counter, and Yassen saw the sign of the bull tattooed there.

Samson's men were watching.

"All right," Yassen said. He would give them a show. Prove that he wasn't as useless as the whispers told.

He unclipped his visor as the guards watched. "But you owe me another cup of tea."

And then Yassen flung his arm out and rammed the visor against the captain's face. The man stumbled back with a groan. The other two leapt forward, but Yassen was quicker; he swung around and gave four quick jabs, two each on the back, and the officers seized and sank to their knees in temporary paralysis.

"Blast him!" the captain cried, reaching for his gun. Yassen pivoted behind him, his hand flashing out to unclip the captain's helmet visor.

The captain whipped around, raising his gun...but then sunlight hit the planks before him, and the brass threw off its unforgiving light. Blinded, the captain fired.

The air screeched.

The pulse whizzed past Yassen's right ear, tearing through the upper beams of a storefront. Immediately, merchants took cover. Someone screamed as the crowd on both docks began to run. Yassen swiftly vanished into the chaotic fray, letting the crowd push him toward the dock's edge, and then he dove into the sea.

The cold water shocked him, and for a moment, Yassen floundered. His muscles clenched. And then he was coughing, swimming, and he surfaced beneath the dock. He willed himself to be still as footsteps thundered overhead and soldiers and guards barked out orders. Yassen caught glimpses of the captain in the spaces between the planks.

"All hells! Where did he go?" the captain yelled at the merchant manning the stall of wild tales.

The merchant shrugged. "He's long gone."

Yassen sank deeper into the water as the captain walked overhead, his subordinates wobbling behind. Something buzzed beneath him, and he could see the faint outlines of a dark shape in the depths. Slowly, Yassen began to swim away—but the dark shape remained stationary. He waited for the guards to pass and then sank beneath the surface.

A submersible, the size of one passenger.

Look underneath the dock of fortunes, indeed.

Samson, that bastard.

Yassen swam toward the sub. He placed his hand on the imprint panel of the hull, and then the sub buzzed again and rose to the surface.

The cockpit was small, with barely enough room for him to stretch his legs, but he sighed and sank back just the same. The glass slid smoothly closed and rudders whined to life. The panel board lit up before him and bathed him in a pale, blue light.

A note was there. Handwritten. How rare, and so like Samson.

See you at the palace, it said, and before Yassen could question *which* palace, the sub was off.

if you enjoyed
THE JASAD HEIR

look out for

THE SUN AND THE VOID

Book One of the Warring Gods

by

Gabriela Romero Lacruz

Set in a lush world inspired by the history and folklore of South America, discover this sweeping epic fantasy of colonialism and country, ancient magic, and a young woman's quest for belonging.

When Reina arrives at Aguila Manor, her heart stolen from her chest, she's on the verge of death—until her estranged grandmother, a dark sorceress in the Don's employ, intervenes. Indebted to a woman she never knew and smitten with the upper-caste daughter of the house, Celeste, Reina will do anything to earn—and keep—the family's favor. Even the bidding of the ancient god who speaks to her from the manor's foundations. To save the woman she loves, Reina will have to defy the gods themselves and become something she never could have imagined.

1

Food for Tinieblas

There were many warnings about the Páramo Mountains, tales of ghosts and shadows now bound to the land after their tragic demise. Yet no one had warned Reina about the cold. How the air filtered through the inadequate layers of her vest and jacket. How every breath she took was a sliver of sustenance, so thin that each gulp left her starving. They'd never told her crossing the Páramo would feel like a journey without end.

The mountains rose ahead of her with their sugar-powdered peaks showered in the violet hues of the arriving dusk. And they opened up behind her like boundless rolling hills blanketed by cold-burned shrubberies and the jutting frailejón trees, which stood alone on a territory perhaps too cold or elevated to be hospitable to anything else.

An icy wind buffeted her forward. Reina fell to her knees like a scared child, her scabs splitting and streaking red on the jagged rock beneath her, but her prehensile tail looped around the rock, reassuring her with balance. When she gathered the courage to continue her climb, she glimpsed the gray fogginess of smoke far ahead, and it filled her with hope. A fire meant a hearth, which meant civilization wasn't too far off.

The way forward was treacherous, but so was the way back. One more day on foot, and Reina was sure she would reach the lower valleys. Images of an inn's warm bed kept her company. She entertained herself with dreams of reaching the farmsteads bordering Sadul Fuerte, when she finally arrived in the city and could share the reason for her journey with the first stranger who asked. She imagined pulling out the invitation marked by the mauve wax seal of the Duvianos family, the elegant loops of Doña Ursulina

Duvianos's cursive beckoning Reina to come meet a grandmother estranged by Reina's father's broken heart. From her breast pocket she would produce a golden badge proving the missive's legitimacy, which had been delivered along with the letter.

The engraved medallion was a metal translation of the Duvianos banner: an orange flower crowned by a red sun rising over a mauve sky. Reina recognized the crest, for she had seen it on jackets and correspondence her father owned from his time as a revolutionary, before he had renounced his old life. Juan Vicente Duvianos had never spoken much of his mother, and when he had, it had been with the rancor and disappointment of a schism. Even after he'd died, Reina had discarded the possibility of a relationship with her grandmother. But after reading the words inviting her to the faraway Águila Manor, where Doña Ursulina was employed, Reina couldn't be sure who had disowned whom.

When the cold ached her bones and the mountain rebelled against her, Reina clutched her objective and reminded herself why she was fleeing to Sadul Fuerte to begin with. Behind her, in Segolita, she was nothing more than a jobless nozariel living on the charity of humans. The laws enslaving nozariels to humans had changed, but not the attitudes. The streets of Segolita had been her home—all crooked townhomes of peeling baroque façades and roads muddied from shit and the latest rainfall—and her hell. Reina was of age, too old for the family for whom she had worked as a criada and accidentally caught the eye of the oldest son, and too undesirable to be welcomed by any other human family or employer. The invitation gave her an opportunity, and hope.

Her path opened up to a crossroads, where a naked, knobby tree sustained two planks with carved directions: Apartaderos, where she had come from, to the north, and Sadul Fuerte to the west. A chill ran through Reina as the air grew cooler and the shadows elongated. No longer was the sky streaked in the stark mauve she imagined had been the inspiration for the Duvianos banner. Dusk spread through the mountains, and with it came a howling wind and faraway yaps that turned her jumpy. "There's nothing but frailejones and demons in the Páramo," the inn owner at the foot of the mountain had warned her, shaking his head in disapproval. She would gladly trade the devils of Segolita for the ghosts of the Páramo.

Camping for the night was the last thing she wanted to do, but the path ahead was long and even more treacherous in the dark. Reina broke off course from the well-trodden road and followed a small creek downstream, looking for a burrow or shelter. The creek entered a patch of frailejones, each tree reaching for the sky with its cluster of hairy succulent leaves. Reina followed the stream, plucking the marcescent leaves hanging from the frailejón trunks to build a fire. The night was still. Her huffs of condensing breaths and footsteps crackling the underbrush were all that disturbed an otherwise deathly quiet, which was odd. Just moments ago she had noted the rising cacophony of night: crickets and the croak of amphibians and the occasional hooting bird. The moon was rising, its light creating odd bipedal shapes in the shadows of the trees she passed.

A branch snapped. Reina paused, thinking it must have been the wind. Then a second rustle set the hairs of her back on end. She whirled around. There was nothing but the moonlight and the shadows it created. Fear fell over her. The shadows breathed. Like they were hunting her.

When the silence was shattered by a second snapping twig, she ran.

Guttural snarls erupted behind her, and stomps. With her blood pumping hot in her ears and her heart panicked, Reina breathlessly pelted through the underbrush. Could there be bears in the Páramo, or lions? The sounds were wet, and the hunting creature sounded heavy. She glanced behind her, cursing when it slowed her down, and saw a shadow crowned with horns. She cried and tripped on a protruding root.

Pain lanced through her ankle, but she had no time to nurse it. She pushed herself back to her feet as several pairs of stomps joined the pursuit. The bared trees closed in around her, their marcescent leaves stretching like claws to pull at her clothes. Thorny bushes sliced her calves and ankles. Fog blanketed the mountain. Unable to see, she stumbled into a gully. She shot another glance at her pursuers as she scrambled up. They carried the shape of people, bipedal, with long, naked limbs coated in the grime of the wild. They had the ears of a bovine and the curved horns of a goat. Moonlight gleamed off small eyes reflecting a single line of intention: the desire to devour. But the worst part of it all—what made Reina realize this would be the brutal, bloody end of her journey— were the grinning teeth. They were blunt, like a human's, but with twice too many shoved into the hanging mandible of a monster.

The first one yanked her by the tail. Its clammy touch leeched all the heat from her. The thing tossed her against a bush, thorns impaling her side and scratching her cheeks open.

Reina brandished her knife, which was a rusty, untrustworthy thing she'd brought for skinning game—not for fighting. She screamed as she slashed at her attackers' limbs to no effect. They regarded her with snarling laughter, the sounds warped as if they originated from her own imagination. As if they had one foot in this world and another in the Void. Tears flooded her eyes and blurred an already black night. They slapped the knife away, their claws ripping her clothes and skin.

Desperate, Reina kicked at one with all her strength, sending it toppling back. She scrambled to all fours and sprang up for another getaway. One jerked her braid, then clutched her tail; another grabbed her by the wrist; and the third reached for her collar and ripped her jacket open.

"Stop!" she cried uselessly, for deep down she knew there would be no stopping them until they had all of her.

She shrieked as one of the creatures dug its teeth into her flesh. One moment its face was close, blank eyes reflecting nothing but instinct, and the next it was pulling out her skin and muscle and sinew as it ripped her forearm open.

White-hot pain surged through her. Reina's screams reverberated across the mountain. The other monster tore her cotton shirt open. Her grandmother's badge flew out, and she caught it, by instinct or by a miracle. The thing was heavy in her hand. She smacked the creature gnawing on her forearm with all her strength, imprinting her family's sigil on its sickly forehead.

A glow spread from the badge upon impact. A bubble of yellow light swallowed Reina and the creatures devouring her, revealing their hairless bodies covered in black welts and boils. The light burst out of the badge like a spring of water. Anywhere it touched, their hideous skin sizzled and smoked, earning their wet, agonized hisses.

The creatures were relentless. Their claws went for her chest as if digging for a treasure within, scraping her ribs, her final barrier. Reina swung their mucus-covered arms away with the lighted badge. She swiped left, then right, forcing the light to repel them. Bloodied and battered, she twisted around to her feet and scrambled away. The monsters remained at the perimeter of the badge's light, their growls following her. They wanted her flesh, but something about the light deterred them.

The frailejones opened to a clearing showered in moonlight. Reina limped to it, her wounded arm gripping the remains of her ripped shirt and jacket over the bloody opening on her chest. Her other arm waved the badge like a beacon. She wasn't sure if the monsters still followed.

Swaying deliriously, she stepped on loose mountain terrain, and the stones beneath her gave. She slipped. Her limbs and head crashed against stone and bramble as she rolled down a scree. When the fall finally ended, Reina took a desperate gasp of air, then curled into a ball. Her spine and skull were miraculously unbroken. Somehow, she was alive. But every inch of her ached and burned, and maybe, just maybe, she would have been better off dead.

"Is that another one?"

"No—that's a person."

Voices echoed in the vast void of Reina's darkness, stirring her. Grime coated the inside of her throat when she took in a big gulp of crisp Páramo air. The brightness of a cloudy sky blinded her as she turned her head. She was rewarded with a headache. Reina found herself cushioned by a mossy blanket. A beetle scuttled dangerously close to her eyelashes. She sat up, and a sharp pain lanced her arm. There was a bloody, gaping bite on her forearm.

She had nearly been eaten.

Tears flooded the edges of her vision. Reina felt a renewed vigor to live. She moaned a reply to the voices, which approached with several pairs of squelching footsteps. With the effort came a thunderous ache in her chest, which was crusted with blood, her skin reduced to flaps barely hanging on. Trembling, her hand hovered over the injury. Her broken skin burned, but the ache came from within. A blazing pain. Even the simple act of curling into a ball, to shield her soul from squeezing out of her wound, was torturous. She cried again. She would never make it to Sadul Fuerte.

The footsteps reached her. Someone grabbed her by the shoulder and twisted her around for a better look.

A "No!" blurted out of her from the pain, but she hadn't the strength to fight them off.

"This one's basically dead," a man said.

"But she lives," the second voice said. This one belonged to a woman who crouched close. Her leather gloves gently wiped the grime from Reina's cheeks, and she shushed Reina's sobs.

A pair of blue eyes peered down at her, brilliant, like the sunny skies in Segolita when not a single cloud marred the sky. The woman had clear pale skin and a sharp nose. Blunt black bangs covered her forehead, and the rest of her silky hair was pulled up into a high ponytail. From the crown of her head curled a short pair of antlers, smooth, the color of alabaster.

The young woman was valco.

Reina couldn't believe it... to be able to see one in the flesh, even if right before her death.

The woman's hand hovered over Reina's torn chest without touching the wound. "You were attacked by tinieblas. But you lived—how?"

"I would hardly call that *living*," the man behind her said, covering his nose with his jacketed forearm. He was crowned with a pair of antlers, too, but his were taller and better developed, with sharp edges surely capable of being made a weapon to impale. His hair was as silvery as the clouded sky. Boiled leather armor peeked out from underneath his ruana—a black shawl-like covering, triangular in shape, which covered him from neck to waist.

"The wretch is nozariel," he added, noting her tail with a grimace. A typical reaction from humans when they realized her parents hadn't cut it off after birth to conform. Perhaps valcos were also in agreement.

The pair had other companions lingering behind, awaiting orders or standing as sentinels.

"The rot is going to get to her one way or another. Leave the creature be," he said.

Reina reached for the woman's hand. She gripped it without permission and begged, "Help, please."

"Unhand her!"

"Oh, hush, Javier," the young woman said. She couldn't be older than Reina, but she was beautiful, in the regal sort of way Reina imagined the princesses of the Segolean Empire were raised to be. She was wearing a woolen ruana like Javier, woven in blue and white with fringes decorating the bottom. She took it off and draped Reina in her warmth, and her scent. "Don't you care to know how she survived the tinieblas? They went for her heart."

"Not particularly. We banished them. Our work here is done."

Panic bubbled in Reina's belly. She knew what the man's look meant. She'd been a recipient of it time and time again in Segolita—had seen it directed at the starved and wounded nozariels on the streets. They were going to leave her to die because of the part of her that wasn't human.

Her heart palpitated uselessly. The spasms shot up her chest again, leaving her without the words to beg for mercy. Tears streaked her cheeks as she lifted the engraved badge with her bitten hand. The trinket was half-coated in the red crust of her blood, but the faint light emitting from it was unmissable. Warm magic pulsed from within the metal.

The woman was even more beautiful when her eyes and mouth rounded inquisitively. She took the badge from Reina, despite the dried blood. "It's the crest of Duvianos," she said, rising to her feet and taking the badge with her to show it to her companions.

"No—please," Reina begged, desperate not to be abandoned. Her chest flared again, punishing her. She moaned and twisted in agony like an earthworm under the sun.

"Javier, you must heal her!" The woman's words were faint and far away. "Use healing galio."

Reina couldn't keep her eyes open any longer. She knew she was slipping away.

"Do I look like a nurse to you?"

In some ways, Reina was grateful for it.

"Please, act like you have a droplet of human blood in you for once in your life. I command it."

She had failed in her journey, right as she was reaching Sadul Fuerte. If anything, she was a fool for thinking she could escape her fate at all.

"Please, Celeste, pay no heed to her baubles. The wretch is a thieving nozariel. How else would she get her hands on something like this?"

Reina's trembling fingers reached into the torn jacket and produced the letter. She had the strength for a few last words. And if this was going to be the end, then she might as well say them. "I am no thief. I'm here to meet my grandmother, Ursulina Duvianos."

The impact of her head against a hard surface yanked Reina back to reality. It flared every nerve of pain like jabbing knives. She had been thrown into a shadowed room, where the scent of dust and manure pervaded the stagnant air. At least it was warmer than it had been, and the bedding was softer than the mountain ground. Voices approached and someone entered.

Reina bit down the ache to sit up and take stock of her surroundings. The dormitory was small, with plain walls and a wooden rosary nailed to the wall opposite her. The young valco woman named Celeste stood by the doorway. She fidgeted with Reina's badge, which was the only source of light as dusk settled over the world outside.

As if she'd been waiting for Reina to wake, Celeste said, "Stay here, and don't go anywhere else."

"I couldn't move even if I wanted to." Her heart pounded in a mad race to outrun the pain. A contest it couldn't win. "Please return my badge."

"If you are who you say you are, then I must take it with me." Celeste didn't give Reina a chance for rebuttal, and Reina would have howled at her for leaving the room with her badge were she not so weak.

She wished sleep would claim her a second time. Was she going to die? The memory of the shadowed devils with the grinning, blunt teeth returned the moment her eyes closed. So she forced herself to stare at the ceiling instead.

Soon, the hum of a hushed argument filled the hall outside the room. The argument ended the moment the newcomers reached the doorway. Celeste brought reinforcements: a middle-aged woman who commanded Reina's complete attention as she entered the room. The woman wore a billowing long-sleeved blue dress with fine golden embroidery. She had bobbed black hair, pale skin, and a strong resemblance to Celeste. Her mother, a human lacking the valco antlers.

She approached Reina's bedside, cautiously, and sat on the stool positioned next to it. Another woman also entered, heralded by the clicking footsteps of heeled black boots on the stone floor. "Doña Laurel?" she said. "What is the meaning of this?"

The second woman was the tallest in the room. Her umber skin was lustrous and free of marks, and her black hair was braided in a circle behind her head. She wore black pants, and her high-necked jacket was partitioned into red silk sleeves and a black silk bodice embroidered with golden laurels down the middle.

"Doña Ursulina," Doña Laurel said by way of welcoming her to the room. "That is precisely what I'm trying to figure out."

Stunned, Reina looked to the taller woman, her heart racing again. Suddenly everything about her features became familiar. The high cheekbones; the fullness of her lips. Yet there were other things Reina never saw in herself: The confidence and commanding presence. The opulence of her clothes.

"She was a victim of tinieblas. We found her on our way down from the Páramo," Celeste said.

"There are tinieblas on my lands?" Doña Laurel raised her voice, accusation dripping off her words. "*You* found her?"

"Yes, mami."

"I've told you time and time again that I do not want to see you hunting tinieblas," Doña Laurel said, disappointment and concern simmering beneath the surface. The words took Reina back to that moment with those creatures, reminding her of the determined hunger in their eyes, how their blunt teeth tore chunks off her skin. Every mother *should* be concerned.

"It was Javier's idea," Celeste added, quick like a white lie.

Doña Laurel pursed her lips, her attention drawn to Reina, who was finding it hard to restrain herself from squirming in pain in front of these women. Cautiously, the woman lifted the covers shielding Reina's chest for a peek at the wound. A metallic stink filled the room.

"The tinieblas' rot," Doña Ursulina said.

Doña Laurel clicked her tongue, but her façade was unbothered. She reached out and wiped the sticky bangs away from Reina's temple, her pity clear in her eyes. "You survived the tinieblas? With your heart intact?" Then she turned to Doña Ursulina and asked, "How is that possible?"

"My badge," Reina croaked.

Celeste presented Doña Ursulina with the trinket, then the letter. The taller woman's eyes doubled in size, then her face contorted into a scowl as she recognized the medallion. She hesitated before accepting the letter with fingers bedazzled in fat gem-encrusted rings.

"What is your name?" she asked without lifting her gaze.

Reina choked on her own spit but answered.

Doña Ursulina unfolded the stained letter, her jaw rippling as she read her own words inviting Reina to these cold lands across the mountains.

Reina met her black gaze as a chill shook her from neck to toes. This was the moment she had dreamed of during those lonely days as she crossed the Llanos and the Páramo. This reunion with her grandmother. How flat and painfully disappointing it had turned out to be.

Doña Laurel watched them. "Do you know this woman?"

"This badge belongs to me, just like it used to belong to my father, and his father before him," Doña Ursulina said, slowly turning it over in her hands. "I enchanted it with a powerful ward of litio protection and bismuto—enough to allow you to see the tinieblas and ward them away. I knew the journey here would have its dangers—I just didn't expect to be...so right." She crossed the distance to Reina and lifted her chin for a better look. "A nozariel like your mother, aren't you?" she said, eyeing the black spots of pigmentation on the iris that made Reina's pupils look oblong, almost like a cat's; the caiman-like scutes over the bridge of her nose; the long, pointed tips of her ears. The marks of her nozariel breed, undiscernible from far away but never failing to earn her a scowl or a grimace from most humans. "You actually came."

"Explain yourself, Doña Ursulina," Doña Laurel commanded.

"I sent the badge to Segolita, along with this letter, to my granddaughter."

Doña Laurel's mouth hung open. "As in, Juan Vicente's daughter? He has a daughter?"

The way they said his name, with the familiarity hinting of a past Reina wasn't privy to, reignited the agony in her chest. She chewed the insides of her cheeks, tasting her own blood, and forced the words out despite the pain. "I came to meet you." She tried sitting up again, only to collapse with a moan. A violent spasm shook her, made her want to scream.

"She needs a doctor," Celeste blurted out from her spot by the doorway.

"The tinieblas hungered for her heart, and they have tainted it. This is dark magic, and it will not be cured by a mere doctor, if at all," Doña Ursulina said.

It was a blow, renewing Reina's fears. She let out a shuddery breath. With an angry hiss and the last of her strength, she said, "I came from Segolita—I traveled this far—to be your family. Not to die!"

And the witch who shared her blood smiled.

"Then it must be fated that you live, child, for if there is one person capable of salving a tiniebla's rot, it will be me."

Follow us:

 /orbitbooksUS

 /orbitbooks

 /orbitbooks

Join our mailing list
to receive alerts on our
latest releases and deals.

orbitbooks.net

Enter our monthly
giveaway for the chance
to win some epic prizes.

orbitloot.com